Incarnation
The Cube Master

SARAH GERDES

Incarnation

The Cube Master

CHAPTER 01

Kyle left Billy's house, hunching his shoulders against the icy bits pelting his skin. He had no choice but to harden the emotions he felt for Billy, her leaving town non-negotiable until the identity cubes were in the hands of the right people. It was his responsibility to keep them safe, helping turn random lines of codes into new faces.

All four hundred million of them, give or take.

Ironically, that wasn't his only concern. He'd made an enemy of the most prominent man in the town, Mario was now his former best friend and senior agent Brayden Cox, his ally, was handcuffed, on his way to FBI headquarters in Denver.

Not a good way to prepare for the New Year.

"Mom? Dad?" he called as he opened the door to his home.

"In here." Kyle winced at his mom's tone, dreading the discussion to come. "We'd like to speak with you." He turned the corner to see his parents sitting side by side on the couch. It was an uncommon scene in regular life, let alone the night where the entire basketball team had been rounded up for polygraph testing.

"Can you spare me five?" he asked, pausing until they gave a nod. He jogged down the concrete steps to the basement, quietly lifting the crowbar from the wall. The professional kiln his mother used for her work was five hundred pounds of metal and steel, liftable only with a professional tool and muscle.

He carefully positioned the crowbar between his chest and shoulder. As soon as he raised the kiln, he realized his dilemma—he had to keep the kiln lifted up while he looked underneath. He searched the floor with his foot, hitting a cement block. Nudging it with his toe as sweat ran down his back, he lowered the kiln back down on the block. Dropping to his knees, he ran his palm over the dirty floor, feeling the latch and pulling at it.

His fingers felt the stacks of money, knowing it were his parent's entire savings, the result of their inherent distrust of the government. Each stack contained ten grand, three years' worth of taxes and expenses in fire proof storage. He deposited the stolen cubes in the far left corner, readjusting the money.

Satisfied, he lifted the kiln back up, moved the block out of the way, then lowered the crowbar. As he jogged up the stairs, he wiped his palms on his jeans, removing the sweat from his forehead with the back of his hand.

Upstairs, he went directly to the living room window, his back to his parents. "Lots of snow falling," he said, forcing his breath to even out. The white layer had covered the black ice from earlier in the day, the slightly warmer weather creating a dangerous condition. It was going to be hard driving tomorrow, but his ATV would make it.

It was his father who spoke first.

"You want to talk about why you dumped Stu's daughter in front of the world, or why you lied to us?" his father asked.

"Neither," Kyle admitted. He watched from across the street as Stu pushed the snow off the front porch, his routine so predictable Kyle could set his watch to it. He pulled the curtain over the window, the thin fabric concealing the details of the Fine home, leaving the outline of the house.

"That's not going to help," his mother grumbled.

"I know," replied Kyle. "But at least Stu can't get a clean shot at me."

Kyle turned, dropping on the inset window bench, wishing the moment away. He suspected his parents were wondering where it all went wrong; his fall from straight-arrow captain of the high-school basketball team to a kid who was now like everyone else: disappointing.

Kyle's back scratched against the faux Christmas tree behind him. "To answer your first question," he began, "I told you there was no good way to break up with Ashley, but in my defense—"

"You have no defense," his mother interjected. "You kissed her in front of the whole town. Her family plus the entire audience got to experience Ashley's humiliation."

"Mom, you never liked her anyway."

"True, but that doesn't mean I wanted you blackballed any more than you will be because you blew the game winning shot."

Kyle's father cleared his throat and raised his eyebrows.

"Harsh, Mom."

"Well, am I wrong?" she challenged.

Kyle threaded his fingers together, elbows on his knees. "No. When Billy put her arms around me after the buzzer rang at the game, it was unexpected but I was so happy to see her, I only cared about one person and it wasn't Ashley."

As he verbalized the emotions of the memory, the ache of loss spread like winter crystals across his chest, wide and cutting.

The impact of his words softened the moment. He'd never expressed any real feeling towards Ashley, or any other girl during his high school career, and his parents had noticed.

"Did losing your scholarships occur to you?" she asked, her face pale with worry.

The question snapped Kyle out of his self-pity.

"I'm glad so many people think my ability to get out of this town is dependent on Stu Fine putting in a word for me. No," he said, cutting off his father who had opened his mouth. "I had three legitimate athletic scholarship offers before tonight from top tier engineering colleges. If they don't stand, screw them."

"You underestimate Stu," warned his dad, running his fingers through his chin-length hair.

"And maybe this entire town *overestimates* him," Kyle muttered. He stared down at the taupe carpet, seeing the image of Billy's platinum hair poking out from under her snowboarding cap, feeling the light touch of her fingertips along his cheek. "Like I said, I just don't care."

His father brushed Kyle's leg with his knee. "And is that why you told different stories to us, Deputy Hancock and your coach about how you hurt your shoulder?" Kyle broke eye contact. "What do I always say? Where there's one lie, there's more. So are there?"

The silence was deafening as Kyle remained quiet. "I see."

Kyle scratched his jawline with his fingertips. "Look, Mark knows most of the truth, but he's keeping it quiet regardless of his position as Deputy. My coach just thinks I'm an idiot who didn't want to admit I was ice climbing because I'd have caught his wrath before the big game. You guys..." he paused, struggling to figure out what to say. "All I can say was it was well intentioned."

"Tell me under what circumstances lying to your parents gets a pass under the guise of good intentions?"

Kyle locked eyes with his mother. "When knowing more could get you killed, that's when." She bit the inside of her lip, eyes narrow, assessing him in the way she'd always done when he'd broken curfew. "The danger isn't gone just because Brayden has left," he added.

Kyle wasn't sure what bothered him more: her disappointment or the lack of trust she now displayed.

Her eyes had grown wide, her voice dropping a notch with each word. "It was that Friday, the night of the break-in," she continued, her voice now barely a whisper. "No. *You couldn't have*."

Kyle felt his father's questioning eyes on him and avoided looking up. "You did it, didn't you?" his father asked. "And that's why you lied about your shoulder. It happened from getting off the mountain and evading the military choppers, not ice climbing or weights."

6

Hands still clasped, Kyle nodded.

"Jesus, Kyle," exclaimed his father. "The FBI have been turning this town upside down for the past week."

For a moment, both parents were speechless with fury. "Why in the world would you risk all that you've worked so hard to accomplish?" his mother demanded.

Kyle rubbed his face with his palms, cupping his thumbs under his chin, elbows resting on his knees.

"It started when D told me there was something inside the mine and I went to see for myself. I thought he was just rambling in another drunken stupor..." he continued, remembering back to the conversation. "He gave me a passcode which I used, and no, I didn't damage anything," he finished, not disclosing his theft of the cubes. He hated to lie to his parents yet again, but the information might send his mother over the edge. "The point is that in a few days, the town is going to get back to its boring self."

"Then why was Brayden arrested?" she pressed. "No one arrests the FBI agent responsible for leading an investigation without a reason. Was he covering for you?"

Kyle felt a pain in his chest as sharp and real as metal. Brayden knew everything Kyle had done, with one exception, and he wouldn't—*couldn't* be honest about that.

"Mom," Kyle began again, his voice as close to soothing as he could get. "I'm not sure entering a closed mine should register on anyone's radar. Like I said, if they'd have found anything connecting the break-in to me, I'd be in jail."

Kyle glanced at his dad for help.

"Your biggest issue now is going to be handling Ashley," his father said, changing the subject. "Your mom thinks she's is going to make the rest of your senior year miserable."

"I *know* she will," quipped his mother, a bit of color coming back into her cheeks. "You're not going to be very popular for a few weeks around town. For that matter, neither are we by association. Thanks," she grumbled.

Kyle reached over, taking her cold, weathered hands in his. He could handle putting himself through pain, but not her. She'd done nothing to deserve being mistreated.

"I'm sorry Mom," he said sincerely. "If I could take it back, I would—but now that…well, we are where we are. I'll just do my best to keep life normal for you, how does that sound?"

Kyle turned to stretch his back, and movement at the Fine home caught his attention. He reached over to adjust the thin curtain. Marty, Ashley and Stu were talking, and he didn't need to read lips to understand the gist of what was happening. Kissing Billy after the game had opened the door for his best friend to make his play with his ex-girlfriend. Despite her always being slightly annoyed with Marty's attention, Ashley was going to go out with him simply to spite Kyle.

Marty shook Stu's hand, asking questions which Marty appeared to answer before Ashley cut him off. Marty's mouth was still hanging open as he looked at her.

Kyle smirked. For all Marty's yearning for Ashley, her shoulder-length blond hair hitting her full chest enticing to every heterosexual male in town, Marty had no idea what the full Ashley experience entailed. Another handshake and nod to Stu's dad, and Marty led the way for Ashley down the front path to the road.

Kyle let the curtain drop and turned back to his parents, still smiling. Marty's father had more money than Stu's, but as the owner of a construction firm, nowhere near the social status or attitude.

"Mom, we are all going to be okay," he assured her, feeling a little better. "It's only five days until New Year's then school starts up again. Work will keep me busy enough."

"Perhaps you're right," his mother finally conceded. "Fresher, juicier gossip will fill up conversations and in a week, you'll be old news."

Kyle kissed his mom on the cheek and went to bed after taking two Ibuprofens for the pain in his shoulder and a Melatonin to sleep. When Mark had advised him to stay up twenty-four hours and live on caffeine to beat the polygraph, he'd done it, adrenaline and nerves carrying him through the game. But now that he was finally allowing his body to rest, the sleep was so deep, he didn't hear the banging at the door or even register his parents shaking him. Then rougher hands took over, the deep male voice authoritative. He mumbled he was sleeping.

"Get up, kid. This isn't a dream. You're coming with us."

Kyle's initial grogginess faded immediately when he saw the two men in tactical gear, the NSA insignia on their jackets. As he pushed back the covers, his mother started shoving the man closest to him. He stood immobile, holding the automatic rifle in his arm, barrel down and eyes on Kyle, not her.

"Mom, it's OK. I'm going," he said, putting on his pants and sweatshirt as fast as he could. In the corner of his eyes he saw his mom push the officer.

Kyle grabbed her. "Mom, stop! You aren't helping." Her hand was to her mouth, stifling a cry as his dad came around the other side and put his arm around her bony shoulders. It was the last image Kyle had before he was cuffed and led out the door.

CHAPTER 02

Deputy FBI Director Gary Forland continuously turned the pencil between his fingers, the motion preventing him from breaking the wood in two. His top agent had been arrested by his NSA counterpart, and Janet was going to give him a satisfactory explanation or a call to the President was going to be the next thing he did. The cyber terrorist activities were consolidated under Janet, and she now held the titles of the Commander of the United States Cyber Command as well as the Chief of the Central Security Service. Gary often quipped the titles were better than the President's and straight out of the Kremlin for their overreaching pompousness.

Gary waited for the line to connect, thinking it ironic that his organization received the brunt of the public outcry over intrusive, tactical activity with suspected criminals but in fact it actually caught the vast majority on the street hurting actual citizens. Cyber terrorism, for all the scare tactics of launching nuclear codes, was more about surveilling a billion people worldwide, purchasing data from a hundred different brokers with better technology and using boomerang methods to find the suspect instead of the actual legwork involved. It was FBI personnel like Brayden and Saachi, now in the burn unit of Denver Medical, who were in the line of fire while the NSA cyber spooks sat in cubicles, protected and preserved from the real danger.

When Janet answered the phone, Gary skipped the pleasantries. "Brayden Cox. Really?"

"Professional courtesy dictates I should have told you first," Janet answered smoothly. "For that, my apologies. It had to be done this way." The pencil snapped in Gary's meaty fingers.

Better it than my temper bursting through the phone.

"During our last conversation, you inferred the lab explosion was a result of arson and likely done by an insider from your team, the very incident that landed Brayden's partner in the burn unit," Gary's voice sound like a paver crunching gravel.

"Cool down Gary and let me explain. As much as you might disagree with our tactics, you might concur with our analysis. Can you do that?"

He wanted Brayden released and back on the job, not in a cell. "Go."

Gary took the pencil half with the eraser, randomly rubbing it against the metal desk as he listened to the NSA Director's justification. By the time she'd finished, the tip had completely worn down.

"You did the wrong thing for the right reason," he concluded, a grudging respect balancing his fury.

"It was approved by the President's advisors—"

"I get it," he broke in, "but I stand by my statement: right reason, wrong action. Planting the information about the data in the mines with a local, hoping to lure the Naturalists and trap them was one bad move. But arresting Brayden to create the illusion he knew something in order to entice the Naturalists to give chase?"

"It was a sound strategy—"

"Which didn't pan out. As you said last week, the Naturalists had it right from the beginning; that their own government was behind the mutating gene, not the Chinese. They're smarter than you give them credit for, and probably saw the move for what it was: a trap. It's over Janet."

"Not necessarily," she answered. In the intervening pause, Gary heard a sigh on the other end, a rare show of emotion for the seventy-something woman leading the government's most powerful division.

"There is one student who took the polygraph and also worked with the man with whom we'd planted the information."

"Yes, the straight-A captain of the basketball team. We both read Brayden's report of the polygraph: he passed."

"Further," Janet continued, as if he'd never spoken. "His job at the mine was repelling over crevices, stringing netting. He knew the area, how to get up and down easily."

"As do the majority of locals who ice climb on frozen sheets that would make a Navy Seal puke," Gary countered. "An entire gym saw the bruises on this kid's shoulder, which could have been caused by him sliding down the mountain after the break-in."

"Which the coach and Deputy Hancock said were from falling because he does in fact, climb ice, apparently with balls of steel," Gary added with unforced admiration. "How far are you going to go to connect this kid with a now-deceased miner and the missing cubes?" His challenge wasn't empty. "The Commander in Chief also said containment at all costs, didn't he?"

"Yes," she agreed, "and containment means keeping knowledge of this situation to the smallest number of individuals possible. That's exactly what Saachi did before the lab blew, narrowing down the list of potential suspects to a handful. Among those is the young man in question, Kyle Smith. Going back to my earlier point of knowing the area, he could have made it down the hill in the middle of a blizzard.

Furthermore, at the bottom, blood was found." She paused for effect. "It was Smith's blood."

Gary dismissed her big reveal.

"I read that too, Janet. It means nothing. Ouray is nearly 8,000 feet above sea level and nose bleeds are common. But since you seem laser focused on this kid, I'll point out the biggest evidence disproving the theory: Smith had no lacerations on his shoulders, only bruising. No scabs or evidence of a tear whatsoever. Someone doesn't make it down the side of a hill without getting serious lacerations."

"But—" Janet began.

"But," he said loud enough for his secretary to poke her head around the door. "Why aren't you bringing up the fact that this kid was with his boss at the pool during the time of the intrusion, then at local eatery where half the town saw him? Brayden noted over a dozen people attested to it."

During the intervening silence, Gary shook his head in frustration. This was so inanely stupid of a woman so perennially smart that... "Wait a minute," Gary began. "Are you implying that Brayden found Kyle out and is letting him off the hook because Jarod, his own son took his life?"

"It fits the profile, Gary," she said with prescriptive pacing. "The now-deceased David Sherman would have told someone capable of pulling off this break-in who has nothing to lose.

That's another similarity to Brayden, who also has nothing to lose."

Gary ignored her comment about Brayden and pulled up the file on Kyle Smith. "Looks to me that the valedictorian has a *lot* to lose if you include the three scholarship offers he has in the bag."

"You have to admit that it *is* possible, about both him and Brayden."

"Sure," Gary drawled, the sarcasm unveiled. "But let's not stop at the possibility of the two being in league with one another. Let's take it a step further: the kid took the cubes and passed them to Brayden, who is going to have his surgeon-scientist wife reverse engineer them. How's that?"

"It's one scenario our analysts created."

"Good Lord," he muttered dismissively. Gary avoided picking up another pencil and swiveled his chair, looking to the scene below him. The icy roads of the FBI headquarters didn't keep visitors from coming day and night, many of them tourists going to the forensics center where the world's best fugitive profiles were created. He didn't require a sketch for Smith because his photo was everywhere, from the local papers to the national magazines on stand-out athletes. His eighteenth birthday was two weeks away. No siblings, adopted father, parents still together and living on Main Street. Sounded just like Brayden's description: an All-American kid.

"When does the hypotheticals end, Janet?"

"When we get our answers," Janet answered, the words coming softly like a panther crossing the grass. "You should know we tracked the movement of one of the Naturalist leaders as far as the Colorado border, then lost him. We anticipate he'll return since the remaining cubes are still in the mine, but we're not going to wait until he does. We're going to use the serum."

Gary visualized the act which usually accompanied those words. "When?" he asked, thinking that about how the close-knit community of 500 would react to needles full of chemicals designed to extract the truth being used on their own kids.

"My field team are rounding up everyone who was polygraphed as we speak. We are going to inject Deputy Hancock as well since he was one person who vouched for Smith and knew him in high school."

"The entire basketball team *and* the Deputy? You'll be alienating the police force who we may need in the future."

"We have no choice," she argued. "He may have the small town allegiance behind him which overshadows his loyalty to a government two thousand miles away."

Gary increased Kyle Smith's image on his desktop screen. Clear skin stretching over high cheekbones, cropped, sandy-blond hair on the sides with a wave at the top. Yep. That kid was about as All-American as you could get, and if it got out that he was being chased by the government for no reason...

"The entire town and surrounding communities may revolt if this goes haywire and the kids suffer long term effects from the chemicals."

Janet agreed with the first part of his statement, not the second. "These *kids*, as you continue to refer to them are actually vote-casting, almost military-age young men. Historically, the age group who cause the most disruption to the country, far more than any single injection."

Gary, powerless to stop her from using the chemicals, ended the call with a request for Brayden's release.

"We can discuss it when we have our next update with the President."

Gary hung up. He had one agent in the hospital and another in cuffs, coincidentally, both assigned to the most volatile situation currently in the United States.

Gary gazed at the picture before him. If Kyle Smith was all that the analysts thought he was, then it was the government who should be concerned, because anyone who could race up and down the mountain in a blizzard, take and keep the cubes, outwit the polygraph and remain alive this long was someone to be feared.

And perhaps Janet knew it.

When he'd been shoved into the backseat of the police car, hands behind him in cuffs, Kyle wasn't sure he'd ever return home. To end up at the local police station two blocks away was a relief.

The man across from him spoke in a monotone, his light blue eyes revealing nothing. "Roll up your sleeve, palm toward me." Kyle did as he was asked. A rubber tourniquet was tied above his elbow as the second officer stood guard at the front door. Both men wore NSA badges; the full tactical gear and machine guns saying it all. This activity didn't require his parent's permission: to resist wasn't an option.

Kyle watched Mark Hancock pace outside the station. Kyle wondered if he'd been woken and asked to stand guard or had come on his own.

Abruptly, Mark turned and they made eye contact. Mark's gloved hands were on his hips, clenching the wide police-issue belt. An almost imperceptible shake of his head informed Kyle he didn't agree with what was happening inside, but was prevented from doing a thing about it.

The faint sounds of Christmas music carried over the sound system. If it was meant to comfort those unfortunate enough to find themselves in the station over the holidays, it wasn't doing its job.

Nothing about watching a syringe fill with liquid was comforting.

Had Brayden known Kyle would be taken and chemicals injected into his system? He must have, or else he wouldn't have slipped Kyle the single white pill following the polygraph test, telling told him to take it before he himself was placed under arrest.

Kyle remained still as the needle disappeared under his skin. As the liquid traveled up his arm, he felt a head rush, his fingers involuntarily twitching, only partly due to the sudden chill.

"That was weird," he muttered.

"It gets better," said the man who pressed the plunger of into the barrel of the syringe, allowing the last of the chemical to flow into his system. A moment later, the needle was extracted and the tourniquet removed.

"I'm feeling that," Kyle remarked. It was the sensation of standing too fast after sitting too long.

"My name is Jim and I will be asking you a few questions," the officer said, replacing the syringe in a metal container.

"Answer directly. That's Lex who's going to help me get the right answers if you have issues responding. Are we clear?"

Kyle nodded, trying to remember what he'd read about truth serums, only recalling they'd stopped using the technique at the turn of the century.

"Isn't this illegal?" he asked Jim, his lips feeling thick.

"They were reinstated for cases of suspected terrorist activities."

I'm considered a terrorist, Kyle realized, the pasty, thick film he now tasted covering his tongue and teeth. He tried to focus, processing what he'd been asked.

"Tell me about your work at the mine."

Kyle gave the facts. "Started working at fifteen during the summers," he began, unsure if he was speaking quickly or slowly. "...hanging nets over the ravines so the skiers and snowmobilers won't die. This year will be my fourth..."

"Skip to when you were on the inside of the mine," commanded Lex. Kyle looked up. The tight threading of the black polyurethane nylon of the man's flack jacket had a shimmer, the seamless material blending into gloves which held the semi-automatic. "Kid," Lex barked. "Concentrate."

"Sorry. I was wondering if your bullet proof jackets were fire proof. What was the question again?"

The man tapped his index finger on his automatic weapon. "You were going to tell us about being on the inside of the mine."

Kyle concentrated, focusing on what he *wanted* to say, not what he *should* say.

And this will prove if the pill Brayden gave me works.

"I worked stringing lines across the crevices left over from the mining. I never had much need to go into the mine itself, which was being decommissioned." He paused to visualize the original mine he knew, not the latest version he'd seen. "It had dirt floors, big entrance, hollow. It was a working mine. Nothing special."

Jim rolled his knuckles on the table. "Why would one of your basketball teammates say that if anyone went into the mine, it had to be you?"

"That must have been Marty, and I'd say because jealousy is a strong motivator."

"Elaborate," requested Lex from his standing position.

Kyle closed his dry eyes for just a moment. The next moment a palm cuffed his cheek, jerking his head to the side.

"Lex, hold it back," commanded Jim.

Kyle moved his jaw. The slap *had* helped clear his mind. He was soo tired.

"Marty's dating my last girlfriend now, or…at least trying to, I think. My memory isn't so good, and I'm not being a jerk, I just—I don't know."

A sharp banging on the window stopped the session. It was Mark shaking his head, a displeased frown cutting into his cheeks. Lex shook his head back and forth, a clear indication Mark's opinions weren't needed and wouldn't be considered.

Kyle straightened his back, nodding at Mark, letting him know he'd survive. Mark watched for another moment, then turned back around.

Kyle refocused on Jim.

"Describe your job inside the mine for me."

Kyle's mind wasn't as sharp as usual, but he still caught the wording in the command. "I only worked *outside* the mine, like I said, stretching netting across crevices to save the skiers and snowmobilers from dying as I already told you."

"You couldn't make the grade to work inside the mine?" asked Lex, a sarcastic challenge in his voice.

"Yeah, sort of like the skill required to pull your forefinger back a half an inch."

Kyle didn't see the fist before it hit his jaw. He barely caught the edge of the table as he lurched left, preventing him from falling to the floor. The door flew open, rattling the bell at the top.

"What was that for?" Mark demanded.

"His attitude," Lex replied, his fingers hovering on the trigger.

Mark looked between Kyle and the two officers. "You said no physical contact outside the needle."

"Correct," replied Jim evenly, "but as Lex said, he was out of line. Let us do our job." The pink in Mark's neck shot to his cheeks, the dismissal an insult in itself. When the door shut, Jim turned back to Kyle. "You were saying?"

Kyle moved his jaw around, It wasn't broken, but it hurt. He rotated it the other way, thinking Jim's buzz cut was so close it could have been used as a golfing t.

"I was saying I'd really like to answer your questions," Kyle finally got out, his words sounding uneven.

"That's what I thought. The night of the break-in, you said you were with your boss at the pool then at the bar with the bar owner's daughter, correct?" Kyle nodded. "And in between?"

"I was walking to the bar with Barrett, my boss and when the Sheriff came by and we spoke to him. Then inside the bar we were eating and drinking Cokes when Deputy Hancock came in."

Kyle visualized Billy sitting in the corner, her textbook open, taking notes and how he'd been desperate for her help. She'd looked so intriguing, studious and distant, all that a disguise for who she really was.

"Kid. Kyle!" A thick hand shook his neck, bobbling his head side to side. Kyle groggily opened his eyes. "You said you were drinking Coke with Billy at the bar. But she's gone and we can't verify your story. Where'd she go?"

Kyle rotated his head around, knowing the room was less clear than it had been a moment before. He paused, looking at Jim, trying to get clarity on the man's face.

"Actually…we had lunch Friday, I think, then I'm not sure what happened. I didn't know she'd left."

Kyle missed the glance between the two men. He was visualizing Billy nestled in the corner of the long, worn leather couch, a Coke on the end table, the deer antlers hanging above and the awful cowboy Christmas music playing in the background.

Lex cursed and began pacing. "You waited too long," he complained. "It's acted too fast."

"What about the game?" Jim asked. "Lex and I were by the door, watching the end of the fourth quarter. Do you remember that?"

"I think we were in a crowd, bunch of people…" Kyle shook his head in frustration. "Now I'm not sure it was real. Did we win?"

Lex grunted while Jim answered, "No. You'd just lost and you went to Billy. That ring a bell?"

Kyle stared at him, the alternate universe of another human being telling him about his own life that he didn't recall.

"Nothing," he said.

"Too bad," Jim remarked, leaning back. "Lex, you're right. His short-term memory's already gone. Kyle, I've got one last question for you. According to the transcript of the polygraph, you said no. But you could have outsmarted that device. It's unlikely you can fool the chemicals. Have you seen or heard of titanium cubes?"

Kyle rolled his head to the right, his tongue tasting blood. He knew the best lies were the ones told with half-truths, so that's what he decided to do.

"Old D told me and everyone else about *big secrets* in the mine," he said, using his forefingers for quotes, "and said that the government would kill the entire town if they knew."

Kyle had the satisfaction of the officers going quiet.

"And?" Jim encouraged. Kyle stretched his neck, determined to tell them just enough to get them out of town, chasing ghosts in the wrong direction. "Come on, Kyle. I can tell you are holding something back."

"What he said was so stupid, you know?"

"Let us be the judge of that."

Kyle tried to appear reluctant, as though the dead man might rise up from the grave. "He said the mine held the records for our faces, the codes to create them." He paused, patting his face, wincing because he'd touched it too hard. "I mean, I know he was a drunk, but to say that the most important thing in the country would be hidden here was ludicrous."

"Yeah," agreed Jim, nodding. "That is pretty far-fetched."

Kyle was pleased with himself. His father had always said that the best way to get past a conflict was to 'catch the ball instead of trying to hit it out of the ballpark.

"It might have been believable," Kyle started, "but then he said that the government put the cubes in the mine on purpose, just to lure the Naturalists so that the government could catch them. What a joke. The Naturalists, coming here, to the middle-of-nowhere Ouray, to get something that's probably not here in the first place."

Kyle had started rubbing his back against the chair, doing his best to scratch, the sensation of heat and pinpricks moving up and along his arms, then his neck.

"Whatever you gave me is making me itch and feel hot," he complained. "This feels like ants are inside me."

"It's a secondary effect of the chemicals," Jim explained. "It's temporary. So aside from your former co-worker who filled your heads with stories of secrets about metal cubes and Naturalists, who do you think had the motivation to get inside the mine to check things out? Your basketball buddy Marty?'

As much as Kyle wanted to get Marty back for crucifying him over the game, it wasn't his style. They'd all go their separate ways in a few months, only to see each other on random 4th of July events.

"I doubt his aspirations include going up a hill in the middle of a blizzard." Kyle paused. "Certainly not sliding down the side of it to avoid the helicopters."

Kyle was still smiling when he caught the quiet in the room.

"Kyle," said Jim, his voice smooth. "How did you know the person who broke in came down the mountain, sliding as you say? It wasn't publicized."

An itch jerked his left shoulder, the split moment of time giving him all he needed.

"Small town, people talk. Deputy Hancock was with the FBI guy Cox when I was out with Ashley Saturday night. We came around the corner and they were at the base of the hill looking at the blood in the snow," he explained, shrugging away the last of the itch.

"Blood in the snow is common?" the officer asked, watching him closely.

"Very," Kyle replied, moving his own nose in response. "Our altitude is 7,792 feet. Out of towners are always getting bloody noses. You know," Kyle continued, as if a thought had come to him. "A Naturalist would be an out of towner. The elevation in Denver is nearly four thousand feet less than Ouray. That would make sense then with what Old D said, wouldn't it?"

Jim's eyes roamed his face. "Yes, it would, except that the blood on that particular spot on the ground was yours. Can you explain how it got there?"

The itching Kyle had experienced on his back and neck turned to pain, merging like two, electrified rods that started cresting over his cheeks, to his ears and up his temples. *Think!*

"Guys, do you have any aspirin?" he groaned, purposefully ignoring the comment. "That stuff you injected is killing me. For the blood—I work right there and go back and forth from there all the time. I get nosebleeds same as everyone else."

Kyle heard the tapping of finger on metal. Lex's dark fingers were nearly invisible against the charcoal casing of the semi-automatic.

"Holding a gun make you feel powerful?" he asked Lex.

The crunch felt like an explosion under his eyes and to either side of his cheeks, the force knocking him back and off the chair to the floor. He'd never had a broken nose, but was pretty sure this was it.

At least the bruising will be even on both sides.

Kyle spat up blood, the warm liquid spilling over a bottom lip he could barely feel. Kyle wondered what in the world had possessed him to aggravate the officer. He then felt a kick to the ribs, his legs curling in protectively.

The door crashed open and Kyle heard the shuffling and grunting of a fight. In his peripheral vision, he saw Lex's left elbow shoved under Mark's chin, pinning him to the wall. Mark was a big guy, but the Patrol officer had the tactical technique.

"We asked you...politely...to stay outside," Lex told Mark, emphasizing his words with an upward shove.

"Drop him," ordered Jim. The scraping of a jacket against the wall was followed by feet hitting the ground.

Kyle saw a body flying into the desk, sending it crashing into the wall, the assault rifle sliding across the floor. He fully expected the man to be Mark, but it wasn't. By the time Lex got to his feet, Mark had the end of the gun pointed at his chest.

"Up here, you are no different to me than a buck on the ridge waiting to be dropped," Mark said, his voice low. Without another word, Mark chucked the gun at Lex who caught it expertly. "You gonna use that?" Mark challenged. "You better make sure you down both me and Kyle, and don't forget those cameras up there streaming straight to State headquarters in Denver." Kyle glanced around, seeing cameras in each corner he'd never noticed before. "Your move, big shot."

Kyle had never seen this side of his hometown friend; the one that assured him Mark didn't have a problem killing a person under the right circumstances.

"Thought so. I'll be waiting outside for Kyle." Mark positioned himself beyond the door, turned half-way, ideal viewing for both the street and the office.

"Lex, if you're going to carry out Reese's order for containment, you don't do it in front of the town's only Deputy and on camera," Jim admonished. "Here kid. Lift."

With the quick motion, Kyle groaned and hurled on the floor, barely missing Lex who jumped to the side.

"Just like Marty told us," said Jim. "An athlete but a complete lightweight. Go have Hancock see if there's a local medic who can come by on the quiet. He may have a concussion; chemicals don't do this."

Once Lex left the room, Kyle felt Jim's hands on his back. "Easy as you go down," he murmured. "We have enough necessary deaths without adding one that's not."

Kyle had one hand on the wall, the racks of pain spiking up his neck and into his eyes, the agony in his face causing another round of black and white spots. The partially opened door let in a sub-zero breeze, momentarily removing the stench of puke, simultaneously helping Kyle clear his mind.

He choked back another heave, doing his best to control the ache in his body that threatened to overpower him.

"But I'm a good object lesson for anyone else who wants to rebel?" he assumed.

"You're only an example if people see you."

Kyle just wanted the world to stop spinning. He tried not to move any part of his face other than his lips.

The door clicked and three people entered. Lex, Mark and a woman Kyle first thought was Billy, then squinted.

"Ruth?"

At the southern tip of Colorado, Billy stood beside her Uncle Roy. They stared through the glass wall as men and women moved efficiently between the dust-free appliances. Instruments, hanging and self-standing covered the grey steel counters. The room resembled a high-end modern kitchen in Paris—on steroids.

A tall man with black glasses popping against his salt and pepper hair appeared in the outer hallway, the door whooshing open as he pressed his badge against the code pad. He went directly to a book, scribbling then left to another room.

"He's logged in and now needs to change," her uncle explained.

Billy heard a whoosh and looked up.

"The air handling system," her uncle said, anticipating her question. "They stay on 24/7, preventing even a single errant particle from getting into tissue cells. Just because we are here on the reservation doesn't mean the tribal procedures vary one whit."

Billy pulled her eyes away just long enough to see a nearly invisible sticker on the window. It looked like an accreditation of some type, and asked her Uncle.

"Yes. It's the CGMP, the pharmaceutical standard for ensuring the quality regulation for human pharmaceuticals."

"Pretty sophisticated for a reservation isn't it?"

"On the contrary," said her uncle. "We started building our own labs before the turn of the century, around the time the government allowed full blown medical centers. With that went a parallel scholarship program to fund any likely physician on the reservation. Most took the money and left, but a few stayed. Those who did helped build the foundation of what you see today, thirty years later."

The man returned in full gear, his head covered with a bouffant cap Billy had seen on surgeons. He wore a blue mask on his face and on top of this he wore a clear shield. On his hands were thick gloves reminding Billy of the cooking mitts worn by the chefs at her father's restaurant, his body and feet also covered.

"In the four days since we've transferred the DNA, the epithelial cells for the faces are half-done. In another three, they'll be completed."

She looked at him, skeptical. "No way," she disputed. "It used to take three weeks to grow organs, like blood vessels."

"Thirty years ago," he said with an educated smile. "With the use of human growth hormones and technology, that time has collapsed by two-thirds, so has the surgical time. Let me show you."

As the man walked into another room, they followed in the hallway.

"This is the room for liquid nitrogen, where they freeze the samples." Another technician joined the man, in his hand a clipboard. "Those are the cryogenic tanks filled with the liquid nitrogen," he explained. Billy thought they looked like giant milk jugs, the off-white barrel like containers on rollers with a wide, round red lid. They watched as he opened the top, releasing the gas into the air. "Those giant metal hooks are called canes, and each cane can hold hundreds of samples. They are likely checking out a sample in order to thaw it and use it."

"Are all those facial cells?"

"No. They freeze any type of cell cultures they need, be it blood, tissues, organs, you name it."

Billy watched the man in the bright blue uniforms working in unison, the tall technician carefully removing a vial.

"Cane 1, position 205," said the tall technician.

"Cane 1, position 205," the second technician repeated.

"For redundancy," guessed Billy.

"All heck would break loose if a strict checks and balance didn't exist." Billy could only imagine; thinking you were pulling out a bladder sample and ending up with a heart sample.

"Shouldn't they close that door back there?" she asked, suddenly worried they'd missed something.

"That's open on purpose," he informed her. "Anytime you are handling a sample within the liquid nitrogen area, it has to have good ventilation or you could suffocate. You're never going to find a cryogenic tank in a closet for example."

The white mist in the air dissipated when the lid was closed back down. "What's the temperature in there?" she asked.

"-346F to -320.44F is the point at which nitrogen exists in a liquid state, that's the reason for the heavy duty gloves and outfits. If a drop of liquid nitrogen gets on you, it freezes and your skin necroses. Dies," he clarified. "If it hits the floor, it will hit the ground like b-bee's and roll around until it evaporates into a gas."

They both walked into the adjoining room where two technicians stood at the door. These were dressed in similar outerwear, with head bonnet and masks, but the white plastic sleeve covers ran up past their elbows.

The technicians repeated the cane and position number, one logging it into the book while the other held accepted the transferred vial.

"Now that they have the sample, its gradually warmed up in a water bath," he explained. "If warmed too quickly it will destroy what you've so painstakingly created."

Billy observed the containers on the brushed stainless steel counters. Electronic gauges identified the temperature, the technicians moving efficiently between the areas, selecting those ready to be worked with.

"Once thawed, the tissue goes into the next area, which is the incubator lab. It's really where the magic happens."

The third room was double in size of the others, large, refrigerator-size lockers lining the back wall, their glass fronts disclosing floor to ceiling shelves. Next to those were a bank of smaller, clear fronted fridges.

"What is it that humans need to survive?" he asked her.

"Food and shelter."

"Exactly. Cells are no different. They need food, which is called media, and then a shelter to grow. Different cells like certain mediums. The main food is a bovine serum from cows for a lot of human tissue. It gives them food to chew on, and then they are put in the growth environment with a specific temperature, gas mixture and humidity. Ah, see here," he said turning her attention to very large flat-bottomed bottles neatly stacked inside the incubators.

"It's like a flask that you would drink hard liquor from, but it's clear," Billy observed. "But what's that red stuff?"

"That's the food for the cells," he said. "And notice that the bottom of the flask is flat. That gives these adherent cells a surface to grow on. What's really cool is that the flask has been tissue culture treated, referring to the process by which hydrophobic polystyrene surfaces are made to become hydrophilic, usually by increasing the negative charge through chemical means. This increased negative charge is important for cell attachment---"

"Oh—" she interrupted with excitement. "I remember this from biology. Some cells like to stick to things and some like to float around."

"Correct. You put the cells in with their food, lay them flat they stick down and grow. You can stack hundreds of flasks up which collectively can hold billions of cells. Each flask of cells goes inside the incubator, and you have a Garden of Eden growth environment."

"It's like glorified chicken eggs," Billy quipped, knowing her uncle would laugh. "Question," she said, turning serious. "Why the purple gloves?"

"Ah, all the technicians wearing purple nitrile gloves, because so many people have latex allergies. They've long since become the standard in the surgical centers."

Billy stood in awe as she watched samples being removed from the incubator, examined and then placed back in the incubator.

"This next part is important," he said. "Watch."

"Cane 3, position 49," said one technician.

"Cane 3, position 49," repeated the other. The first technician took the vial over to a three foot tall canister.

"Not all cells live after being thawed," he told her. "They are putting the vials into the centrifuge. A centrifuge spins the cells at a high rate of speed, forcing the contents inside the tubes to separate. The living cells drop to the bottom and form a pellet, the dead ones usually stay floating in the liquid or what we call supernatant. We repeat this process several times to separate the viable vs the dead cells."

They watched the technician place the vial into a container, shut the lid and start the machine, the vials whirling within. A few minutes later, she removed the vial, giving it to her partner who sat at a counter.

"Now she's taking the live cells, getting rid of the waste which is the old food and giving them new food. Remember I mentioned the magic? To grow the cells in mass quantity, you provide food that causes them to start interacting and talking with each other. The cells literally self-determine what function they are going to be. Some will decide to be the outer layer of epidermis, another says: I'm going to be the dermis or connective tissue part. We use a human growth hormone in the cell development to reduce the time from three weeks to seven days."

One of the technician's stood, opening the largest incubator. "See those?" he asked her. "The cells for the faces are floating in their own food. We are now just a couple steps away from a new face. Come with me."

Billy walked beside her uncle, and he led her to an adjoining series of rooms reaching one resembling a Claymation studio more than a lab.

"Our relatives down in the Mesa Verde area worked for decades to form and mold clay around the skeletons just as forensics specialists. Today, we are using 3D CAD drawings to create the biomesh for the newly-grown skin. Think of it as dissolving scaffolding that can be removed once the face adheres."

Billy's eyes went to three people sitting on metal stools, each involved in a different task.

"You see," he continued, "the skin itself can't just lay flat over the bones and facial structure. When the government inserted the transmutated gene, the bone structure underneath was also likely changed to fit the face. We got around that by 3D modeling for bone and facial structure."

Billy looked at a CD image of a person. "The cultivated cells are carefully removed from the bottom of the flask using a proteolytic enzyme called trypsin dunked into a new food medium, and then seeded on top of the biomesh. The cells start to adhere to the mesh and start growing into epidermas skin. Watch here."

Billy felt her breathing go shallow as a technician removed a single piece of skin that was adhered to a biomesh from the incubator. It had its eyes, nose and lips cut out. She carefully lifted the attached skin with prongs and dipped it into what looked like red juice. It was nauseatingly fascinating.

"This is the final stage of growth," he told her. "The last few days of the process. The entire face is floating in medium and accelerator. Think of it like putting down seed for a lawn, and needing to fertilize it and hook up the hose for watering. Those cells are going to attach to the mesh because it's built out of something they want to grow on."

Billy thought of Kyle's intended career in the biotech field which had begun long before this went down. Computer science was cool, but this was revolutionary.

"Now the entire organ—the face—is going into the bioreactor to complete the growth cycle. What's unique about the face is that unlike a bladder or other organ, which would be put back in the body and grown, the biomesh just dissolves. For faces, once the final growth is done, the transplant will take place."

"There's one major question mark however." He hesitated, looking around her face instead of at her eyes. "We don't know if the skin from the DNA cubes is legitimate and will take as expected. A regular facial transplant has always been done from a cadaver, which requires days of pre-antirejection drugs. Add on top of that a week or two of recuperation and months or years of healing with a high possibility of rejection. *But*," he continued, emphasizing the word, "with the recipients DNA being placed atop a modified face—"

"You wouldn't have any rejection," she anticipated, "in theory. I can see the problem. No trial patients." Only the most adamant person would strip off their perfectly good face without having a high probability it was going to work.

Billy's heart pounded equally with excitement and fear, the image of Kyle in her mind's eye.

"You can use me," she volunteered. "My face should be an exact replica of what I have right now, verifying if what's on those cubes is real and correct. No one would ever know either," she added, "a complete bonus."

Her uncle was quietly assessing her. Something in his manner struck him as odd, and she guessed.

"You were thinking of this the entire time, weren't you?" He slowly nodded. "And that's why you wanted me to come back, not to be away from the town, but to test out the faces."

"I wasn't going to force you—but I was hoping."

"You hoped correctly I'd be all in on this."

Her uncle nodded, then tapped the window. A female technician looked up, acknowledging her uncle's head nod. The woman moved to the largest, double refrigerator on the left. Billy involuntarily gasped when she saw what was on the inside: it was full of individual flasks containing facial skin growing on the biomesh.

"There must be hundreds," she whispered.

"In that one alone. Thousands are already being cultivated in the others. We have almost no limits to the number we can grow."

The woman reached to the top tray, removing it. She approached to the nearest table, setting the metal tray in front of them.

Billy was at a loss for words. They were her faces, all five of them.

"Perfect replicas," said her uncle quietly. "They allowed for cell disintegration and death, creating extras, but nearly all survived the process."

"It only takes one," Billy responded, her resolve weakening a little at the faces. It wasn't hypothetical, it was real. The skin on her face would be outlined with a laser, removed and replaced with this perfect skin, one lacking her freckles and smile lines on the corner of the eyes.

"How long will it take for the surgery and the recuperation?" she asked, her voice subdued.

"Three surgeons and a small team will have you out of surgery in about twelve hours. As to the recuperation, assuming no rejection, it should be two weeks, the same as any other major surgery. The exactness of the DNA allowed us to enter it into the computer system and come up with a dot to dot alignment of nerve endings, which was both the reason facial transplants use to take up to 36 hours, and but also where you'd have dead zone spots on the face that looked a stroke victim."

Billy clenched her jaw, feeling the sensation of the muscles rippling under the skin.

"What about scarring?"

"Modern medical science applies to that area as well," he said with confidence. "Sutures will be under the skin, but topically, we won't have any sutures. They use skin glue, which is essentially super glue for the epidural layer. No scars whatsoever."

Billy pulled her eyes away from the skin in front of her.

"We?" she asked.

"I'm going to be having this same experience at the same time, same surgery, different rooms," he revealed. "We need more than one sample set."

That was slightly comforting; she wouldn't be alone. They'd be going through it together.

"You said in four days, give or take?"

"That's right."

Billy mechanically nodded. Would Kyle like the revised her as much as the real one? And the bigger question loomed. Would she?

CHAPTER
05

The rhythmic tone of a pulse monitor woke Brayden, the darkened room partially lit by the fluorescent lights above the sink at the end of his hospital bed. The curtain to his right was pulled back, the bed empty. He was alone, his right wrist handcuffed to the rails.

Next to his palm was a call unit. He pressed it, recollecting his last clear moments. It had been at the high school interrogation where he'd polygraphed the basketball team. Then a car, flanked by NSA agents. Now he was here in the room.

Many chemicals could erase the memory, but he suspected this kind was preceded by an interrogation.

The door opened and shut, the side angle of the face in front of him shielded by shoulder length blond hair. He felt unsettled and comforted, the meeting point of the emotions he associated with his wife.

"Hello, Brayden."

"Laura," he responded, as though greeting his wife while he was in handcuffs were nothing out of the ordinary.

She came to his side, her warm fingers checking his pulse, the smock of her physician's uniform wrinkle free.

"Surgery today or are you on call?" he asked.

"Both."

He watched her eyes, wondering if all she were considering was his health. In a world where she'd told him she was moving to another city but wanted to remain married, nothing about their relationship was normal.

"Anything interesting?" he prompted, hoping for more than one word answers.

She nodded, her attention on the monitors beside him. "A forty-one year old mother of three came in with a migraine, her speech garbled. Within the hour, she had died, the brain aneurism exploding before we had the chance to stop the bleeding."

"God," he mumbled.

"That's who she's presumably with," Laura said, the monotone of her voice keeping a high and thick wall around the thought that their own son was in the same place.

"Last week," she said, continuing in her detached tone, "we had another female who came with similar symptoms. In that case, the x-rays showed two aneurisms about ready to go. Open your eyes wide," she requested. She gently lifted his eye brow, speaking as she shone the light in his eyes. "So few survive the surgery, we suggested she say her goodbyes to her family members, but," she paused, going to the other eye, "survive she did. Only after we'd sown her back up did the x-rays uncover a huge miss on our part. She had a third aneurism."

"You're kidding."

His wife clicked off her light. "I wish. That time, we completely removed the skull..." Brayden listened to his wife's clinical recounting of the procedure, inspecting her face as she continued her tasks.

"Will she make it?" he asked, genuinely curious.

"She probably has about thirty angels over her shoulder to have made it this far, so I'm guessing yes. That said, statistically she'll have problems down the road. Paralysis, multiple sclerosis. Other issues."

Brayden thought about the angels notion. "Angels or not, your work must have been exquisite."

His wife's eyes softened. "An uncommon word associated with surgery, but yes, it was the best we could give. Dr. Natter assisted."

Brayden didn't respond. When Laura had initially said she'd taken a job in Coeur d'Alene, Idaho, she'd mentioned it was because it was the fastest growing surgical center in the West, but Brayden had hypothesized it was more probable that she'd met a doctor at a conference, hooked up and this is where he was located. Natter usually attended the same conferences as Laura did, and it had fleetingly occurred to him that the two had started an affair. It wasn't until a teenage boy in Ouray had opened his eyes to another possibility for his wife moving--a reason so shocking, so infuriating and yet hopeful-- that he'd decided to give Laura the benefit of the doubt.

He was glad he did. That choice had saved Kyle Smith's life, maybe Mark Hancock's and most certainly his own.

"That's a thoughtful look," Laura observed. She sat in the chair against the wall, legs crossed, her elbows on one knee, leaning forward with interest.

"I was thinking about Idaho and your upcoming move. By the way, what day is it?"

"Next Friday."

They assessed one another, Brayden contemplating their unique situation. He was in the FBI. She was a surgeon specializing in brain and trauma. Laura also had been a government research scientist and advisor for years. He guessed she likely knew the chemicals he'd been given and how long it would take him to fully recover.

"You are over the worst of it now," Laura offered, as if she could read his mind. His tongue still felt thick and his mouth dry, but the metallic taste was already dissipating. The remaining after effects would be gone in the next twelve hours. That wasn't what bothered him.

He lifted the handcuff. "You think so?"

"That's on your side. Medically, we have no reason to keep you here."

"Laura…" he had so much he wanted to say, but in his new world, he wasn't sure what would qualify as safe any longer.

He turned over his free palm, the invitation hanging. She came to his side, placing her hot hands on either side of his. For the last year, her increasingly warmer temperatures had bothered him. Today, it was welcome.

She looked at the monitor, the upbeat tone of her voice at odds with her serious expression. "How's your head now?"

"It would be a lot worse if you hadn't given me the migraine pills," he said, the little white blockers what he'd shared with both Mark Hancock and Kyle. "Thanks for that."

She ran the top of her fingers along his palm. "I thought they might come in handy."

"Did you hear about Saachi?" he asked.

"She arrived by Life Flight Friday night. She's sedated and is in stable condition."

Brayden stroked the top of her hand with his thumb. "Prognosis?"

"She might regain the use of her arm. Her face should take to the skin grafting as well as anyone's does, but due to the color of her skin, it won't be a perfect match."

Saachi was a beautiful, small spitfire of Indian descent, her warm coloring and complexion the best of what India produced.

"What would it take to match the skin if you could grow it?"

"Depends on lab availability and money," she answered. "Labs are scattered around the country by region, and they have a list of orders for life savings organs like livers. Typically, a facial transplant recipient is a full-fledged burn victim due to domestic abuse or another fully violent incident. Not sure this would meet the criteria."

Brayden blinked. "A burn caused by a lab explosion doesn't count as violent?"

"To clarify," Laura said kindly, "while unfortunate, only part of her jaw and neck are affected. Her eyes, nose and lips aren't compromised. Like I said, she needs to agree for the grafting on what she has right now, which she may not want. To have a complete facial transplant..." His wife left the comment hanging.

"Is she coherent enough to ask her what she wants?"

"In a few hours, yes."

Brayden wondered whether Saachi would rather keep what she was born with, even with these new scars or imperfections.

"After all, that's what makes us unique," Brayden said more to himself.

"What makes us unique?" Laura asked.

"Our experiences," he answered, feeling a rush of love for the wrinkles at the corner of her eyes, created from bright smiles and deep, gut-wrenching tears. "The events that show up on our face, which can't be hidden away in our heart or underneath clothes. I'm glad I'm going through this with you."

The door clicked and with it, so did the momentary tenderness in his wife's eyes. "Let's hope so."

On her way out of the hospital room, Laura was given a big hug by Brayden's section boss, Mitch Cooper. Brayden thought it was the least she deserved after twelve years of Christmas parties and summer socials. When they released their embrace, Laura gave him a final, detached look and left.

"That doesn't look like fun," remarked his supervisor, his eyes on the handcuff.

Mitch rested against the counter opposite Kyle's bed. Brayden's chief was a fifty-three year old former triathlete who'd applied to the Air Force Academy and was accepted, but dropped out when he failed the eyesight exam. Eight miles away was the University of Colorado in Colorado Springs. Swapping flying for football, Mitch went on to become a first-string running back. After graduation he couldn't shake the itch for the military, joined the FBI and never looked back. Technically, Brayden had two bosses: one for the local activity which was run by Mitch, and Gary for the projects out of headquarters. Most of the time, the two didn't overlap, operating independently from one other, except for details provided to the other on a need-to-know basis. Brayden wondered how much Gary thought Mitch needed-to-know now.

"It was a set up to flush out the Naturalists," Mitch said bluntly.

"Did it work?"

"Not even close," said Mitch with disgust. "All the young men you polygraphed were subsequently injected without the resulting benefits. Seriously," he added, responding to Brayden's dark look. "You have a lot of pissed off parents, including one mother who is raising holy hell with the state police, even tracking down O'Connell at State."

Brayden could only think of one woman who'd be so bold, or naïve, to do such a thing. "Kyle Smith's mom?"

"You guessed his mother because he was called out in your report?"

"It was only logical. In a town of people who toe the line, she's the nonconformist."

"She's going to be the dead nonconformist if she doesn't keep her mouth shut," predicted his supervisor without sympathy. "The simple reality is her kid couldn't handle the effects of the juice. He got mouthy, catching several punches from the guard."

"Kyle got hit?" Brayden asked with surprise.

Mitch nodded. "Broken nose, two black eyes. She took a picture and that's what O'Connell got at state." He pulled out his phone, turning it around for Brayden to see. "She threatened to go to the press because her kid was essentially catatonic when they dropped him at his home. She started with the Deputy, then it went upstream to O'Connell, who sent it along to Gary…"

"Then down to you," guessed Brayden.

"Full circle it came," Mitch finished, putting the phone back in his pocket. "The irony is that the kid was clean, in fact, the entire group of them were."

"Everyone passed?"

"Including the Deputy." Brayden opened his mouth in surprise. "Yep. They wanted to be sure he wasn't protecting the locals, but nothing."

The pills had done their job, Brayden thought with satisfaction. Way to go Kyle *and* Mark.

"What now?" he asked his boss.

"You're going to be released after Gary's next meeting, with the other department heads and President."

That was impressive. In the dozen years Brayden had worked under Gary he'd not seen him go to battle for an underling. "You will remain in custody until the final paperwork is complete. You know what that means."

Brayden nodded. "More breadcrumbs for the Naturalists to follow?" His records were being manipulated, the details of his circumstances altered just in case a hacking occurred. The set-up ruse would continue. Brayden could only hope Gary didn't get fired, in which case he'd be taking Brayden's veil of innocence with him.

"If the Naturalists really thought you had valuable information, they would have found a way to take you alive," Mitch volunteered. "In fact, Gary thinks that's what might have happened to Saachi. She was close to knowing who got into the mine, perhaps the Naturalists knew it and wanted to stop her from communicating the facts."

Brayden hadn't thought about that possibility. "Then you think they are going to go after her again?"

"It's possible, but unlikely. She's likely to be in and out of surgery for several weeks. The Naturalists have better things to do."

Brayden considered telling Mitch about the Naturalist who attacked Kyle, but decided against it. That would lead back to Mark, who had helped clean up the mess, sparing the community from the full-on intrusion of the Patrol coming to town, preventing mass devastation.

"What you're saying is the Feds think the person who did all this is still there?"

Mitch nodded.

Brayden listened as Mitch described the strategy Janet had outlined to Gary. "Why would the NSA bother with a hunt for something so small it can be carried by anyone, anywhere, including oral crevices?" he asked Mitch.

"That's why they are meeting with the President. The spooks at NSA believe they have a link to the Montrose blowup and one of their own people."

"Someone in the NSA is a Naturalist sympathizer? The irony increases."

Mitch crossed his arms. "I'll tell you what. You get me in a room with any one of the Naturalists without a camera and it would be all over."

"You think?"

Mitch whistled, the sound of a man confident that killing someone could easily be accomplished without a firearm. "You take nearly forty years of progress and want to turn it back, to what? I like this version of me," Mitch continued, turning his head to the right, pulling the skin tight. Brayden laughed, the man's ego fitting his looks perfectly. "I might volunteer myself to go track and smack whoever it is."

Brayden forced the smile to remain on his face. Thoughts of Kyle and Billy permeated his visual. Mitch was a lifer, a tried and true believer in all things government-issued. Things would be very different had Mitch been sent to do Brayden's job. Kyle would be dead, and the cubes would be back in the government's hands. But they wouldn't have their ultimate target--the Naturalists--who were still on the run.

"Be careful what you wish for Mitch, you might get your chance."

"And I'd like that," said his boss, standing. "Given what Gary said, I'm thinking the paperwork will be done in the next twenty-four hours, then we are back to task. You going to be up for it?"

Brayden nodded, ignoring the throb at the base of his skull. "More than."

"Good. I'll get on that paperwork."

Brayden thanked him and closed his eyes when the door shut. He had no idea what he was in for next.

Eight miles away, Danny Amato stared at the screen in front of him, the blue illumination bouncing off the green glass of his modern desk, a mirror version of the glow of the window to his right. The streets were full of pedestrians immune to the cold of the mile-high city, the bars of the Golden Triangle district busy no matter the time of day. The area was new, sexy and hip, everything that he was not. But he could more than afford half the floor of glass and steel on the eighth floor from which to command a piece of the world. He was the top of his field, and tonight, he'd found something unique.

"There you are," he murmured to himself. His day job included running Danny Amato Consulting, a perfectly legitimate consulting firm allowing him to use his best hacking skills to ferret out criminals in the government system. It gave a salary and best of all, an insight into the most advanced military happenings in the world. In truth, seeing what no one else did was more of a turn on than any drug or woman; the high incomparable to the sometimes obscene amounts of money he received just to detect and deter foreign entities from stealing his country's own secrets.

"But sometimes it is our own that are doing us wrong," he said aloud. His primary task for the NSA included monitoring the satellites in and around the western states. Doing a routine check of the data log, he noticed files had been swapped out.

As though copying and pasting would do the job. Even if you changed the time stamps it could be tracked if it wasn't done properly.

"And that's when I found you," he mumbled. The individual was clever enough to replace footage capturing a person entering and leaving a mine, but not smart enough to cover his or her tracks. The person also didn't know about the redundancy Danny had put in place, allowing him to access the original files himself.

The break-in was followed by internal threads between the NSA and FBI.

"And every keystroke, word and sentence recorded so the ultimate big brother can spy on all of you," he said, slightly gleeful. It had been his group who was hired to deploy the code tracking software on every computer in the bureau and NSA.

The FBI had gotten involved, sent personnel to Ouray in the hopes of retrieving these things. Teenagers had been taken, an FBI agent hurt in an explosion and another arrested.

All for some cubes referred to as storage devices.

What, he had wondered, could be so important that both the NSA and the FBI had sent personnel to a remote town only to come up empty, and two of their own hurt and in custody?

Answering the question had become a side distraction of his work, like an episodic reality show providing entertaining installments. He waited and watched, knowing someone would type too much or make a mistake. And they had.

"And now, whoever you are, I have you, and I'm tracking you, without you even knowing it."

Danny wasn't doing anything with the information he was gathering. He was watching and waiting. He hadn't been hired by the government to look after its own people, at least not on this project, and he wasn't compromising any deep, dark secrets. He was just being a voyeur. It was a feeling of power and control.

And it was harmless, he told himself, glancing down at the streets below. If and when what he saw went cross grain to his contracts, then *maybe* he'd say something.

In the meantime, he'd just follow along, the entertainment value worth the time, the boost to his ego more than worth the effort.

CHAPTER 06

Mark hovered behind Ruth, positioning himself between her and the door. Not that someone in town was going to be strolling by the police department at five in the morning.

Except for Kyle's dad. Ed was the town's earliest riser, his dawn walks legendary in the fifteen years they'd been residents. And now that his kid had been taken, Mark was rather surprised Ed hadn't been hovering in the dark with a pistol, demanding an explanation.

"Eyes dilated and the bump is a good size," Ruth was saying, her tone objective and reasonable. "A doctor wouldn't prescribe anything other than keeping him upright and awake for the next few hours to prevent a clot. Kyle?" she said, cupping his chin with her fingertips. "You need to stay awake for the next six hours or so. Can you do that?"

Kyle slowly nodded his head, causing Ruth to look up at him. "After that, no running, jumping and no more fighting," she counseled, her humor overlaying genuine concern.

"I'll tell his parents," Mark promised. He felt eyes on him and stared straight at Lex. Had Lex lunged for him, he would have shot the gun in an instant, claiming self-defense. He supposed Lex knew it as well. No one was going to come into his town, harm his people and leave unscathed.

"We'll take him back," Jim said, already preparing to lift him up.

"No you won't," Mark countered, his hand on his gun. Ruth was right beside him and threaded her arm under Kyle's shoulder. In the face of the two locals, Lex remained in place, motionless.

Mark took the other side, and without a word, they lifted up Kyle.

"Keep your head up," Ruth coached. "You need deep breaths so you don't get nauseous again."

"I'll come back to lock the doors," Mark promised.

"No you won't," replied Jim. "We've got two kids done, seven more to go."

Mark caught Ruth's worried look as they guided Kyle outside. "I have my car," she said, but Mark shook his head.

"Ruth, I appreciate your help, but you can't do anything more here. I doubt his parents have the insurance to take him to the doctor and you can't risk Stu seeing you."

She snorted. "Forget about my dad, and I'm no plastic surgeon, but I've helped on enough of these in the emergency room to know how to get him set up."

Mark unlocked his car and they eased Kyle inside. "If you can do it, I'm sure Kyle will greatly appreciate it."

Ruth laughed. "I'm doing it only partially for him. The other part is for my sister. I want him back to his perfect self so Ashley can see exactly what she's missing and regret every single moment she mistreated him."

Mark sat Kyle upright, his hands on either side of his shoulders in case he fell over. "Kyle, we're only going down the street. Can you stay upright?" Mark's concern increased as Kyle's eyes rolled. "Are you sure he's going to be okay?"

Ruth pulled her lips in. "Okay is relative, Mark. His memory for the last twenty-four hours and for the next day or two may be completely shot. Whether or not he will ever recall what's happened is anyone's guess. I'll meet you back at his house and we'll be able to tell his parents what to do."

"Or what not to do," Mark muttered. "Having his mother run to my bosses yet again is only going to make life worse for Kyle."

At that, Ruth gave him a worried look. "As if that's even possible."

For Kyle, the hours passed in a blur of pain, visions of Billy coming to mind. When he finally felt coherent long enough to concentrate on his surroundings, he realized just how much his face hurt.

"Do I look as bad as I feel?" he asked his mother.

"Worse," his mother quipped. "Ruth fixed your nose as best she could, but made no promises about what she suspects are needlepoint fractures on your cheekbones"

Needlepoint fractures? He moved slowly to touch his nose, this time dancing his fingertips on the surface of the skin. "Is my nose broken?"

"Uh-huh," confirmed his mother. "You're lucky. Mark got Ruth to come over without Stu knowing. And now I'm going to insist on you sleeping, which is what you've been wanting to do for the last day. Here. Take these. You need to sleep."

Kyle swallowed the pills, thinking of Ashley's sister. "She'll get in trouble with Stu."

His mother chuckled. "Oh no she won't. She's too smart and Stu too stupid to think his least favorite daughter is going to help you out."

"She has no idea what she should look like," Kyle mumbled, his eyes already closing.

"What'd you say hon?"

"Nothing. Tell her thanks for me if she comes by and I'm asleep."

"Sure thing."

At ten a.m. Monday morning, Billy had changed, wearing the white, open-backed top and drawstring bottoms, and got under the covers of the bed as directed. The room wasn't warm, and she wished the thin blanket was heated. The research scientists had patiently responded to her questions, but each answer was invariably accompanied with a caveat: this hadn't been done using a person's own skin cells; perhaps it would be tougher than what was on her face now, or maybe less so. It had been four days since she left Ouray, and over a week since Kyle had transferred the DNA data.

Today, they were going to use one of the five biomeshes created from her DNA and place it on her face. It was still four days until the skin would be considered fully developed, but this procedure was to check the form more than the finality of the skin. The entire surgical team wanted to see if the DNA records were true to life.

Billy took a deep breath, closing her eyes. She'd not told Kyle what she was doing, but of course she hadn't had the chance. He'd not contacted her, and she was unsure why. All he had to do was get the USB and media card from under Fred's rock and they could communicate.

"Hello Billy."

"Dr. Pike."

He came to her side as two other nurses followed behind . One carried a tray with a glass covering while the other held what looked like a portable imaging machine.

"Charlotte is going to put a covering on your upper body since this is going to be a little wet," he began, nodding to his nurse. Billy thought it resembled the lead jackets used by dentists before an x-ray, but it was lighter. Remembering what Uncle Roy had told her about food for the cells, she visualized her new face still eating the nutrients from the red juice right up until the time it was placed on her skin.

Billy shivered.

"I'd mentioned before it's going to feel both soft and hard," he said, watching her expression. Billy nodded, breathing deeply. "The firm aspect will be against your skin," he continued. "That's the biomesh or scaffolding. On top of that, the billions of skin cells are still feeding, so the media will seep through the biomesh and onto your skin."

"Can I look in a mirror?" In her peripheral vision, she saw the nurses glance at one another, then at Dr. Pike. "Is that a problem?"

"Not a problem per se," he answered, coming to her side. "In some ways Billy, the surgery is the easy part. The element that is completely out of a surgeon's control—and to a degree—the patient's, is the reaction to a new identity. In this case, you're not getting a completely new look, but more of an upgrade."

"Like a face lift twenty years before I need it," she quipped, her lighthearted response a cover for a deeper concern that she felt. Dr. Pike nodded somberly.

"Roy believes you are mature enough to handle it, but I have to say that a facial transplant is a lot for even a grown adult to deal with, but at any age it would be a shock. You'll be covered in red mesh, oozing liquid with the patchwork of cells resembling gauze more than skin."

Billy assessed his expression. She was sure he wanted her to be in a positive state of mind going in to the surgery, not obsessed with the outcome. But how could she not? This was her life, and once the surgery was over, there was no going back.

"Maybe you're right," she admitted. The final result was going to be different than a bloody mask overlaid on her face.

Dr. Pike looked relieved. "Lean back and try to relax. The more still you are, the better the 3D imaging will show if this new face is true to the DNA structure.

"Close your eyes, hon," Charlotte requested. "Breath deep, in and out. That's a girl."

Billy visualized Kyle, sleeping peacefully in his bed, the snow falling outside, his mom and dad working away in their front workroom. She felt the top move to her neck, the covering complete and now warmer than it had been.

"It's coming on now," said Dr. Pike. "Keep your eyes closed and body still."

Billy felt the wet, cold material from her chin, around her ears and up to her scalp, ending at her hairline. She envisioned Kyle in her front room, watching her closely. She'd recognized the look of interest, then desire, all the while maintaining a distance. She adored his admiring gaze and wondered if she'd still be on the receiving end of it after the surgery.

"Just doing some adjusting now," Dr. Pike told her. Billy thought she heard a gasp from one of the nurses, the sound turning into a hum of approval. "Yes," agreed Dr. Pike. "It appears to be a perfect fit. Nan, it's in place. Proceed with the imaging."

"Billy, I'm going to ask that you take a breath and hold it for ten seconds so your chest doesn't move," explained a new voice. "Raise your right index finger if you can do that so as not to move the position of the face." Billy raised her finger in response. "Good. Now let's begin….Hold…"

Six times Billy held her breath for the nurse. By the end of it, Billy was starting to feel claustrophobic. She unconsciously began moving her fingers against the bedding.

"You doing okay?" asked the doctor. Billy raised her index finger and moved it left to right. "The enclosed sensation bothering you?" Billy pulled in her finger as a yes. "We're almost done. Hang in there. And...now I'm going to start lifting off the biomesh."

Dr. Pike began from her chin, the biomesh covered skin coming off as a single piece from one end of her face to the other.

"Eyes closed until we clean you," requested Charlotte. A warm, wet cloth was placed on her face, the sensation calming. Charlotte moved the cloth across her skin, telling Billy she could open her eyes. The tray with her face was gone, along with the other nurse. Dr. Pike was examining her.

"How are you feeling?"

She was honest. "I hadn't realized how confining the experience would be."

"The good news is you'll never have to experience the sensation again. You'll be out for the duration of the actual surgery. Do you have any new concerns now that you've gone through this preliminary experience?"

Billy nodded, thinking of Kyle. "How do you anticipate what others will do when they see me, or how they'll react?"

Dr. Pike sat on the edge of the bed. "You can't. It's one of the great unknowns, but you hope those who care and love you will embrace whatever version of you emerges from the operating room. Do you have the support system around you to do that?"

"I only have my dad and boyfriend…"

"And they don't know what's going on."

Billy shook her head. "They don't even know where I am let alone what I'm planning on doing."

"Hmm. Well, you are going to hope for the best, because there's nothing else anyone of us can do at this point."

No there wasn't, but she could tell Kyle when he called her up. She'd left the burner phone and notations, along with the details of how to reach her on the dark net under the rock with Fred. All he had to do was remember she'd told him where.

What was he waiting for? She wondered. Because she'd not told her dad where she was going, calling him was out of the question. Reaching out to Kyle's parents also a bad idea; his dad Ed couldn't keep his mouth shut once he had a few beers in him and was up at the Elk Club.

No. She had to be patient and wait. There must be a reason Kyle wasn't calling. She only hoped the conversation occurred before she had the surgery and not after. She was going to be living with a new face in a few days, but he was the one having to look at her.

An hour later, Dr. Pike was sitting in his office when Charlotte entered.

"She's one brave young woman," admired his nurse.

"That she is," agreed Eric, continuing his examination of Billy's paperwork. "The scaffolding materials are working perfectly, just as we'd hoped."

"Check this out." Charlotte handed him a sheet which he quickly scanned. "All four dozen in our lab are on schedule," she said with satisfaction. "No deterioration or weakening of the cells as we feared."

The reservation labs in three states were growing hundreds of faces. In another week, it would be four times that amount.

Charlotte sat down, her expression transitioning from enthusiasm to discomfort. "Dr. Pike, I don't want to overstep my bounds, but may I ask you a question?"

He looked up, guessing. "Why are we doing this?"

She pursed her lips. "At first I thought it was for the scientific challenge but beyond that...."

Eric didn't expect her to understand. She was of the younger generation, her father married off reservation, their legacy within the Tribe marginal. Her memory of the greatness of the Native American people was relegated to the history books, just like the forgotten language of their people.

"Our tribe lost millions of acres of land, along with gold, silver, mineral and water rights, and my great great great grandfather gets a peak named after him."

"Pike's Peak," Charlotte said with reverence. "But that's exactly why I'm even more confused as to why you are helping the very entity that has screwed, blued and tattooed us."

Eric grinned.

"Help? No, no my colleague. We are going to hurt the government so catastrophically that they will be the ones fighting to retain control."

Charlotte pulled a metal chair beside him, her eyes bright. "You think this will help get our lands back?"

"Yes, and at first the government will have no idea what has happened. Then the general public at large will learn they've been betrayed; no one was spared except for the outliers, the non-conformists---"

"Or those on reservations who weren't susceptible to government oversight," she finished. "You want a revolt?"

Eric peered again at the samples she'd put before him.

"I want change, fair and equal, across the board," he answered. "And thanks to the sovereign-nation status afforded to the tribes, we'll have that. State of the art hospitals and medical facilities on every reservation, skilled medical personnel..."

She paused, rubbing her gloved fingers over one another. "But they need the DNA like we have."

"According to our source, that's being worked on as we speak."

As Eric said the words, his sense of justifiable retribution was high. They could start conducting facial transplants around the country and the United States Government would be powerless to stop them.

Over the next twenty-four hours, Kyle mostly slept, made the occasional bathroom trip and graduated to a bath and chicken noodle soup. His face had improved from blue to deep purple, the swollen skin stretching the stitches. He resembled a racoon after a night-long bender, the black extending from his eyes down his cheeks.

"Zombies look better than I do," he remarked to his mother as he stood in front of the fridge

"Perfect for Halloween, not so much for New Year's Eve." Kyle pulled out the milk, drinking it straight from the container.

"Hey now!" his mother scolded. "Just because you look like the walking dead doesn't mean you forget your manners at home."

Kyle replaced the gallon, searching the fridge for a meal. "New Year's Eve is tomorrow. I'm thinking maybe I can try going out."

"Hon, you've gotten a lot better in the last day, but you won't be going anywhere tomorrow night."

"It's Wednesday," he said. "What's going to be going on mid-week?"

He zeroed in on ham and cheese. "Mind?" She shook her head and he pulled out pickles and applesauce. "I'm more than well enough to sit lifeguard duty, and I'm sure Barrett's pissed I've been gone so long."

He sat down, shoveling the food in as though he'd been in the Ethiopian desert for a year. His mother watched him with interest.

"Your dad said business at the hot springs has been slightly slower over the last few days. Maybe it's the rumors going around about you and the boys. Lord knows after what I've seen and heard, I was ready to take up arms and start the next revolution, one officer at a time."

"I would have liked to see that," he remarked.

"Actually, you did," said his father as he entered the kitchen. "They took you in the middle of the night and your mom assaulted a member of the group who took you."

"I didn't assault anyone!" she protested.

"No, you took him down and left him begging for mercy?" Kyle suggested with a smile.

"Then I brought you home with your face all beat up, and Ruth performed back room surgery…" added a male voice.

"Well, hello Mark," his mother drawled.

His father offered Mark a cup of coffee, speaking as he poured. "Now your mother's probably on some government watch list, which is bound to help business."

"I'm sure of it," agreed Mark somberly, taking the cup from his father's outstretched hand.

His mother's laughter filled the small room, and Kyle couldn't help smiling.

"Kyle, I know this may look like a social call because I'm drinking your father's organic coffee," Mark began, "which is only tolerable because it's warmer than the 17 degrees it is outside, but this is actually business. Would either of you mind me having a few words with Kyle in his room?"

The laughter stopped immediately, and his mother's eyes grew wary.

"Go on," she said, the angry edge in her voice back.

In Kyle's room, Mark went to the window his attention on Ashley's house.

"Anything going on at the Fine's?" Kyle asked.

"Hmm," answered Mark, swallowing. "Depends by what you mean. Marty's on the front porch looking awfully uncomfortable. He just shook Stu's hand who looks like the funeral director at a mortuary. Ashley...well, she's probably never looked better."

"Being with Marty must agree with her."

Mark grunted. "Unlikely. The more realistic scenario is that she knows which direction your room faces and is gambling you will see her."

Kyle pulled out a long-sleeve wool shirt.

"You don't think she's going to see me and want everything my handsomeness promises?" Kyle had the satisfaction of seeing Mark's cheek wedge up with his smile.

"I like the new you," Mark observed. "A bit more rebellious and beat up, in other words, normal like the rest of us instead of the walking Greek god you were before." He turned to Kyle, his face empty of humor. "Anything coming back yet?"

Kyle pulled on his shoelaces, frustration evident in his face.

"When I do have a memory, it's like snapshots without the frame, the context doesn't make much sense. It makes me doubt if it's real or imagined. The last thing I remember is seeing Billy for lunch on Friday. Want to fill in the blanks?"

Mark inhaled, his broad chest raising his equally big belly up a fraction. "Be happy to. What you don't know could actually get you killed and me in jail, which is not a place I want to be."

Kyle sat forward, elbows on his knees. "You're serious."

"Unfortunately yes. The entire team was injected with a concoction civilians call truth serum. You also got beaten up because you mouthed off. If you didn't get any sympathy points from me before, this might be your ticket."

Kyle glanced at the side mirror. His nose and part of both cheeks were covered with gauze and tape, the open skin moist with some type of Vaseline.

"Did I deserve your anger?" Kyle asked.

"Deeply," Mark growled. "I believed your story and stood up for you only to look like a fool because you told me one scenario and your coach another. It got worse when it was Brayden who told me the truth about the mine, you and the cubes. Now this. Jesus, Kyle. What were you thinking?"

Kyle blew air out his swollen, sutured lips. "I don't remember."

A laugh of disbelief escaped from Mark's lips. "That's what you said before, so at least you are either consistently lying or consistently truthful."

"I'm sorry," Kyle said lamely.

"I hope so, but that's the problem with someone who lies, Kyle. You doubt the truth until trust is established."

"That's comforting," Kyle said sarcastically. He made the mistake of placing his head in his hands, yelping at the pain. He heard his parents and he called out he was fine.

"Mark," he began, hesitating for a moment. "I can't risk sharing more because you could be danger. What they did to me they could do to you."

"Too late. It's already happened." The town's lone deputy sheriff took another sip of coffee. "The bigger issue is the cubes. Before they had just gotten you in trouble. Now they have personal meaning for one reason: Saachi." Kyle didn't follow. "The lab was blown up, leaving another technician dead and Saachi badly wounded. She's at Denver Medical in the burn unit, alive, but badly injured."

Kyle was sympathetic and caught the implication in Mark's words. The DNA on the cubes could be used for Saachi as much as anyone.

"My news isn't as bad, but it's not good either," Kyle started. "I don't remember where I put the cubes."

Mark cursed. "Well, pray that part of your memory returns. In the vein of other bad news, Billy's gone. She left without saying goodbye, writing a short note to her dad not to worry. But her father's blaming you— no," he stopped the interruption, "let me finish. Ty believes you're the root cause because she was falling for you. That said, he also suspects she was being bullied by Ashley, her dad or both, so elected to skip town." Mark stopped talking and chuckled. "Do you remember the game and the kiss?" Kyle shook his head. "You blew the final shot, the entire auditorium erupted with boos, but instead of going to the locker room in shame, you went to Billy and you kissed her right there in front of God and country, just feet away from the Fine family. Stu about ripped you a new one for making Ashley look bad, then promised to send me back to being a private security guard when I tried to calm him down."

Kyle tried to recreate a scene he didn't remember.

"I bet Billy liked it," he said to himself.

Mark grunted. "I can see your ego didn't get the thrashing that your face did."

"Well, you clearly saw it," Kyle retorted, an ounce of happiness in his voice. "What did you think?"

A reluctant but clear look of admiration changed Mark's expression. "I can't lie. It was a Gone-With-the-Wind type of kiss if that tells you anything."

Kyle didn't remember the event, but felt all the love that must have accompanied it. The emotion was short-lived.

"Did Stu or Ashley really chase Billy away?"

Mark took another sip of coffee. "I can't imagine anyone getting under Billy's skin enough to make her leave, but from what I've seen in the last week, I put nothing past people now. Just be careful with Ty. I had to threaten him with imprisonment to prevent him from breaking down your door."

"But I don't remember anything anyway!" Kyle said, frustration and loss compounded.

"Billy's a teenage girl, but a brilliant and even-tempered one," Mark said evenly. "She's not a runaway, but someone who left with a plan and intent. Ergo, I didn't file a missing person's report, although Ty doesn't know that part and thankfully, the Sheriff had to go back and be with his mother who's still recovering from her heart attack."

"You're saying you have the run of the town for a while and Billy is where she wants to be, even if none of us know where that is?"

"Precisely."

While Kyle agreed with Mark's inaction, they both knew that after Ty's wife left him, Billy was his everything. Of course he was going to take it out on the person who'd raised Billy's emotions in the last two weeks.

Mark went to the door. "You're coming back into a world very different from the one you left Kyle, so get ready for it," he cautioned. "On the bright side, you've been out so long, the drama that you left in this town *might* have settled. Emphasis on the word, might."

"Wait," called Kyle, uncertain. "Where does that leave me?"

Mark's hand was on the door. "Friendless and hopefully insignificant enough to not attract attention. Exactly what I think is the best for you."

CHAPTER 08

After Mark had gone, Kyle got ready to leave. His time was going to be split between work and finding the cubes.

Kyle reached to the top shelf in his closet, expecting to find his hat with ear coverings. Instead, a box toppled onto him, crunching his nose. He groaned, seeing spots.

"You okay?" his father asked, coming to his side.

"Eventually," Kyle answered, breathing through the black spots.

He put his hand on Kyle's right shoulder, who dropped back in pain.

"Oh, sorry about that, wrong one," apologized his father, laughing. "Every part of you is beat up, and it wouldn't be so funny if it weren't so bad."

"Why are you still laughing then?" Kyle grumbled.

"Because it's now slightly worse. Stu delivered the message you're never to speak with his daughter again. He said if you come within one hundred feet of his home, a restraining order will be placed against you."

"Did you point out we live within one hundred feet of him? What's he going to do every time I walk to work?"

His father's focus landed on Kyle's nose, lips then cheeks. "Actually, I'm not convinced someone who's drowning is going to be comforted if you're the one doing the saving."

"Funny Dad, but they don't have a choice. Everyone knows I need the money."

Kyle headed out the door and stayed to the right, keeping to his side of the street. He crossed over Main just before the open field, fifty yards beyond Ashley's home. His annoyance turned to gratitude when he saw the parking lot was emptier than normal for a holiday. Maybe his absence wasn't the burden to the owner his father feared.

He said hello to Mandy at the front desk, pointing to the Barrett's office.

"Whoa!" Mandy exclaimed, scrunching her lips and nose. "Can you even breathe...or *see*?"

Kyle scowled. "I made it here didn't I?" Mandy tried to be polite but couldn't stop her eyes from darting up and around his face. "I know," Kyle admitted. "I'm a walking car wreck."

Mandy giggled. "Walk yourself into his office. I saw you coming down the field and let him know. He's waiting."

Barrett was on the phone when Kyle appeared in his doorway. Kyle's ego bumped up when Barrett's eyes expanded into what seemed to be admiration. This high was followed by a low when he turned to large pool area, catching a reflection of his face in the window. Perhaps his dad's insinuation was right: the patrons were likely to die if given the choice between Kyle saving them and drowning.

Well, maybe I can mop the floors and wipe down the weights in the upstairs gym until I heal.

Barrett waved him to a chair, gesturing for Kyle to shut the door behind him. That was a first. Nothing said at the pool required a closed-door discussion. The closest they'd come was Christmas Eve when his then-girlfriend had demanded Barrett give Kyle a desk job in order to give him more flexibility in his schedule. Kyle told him he'd quit if consigned inside. Barret had ignored Ashley, Kyle had kept his lifeguard job and life had continued.

Waiting for the Barrett's call to finish, Kyle examined the lap pool, then the hot tubs and sulfur ponds where Barrett kept the exotic fish and turtles. Not one area was more than a quarter full. Maybe the roads were bad coming out of Montrose, snarling traffic.

He focused on fish pond, knowing Fred was likely perched on one of his favorite rocks, perhaps even the very one where

Kyle had first hidden the cubes after he'd come down the mountain.

I had to have put the cubes there. It had proven to be the safest place over the last two weeks.

Kyle's thoughts drifted back to Billy. He recalled the first time he'd seen her body at the pool. She was slim but with athletic curves, not the straight lines of Ashley. Was Billy ever going to return, and when she did, would they start back at the beginning—before the famed kiss he couldn't remember--or somewhere else entirely?

Kyle crossed his legs, bouncing his foot to fend off the lethargy that was starting to hit. The heat drifting from the hot springs was having an effect.

Barrett finally hung up, his expression sour. "That's a good look on you."

"I think so," Kyle agreed, giving Barrett his profile. "The girls will be all over this." Kyle expected his joke to get a laugh, Barrett always being one to appreciate his humor.

Not now.

"Light crowd today," Kyle remarked, not wanting to make more of the weekend incident. "Was it like this over the weekend, too?"

Barrett followed Kyle's gaze, surveying the domain that had made the spa one of the more cash-flush businesses in the community.

"It was filled to capacity Friday night after the game, but you weren't here to notice," Barrett told him. "Saturday it eased off dramatically. Then you see today, where we are practically empty by comparison to years prior."

Kyle watched Matt and another lifeguard on duty, the two looking cold and bored on the metal stands. Maybe his dad was right about him not working, but for the wrong reasons. Kyle's face had nothing to do with the lack of swimmers.

"Sounds like you don't need me today."

Barrett put his hands on his rotund belly, inhaling deeply. It was a look of regret.

"I'm not going to be needing you at all for the foreseeable future. I'm letting you go, Kyle."

Kyle was stunned. He'd worked since he was old enough to push a broom and had never been fired.

"Because of this?" he asked, pointing to his face.

Barrett jerked his head to his right. "I could care less how you look. It's because your former girlfriend's father paid me a visit requesting I fire you. I told him to get out. This is my business and I'll run it as I please, including hiring those I want."

Kyle ran his fingers through his thick hair, absorbing what Barrett hadn't said. "How'd he get the people to stop coming?"

"That, my sharp friend, showed me just how far Stu's slimy tentacles reach. When the buses didn't arrive Saturday morning, I called the transportation company. Someone had paid them to take the visitors to the springs in Grand Junction."

"Two hours away?" Kyle asked in disbelief.

"With a free hotel stay overnight, meals included."

"All because I kissed Billy at the game?" Barrett looked grim. "Bribes can't last forever."

"Beyond money, Stu wields influence. Coincidentally, word of the Christmas Eve event wherein a patron had his or her diaper blowout found its way into the Telluride, Montrose and Durango rags—"

"No," whistled Kyle.

"Yes. And *somehow*, the words 'unsanitary', 'health risk' and 'may close for the season' were wrapped into the articles. Reservations have plummeted and the tour buses started rerouting nearly all their scheduled visits for next week. Even if Stu hadn't paid for the first bus to be misdirected, our fate was sealed, at least temporarily."

Kyle's jaw muscles flexed under his bruised skin. "I'm sorry, Barrett," he said, putting on his gloves. "The sooner I leave, the faster you can get back to running a business that's core to the town."

"An awfully mature comment coming from a seventeen-year-old."

"Eighteen next week," Kyle corrected, standing. Old enough to vote, be drafted for the military, leave town, and certainly go head-to-head with Stu.

Kyle swayed, the black spots returning. Barrett was by his side in a second, his girth at odds with his agility. Kyle gripped his boss's forearm, grateful for the hand. When he nodded, Barrett cautiously stepped back.

"For the record, I'm sorry along with you kid. There's no one in this town I'd like to stick it to more but..." He trailed off, his face red with the reality of being the lesser businessman.

"You have a family and employees. I get it." Kyle zipped his jacket. "Can I come back to use the pool? Maybe in the early morning or late at night when no one's around?"

"For now, give it a rest for a month, until February. I don't want your presence to be confused with you working here."

Kyle understood. Barrett needed business to return to normal; until then, Kyle was an unwelcome presence.

"Thanks for all you've done for me, Barrett. And sorry you've been put in this position."

Barrett extended his hand. "Me too, kid. Good luck."

Luck, thought Kyle. Not something I have a lot of at present.

But the cubes...

"Barrett, since I'm no longer welcome here, can I say goodbye to Fred one last time?"

His boss nodded his head. "Make it fast."

Kyle did, petting the turtle and pretending to rub the underbelly. He found a package under the rock where he'd initially told Billy he'd hid the cubes. Feeling under the water, he could tell this didn't contain squares but flat objects. He slid the items under his jacket and in less than five minutes, left the pool area.

From his living room window, Stu watched Kyle come out of his home and walk along his side of the street, cutting over to the pool at the second cross walk, closest to the facility. Even from the distance, Stu could see the kid's patchwork face of gauze and tape. It was worse than he'd been told.

An added bonus.

Stu stayed at the living room window after Kyle entered the rec center, anticipating the boy wouldn't be long. He was proven right. Barrett's job-terminating conversation had been efficient, less than fifteen minutes. Kyle returned to his home using the same path.

Kyle's now out of a job, thought Stu with satisfaction. His every move from here on out was going to be tracked, any chance he had of a life inside this town or outside shut down and shut off. He would be stymied in his goal to get out of town on a scholarship, his immediate dreams destroyed, just like he'd destroyed Ashley's heart on Friday.

As Kyle walked along the street, Stu caught his profile. To his dismay, Kyle wasn't hunched over. He was walking straight as an arrow, focused and sure, as though this were just the latest challenge in his life and he were going to face it head on.

"So he thinks," Stu murmured to himself.

"Thinks what?" It was Ashley, who'd come from behind. Before last week, Stu had sympathy for Kyle's situation in life, his parents and lack of Christmas activities while applauding his determination and drive. Then, Stu had been convinced Ashley wasn't good enough for the young man.

"He thinks he can outdo what he's done," Stu answered. In his peripheral vision, he saw Ashley's lips turn up with glee.

"It's over?" she asked.

At this, he turned to his favorite daughter. "Actually my dear, it's only just begun."

The knowledge that a USB and smart card were on his person urged Kyle to walk home faster than he would have. His pace, combined with a fragile nose ecosystem, caused waves of nausea along the way, forcing him to slow periodically, crossing from Stu's side of the road later than he would have. He knew how far 100 feet was, and he didn't care. The restriction only added to his determination and defiance.

Let him think he's hurting me. The man won't know what hits him when his world shatters before his eyes, hopefully, with the entire town watching.

Once he got home, Kyle poked his head into his mother's workspace, telling her he was going up to Ty's. No matter what was on the finger-sized devices, first he had to speak with Billy's father and make things right.

"Wear your face mask," his mother shot back.

"I wasn't planning on taking the ATV."

"I didn't say that because of the snow. It was additional facial-damage prevention."

"Funny, Mom," Kyle muttered.

"Actually, in all seriousness, your ATV didn't come with a first aid kit and doesn't have a compartment for a kit, but it might be good to find something that would work for that purpose."

"Like a tank bag?"

"If that's what you call it, then yes. I think we have a man's bag under the bathroom sink that might do for now."

Kyle nodded his head as he sat down in the office, inserting the smart card into the computer. He quickly scanned the three pages Billy had written, his smile increasing with his adrenaline which flowed like gas lines through a pump. He did as instructed, inserting the USB to double check the items Billy said were on it.

Perfect.

Kyle put on his heavy jacket, hat and goggles heading outside. He sat on the cold seat of the ATV, pausing. Thinking of his mother's advice, he returned to his bathroom, digging under the sink, finding what he wanted. He took an extra flashlight from the kitchen drawer, adding it to the basic emergency kit. Back under the carport, he unstrapped the two

Velcro bands, looping each under the front handlebar then pressing tightly over the strap. First aid kit ready for use.

He took the adjacent alley, thankful for the back road and buildings that shielded his coming and goings from Stu.

Kyle drove to the rear door of Ty's restaurant, slowly opening the door. He saw Dan the chef in front of the stove.

"Ty around?" It took Dan a moment to recognize him. "Yes, it's me. Kyle Smith."

"You're not real welcome around here at the moment." Dan had been on the job for less than a week, but already knew Kyle and Billy were a thing.

"Is that a yes or a no?" Kyle asked, maintaining his politeness. Dan hesitated a moment, then glanced at the side hallway, as though he were on the fence about Kyle's guilt or innocence. "Thanks. I'll try him at his house."

Kyle went around the corner, to the side of the building where Ty and Billy lived, waiting impatiently after he'd knocked twice without an answer. He was about to give up when the door opened. Seeing Ty's face, he involuntarily took a step back.

"Ty, before you say a word—"

"What did you do to her?" her father demanded.

"Nothing, I swear it. You saw what happened at the game, same as everyone else. You know how we feel about each other."

"Or felt," Ty roughly suggested. "Something changed and I want to know what."

Kyle grimaced, shaking his head with frustration. "That's half the problem, Ty. I don't remember what happened after the guys took me; my memories are gone."

"Sure they are," Ty drawled. "The excuse of getting jacked up by the Feds isn't flying with me."

"If you don't believe me, then give your daughter more credit," Kyle countered. "You know that if I'd done something to harm her, Billy would have lacerated me in epic fashion then told you about it. Her MO is not to run and hide. Even Mark said so."

"Whatever you did could have changed that."

"Ty, for all I know, you might have told her to stop seeing me, or done something else and she left because of you."

Ty's punch to Kyle's stomach doubled him over. He caught the door frame with his hand, spitting up phlegm. The blood seeped through the cracks in his lips that hadn't healed from his last beating.

"Hit me as much as you want," he groaned, grateful Ty chose his stomach, not his face. "But I want to know where she's at and why at least as much as you, maybe more."

"Shut up and leave."

Kyle pulled in his core, forcing himself to stand up straight. "And join your daughter?" Kyle demanded, knowing his words were personal and biting. "It's only four more months until we both leave anyway. Probably each of us our separate ways, but at least gone from this no stop-light town."

Ty's hand cocked back again, and this time, Kyle was ready. He blocked it by lifting his right arm, cutting up and into Ty's soft belly with this left.

"You son of a—" Ty choked, catching the door with his free hand. Kyle's intent was to send a message, not hurt the man.

"I only hit you because I'm not going to take any more abuse that's undeserved, from you or anyone else. There's a third possibility, Ty. You're not so mad that she's gone, but that she was actually happy to have fallen for someone. She's her own person, and you can't keep her here forever; just because you're alone and lonely doesn't mean you should consign her to the same fate. "

Ty looked up, his face black. "Get out before I call Mark and have you arrested for harassment and trespassing."

Kyle wanted to hit Ty again out of frustration, but it would only turn his one possible ally in town against him.

Kyle inhaled his pride, trying another approach.

"Ty, will you listen for a minute," Kyle pleaded. "You have to believe me when I say that I don't know what happened after the game. And no one can place me with Billy at all after that, not you, my parents, Mark—no one. How could I possibly have seen her, or done something to her, without anyone knowing?"

Ty's face was still flush from the punch, but less fierce.

"But it was you leaving Ashley—"

"That's right," Kyle interrupted, not with anger, but passion. "I left Ashley *in the past*, where she belongs. Instead of being pissed at me, your anger and efforts should be focused on Ashley and her dad. I mean, in the last twenty four hours, he's already gotten me fired."

That got Ty to focus on Kyle's eyes.

"Barrett fired you?" Now that Ty knew, he'd have no problem telling the half of the town who didn't already know it.

Kyle nodded. "Maybe Stu said some choice words to Billy and she took off, not wanting to deal with his crap. But there's one thing I agree with Mark on," he continued, feeling energized his words were now making an impact. "I'm sure it's going to get worse before it gets better."

Ty finally stood up straight, meeting Kyle eye to eye.

"I don't know what to do, or to think, even," Ty admitted, the words spilling out from a father desperate to hear from his only daughter who'd now disappeared. "I'm mad as hell at you for dropping into my daughter's life, which was—I don't know, maybe she'd say dull, but it was better than having her gone. And you—"

"Changed that, I know, and I really am sorry, but..."

Ty's facial expression vacillated between anger and resignation. "But you two were in love," Ty said. "I saw a little of that the other night in the kitchen, when Ashley stopped by unannounced."

Kyle nodded, dropping the last of his aggressive stance. "Ty, look, I know this seems quick for you, how fast we discovered how we feel about one another, but you can't make that up. It's there. Can you possibly understand?"

The man's shoulders dropped from the force of Kyle's words, his expression finally free of the hate he'd first expressed.

"I understand you've caused this and that can't be taken back."

With his words, Kyle felt a body-slamming hit of guilt. Had he not involved Billy when he'd come down from the mountain, had she not been the only person smart enough to help him figure out the cubes, or contact the Naturalists, Kyle was sure he'd have been caught, most likely now dead.

"You're absolutely right, Ty," Kyle acknowledged. "Had I just left her alone, and us continuing to be nothing more than academic adversaries she'd be here with you. I can't say I'm sorry enough."

Ty's exhale was thick. "I guess that's where we leave it then."

"I'm going to find her, Ty, but…" Kyle hesitated, unsure how the man was going to react to his honesty, "but I can't guarantee I'll bring her back if she doesn't want to come."

Ty's eyes traversed his face, his eyebrows raised up in distaste. "Not sure she'd want you anyway. You resemble the devil. No one's going to want you."

That's what Kyle was hoping.

CHAPTER

10

Gary nodded to the Secret Service security detail, entering the soundproof conference room where Janet and Peter Rone, the director of the CIA, were already engaged in a debate about the handling of the events in Ouray. Sitting at the head of the table was the President of the United States who gave him a nod. Gary thought the downturn of the President's mouth indicated his feelings on the situation.

"The likelier scenario is that whoever has the cubes is going to open to the highest bidder," argued Pete, his pale skin tinted with a flush of red. It wasn't the room that was hot, thought Gary. It was the intensity of the conversation. "The DNA being the currency, going to the highest bidder regardless of government alignment or loyalty."

The President's silver eyes turned matte as he absorbed Pete's comment. The faint white of scars on the President's hands were the only outward sign he'd once seen battle, his Purple Heart medal and bravery seemingly left on the field.

War wounds replaced with manicured nails.

Gary took his seat by Pete. "Trafficking of every product imaginable from people to products is nothing new," Gary began. "And while the stolen cubes include information on residents in two of the most populated states in the country, they are nothing compared to the six missing master cubes. Janet," he turned, hoping his black eyes matched his skin color, "you've been collecting the financial, genealogical, medical and god-knows-what-else data on over a billion people by your agencies and data brokers for decades. Now 400 million of that billion are at risk—all here in the US." His stare was hard and uncompromising. "Between the mutating DNA thread and this, you have overseen the broadest and grossest misuse of government I've ever heard of."

"She did it with the support of the US Presidents, up to and including myself," inserted the leader of the free world. Gary didn't blink. He and Scott had served in the Marines together, saved one another's lives, killed enemies and watched those they cared about die in their arms.

"Good," Gary responded. "Then let's identify what in the hell we are going to do about it, because I'm telling you this," he paused, pressing his fingers on the table until the ends turned pink. "It's going to be my organization that has to deal with every criminal group in the world who will be canvassing and killing each person they come across until the cubes are found."

The silence was long, but Janet was unbending. Gary forced his hands and feet still, as though he could get her to admit a portion of regret, or even wrongdoing, in her acts. Her cropped white hair was as motionless as her eyes were alight. Apologies were not forthcoming.

"You are assuming they will fall into hands of an entity who can do something with it," Janet said calmly. Pete's lower lip dropped open, incredulous.

"The wealth in this country is in the top ten percent," Pete said, his tone more of banker than intelligence agent. "With all that information stored on fingertip sized devices…" he left the comment hanging.

Gary caught a look between Janet and the President. For some reason, the potential financial catastrophe Pete brought up didn't seem to raise the pulse of the group.

"What are we missing?" Gary asked point blank, his eyes not leaving the President.

The President stood, arms crossed, and started to pace. Had he taken an FBI course or two at Quantico, Scott would know that standing and turning meant avoidance and deceit. Too bad he'd traded the military uniform for a single term as a state senator before jumping ship to the Presidency.

"Financial crises come and go," he started, brushing his forefinger over his lips, another sign of indecision. "We can adjust monetary policy to stimulate the economy while we back up and guarantee the banks who will lose the funds. That's much less of a concern in the long term."

Gary glanced at Pete, who peered up and over the top of his metal rimmed glasses. He resembled a thirty-year old runner not a fifty-something intellectual that he was. It was rare that someone from money and privilege elected to skip training for the Olympics and join the ranks of government, but he'd done it in his twenties and never left. In Gary's opinion, Pete had the best of both worlds: ferreting out the bad guys, but sleeping easy at night because he didn't have to worry about his retirement.

"Losing the wealth of this country hasn't happened in two decades, sir," Pete noted. "I'm not sure it's quite as easy as what you are saying."

The President turned. "Don't misunderstand me. I'm not making light of a potential crisis. I'm simply saying that it's preferred to thousands or hundreds of thousands dying in the process. Janet?"

All eyes went to the calm seventy-three year old. She took the baton as easily as the last sprinter on a 400 yard dash.

"Right now, you and Gary are rightly supposing the criminals will be after the financial and personal data," she began. "The President and I, and those before him, are worried about a complete and total uprising of the population of this country, all because of one thing: they've been deceived. By us."

She paused half a moment to receive the head nod from the President before continuing.

"You must go back thirty seven years ago," she told them. "The Chinese pulled their bonds, collapsing the currency then pressuring Canada and Mexico to starve us of natural resources and food through high tariffs and tough sanctions."

"We were decimated economically," interjected Pete. "Then they added the devastating mutation as the final act of supremacy. We know our history."

Janet's stare lasted a moment longer than Pete's statement.

"Wrong," she said. "The Chinese were preparing to invade, wipe us out and take our natural resources. We had to make our country unappealing from a physical invasion. We did it by administering a mutating gene. It saved the country, the notion of a mutating gene protecting our borders in a way no machine gun could."

Pete removed his glasses, inspecting them with the peculiarity of a scientist, as if ridding himself of the offending object would do the same with what he was now hearing, which was equally offensive. He had a minute to absorb what Gary had known for two weeks.

"So, putting aside my disgust, because I don't have the luxury of doubting the leaders responsible at that time, we are nearly four decades after the fact. What caused the disruption we find ourselves in today?"

"The Naturalists," answered the President. "Their obsession with proving the government was involved, resulting in hacks to the NSA systems, some of the biology research labs and even our satellite systems. It's gained ground in the last year, so the NSA created a plan to trap them."

"That's what led to the situation in Ouray," finished Janet.

After a moment of silence, Pete looked across to Janet.

"Instead of eliminating the Naturalist cells, you placed everything they wanted in a single location hoping for the big attack? But now the situation is worse and we," he pointed to Gary with his finger, "get to clean up your mess."

"Containment has been and still is the strategy," offered the President, as if trying to avoid a conflict between his three department heads.

Pete's expression of incredulity bordered on insult.

"Had you picked anywhere but the Little Switzerland of America, maybe, but travelers from every corner of the world come to ice climb in January and jeep in the summer," he said. "I've been there, sir. You have grandmothers driving four-wheel vehicles over boulders along thirteen-thousand foot edges without breaking a sweat. If your plans include wiping out that town, it will guarantee a thousand more conspiracy theories to those already in existence."

Pete rolled his thumbs over one another, thinking.

"Janet has governance over every lab in the country authorized to grow human cells: organs or skin. Even if, somehow, a few labs were growing facial skin, they'd be found out. To pull this off, you need dozens or hundreds of labs, all operating under the radar and in the black. It can't happen."

"To add onto Pete's hypothesis," Gary said, "these faces need to be matched to the donor. I just don't see the person in possession of the cubes starting a call down campaign, telling people that their real faces are now being grown and asking whether they would like a 'put order?'"

A slight smirk appeared on Janet's lips, the mannerism annoying. What could she possibly find amusing about the situation that her organization had caused?

"Actually Gary," she began, "you and Pete have just zeroed in on the NSA's theory. We believe the DNA will be taken overseas and grown in foreign labs, out of our reach and control."

Pete cocked his head. "To what end?"

"The Russians and the Chinese are just two countries on our list of adversaries who would love to see our own people revolt against the government."

The CIA man didn't argue with her statement. Every branch knew the threats were constant, despite the polite rhetoric espoused by country leaders during agreement signings.

"You're supposing foreign governments will take the data and use it to create civil unrest which could make an external invasion look tame by comparison," Pete concluded.

"They did it with the President election, why not this? It practically guarantees an invasion," finished the President. "Either way, we are at war internally and externally. All roads lead to vulnerability for this country."

Pete nodded with grim understanding. It would be the CIA's job to use its reach in dozens of countries to find and counter those who ended up with the cubes before they had a chance to execute their plans against the US.

"And what you originally thought was on-the-ground containment within Ouray is now over," Gary added.

"Not over," corrected Janet. "Likely just moved. The data must get across the wires somehow, either physically or digitally. As Pete noted, we monitor every authorized lab in the country."

The FBI was being relegated to a ground unit, only using its tactical or digital forces when necessary.

"Sir," Gary started, addressing the President. "It would be irresponsible to assume a financial catastrophe can be managed. I contend that we need to put the failsafe in place to avoid the economic Armageddon, because that puts our entire country at risk."

"Your proposal?"

"My cyber security team and financial white hats work with the top five banks in the country who control 56 percent of American money. There will be zero oversight and knowledge of the work by anyone other than the head of the treasury. To communicate it broader makes rumor and a crash inevitable."

The President looked at the other two for agreement and received it.

"How long do you think it will take to preserve the financial side?" he asked.

"I'm not prone to making guesses, but given historical precedence, I'd say two to three months," Gary estimated.

"About the time we believe is needed to create new skin for faces, conduct the transplant surgeries and take it regional, national or God forbid, international." Janet added.

"It seems that's our target then," the President concluded. "Unless Pete intercepts the cubes prior."

After the group disbanded, Gary was almost at the elevator when he felt a tap on his shoulder. The Secret Service agent asked that he follow him. He turned and went back to the conference room. Scott was on the phone by the window, his back turned. When the conversation ended, Scott glanced over and motioned him forward. Together, they looked down, watching as Pete and Janet entered separate vehicles.

"Her work is so secretive I likely don't know the half of it, nor is it safe for me to know."

Only in private did Scott talk to him like an equal, the privilege of one former Marine to another, titles be damned. "There's a reason she's been in her position for nearly four decades."

Scott's comment wasn't what unsettled Gary. It was the fear he saw in the President's eyes, one that had never been displayed even on the battle field.

"All problems have a solution," Gary remarked, the language and tone familiar and clandestine. The nod of Scott's head was nearly imperceptible.

"We want the same thing Gary, but it must come to a conclusion at the right time and way." Gary placed a curled index finger to his mouth as though in thought, the Marine signal for confirmation received. "You have four months. Less if the cubes get out and a crisis erupts. I'm not sure the Presidency will survive if that happens."

"Mr. President," said Gary, purposefully using his formal title. "Have you considered that might be exactly what Janet wants?"

CHAPTER 11

Kyle drove over the bridge, the dry, compacted snow easily managed by his ATV's triangular tires that provided a balance not found in his emotions.

Hitting Billy's dad on New Year's Eve?!

He still couldn't believe they'd both thrown punches, but then, two weeks ago, he wouldn't have imagined himself in love with Billy either.

At home he stripped off his outer layers in the mud room, going directly to the basement and coming back up with his arms full of empty boxes.

"Mom, my New Year's Eve party of one is taking down the Christmas tree if that's alright with you." Neither parents looked up from their work; his mother hunched over her current project, carefully soldering the liquid metal around stained glass, his father cutting out a shape from lapis colored glass.

"Your shift end early today?" asked his father.

"Nope. Fired," he said simply.

"You sound happier than you should," his mother observed.

"Because the thought of making Stu's head pop off is a good one," he answered, stripping off the garland.

Kyle related what Barrett had told him as he lifted the angel off the top of the tree, carefully wrapping the porcelain figurine as he spoke.

"I'm confused," said his mother, finally looking up. "Why are you so happy?"

Kyle smiled. "Because of the gauntlet Marty is going through in his pursuit of Ashley." His mother's eyes slid from him to across the street. Marty stood beside Ashley. Her cheeks were slightly flushed from the cold, the fur around her face accentuating the color of her lips and blond hair. She was a beautiful girl...at first glance. Mascara-enhanced lashes couldn't hide the dark look in her eyes and gloss would do nothing for the downturn at the corners of her lips. She looked miserable; a person carrying on a charade because she had to, not because she wanted to.

Marty looked equally unhappy. His hands in the pockets of his ski coat, his shoulders hunched against the cold, his eyes on the doorway, not Ashley.

"Oh, kiss her already and get it over with," muttered his mother. Just when Marty looked like he was going to make his play, Ashley turned her cheek to him, putting her hand on the door.

Kyle sniggered. "That right there makes me happy even if it hurts my face to laugh," he said dryly, returning to his task of removing the multi-colored lights. "In other small-town news, you both should also know I spoke with Ty. He punched me and I punched him back."

His mother gasped, causing his father to swear at Kyle for his delivery.

Kyle laughed. "Mom, it's fine. He blamed me for Billy leaving, I suggested it could have been his fault because she fell for me hard. It all worked out. Mom, you can start working again. No more surprises, promise."

She scowled at him. "You both probably deserved a good punch." She was still grumbling as Kyle finished with the lights. He dissembled the tree in two pieces, packing it away and making a last trip downstairs. He offered to vacuum the floor before he left for Montrose, but his mother shooed him away.

"Go, get out," his mother muttered. "I'm furious at so many people right now: Stu for getting Barrett to fire you, Barrett for doing it. Ty for hitting you and you for starting all of this! Be gone with you."

Kyle bent to his mother's ear, knowing fear underlined her worry, like the motion of frigid water moving under the frozen ice above.

"I'm really sorry Mom, and I do love you." He kissed her cheek. "Thanks for keeping the faith in me."

His mother paused to place a small, dark blue piece of glass in place. "As I'm not a religious person, I don't keep faith in anything, but I do have belief in some things, including you."

Kyle's throat relaxed when he joined the line of cars leaving Ouray. Traffic was light compared to the number of vehicles entering the town, no doubt for the New Year's Eve festivities. Those wanting peace kept to the warm water of the hot springs while the locals were up at Ty's. The rowdier bunch went to Durango or Montrose, and the affluent were partying like rock stars over in Telluride.

Kyle entered the lobby of the Montrose library. Billy's directions on the USB had been specific about where to sit, causing him to wait for an older woman to finish up. When Kyle took his place at the end of the rectangular bank, he knew why Billy had selected it. A wall of books to his left and behind him blocked two of the three ceiling cameras. One existed on his right, but it was faced towards the front entry.

Locating the data slots, he slipped in the USB drive Billy had loaded with TOR, the application to connect to the dark web. He'd listened to Billy's explanation of accessing the dark web, her recorded file identical to the written notes she'd also included. Step by step, he methodically followed the directions, the screens appearing as they should. As instructed, Kyle selected the "Make tails look like Windows" option. Anyone walking by would have no idea he was using a completely unauthorized and illegal operating system to access the dark web. Not even the random librarian who walked around the computer center to monitor the content.

His chest beat strong as the screen changed once then looked normal. He entered *Sunsetmoon*, and waited.

Olde Town Arvada in northern Denver wasn't what anyone considered a hot bed of criminal activity. As Danny drove down Main Street, he decided the cowboy-style and hometown hardware store looked positively Rockwellian. On a recommendation, he'd stopped in at Steubens, ordering a lobster roll and Cuban sandwich, wondering if the comfort food was meant to alleviate the stress he felt at the meeting he'd arranged. The aftertaste of the Latin spices were still on his tongue as he drove by author Clive Cussler's auto museum.

Arriving at the designated meeting place, Danny checked his directions again, doubting the non-descript, one-level red building was the right location. Sure enough, this was it. The Old Man Bar.

Only in Arvada. If this were his only experience with the outskirts of Denver, he'd leave with the impression that a wholesome, quiet and safe America did exist, and it was here.

He took the last open seat at the counter, pressing his hands against his stomach. Too much rich food, but given the source of the advice, he'd done what had been suggested, just as he was doing now.

Danny ordered Black Velvet, impatient for the arrival of his guest. Neither the meeting nor the liquor were smart, but one was a necessary tonic for the other. A month ago the doc had told him the blood in his urine was an ulcer and he needed to lay off the hard liquor. Danny had requested a prescription and kept on drinking. The meeting had to happen, so did the ulcer-producing drink.

Danny noticed a red-head walking towards him and he smiled. She met his eyes briefly, sliding away with the ease of a woman who decided to look through him as opposed to at him.

Typical. He swallowed the liquor, the brief encounter affirming his decision to meet with Philip Rush. Unlike himself, the twenty-five-year- old Russian-born, London raised kid didn't operate behind the scenes on the dark web; he ran it, the unofficial diplomat of the underworld. Urban legend had it that Rush put his own father in jail after the man had abandoned the family, the underage pornographic material on his computers ending up at Scotland Yard. After that, Bitcoin credits had flooded the young man's account from anonymous Eastern European sources who'd heard of his feat. The kid had practically coined the term crime-for-hire, the Russian computer prodigy earning millions before he could vote.

Once Rush landed on American shores, his ambition increased with his exposure to the umbilical-like attachment between cybercrime and physical enforcement. He helped the west coast Russian groups gain control over thefts and fencing of auto parts from Idaho to Los Angeles, and the Bulgarians who covered the trafficking of stolen jewelry and clothing on both coasts to the inland empires of Vegas and Chicago. In both cases, Rush had used electronic systems to manage the product supply chains, identifying internal theft from within each crime syndicate.

Even bad guys had stop-loss issues, Danny mused. Retaliation and change had been immediate and merciless; the mob bosses practically kneeling at Rush's digital feet for helping them save millions.

Nothing like that would ever occur among the Italian families. It wasn't about losing the arm, it was about the shame on the family. His own father never had to tell Danny to stay on the right side of the law; he simply invoked their Sicilian ancestry and the honor of being an Amato, which meant beloved one.

"And that's why I'm doing this," he murmured to himself.

"Doing what?" questioned a smooth voice. The man he assumed to be Rush had taken the seat next to him with the silence of a ghost.

"Having a meeting with a person who's the Ambassador of the Internet," responded Danny, glancing uncomfortably to his right. Rumor had it Rush had a scar running from his jaw to his ear, collateral damage of an altercation with a cousin after his father had left, but Danny didn't see it. Must be covered by the trendy facial hair.

"I won't kill you, at least not tonight," joked Rush, ordering a dark beer on tap.

"I'm too valuable for that," remarked Danny in complete seriousness.

"Really?" drawled Rush, thanking the bartender. "Half the dark web would praise me if I had one of my friends break your fingers."

At forty-five, Danny looked old and physical unfit, but he wasn't worried about his safety. In fact, Danny's anxiety about what he intended to reveal diminished in direct correlation to Rush's arrogance. He had taken a day to verify and reverify what he'd found, and he kept coming to the same conclusion.

He needed a partner, and that person had to be of the criminal mindset.

Danny grunted. "If I wasn't around to help my clients, you and your ilk wouldn't have an economy from which you could steal."

Rush cocked his head back and laughed, taking another Black Velvet. "So true. You keep me in business so I should thank you."

Danny caught the eye of the bartender and ordered another drink, using the opportunity to glance at his adversary. He resembled a fresh-faced, Wall Street professional, his grey-blue eyes popping against his thick, light brown hair, the top lifting up and over, the sides cut fashionably short. His neatly trimmed beard had tinges of amber, the effect upping his age to thirty.

A better looking, hipper Prince Harry.

"You're not going to thank me at all, Rush," he said prescriptively. "When you hear what I have to say, you're going to anoint me. I'll be the Cardinal to your Pope."

At this, the handsome young man raised an eyebrow and laughed harder. What Danny would give to have the younger man's looks, the physical form matching the brilliance inside. But Danny kept his stare even and face placid, ignoring the two, wide-shouldered men who'd positioned themselves behind and on either side of their employer.

"What could possibly upgrade my digital enemy from one I loathe to one I admire?"

"I'm proposing a deal Rush, you and me, counter forces working together to change the face of the country."

"Sure," responded Rush, rolling his eyes, an indication to Danny he'd probably taken the meeting more out of curiosity than real intent. "You want me to throw you some digital bones for your corporate clients to make you look good, and in return you'll reveal a few weak spots for my own financial gain?"

Purposefully, Danny finished off his drink, setting the glass on the counter with the precision of a bomb technician. He turned his dark, Italian eyes to Rush, visualizing his father's look of disappointment at the deal he was about to offer. Rush's laughter stopped short, catching the subtle change in Danny's demeanor.

"I'm going to give you clues as to what has the federal government mobilizing every secret force they have, and then I'm going to tell you what I want in return."

Although his eyes showed some interest, Rush tilted his head as though Danny couldn't possibly make good on such a claim. "And this is going to be big enough to make us two work together?"

"Yes," he calmly replied. "I think you'd like the financial data from a few hundred million people in this country so you can cherry pick here and there for the rest of your life."

What sarcastic comment the European was going to make stopped as he assessed Danny's words and demeanor. Liars and thieves were the best spotters of their own kind, which meant they usually knew when the truth was before them. Danny was telling the truth, and Rush knew it.

"What do you want in return, a few hundred million? But my bigger curiosity is why me? You could have gone to my competitors who probably dislikes you a lot less than I do."

Danny pushed his lips out, then rolled them in. "I chose you for very specific reason, and it's not just competitive admiration," he answered, tilting his head with the compliment. "You're an enigma, unknown to the real world, which means you are the only person who can get close enough to the source of the data without attracting attention."

"Hold on," interrupted Rush. "I actually have to be involved? No," he said, shaking his head. "No way."

"Hands on," Danny reiterated with a half-grin.

"But you said the money isn't the primary motivation for you so…you need someone to disappear?"

"Yeah, me," Danny responded, enjoying the look of shock on Rush's face as he interpreted the statement incorrectly. "My face, Rush. You're going to help me get it back, and in the process, destroy the very organizations who have been tracking you for the last five years. The same ones who have screwed me and my countrymen for decades."

Rush had the advantage of missing the joys of being an American citizen losing his face, but that didn't mean he wasn't aware of the virus. Heck, he probably imported girls so he could continue the pure Russian strain of good looks, and Danny didn't blame him. If he resembled Rush, he'd want the genetic line to be kept pure too.

As Rush grasped the implications of Danny's revelations, his skin stretched over his angular jaw, the magnitude of the opportunity lighting a fire in his eyes.

"You and me partners?" asked Rush as though he were testing the words out and ended up liking how it sounded.

"That's right," confirmed Danny. "The good guy Italian and bad guy Russian, joining forces to rework history, and you becoming rich in the process."

Rush shook his head, disbelief and humor merging with monumental change. "The country will never be the same."

Danny raised his glass. "That's what I'm hoping."

CHAPTER 12

Mark hung up with the hospital receptionist, annoyed the front desk had refused to allow him to speak with Saachi even though he'd provided his law enforcement credentials. Brayden had said one side of her face had been badly damaged...maybe she was physically unable to talk. That made sense.

He opened a can of beer, considering his options. What had Brayden said? The busiest time of the year for medical staff was after the holiday meals, requiring his wife to take extra shifts at the hospital.

On a whim, Mark pulled up the staffing list at Denver General. Sure enough, Laura Cox was listed as a surgeon.

I love it when my hunches pan out.

Mark called the hospital again asking for Dr. Laura Cox. He was put into her voice mail but hung up. After accessing his police database in a matter of seconds, he had Laura and Brayden's home address along with cell phone numbers.

On the second ring, she answered. "Dr. Cox."

"This is Deputy Hancock of the Ouray Police Department…" he began, using his professional, authoritative manner. He inquired about Saachi, revealing his inability to gain even the barest of details about her condition from the hospital staff. "She was working with Brayden in Ouray and I'm concerned about him, and very much so about Saachi," he added.

"Just a moment, officer," Laura requested. The background noise receded, as though she were walking away. "Sorry about that," she said. "I needed the privacy only an authorized room can offer. Deputy Hancock, before I answer your questions, are you aware of…the situation?"

That was a broad question, thought Mark, but he'd had a lot of time to consider the white pills Brayden had given to him and Kyle. They could have come from Laura. He took a gamble.

"To a degree, yes," he answered. "Brayden was taken from here in handcuffs for reasons I don't understand. Do you have clarity on that which you can share?"

"Yes and no," she answered. "He was in the hospital and released. The bad news is the situation from which he left is still in…turmoil, shall we say."

Mark considered his next words.

"Laura, I don't want to alarm you, but do you think—is it possible that whoever went after Saachi might come after you? Brayden is the one connection between you both."

"I'd not thought of that," she answered, the physician's confidence gone.

"Can you update me on Saachi's status?"

"We performed skin grafting on her arm using the epidermal layers from a cadaver, the typical skin donation suited for critical situations," she added. "But she doesn't want to wait for us to take new skin or grow new skin to match her face. She wants to get back on the job."

Saachi was a woman who'd wear her scars with pride. Mark's admiration for her expanded like a helium balloon, accompanied with the overwhelming desire to wrap his arms around her.

"One of my personal theories is that the lab explosion wasn't some random accident. The timing was too precise to when she was going to deliver results."

"Don't think, Deputy," Laura said. "I know it was."

Her conviction stopped him cold. "Do you know who?"

"All I have is a suspicion."

Mark's heart rate increased with his line of thought. "Which means you can't go to the authorities, another way of saying they may be involved."

"Correct."

Mark heard the waver of her voice, her nerves coming through loud and clear.

"I wonder if it would help for me to have a discussion with her in person. Is that a possibility?" he asked.

"As long as you can get it cleared with the FBI, I won't stop you, and I'll see you, assuming I'm still here."

"Oh, right. You must be looking forward to time off," he said, assuming she was on call.

"No Deputy, I'm transferring out of state on another job assignment."

"Sorry to hear that. Well, hopefully I'll be able to meet you in person."

Mark looked at the snow which was beginning to fall outside. Brayden hadn't mentioned a transfer, but then why would he? It was personal information, and maybe he wasn't going with her.

Mark ran his big toe along the top of his other foot, feeling the ridge created by years of playing icy hockey. The obvious detective's answer was she was running from something, which could be true. But the senior instructor in the homicide unit at the Police Academy always counseled against tunnel vision; try to see things from the opposite angle.

With that in mind, he considered the alternative: perhaps Laura Cox wasn't running from something, but instead was going *to* something.

Not my agenda or my business.

He had to make plans to get up to Denver and talk some sense into Saachi. He and Laura agreed on one thing wholeheartedly: that woman needed to be protected, and that included from herself.

Billy had her Diet Coke beside her, the third in the last two hours. She was used to late nights and early mornings, but not sitting in front of the computer screen for hours on end. It almost made her wish for the easier, but less exciting, high school life she'd temporarily left back home.

Almost.

"How's it going?" asked her Uncle.

Billy looked over her shoulder. "Just killing time searching the net," she answered her uncle. "What about you?"

"Our physicians are waiting for more DNA."

"Don't have it," she said, annoyed something so obvious had to be repeated.

Roy sat down beside her, elbows on his knees, fingers threaded.

"I know what you're going to ask and what he's going to say," Billy preempted.

"Okay, then what do we do about that?"

Billy kept typing, the rapid tap-tap-tap continuing a moment more until she realized Roy was going to sit and stare at her until she addressed it head on. She lifted her fingers and pushed back the chair.

"*We*," she emphasized, "do nothing. They will spot you on a dime, and I'll get no end of grief for returning, my every move probably followed by Stu Fine and my own father."

"And Kyle," interjected her uncle. "Don't give me that look," he added. "When you guys were saying goodbye, you might as well have been on the bridge of the Titanic." She snorted. "React how you will, but that boy would do anything for you, and we both know it."

She folded her arms and simply looked at him.

"Look," he continued. "He's there. He knows the area. He has the hot rod ATV. He can get just about anywhere on that mountain and outrun them like he did before if he gets in a jam. You know it can be done, you just don't want to encourage him."

"You're right," she fired back, "I don't."

Her uncle unthreaded his fingers, placing a warm hand on her leg. "You have seen beyond yourself and Kyle this entire time or you wouldn't be here in the first place." He was right, and she didn't like or appreciate the path he was going down.

"Yet you want me to put him in harm's way again, the difference being this time I'm knowingly responsible for it."

His silence affirmed her statement.

"If this all pans out as we want, do you think the government will capitulate, making everyone return to what their natural state should have been?" she asked. "An equal playing field for all?"

"Some groups within our movement want that, for sure."

Billy thought of Ashley and Ruth. Strip the looks from one and give it the other.

"We should mandate it," her eyes steeled on the moving bubbles on her computer screen. In her peripheral vision, she noticed her uncle's shoulders shrug.

"Why? Free will and choice was removed once. Why would we or the government, or anyone, come back and take it away a second time?"

She didn't answer. A root of resentment had been growing deep within her. It had been dormant, frozen under the unemotional topsoil she'd created after her mother left. The result had made her teenage years lonely and miserable. She wasn't going to admit to her uncle that she'd like Ashley and the others who'd judged her during that time to feel some of the pain she'd endured.

"I guess we can only hope the government or whoever pushes this out to the masses will force the changes to happen." With a sigh, she realized her uncle wasn't going anywhere, and so she finally relented. "I'll do what I can, Roy."

Billy waited until he'd left to switch the screens. She searched on the tribal reservations in Idaho; four total, two in the northern part of the state.

She looked over her shoulder, just to make sure, then opened two new screens. Between what she'd learned about agent Brayden's wife Laura knowing her own mother, and what Kyle had suggested the timing of the Cox's daughter dying, there had to be a link. If Kyle was right, a daughter was alive and hiding somewhere, and so was her mother, perhaps together.

The question she was going to answer, with or without the help of anyone else, was where.

CHAPTER

13

Kyle randomly surfed the Internet, skimming over the articles on trade wars with Mexico, reading a side bar story on stolen identities. The cartels had graduated from passports to fingerprints and replicated retinas. Labs were in place growing black market livers for those who could pay; the one-time fee of a half of million far more profitable and less risky than carrying cocaine across the border. The trade routes leveraged those used to carrying drugs up through Detroit to the eastern shores and down to Arizona, then up to Seattle or down to Los Angeles. The process hadn't changed, only the contraband.

Kyle's fingers unconsciously paused on the keyboard, his face feeling a chill. It wasn't a big stretch from a liver to a face.

Kyle thought back to the meeting in the cabin when he'd temporarily turned over the cubes to Roy, who'd uploaded the data from three of the individual state cubes. He'd not even hinted at the possibility of criminal activity; it was all about giving people the choice to go back to the person they were meant to be, eliminating the governmental control.

Hello Cube Master. I understand you've been wanting a Sunsetmoon. Took you long enough. Kyle looked at his computer screen in happy disbelief.

How do I know it's you? He typed back, suppressing the smile that had already formed.

Because only I'm sharp enough to come up with the name Cube Master. It fits both the situation and your role, don't you think? Besides, you couldn't be here if I hadn't given you the steps to do so, audio, visual and printed. That good enough?

It was Billy alright, the reality causing a surge of oxygen so great he felt lightheaded.

I miss you, he wrote, unashamed and vulnerable.

Good. You should.

Kyle involuntarily laughed. *So Billy.* He imagined touching her platinum hair, gently brushing it away from her green eyes, giving her a kiss. So easy to visualize but stupid to write.

How are you holding up? I heard you lost your job.

Her comment broke his mood.

Do you have spies around town?

Hardly. I called the pool. Mandy told me you no longer worked there. I made the assumption you were fired.

And beat up, he wrote back. *Your dad blames me for you leaving. He punched me. I punched him. We're all good now.*

Protective dad--sorry

Don't be. I'd probably have done the same.

Did you bring the earphones?

Of course

Time to plug them in and get ready

He inserted the ear bud, leaning forward on an elbow as her voice came in his ear.

"Lean back and surf the Internet like you were doing before," she said. Her voice jolted him upright, and a soft giggle came through. "No, don't look like a cork went up your backside, relax just a little."

"How—"

"Because I can see my Cube Master, that's how," Billy answered. "Look straight ahead. See that little black dot in the center of the computer, right above the screen?" Kyle hadn't noticed it before, but it was clear as day now. "All the monitors come with cameras, but library policy is to deactivate them upon arrival. Before I left, I reactivated this one so I can see your every move."

"Because you're brilliant of course," he said, his smile so wide he felt warm blood as his lips split.

"And you look like the loser in a UFC championship round," she observed. "For future reference, when you logged on, the screen activated and it will shut down when you log off. Don't lose the USB by the way. You may need to get a hold of me and that allows you to do so from any computer anywhere."

She stopped talking, though he heard a muffled chuckle.

"What?"

"*You*. You….are… beat up," she said with sympathy. Kyle closed his eyes for a moment, wondering if he'd heard more in her voice than just words.

"Is that what you were really thinking?" he asked quietly.

"No. I was thinking how gorgeous you are, despite the white bridge on your nose and the exotic looking black and purple eyes." Kyle stared at the black screen, imagining her in front of him, so close he could lean forward and kiss her.

He held her eyes for a moment longer. "I can get past job loss and facial destruction, but what's really annoying is this one way visual."

"Hold please," she requested in the tone of an operator, the request making him chuckle. "Up here, Kyle. No, not at the camera, the box at the upper right of your screen."

Kyle leaned forward, squinting to be sure it was Billy. "New look," he observed. "Total. Hotness." He expanded the screen another inch. "I never thought any hair color other than platinum would make your green eyes pop, but dang girl, you are rockin the brown. And red lips? Really?" he asked, loving the look.

Billy's pursed her lips in a pouty way completely out of character for her. "I told you I needed to prepare for a change, and this was it." She purposefully fluttered her eyelashes, then turned serious. "You don't have much time before you're going to get kicked off," she said, changing both her expression and tone. "Thirty minute limit, remember?"

Kyle hadn't, but now noticed a kid in a green hoodie staring at the rows of computers as though he knew who needed to be off and when.

"Go on," Kyle said in a quiet voice.

"Bad news first. I accessed the national scholarship database and found that your name has been flagged an 'ineligible.' In other words, you no longer have the ability to get an athletic scholarship." He asked about the three already extended to him. "Withdrawn," she said crisply.

"Who has the ability to do that?" Kyle wanted to know.

"Anyone with a deep pocketbook and revenge as a motivation."

Kyle imagined Stu gloating in his home, his success with both Barret and axing the scholarships helping him raise his glass of champagne a bit higher.

"Impressive, but then again, college has been a fading dream for me in the last couple of weeks."

Billy shook her head, the angular drop of hair brushing her eyes, the sexy wave catching on a long lash. "Close your mouth," she chided.

"Can I help it if just looking at you completely distracts me, even when you're giving me terrible news?" he grumbled.

"No, but you need to listen to me," she stated, brushing the hair back. "Stu isn't smart enough to think you'd reapply without the athletic piece. That means if you keep your mouth and go for the academic scholarship only, you have a shot, assuming you're not in jail of course," she quipped with a smile. "Maybe we will end up going to the same school."

"Maybe," he murmured, focusing on her use of the word 'we,' two letters of comfort that meant a bunker as the hurricane swirled around him.

"Don't be getting insecure on me," she said. "Especially since you're almost a legal adult and can be drafted by the Patrol, a scary thought on a good day."

Her honesty and that reality had the intended effect; it reassured him she was in the game as fervently as he was while being pragmatic about his future.

"Changing subjects," she said, "you need to know how far we've come but also what we need from you now." She explained that the upload of the DNA data from the cubes had been successful, and her uncle had already started the process of locating recruits for the new faces.

Kyle noticed Billy's eyes had gone above his head. "Looks like that kid wants your seat," she said, her voice increasing in speed. "Lean forward and I'll keep this short. We have volunteers, three that you know, starting with Joe."

"What?" he whispered, shocked the man who had originally taken him up the mountain in the blizzard to steal the cubes and then disappeared had come back into his life. "How—"

"He found me and Roy after we left town. He told us he wanted to be a part of what he unintentionally started with you."

Billy went on. "People turn up at the reservation desperate to gamble or just desperate, but if they are on the cubes, we can use them, assuming they are willing."

"Reservation?" he whispered. "Your family..." his word trailed off as he put it together. Her mother had Indian blood, and reservations were the only place the government couldn't penetrate.

"The labs you were talking about."

"Yep," she finished, her voice now a whisper. "The tribes have their own hospitals, their own doctors, labs, all of it."

The government could hunt the country, but they'd never think to look on Indian land. And even if they suspected, they were prevented from taking action.

"Billy," he began in earnest. "This means you can come back now, right?"

Her mouth turned down, the shake of her head barely visible. "You need to find a way to get the remaining cubes out of the mine. Three states is a start, but we need them all. On that subject, we hacked into the remote cameras and looked at the satellite pictures of your original break in. The weather prevented the images from being clear. That's why you weren't tracked down."

"All this time I thought it was because of my human toboggan skills." His humor was short lived. "Billy, satellites have been hovering above us, monitoring our every move? Not real excited about that," he admitted.

"Kyle, don't worry about it now. We need the rest of the identity cubes and the six masters. Roy never was able to make sense of them, but you figured it out. We have to know what you do."

"Billy, I can't even remember where I put the cubes I took!"

"Don't worry," she counseled as though talking a cat down from the high branch of a tree. "It will come back."

Kyle felt eyes on him and turned. The kid was standing closer, staring pointedly at him. Kyle lifted his chin in acknowledgement then turned back to the screen.

"The masters are just financial and personal stuff," he argued. "Who wants that kind of thing?"

"Lots of people, including us. It may give us the leverage we need." She paused until she had his full attention. "You have to do it Kyle. Anyone from the outside will be spotted, you know the area—"

"But what if they are waiting for me?" he asked.

"You pick the right time," she counseled without hesitation.

Kyle glanced outside. It was snowing lightly, but the dark clouds usually preceded a good dump. He felt the tingling of nerves pricking at his bruised skin, knowing it had nothing to do with his injuries. "And if I don't?" he asked.

"I know the area as well as you do."

"Billy, don't you even think—" he said roughly.

"I do think, and I'll have to do it for both of us if you don't," she retorted, her voice as challenging as her expression. "So stop and listen for a sec." Kyle didn't know if she was bluffing or not. "That's right. Concentrate on *me*," she demanded.

He caught his breath. "You say it that way and with that look, expecting my brain cells to work?"

Billy winked but kept talking, her expression intense. "I left something else for you. It's how to get in contact with me. It's a burner phone, prepaid and anonymous." Billy relayed where she'd placed the device, waiting until Kyle acknowledged the location.

"I see the section." He also noticed the kid in the green hoodie waiting, now tapping his foot, arms crossed.

"Billy, I wish I remembered kissing you after the basketball game, the one that apparently was so good Stu almost got arrested for threatening me."

Billy's eyelids lowered and she got very close to the camera. "Our kiss *did* rock the world, but not half as much as when I told you I loved you."

Kyle was speechless for a moment. He didn't remember the incident so for him, it was like hearing it for the first time.

"Three weeks Kyle, four at most and I'll be home. Happy New Year's but…Kyle, I may look a little different."

Kyle forgot the kid behind him as his eyes flicked back and forth between her eyes. "What are talking you about?" he asked.

She leaned very close to the screen, as though proximity were going to help him comprehend what she was saying. She'd volunteered to have her beautiful, perfectly fine face cut around the edges, lifted and then replaced with a replica. All the little things would be gone: the tiny freckles on the cheeks, the fine lines when she smiled. Would she have her eyelashes? What about her lips?

A thousand thoughts and images ran through his mind, all of which emanating in a single fear.

"You could die Billy."

"Which I've already told you is an inevitability for everyone, and our risk of that increased dramatically when we started this adventure. Look Kyle, someone has to do this, and both me and Ray are going under the knife along with Joe, two Naturals and one with a mutated gene."

"But I don't want you to," he argued fervently.

Her expression turned stern. "I'm not asking you."

"Then why are you telling me?" he asked quietly.

"Because...I want to know if you'll still think of me the same after?"

The words took the air out of Kyle's chest. "How can you even question that? You are always going to be Billy to me," he said with complete seriousness. "Maybe version two-dot-0..."

"Not all versions are actual improvements," she retorted with equal parts playfulness and pragmatism.

Seeing her determination, there was nothing more he could say or do. "Just come through it alive and well," he requested.

"We have another week, so it's not like it's tomorrow. We'll use the burner to talk between now and then."

The next instant, the small video square disappeared, the light of the camera turning from red to black. Kyle waited a moment, hoping she'd come back. When she didn't, Kyle switched the screens back to Windows and removed the USB. The other kid took his place, wiping down the keyboard with a cloth.

"Thanks," said Kyle. The kid had removed his fingerprints.

Kyle walked out of the library into the snowy night, wishing that Billy had finished the conversation with words about loving him, not the fact her face was going to be altered.

And she had also asked him to put his life back on the line by giving him the task of retrieving the cubes. She was risking no less, and if he were honest, a heck of a lot more than he was.

He'd find some way to get the remaining cubes to Billy and then his role in this was done. When the new year started tomorrow, he was going back to being a regular senior high schooler with four months until graduation.

Until then, to the others in the town and his parents, he was going to be exactly what Mark had predicted: friendless and boring, just what everyone expected.

At home, Kyle found a note from his parents on the kitchen counter. They'd headed over to Telluride to install a window for a client as a New Year's surprise.

"And not getting paid enough for their time and hard work," Kyle said aloud, irritated. They'd saved all these years, living in a home not much larger than a class room, sharing bathrooms with their only child, insistent on paying everything in cash.

"Because what you own outright the government can't take," his mother had repeated as though she were a displaced refugee.

It was true. In his eighth-grade civics class, Kyle had read the fine print on the law; in addition to homes with a mortgage, the federal government could seize bank accounts and even safety deposit boxes.

"And that's why we keep three years' worth of taxes in cash under the house," his mother had told him, the sly comment accompanied by a look which indicated she felt like she was pulling one over on the government.

"Seriously?" he said. "Where?"

She made him promise never to get into the stash, then said, "Where do you think the safest place would be?"

He didn't have to think long. "The kiln."

"Under it, to be precise," she corrected. "The box is fire and water proof. It's the same way grandpa always saved his money."

And that's when it hit him.

I might have stored the cubes there.

Kyle ran downstairs, searching around the kiln. The crowbar wasn't hanging in its normal spot but instead leaning against the cement wall. A good sign.

Kyle had no recollection of lifting or moving the kiln before, the void in his memory still unnerving. He walked around the kiln, dropping to his knees. With this hands, he felt the faint lines of a square on the floor. His heart was now racing, the fear someone would come to the front door greater than ever.

Without a moment's hesitation, he positioned the tool and lifted. He had a moment of déjà vu, feeling like he'd done this before. He couldn't get into the box without something to hold up the kiln. In his peripheral vision, he saw the cement block.

Kyle extended his right leg, curling the tip of his shoes around the block, bringing it close. It easily supported the kiln, and once it was in place, he brushed the surface of the floor, feeling the latch. The adrenaline coursing through him felt electric as he lifted the latch. Moving the money around, he felt the sharp corners of what he knew must be the cubes.

He'd found them. Now that he was sure they were safe, he could focus on Billy's next task.

"Impossible," he grunted as he lowered the kiln back into position. Heading to his room, he caught his reflection in the bathroom mirror and couldn't help but stop. He flicked on the light and grimaced. Carefully, he touched the material Ruth had applied to his nose, the tape expertly affixed to his cheeks. The skin was puffy and swollen, but seemed to have receded at least microscopically from the day prior.

Four days since the interrogation. As the blood seeped out, the coloring had changed, darkening his skin even further. Maybe one day he'd get more details on what he'd said to warrant such a beating.

Probably the type of information that would go on the master cubes.

Kyle's deep sigh was audible. How could he possibly go back up the mountain, enter the mine again and get away, this time unscathed? There was no way. Even with what Billy said about hacking the satellites…it was the government! They were infinitely smarter than a high school kid.

Still…Billy was so adamant.

He stood still, on the precipice of doing nothing or taking action. Waiting and willing life to go back to normal, Billy's return and their reunion would be…

"Broken," he murmured, watching the snow collect on the Fender's backyard shed. Billy would be disappointed that he'd allowed his fear to stop the progress they'd both taken so many risks for. Any thought for a romantic connection would then fall apart, because her respect for him would be gone.

Kyle crossed into the mudroom, putting on his all-white snow gear, hat and goggles. He lifted the lanyard with the keys to his ATV from the wall, thinking only a few steps ahead of his actions.

Going to the mine wasn't off limits, there were no signs posted, and if he were a guiltless, average teenager, he'd do exactly what he wasn't supposed to do, which was just drive around and see what was going on.

That was taking action, he thought.

Kyle was almost out the door when he turned around, going back to his room, retrieving the phone Billy had left for him. She said to use it only in cases of emergency, but then he realized she'd not given him a number to call.

He flipped the phone over. No number there. He turned it on, waiting to access the address book. One saved number existed.

Me

Kyle was smiling when he put the phone in the pocket of his jacket.

It was a quarter past seven when Mark lifted the police issue belt hanging from the metal horseshoe by the backdoor. By law, he was required to put it in a safe with a lock, but it was Ouray, a town which blessedly hadn't had a home invasion since his first day on duty. Now the belt was around his hips, and when he should have been ringing in the new year with a potential girlfriend, he was going to be offering rides home to those who'd had a few too many. With luck, he might break up a fight or two.

Marks thoughts were on Laura Cox and Saachi when he opened the door and heard the rumble of a four-wheeler. If it was Kyle on his ATV, he'd be glad of it. Kyle needed to stay occupied now he was unemployed and didn't have a friend in town.

Other than me.

The vinyl car seats of his patrol car were still warm from earlier in the day, a tender mercy as his God-fearing grandmother had always called them; the little things that made life a bit more bearable when times were hard.

Mark looked both ways and turned left onto 7th. The Historic was sold out, the bar already packed. The oldest hotel on the western slope attracted a particular overseas crowd, and those from the US who wanted to wear their fur coats without getting hit by snowballs. They sat side by side with old-timers who liked a strong drink without the music and flat screens of Ty's place.

It triggered additional thoughts of Saachi and their last dinner together. He could barely think of her without getting caught up in her smile, intellect and warm, brown skin. On Main Street, Mark turned right to the base of the mountain and flipped a U-turn. Driving five-miles an hour, he scanned both sides of the street. The hipper crowd chose the live bands of Telluride, leaving hotels like the Box Springs Hotel and the Weisbaden for the die-hards who wanted the convenience of the internal caves filled with hot, spring fed water.

Of the two, he personally preferred the Weisbaden, where all one had to do was put on a robe before leaving the hotel room, descend into the main floor, hang a left and walk right into the hot springs. No need to go outside. Relaxing, romantic, and unrealistic—for him anyway.

Mark's mouth turned down when he saw a couple he recognized. He slowed the car, rolling down the window.

"Marty. Ashley," he said.

"Hi, Deputy," greeted Marty. Behind them, Mark recognized Samantha James and Ben Gaby. Usually Ashley couldn't keep her mouth shut, but now she was a clam. Samantha smiled and Ben nodded, but not a word was spoken. Mark put the car in park and got out.

"You all been drinking then?"

Ben looked down and Samantha couldn't help smiling, her look accompanied by the giggle of a person who's been caught.

"Marty, are you the only one who's sober?"

"Someone had to be." His response was more of a grumble, accompanied with a shoulder raise towards Ashley.

"Your father will ground you for life," Mark told Ashley, "and will shoot you for corrupting his daughter," he told Marty. "Didn't you learn anything from Kyle?"

Marty's eyes narrowed, but it was Ashley who responded.

"That naïve jerk had no clue how to act when we dated," she slurred. "Wouldn't drink, wouldn't have fun—"

"Ash—" said Marty, touching her arm. She pulled away, jutting out her perfectly painted lips as though Mark was going to feel sympathy for her plight.

"You can touch me when I say," Ashley hissed at Marty, who lifted his hand.

Mark smirked. In truth, he'd intended to get a rise out of one or both of them, believing Ashley was more than to blame than her father for screwing up Kyle's life. Stu was merely doing what he thought would make her happy.

"See this, Ms. Fine?" questioned Mark, putting his hand to the recording device on his collar. "I'm now recording our conversation, so there is no mistaking what's taking place. I'm going to say this one time. You have just admitted to breaking the law by drinking underage. You're eighteen, not twenty-one, and I can arrest everyone here but Marty. Do you understand?"

Ashley was already starting to raise her voice when Samantha grabbed her from behind. "Don't!" she said. "You'll get us all in trouble!"

"Ashley," continued Mark, giving a head nod to Samantha. "I can arrest you three now, or I can keep this to myself and let Marty take responsibility for your safety and welfare this evening. What will it be?"

Ashley's heart-shaped lips turned ugly as she scrunched them together. Mark turned to Marty.

"Are you willing to take on that role?" Understanding the severity of the situation, Marty nodded gravely. "Are you sure?" Mark repeated. "If anything happens to these three, you will be held responsible, by all the parents and Stu in particular. Are you willing to sign up for that?"

Marty looked at Ben who shook his head no.

"I'll be taking Samantha back to her place, Deputy."

"A wise move Ben. Get going." Ben took his date's hand and they walked in the opposite direction.

"Thanks for ruining our night, *De-pu-ty*," Ashley drawled.

Mark smiled. "As an officer of the law, it is my duty to keep the citizens of this town safe, and if that means your New Year's Eve night is cut short due to your own choices, I'm glad for it. If you'd like, the three of us can have a sit-down with your mother and father right now, and I'll play this entire tape back for them. Would that be more to your liking?"

For a moment, Mark could see the girl wanted to call his bluff, but she remained silent long enough for Marty to exhale a breath of relief. It wasn't Stu's daughter who'd get the wrath, but Marty.

"I'll keep this tape on file just in case I need it," Mark told them. "Marty, I expect you'll stay away from the bars, and if you are going to be out tonight, you will be someplace safe?"

"Yes, sir."

"Good." He waited until they'd walked half a block then got back in his car. Ben and Samantha were nowhere to be seen. Mark could only guess where Marty was taking Ashley. Kyle had kept that girl as pure as the driven snow by reputation, and now Mark had confirmation that Kyle really had been the Boy Scout they all thought he'd been.

The Christmas lights glimmered in red, white and green down the street until just before the Smith place. The living room was dark, the tree already down. He guessed Ed had already taken his position up at the Elk Lodge and Kyle's mother...well, who knew?

Mark continued on his route, ending at the hot springs parking lot. It wasn't as crowded as past years, but still busy. Mark parked, surveying the area, his eyes drawn to the southwest corner. It was the base of the hill where he and Brayden had stood, looking up the mountain. Two days later, Saachi had arrived...

Mark found his phone and sent a text to Sherriff Deardon, requesting the weekend off. He wrote that a close friend had been injured in an accident and he wanted to visit, receiving the approval response within minutes.

Mark exited the lot, driving up and down the remaining streets, thinking about Saachi. He knew her type of law enforcement: a deterrent only served to increase her drive for justice, and if it cost her life so be it. She wasn't going to let burns and the threat of additional harm dissuade her now. It was fate then that her name meant truth, because she might die in the search of it.

CHAPTER

15

Kyle wound his way through the town, taking the ATV up and over chest high snow banks, the twenty-inch wide tire tracks practically floating on surface. He wanted to return home, but couldn't.

Because Billy's words are haunting me.

If she were here, Billy might make the argument he was pushing against the inevitable. Someone had to get the remaining cubes and right the wrongs that had been committed during their parent's youth and not just for the residents of three states. For all states, all citizens. And if not him, then who? Her?

Kyle turned the handlebars, heading in a zig zag up the side of the mountain, roughly following the edge of Box Canyon Falls. The metal railing was invisible, well below the snow line. He kept a good ten feet to the right of where he estimated the railing to be. Even with these wide tires, a soft bank of snow could give way at any time, carrying him and his ATV down a hundred foot crevice to the ice water below.

Up he drove, changing his bright white lights to a lower-beam yellow which gave better visibility in the falling snow. He passed the scenic platform where tourists had straight shot views of the ice climbing competition in February, seeing the sign announcing the date and last year's winners by age group.

I'll win again, thought Kyle, his competitive spirit rising. And not just for my age group. Any day now the city engineers would take out the long hoses, turn on the water from the hot springs and start spraying in anticipation of the climbing competition, each spray adding a layer of ice, ensuring the frozen water would be as hard as the rock beneath it.

Kyle passed the top of Box Canyon, turning right, avoiding the known crevices where he'd strung the netting for his summer-time employer. After the snow melt, the catch zones, as they were called, were easily spotted when it was clear and dry, the surrounding trees marked with green signs identifying the area. Today, those signs were covered by snow as was the tightly bound netting. A skier wouldn't know he'd gone over the top, nor would a snowmobiler unless the driver hit it in a steep angle. If that happened, or the snow had melted in the center, no amount of netting would prevent the snowmobile from going nose first or flipping over.

Kyle made a wider-than-normal turn around another zone. He was tempted to test out his ATV on the netting, guessing the two types of off road toys were comparable in weight.

Not today. While he trusted the engineers responsible for drilling the metal posts into the rock surface as he strung the nets, he wasn't going to risk his life or his ATV proving the weight limit. Kyle glanced over his left shoulder, knowing the last catch zone was behind him.

His inattention was ill-timed. A branch whipped across his cheek and broken nose. Tears of pain fogged his goggles and he slowed to an idle as his vision cleared. His white glove showed the dark spots of blood. He turned, going straight until he saw the clear, snow covered path of a hiking trail. As he drove, he passed the jagged, leaning tree which out of towners called the wooden Matterhorn due to its off-center shape. From that landmark, he knew he was about forty feet from the top of the hillside, the large boulders rimming the eastern edge concealing the mining shack where he'd found the cubes.

The wet of Kyle's nose blended with the flakes, producing a chill down the center of his back. The exertion of his climb couldn't conceal the anxiety-created perspiration produced by the proximity of danger.

Nothing to lose by getting closer.

Kyle slowly moved the vehicle forward, emerging from the protective covering of the forest and into the clearing, where the whine of wind vibrated, penetrating his thick cap. He continued to the left of the rocks that now resembled truck-sized puff balls, killing the engine near the back of the shed where he and Old D spent many summer nights.

"This is so stupid," he muttered to himself. What was he going to do, really? Use the same codes, make a run for it and go down the hill without anyone seeing him?

Kyle saw movement under the light of the outbuilding. A figure was walking to a parked snowmobile, carrying two sacks. The man opened a metal box attached to the back of the seat and dropped the sacks inside. He left after speaking to another man who had placed items in a pack on his own snowmobile.

There's no way the government would have left them in the caves unless... *they think someone stupid or crazy enough would go in for the rest of them.*

And Billy and Roy were playing right into their hands by suggesting Kyle do just that, but maybe they knew that.

The two men went back into the mine, and Kyle felt the pressing of his chest from sternum to shoulders, the rush of adrenaline going straight down his inner thighs.

They had to be removing the last of the cubes, but was it all of them? How many more were left? He'd unconsciously started counting the seconds they were gone. How long it would take for the men to walk down the tunnel, retrieve more and walk back up.

When he'd gone in the previous time, he'd sprinted in and out and it had taken only a few minutes. Kyle knew their snowmobiles couldn't make it where the wide, triangular rubber tracks on his ATV could, but their vehicles had speed on their side. His topped out at forty miles per hour, theirs could hit 100 on a straight away.

Do I make a run for it, or wait for another trip? They'd never know I was here…until they returned.

Kyle crept behind the boulders, watching for shadows and listening for voices in the tunnel in case they turned around. Then he ran for the snowmobiles, sprinting in the thin snow, grateful the windswept area had kept the banks low. The first metal box was unlocked and he flipped open the lid, grabbing the small black sacks, closing the lid then getting sacks out of the box on the second snowmobile.

He pelted back to his ATV, focusing as he unzipped the top pack on his machine, cramming the sacks inside. They barely fit, the zipper stretching by the time it closed up. He glanced behind him, thrusting his ATV in reverse. Back he went, almost over the edge before he jammed the gear in forward, cranking the wheel. Suddenly, the night was light up with the pink of a flare gun.

It had been a trap, and he'd fallen right into it.

When Danny lifted his glass in a toast with Rush, it was symbolic, their unorthodox union cemented in mutually beneficial outcomes; one based on greed and power, the other on morality, and if Danny were honest with himself, vanity.

"Here, you're going to need this," Danny said, removing a brochure on Telluride and slipping it across the bar to Rush.

"I told you before, I'm not getting my hands dirty."

Danny used his pointer finger to move the pamphlet an inch closer.

"Yeah, but you said you weren't going to meet me on New Year's Eve either," Danny retorted. "You may have twenty years of youth on your side but not the wisdom that goes along with the it."

The young Russian's fingertips tapped the table, giving Danny the distinct impression the kid would like to give him a personal demonstration of the amount of havoc he could inflict.

"Take my word for it," Danny continued confidently. "I didn't invite you here to get into a verbal pissing match. When you hear the details, you're going to be convinced there's no one else you'll want doing this but yourself."

Danny began with his investigation on the origin of the cubes. It started with the disappearance of a scientist from Microsoft four decades prior, who had bragged about creating solid state storage devices, gave a presentation then was never heard from again. Reality had turned into urban legend: the rumors of the devices being purchased by the government or a technology company were mentioned periodically over the years, then faded away entirely except for the random references that were right up there with voice activated households and self-driving cars. Both had come to fruition, but the item which had started it all had all but disappeared.

Danny paused for effect. "Then a few weeks ago, I noticed an anomaly with a satellite system monitoring a remote area of Colorado." Danny glanced around the bar, unconsciously moving closer to Rush, their shoulders touching. "Part of my job is ignoring all that I see, never using it to my advantage—"

"Which has been your constant failing," interjected Rush.

"Or success," countered Danny dryly. They'd never be on the same moral plain but they could understand and to a degree, respect each other. "The satellite was hovering over a defunct mine in the hills outside Telluride, for what reason I couldn't fathom, and I'll admit, curiosity got the better off me."

Rush smirked. "The angel of the internet is human."

"More than," Danny agreed. "I followed the progress, watching someone enter the mine and leave, then all hell broke loose; marine choppers, military personnel, the works. Soon after I saw floating code from the NSA that the FBI was assigned."

"Hold up," Rush said, the sarcasm gone. "Our contact in the Denver office told us someone had been sent to an obscure town in the four corners area a couple weeks back; something was up because he is known as the best, but the informant didn't know more."

Danny gave a sly smile. "Part of the reason is because I deleted the data on the satellite system."

Rush grunted with satisfaction. "You put your big toe on the line separating our territories when you spied on your clients' activities, but you crossed over fully into our world when you deleted the data."

Ignoring the comment, Danny continued. "I monitored the dark web waiting for someone to brag or a mistake to be made and a few days ago, it happened. Look at this." He pulled up a photo on his phone, an image of metal cubes, each of the eight sides with a flat surface. "My guess is whoever's sending the data across the internet is an amateur, thinking their tracks are covered just because it's the darknet. A juvenile mistake. That's how I found it."

"What's on them?" Rush asked. Danny had been waiting for the question and watched his former adversary's face as he answered.

"The DNA for every American citizen, specifically, their faces. It's also been mentioned that another set exists which include the financial, medical and personnel records of every known US citizen. These," he pointed, "are held on solid state, titanium cubes."

Rush smirked. "Could be nothing more than black mirror stuff," he dismissed.

"Do you think I'd waste my time or yours on facial recognition software? That's *after* the face is created. This is what *creates* the face. Think of it as pure cocaine. You take that and make crack. This is what makes the coke."

With Danny's explanation, Rush expressed slight humility, then greed. "Who has them?"

"That, my new partner, is your job," Danny answered. "Knowing you've got contacts at the FBI I don't, that's the place to start. The user I'm tracking has mentioned more activity in Ouray, the town where the mine's located. But there's another angle. The user hasn't been smart enough or is perhaps arrogant to think that we can't track a Naturalist, and yet it's as clear as day."

Rush was momentarily quiet. "Naturalists and the government going at it? That's nothing new, but their activity keeps the feds out of our business, or at least distracted, and for that I'm continually grateful."

Danny picked up his phone, opening an application before setting the phone down again. Although grainy, the falling snow in front of a light cast shadows on an outbuilding.

"It's a live feed," Danny explained. "Something is happening right now involving the NSA. And another thing," he continued. "This amateur hacker is communicating with someone local."

Rush's eyes went back and forth between Danny and the grainy images as if he were envisioning the person he'd need to find.

"The town is micro, less than five hundred residents, and the NSA was idiotic enough to put a bunch of the teenagers through the truth serums. One got beat up pretty bad."

Danny showed him one of the images he'd captured. The kid's nose was busted, his blue eyes black rimmed, jaw swollen. On seeing this, Rush looked the way Danny felt: furious. They were united in their animosity towards abuse of authority, the damage lasting far longer than the event which caused it.

"But they found nothing?" Rush asked, the muscles under his jawline working.

"Apparently not and left, for a few days at least. The local person is being told by his contact on the dark web to go back in for more. No kidding," he emphasized, nodding at Rush whose eyes were now riveted on the grainy video. "Now you see why it has to be you in that town, ferreting out the cubes," Danny concluded. "Would you allow anyone, even your blood relative with these cubes, knowing what could be on them?"

"Not on my life."

That's what Danny needed to hear. "Take it," Danny said, handing over another printout he'd brought. "This month, people start arriving from all over the world for the local ice climbing competitions. It happens in a narrow gorge right in town. You'll blend right in, assuming your reputation in that area is deserved and not your digital alter-ego."

This elicited a slight grin of conceit Danny had anticipated. "More than."

"Once you get the identity cubes, I want the code to see what my family and I would look like, and determine if we can reverse our face. From all I know it's possible, and I expect you could care less about the DNA threading since you're not an American who had his face scrubbed."

"You understand correctly," Rush responded without sympathy. "I'm getting the better deal."

It's all in the eye of the beholder.

Danny motioned for the bill. "Our business for now is concluded," he said, pulling out his wallet.

"Indulge me a moment," Rush requested, twirling the glass in his fingertips. Danny didn't have to go anywhere, and recognized the change in his rival's disposition. He also noticed the faint scars on Rush's fingers and palm. They had the look of defensive knife wounds.

"You've tracked Mr. Anonymous on line and are now following him," Rush started. "Why wouldn't you just reach out and make contact? Bribes go a long way for 99% of the people in this world. It would be far easier and less time-consuming than me chasing to some small town five hours from here."

Danny wasn't surprised at the suggestion. He'd considered it himself.

"It won't work for two reasons. The first is this black-hatter is an amateur, a person I found through the Hidden Wiki." Rush groaned and Danny nodded. "Right. Total novice, which means if I can catch her, someone else will too."

"Whoa, hold up. A girl?"

"Has to be," said Danny. "The terminology and construct is feminine in tone, and that's the second reason I wouldn't reach out. Even if I got her to talk, she'd likely reveal my identity if she got caught and probably break down in the process. Far easier to observe from afar and use the information."

"Huh," said Rush, gazing at the liquid in his glass before taking a drink. "Girl communicating with presumably a guy in Ouray."

Danny could practically feel the man's intensity increase. Rush was everything Danny was not; lean, handsome. Rush was also dangerous, the characteristic attractive to the female persuasion and probably a good deal of the male. Danny didn't have to leap far to align with Rush's line of thought: he'd have the advantage of his looks and charm, not just his digital smarts.

Danny signed the bill, his attention on the waiter.

"What's going on?" Rush asked, redirecting Danny's attention to the phone. "You said this was the entrance to the mine. Shouldn't it be dead up there, especially on New Year's Eve?"

Although grainy, the black and white image was clear enough to show three figures; two moving toward what Danny assumed were vehicles and another some distance away. They walked side by side then disappeared.

"Looks like they're entering the mine," Danny surmised. They watched in silence as the third figure slowly approached the vehicles then stopped behind a large barrier. "Bet that's a rock. It's solid and roundish."

Suddenly, the figure darted towards the location where the two figures had been and then stood still.

"That there is steel," explained Danny, tracing the long figures. "My guess are snowmobiles." Less than sixty seconds later, the figure darted back to the boulder, the heat from the engine burning red as it fired up.

"That's proves your black-hat female was right on," Rush murmured.

"He runs like a male," observed Danny. Rush grunted his agreement. The video had waves of clarity and distortion, making the images hard to read.

"What's happening?" asked Rush, unused to deciphering videos.

"Weather most likely. Guy's in trouble now," Danny observed dispassionately. "That red shot is a flare. See there," he pointed. Two figures had appeared on the lower right hand part of the screen. Then two more red spots of heat appeared on the left of the screen.

"Looks like there are four chasing the one."

They watched until the feed turned to black. "You think he got away?" asked Rush, the question holding the hope of a fellow outlaw.

Danny clicked off the now dark screen.

"That's what you're going to find out."

CHAPTER 17

Kyle turned the ATV hard, accelerating too quickly. Precious seconds were lost as he straightened the tires, lurching forward, careening over the hillside. He heard the roar of engines, but the sound wasn't from behind; one was coming up from below and another was to his left.

Four snowmobiles. He changed directions, going straight to the narrow ridge just below the actual road leading to the mine. Up and over his head zoomed a snowmobile, the massive vehicle whining, the exposed muffler deafening.

He instinctively ducked, turning left, running straight into another set of lights. They were herding him, the capture complete and total.

If he was going to go down, it was going to be in flames. He sped up, going straight for the snowmobile in front of him, hoping that by now, the one above had landed in the deep snow, perhaps getting stuck, but if not, turning around and coming back up the hill.

Faster he went, the distance between him and the oncoming snowmobile tightening. In his peripheral vision, he noticed lights were pacing him. One of his pursuers had gone up above, and now, below and to his right on the snow shelf was the second mobile.

Kyle braced himself for impact, gripping the handles while simultaneously leaning back. The collision launched Kyle up, the driver of the snowmobile turning fractionally just before the tip of his vehicle met Kyle's front track. As Kyle went through the air, he felt the impact of something scrape the bottom of his ATV, unsure if it was the plastic windshield or the man's head. He hoped the guy had leaned away instead of colliding with him face first, the crunch of Kyle's back tracks hitting a hard surface. He glanced behind him, seeing the front of the snowmobile had buried deep into the hillside.

Above and to his left, the other snowmobile was now at the edge of the road. The driver had the choice to turn away or go over the ledge and risk going right on top of Kyle which is what he did.

Insanity!

Too late to turn or he'd have fifteen hundred pounds of metal on his back, Kyle turned the ATV a hard left into the snowbank himself, slamming on the breaks. The snowmobile careened right over him, the momentum and speed off the hillside propelling it a good ten feet. Kyle watched the landing in slow motion, the back of the heavy rig falling first. The driver had no choice but to hold on, ignorant that the light, front end would rotate backward, crushing him. At the last second, the driver must have sensed the inevitable, because he leaned off to the right, diving for the protective snow. The seconds elongated to minutes as the front end continued to flip back, landing on the snow, the metal skis face up, the chains of the machine still going.

Two down.

Kyle reversed the ATV and turned back around to where he guessed the other two to be. He had to take care of them up here, on the mountain. If he got into town, they'd see him and be able to identify his vehicle.

He knew where he had to lead them, dreading his decision, but it was now survival.

Kyle saw the lights to his right and in front. He kept his speed even, tracking along the mountain at an incline, heading back up. The driver spotted him, turning perpendicular to cut him off.

That's it, thought Kyle. *Follow me now.*

A branch snapped on his right shoulder and Kyle clenched his teeth in pain. He dropped low to the handlebars, hugging the edge of the trees, the coverage giving him better vision with the heavy snow. Kyle jerked, the bump lifting him an inch off his seat. He'd scraped something underneath, probably a stump but the force of his speed had kept him going. He had no choice but to turn a harder right, the angle up the mountain putting him on a known hiker's path. He couldn't afford to get the ATV high centered and stuck on an invisible object under the snow. If that happened, he might as well park his ATV now and put his hands in the air.

His closest pursuer was now within half a football field length, the other set of lights nearing from below.

Two in one, he hoped, knowing he had to get it exactly right or they'd both be dead, not injured or out of commission which is what he intended.

Nearer....nearer... searching for the Matterhorn tree. Kyle intentionally slowed, pushing down the pressure he felt in his chest as he released the gas. The driver did the opposite, coming at him full throttle as if Kyle were going full out.

Now! Kyle's thumb depressed the gas, and he veered a slight left, making for the Matterhorn. He expected the slight drop in the snow, knowing the catch basin of the thick cable netting he'd strung below was in place. The snow had to be four, maybe five feet deep, but not compressed or packed. The cables were tightly knit: close enough to prevent a body from going through but not a foot or a leg.

The broad, evenly pressured tracks sank at first then lifted up, easily passing over the fifteen-foot wide cable netting. He was just over the edge when he heard the high whine of the snowmobile coming straight for him. Kyle moved another ten feet, then paused, watching. Down the steep mountain side the snowmobile came, following Kyle's path. Straight on it hit the covered cable, the pointy front-end making a knife-life incision in the snow, its heavy back end pushing it further into the white, powdery flesh, its rider launching forward, the face plant funny but not fatal.

Kyle didn't wait around for the screams of frustration as the man attempted to extract himself from the powder. Given the depth of the snow and angle of the vehicle, it would take a winch on another machine to pull it out backwards. That, or wait until the snow melted.

Before Kyle's satisfaction abated, another vehicle came from his left, slowing as the rider saw where his compatriot had landed. He gunned it, going up and around the Matterhorn. Kyle guessed he had a few seconds lead time to get away, thinking through his options. Kyle headed for Box Canyon, knowing the hidden fencing was no more than a quarter mile away, the stream running at a diagonal to the town, the high, rock glaciers on either side making for the perfect ice climbing conditions but mortal tragedy for those who didn't know the area. His only chance at saving the rider was to get him near the metal platform; it would stop the snowmobile and only incapacitate the rider.

The customized rubber tracks helped the machine float to the surface as he increased his speed, grateful the snow was continuing to dump, the identifying marks of the rubber hidden for hours.

His lights bounced off the large metal platform hanging from the top of Box Canyon Ridge. He was too far west, the only thing across from that area was a two hundred foot drop. They'd both be dead.

Kyle cranked it a hard left, the jolt into a metal post underneath wedging him to a stop. He flew over the side of his ATV, the release of his throttle keeping the motor running, but his vehicle was motionless. He was waist high in the snow and barely reached over the front to push the knob to off then struggled to the back. With all his strength, he lifted the back end up and right.

What am I thinking?! He held his breath and lifted, this time the other direction. He could see the right tire was still stuck on the bar. Kyle had no choice. He pushed down into the snow, burying his knees as deep as he could, placing the top of the tire on his left shoulder, the rubber scrubbing against his neck. Using the force of his thighs, hips and upper body, he lifted, pushing on the diagonal as he did so. The tip of the metal shone, the flat edge running into a point, obvious and innocuous in the summer, fatal in the winter.

I hope this works.

The snowmobiler was headed straight towards him, the force of a side hit would be the equivalent of an off-road T-bone. Kyle knew that with the depth of his tracks in the snow, it would be a miracle if he could get out.

Kyle had one leg over the ATV, simultaneously moving the on-switch with his left thumb, when he thought to use the fence as both barrier and a sprinter's block. Costing him precious seconds, he changed directions, going back several feet, though now he was at the correct angle.

The man lifted up his arm and Kyle instinctively ducked, the bullet hitting the frozen wall of ice behind him. He crouched low, waiting until he saw the white rimmed goggles.

Unsure if he'd get stuck on the railing again, he chanced it, backing up, holding his position. A split second before Kyle thought he'd get hit full on, he gunned the ATV, leaning back off the end to give it extra power, the front end lifting up and off the railing he'd used as the platform. The driver took evasive action, making a turn so sharp the snowmobile lifted its left side, leaning on the right.

Kyle shifted forward over the handlebars as though his weight were going to help avoid the inevitable crash that was sure to come.

But it didn't happen. The machine on his left was now propelled forward by both its weight and the downhill slope, listing further on its right side as the driver tried to correct.

With his right thumb still engaging the accelerator and wary of trees in his path, Kyle looked past his left shoulder. The snowmobile had hit the edge of the railing, the metal edge serving as the intended guardrail, but it wasn't enough. The force was so great the man flipped off the side as his vehicle continued to slide without going over.

Kyle didn't want to know what happened to the guy, but couldn't help it. He turned off his vehicle, listening. The eerie calm of the falling snow was like a cemetery after a funeral, interrupted only by the catching sound of the snowmobile engine.

Kyle hoped the man had fallen on the metal platform five feet below, only injured. If not…

He turned back around, changing course. The drive back down was all the time he had to figure out how he was going to literally and figuratively cover his tracks. At least three of the guys were alive, and they would eventually be found and tell what they knew. Then they'd come after Kyle again. And this time they wouldn't let him go.

CHAPTER

18

Mark had finished his fifth pass of the town, disappointed and yet relieved the highlight of his night was encountering a semi-drunk Ashely Fine.

He'd just passed the Stagecoach and crossed Main Street when he saw the recognizable lights of an off road vehicle coming into town. He guessed it was Kyle. The lights flashed and the vehicle slid over to the side of the road. They flashed again and Mark approached, driving right alongside. Sure enough, it was Kyle. Mark lowered his window, relaxed.

"Hey Kyle—"

"Mark, please," interrupted Kyle, looking panic stricken. "I was up at the mine and..." Keeping his own emotions in check, Mark listened to the kid who sped through a description of what just happened.

Kyle confirmed he wasn't injured or bleeding, but his tire tracks could have literally made impressions on the other vehicle.

"Get rid of your ATV now," Mark told him, thinking about where Kyle could take it. The entire town could be flooded in hours depending on whether they pulled in other FBI, Patrol or who knew what else. "The old mill on the river," Mark decided.

Kyle took off, out of sight almost immediately as he traversed the backroads that paralleled the stream flowing down from Box Canyon. The Christmas lights were still on at most of the homes, the revelers inside having no idea another federal crime had been committed in their idyllic valley. The decrepit mill sat in the shadows of the mine tunnel, the old, unused area not even on the historic registry. There it could sit indefinitely.

Mark followed at his usual pace, the one he'd used for going up and down the streets of Ouray for the last hour. Kyle was already off and looking for dents or impressions on his ATV when Mark arrived. Mark told him to get back on and drive around to the far side of the snow-covered building. With a jerk and a pull, Mark opened the sliding door. "Haven't been here since high-school smoking weed," Mark muttered to himself. The place looked like it hadn't been used since, save for a few more beer cans which were on the floor. Portions of the metal room had warped, but overall it was dry and clear of debris. Kyle pulled in and parked.

"If the stench or trap holes don't kill you, it should be safe," said. Mark. "And sorry to do this but you've got to jog back," he said, then added, "fibers in the car---"

"Got it," Kyle said, removing the pouch with his precious cargo from the front handlebars.

"Kyle, stop and think carefully. This place could be swarming with officials in hours. I know you believe the cubes are safely hidden in your home, but that's the first place they'll look. You've got to move them and do it tonight."

Kyle didn't stop to answer as he shoved the entire pouch under his jacket.

"I know exactly where but I have to ask you to cover for me," Kyle said, looking up. Mark involuntarily took a step back. It wasn't Kyle's slightly disfigured face or the unsettling bruising that caught him. It was his fierceness. Gone was the innocent, trusting and believing Kyle; the image he'd had even after the NSA guys had given him a beating. This was....

"Kyle," he began. "Those guys on the mountain are probably alive; you didn't kill them. It was—well, not quite self-defense," Mark admitted. But Kyle shook his head, his eyes wide with the same dazed look that he'd had when the shot to the Naturalists had left him with blood stains. Mark knew what he was going through, but he couldn't have Kyle lose it now.

"Don't go there," Mark said forcefully. "I'd knock you or shake you but as I was starting to say before, I can't risk fibers transferring from me to you. I'm telling you now: you did what you had to do, for yourself, for Billy, for Saachi and Brayden. Now let's go through this because your life and now mine are going to depend on our stories being straight."

"Okay," Kyle breathed in, nodding his head.

Mark quickly went through the timeline they were both going to follow, keeping as much to the absolute truth as possible. Kyle returned home, found his parents gone, decided to watch television for a half hour, then walk up town, where he saw Officer Mark Hancock at the Stagecoach Hotel. They would match exactly with the timing of the mountainside chase. Kyle returned home and Mark drove by, seeing him in his living room watching television approximately ten minutes later.

"But what about the ATV?" Kyle asked.

"What time did you leave your house?" Mark responded. "I need it down to the minute." Kyle told him, along with all the details Mark required to write up a stolen vehicle report. Mark was now his alibi, and also one hundred percent his accomplice in crime.

"Now where to hide the cubes?" Mark asked.

"I know where, just not how to get in. The Weisbaden caves."

Mark thought for a moment, then nodded. "In the crevices?"

"Either in the vapor room or in the very back of the general soaking area." Mark congratulated him. Not in a million years would anyone think of a tourist spot where the temperatures ran above a hundred.

"Good man, just don't cross Linda. She hasn't mellowed since semi-retiring to Littleton."

"Are you kidding me?" Kyle retorted, thinking of the owner who could be as sweet or ornery as any grandmother. "She'd fry my balls for breakfast if I step one foot out of line."

Three minutes later, Kyle had run into the black night, jogging back to his home. With his athletic gifts, Mark knew he'd be home in less than five, showered and changed in another five, then adding the existing cubes with those he'd just collected and heading up the street to the Weisbaden. With any luck, the guys on the mountain were alive, but dazed. In the deep snow, it could take thirty minutes to get down, and if their cell phones were working, another hour for reinforcements to come up from Montrose or Durango.

Mark took the time to use the materials to cover all traces he'd been inside. He shuffled the snow, careful to disguise the boot prints should they have left an impression. Once he was on the main road, he took an alternate route back to the town, his gratitude the deep snow had continued falling unabated.

With the cover story he and Kyle now had, the ATV hidden and Kyle on his way back home, the rest of the evening could resume as normal.

Mark parked on Main to write up the false police report on the stolen ATV. Then he began his routine of surveying the city, his eyes periodically looking up the mountain for signs of activity. In the next few hours, the town would be receiving visitors.

Rush required only an hour to get his team assembled: Marcus, Alexie and Raze, enforcers and bodyguards, all equally adept at guns and intimidation.

Not that we're going to require either in a town of five hundred, he thought to himself.

As the elevator in his apartment building dropped, Rush realized the adrenaline pumping up his system wasn't entirely due to the notion of making a gross amounts of money. It was from the thrill of being the first with access to the stolen government goods, made possible by his unlikely frenemy Danny Amato. Who would have thought?

Rush's cell phone rang and he saw the caller. He kept the details vague, the call brief. His girlfriend of the month didn't have the right to know his schedule. He was headed out of town for business, the end. If she was there when he returned, great. If not, have a good life.

He was smiling as the elevator door opened. Marcus was waiting for him, hand outstretched to take his bag. The others were in the car.

"What about a cover?" Marcus asked. "We don't look, speak or act like locals."

Rush shook his head, dismissing the worry. He'd done his homework.

"All we need is ice climbing gear," he informed his bodyguard. "It will be the reason we're in town, no questions asked. You find us a place local?"

"No luck, boss. All sold out, only a few hundred rooms in a town that size. Closest we have is Telluride, across the mountain range, thirty minutes away."

Rush climbed in the back seat of Defender, comforted that the twenty-year old imported vehicle was indestructible; the hundred grand in modifications made it fire and bomb proof, and the rear bench seats accommodated seven stored guns and equipment in storage compartments good enough to fool the border patrol.

That wasn't going to happen on route from Denver to Ouray, and with any luck, no guns would be required at all.

But Rush's philosophy on guns was like a condom: better to have it and not need it than need it and not have it.

"Let's go," he told Marcus. "Time to go make us a billion dollars."

CHAPTER 19

Brayden finished showering. His release had been efficient and underwhelming, just as Mitch had intimated.

Laura was due home any moment, the anticipation filling him with the excitement of a first date and the dread it would end poorly. For a moment in the hospital, he'd felt they were bound by the pain of their past and the secrets of the present.

Brayden put on sweats and a t-shirt, dropping to the floor, pumping out fifty push-ups before his arms burned. Since his son's suicide, he'd trained himself to use mental distraction as a method to stop his thoughts from overwhelming him. It had worked for three years, right up until the time Kyle told him what he'd learned on the master cubes; that his son's death couldn't have been self-inflicted, due to the shotgun and placement of the device. The information had been kept from Brayden and his wife, but it had been on the cubes, black and white.

Anger fueled another twenty reps, but he didn't notice his teeth were clenched until he moved his jaw. The crunching could have been his rising fury, but who to take it out on? Who could have done such a thing, and why? Every murder had a motive, and his teenage boy had no enemies, debts or hidden secrets. The FBI's own team had investigated him and Laura due to their positions with the government and concern over their performance and even susceptibility to bribes. Six months later, they'd moved on with their lives, but in different directions; he with cases and she with the hours at the hospital.

But thanks to Kyle, that distorted reality had been clarified, like the dirt on a glass removed, giving his relationship with Laura a second chance.

"More than a second chance," he said to himself, a tinge of hopeful anticipation creeping into his chest.

That was the other bomb Kyle had dropped on him. According to the cubes, his daughter Sasha, might be—could be—alive somewhere. The DNA coding on the cubes didn't match what she was given at birth. It had given him a tentative hope, the kind that you want to suppress because the explosion could be so great.

Brayden went downstairs, found the scented red candles and lighters, strategically placing them in the dining room and downstairs guest bedroom. He started the fireplace, the glow giving the cold living room romance that it hadn't had in years.

Brayden paced in the living room, the growing desire for his wife and their new future conflicting with the reality that he still had a job in Denver and the recent activity in Ouray, hopefully which had calmed down. Kyle was smart. He'd take the right course of action.

More out of nervous anticipation than any real intent, Brayden took a notepad and pen out of the kitchen and sat in the armchair. His doodles took shape as he wrote the names of his children and Laura down, the ages when he'd last seen them. He wrote Ouray, Denver and Coeur d'Alene on the paper cities he'd been or would soon be going to.

Outside, the lights from the street merged with those from the fireplace. It was close to midnight now.

Unconsciously his loops of the pen drew circles around children and parents, then places.

Later he would tell Laura he didn't know if it was his unconscious awareness coming through, his mind on her and their family guiding the tip of his pen, but at some point, he stopped, staring down at the paper before him.

The overlap between his daughter, Laura and Coeur d'Alene, Denver and Ouray were concentric.

It was a chest-stopping hit, where he felt the physical impact of the knowledge. Kyle had told him Sasha's recorded DNA was different from that on the deceased body. In other words, it had been switched. Kyle had hypothesized that it wasn't inconceivable that given Laura's position at the hospital, she could have easily conspired to manipulate the records and squirrel away her daughter. And the only place Laura could have hidden the child would have been on an Indian reservation, where even the long arms of the US government couldn't reach. By why?

Brayden's hands started to shake, but no longer from the romantic, passionate intent he'd entertained five minutes before. It had evolved into the very real prospect that Laura had conceivably worked with someone of Native American descent to hide their daughter.

He pondered that further. What had Mark told him? Billy's mother had left when Billy was a baby, disappeared, leaving the family behind.

Brayden looked up the number to Ty's bar, unconcerned if his cell phone call was tracked. A simple question or two could be inserted into a conversation without raising an alarm.

"Ty, please," Brayden requested when the phone was finally answered.

"This is," Ty said gruffly. The noise in the background almost made a conversation impossible.

"Hi Ty-this is Brayden Cox of the FBI You might remember me—"

"I do. Are you calling to give me news about my daughter?"

"News?" Brayden asked, caught off guard.

"Guess not," Ty said sourly.

"Why would you ask? What's happened to Billy?"

"I was hoping you or someone else could tell me. She left after the game Friday night. Not a word from her since. I told the locals about it—Mark, or Deputy Hancock to you. He said Stu and others might be making her life difficult."

Brayden heard the anger, worry and fear in the man's voice, his gruff exterior the only defense against the possibility his daughter had been kidnapped instead of her intentionally leaving.

"You ask Kyle?"

Ty grunted. "I punched him actually, but it didn't work. He said he didn't know why she left or where she'd gone, but I swear…." The man left the sentence hanging.

"Ty," Brayden said firmly, "what I saw between those two was real, and she's one smart young woman. More so than most of the people in that entire town, if you want my professional opinion." The silence on the other end encouraged Brayden to say more. "Ty, let's just say I don't know this for a fact, but there was a reason she left and one why she'll come back. Of all the people in that town to trust, Kyle Smith is it."

"Trust is different than like."

Brayden got that too. "Ty, I have a strange question and please—this isn't meant to offend you. When did your wife leave the family?"

"It was the day after Billy's third birthday."

"And what day is her birthday?"

"October 14th. Do you know something I don't?"

The sudden constriction of Brayden's throat made it impossible for him to speak. He nodded, until he could talk. "My daughter was born October 14th. She died when she was three years old."

"My God," whispered Ty. "What are you saying?"

"I don't know, Ty. But Kyle thought there was a connection of some kind."

"The boys from the NSA beat him up real bad, but I thought he deserved it for chasing Billy out of town."

Brayden thought through the scenarios. "Ty, maybe you should consider the possibility that Billy left town to protect Kyle and not put you in harm's way? And that maybe Kyle was beat up because he didn't share things that could have put the entire town in danger."

The line was quiet, allowing Brayden to hear a customer ask for another glass of whiskey.

"Maybe," admitted Ty.

"I'll get word to you if I learn anything—but Ty, not if it's going to put anyone in jeopardy, understood?"

"I think so," Ty answered. "I'm just…that's my daughter out there, and I can't believe this is happening."

"None of us can, Ty."

The phone was ringing when Kyle threw open the door. He ignored it, dropping his gear in the mudroom, the sweat on his face mixing with the melting snow now that he was indoors. The sound stopped, then started again as he shoved his shoes to the back, unable to control the adrenaline flowing through him from the flight down the mountain then finding Mark. He'd fully intertwined Mark in his problems now, far more worried about the guy than he was himself. If the feds put him in jail, he'd just be another kid to pound on, but criminals hated cops. They'd kill Mark outright.

Kyle ignored the phone as he headed towards the basement kiln. No one he wanted to speak to would be calling his home on New Year's Eve so close midnight.

Unless…

"Mom? Dad?" he yelled from halfway down the stairs. No answer. Crap. Something could have happened to them.

He sprinted back up, taking two steps at a time, answering out of breath.

"Hello?"

"Kyle, Ty." Not the person Kyle wanted to speak with right now as he'd soon have men coming down the hill and he had to get out of the house.

"Look Ty, I said I'm sorry—"

"Yeah, about that," Ty interrupted. "Look, to cut to the chase, I got a call from Brayden and maybe I was wrong about Billy. Maybe...well—perhaps I was too hard on you and shouldn't have been."

"Brayden contacted you??"

"Yes, and all I'm saying is that...me and Brayden have a strange connection and you were the one who figured it out."

Kyle didn't dare risk being wrong but desperately wanted to know. "Does it have to do with his wife, Laura?"

"Seems so," he replied. "Susan, that was my wife, left the day after Brayden's daughter died."

The sweat felt cold on Kyle's body. "What does Brayden want me to do?" he asked, bracing himself for yet another impossible task to add to the one he already had.

"He said nothing for you to do, but on my side, well, he wants me to feed you," he said without a hint of humor.

"Come up and get some takeout, and use the back door. The bar is no place for an underage kid on New Year's."

Didn't Kyle know it. "Be up as soon as I change."

CHAPTER 20

By the time Danny arrived home, the images on his phone had turned from grainy to clear. The satellite was still in position, capturing the mountainside to the edge of town. It was a mistake on the part of the satellite developer, he thought, who hadn't expanded the circumference of the lens to include the small circle of the city center proper.

"Doesn't matter now," Danny said to himself as he positioned the keyboard on his lap. With the rapid tapping of his fingertips, he replaced the visual record with one from the day before where no activity had occurred; the conditions still a white out. Anyone else looking would surmise the blizzard had thrown off the images, causing no internal alarms.

Danny zoomed in on the terrain south of the mine shaft. Four, faintly reddish marks designated the heat emanating from the snowmobiles. None seemed to be running, the leftover warmth of the engine just enough to be picked up.

"And where are the riders?" he asked the computer. He had to zoom out and then back in to make sure he caught any human movements.

Nothing.

His eyes darted back and forth across the screen. It had taken forty minutes to return home, not enough time for a rescue unit to drive up to Ouray from either Durango or Montrose, which were the closest towns. Danny tapped into the Patrol database, seeing their nearest unit was in Grand Junction, two hours away, longer in the bad weather. Even if the guys had called in for back-up...no, the guys still had to be on the mountain.

What was he missing? They could all have died in the last forty minutes, sure, but that also probably defied the odds.

He rolled his fingertips along the keyboard, thinking.

The guys were probably wearing all white tactical gear to blend in with the snow...it would be impervious to the weather.

That's it.

He tapped out another inquiry, finding what he wanted. The all-white tactical gear was sensor-resistant, required technology for dropping spies into enemy lines. And ironically, Russian made.

Danny accessed the darknet, querying on the software code to revert the tactical gear from invisible to heat sensitive, finding just want he needed for five-thousand in bitcoin credits. Using the code he'd been given for the satellite, he took another look at the mountain side.

"There you are," he said to himself. Two bodies crouched within feet of their snowmobiles, motionless. The orange of heat was faint: they were alive but barely. It took him another minute to find the third rider, he was moving very slowly down the hill, inches at a time, which meant a foot or two. By that measure, it would take a solid hour to reach town. Danny couldn't locate the fourth individual.

His felt the adrenaline increasing, a slight pressure on his chest as though he were the 911 operator asking about the vitals on a victim.

He scrolled his fingers over the keys, adjusting the satellite for position and clarity. A long metal post lined a wall, running parallel with a ridge. He leaned close, increasing the zoom. The ridge was the edge of a ravine with a stream below it. The water wasn't frozen, but still moving with a strong current.

The government satellite moved at his direction and he followed the stream. The clear view blocked only when a bridge covered the water. Two additional bridges blocked his view as the river coursed through town and eventually merged with a larger river.

If the body made it under the bridges, there was no telling where it would end up.

Danny zoomed out, taking in the Ouray valley. A large lake was miles downstream, halfway to Montrose. With the speed of the current, a floating body might already have reached the lake, and from there, it would sink with the weight of the gear.

He inhaled deeply, on the edge of his own moral dilemma. Two men were up on the hill at mortal risk. Another was likely already dead, the third living was making his way down the hill, no guarantee of survival.

Danny considered the predicament. The discovery of the cubes and the potential to right many wrongs was a once-in-a-lifetime gift that he was never going to get again. He had to give Rush time to get in and get those cubes no matter what it took, and that wasn't going to happen in the six hours it would take until Rush arrived. It would require days, maybe weeks depending on the situation he encountered. Those guys on the hill had maybe hours, less in the snow and cold.

I've worked my whole life playing by the book, thwarting people like Rush, and now when I have the chance...

Danny stood, pacing the kitchen. He drank a cold glass of water, clearing his head from the alcohol he'd previously consumed. He was Italian who'd been taught to honor his family name.

"That's all you have in life," his father repeated right up until the time of his death. "You have your integrity and honor.

It remains unless you give it away, because no one can take it from you."

That's what helped Danny sleep at night, a luxury he wondered if Rush had ever known, always looking over his shoulder, relying upon beefy bodyguards to protect him.

Danny took another drink and headed back to his computer, finding the cell phone number for Brayden Cox. He used an anonymous internet phone line and placed the call, cursing the entire time. No matter how badly he wanted a new face, he'd regret looking at himself in the mirror if all he saw were the orange-tinted, motionless bodies looking back at him.

Gary was at home nursing a whiskey, having watched the ball drop, when he received a call from Brayden. Four men down, one missing, the informant a black-hat with a conscience.

Thanking Brayden, he'd called Janet for the satisfaction of telling the woman her men were down.

"On one hand, I should congratulate you for setting a second trap that the perpetrators fell for," said Gary. "Your analysts were right. Do I need to say that's negated by the fact your systems have been penetrated and you failed?"

"No, you don't," she coldly replied, hanging up.

Gary's next call was to the President.

"Scott, the ultimate irony is that you have a hacker who has tapped into the satellites, first to monitor the events then to call up Brayden, otherwise we'd never have known."

"We don't know what other surveillance systems they've penetrated," stated the President.

"Sir, Janet's corrupted from the inside---"

"Don't kid yourself Gary. Every organization in our government has people who have been bought out. It has been and always will be a numbers game."

"True, one where we hope our numbers are greater than theirs," Gary finished, the oft-repeated mantra of the intelligence agencies in the United States well-deserved. "But she went around your direct orders and failed again. I get you're sensitive to her abilities, but how long are you going to allow this to continue?"

"Hold on," Scott requested. "Janet's on the line."

Gary was put on mute as the President spoke with his peer and pain in the ass director of the NSA. Gary recalled an earlier conversation with Brayden, who'd contended a local was involved. But if that person or persons had eluded the federal forces a second time, there was no way the individual was going to stay in town.

And Janet could be right once more, Gary mused. The perpetrator would leave town, and Janet's idea to have the drones in the air and the roads blocked by police was reasonable. Her predictions were as good an outcome as bad, which is what he told the President when he came back on the line.

"Evac is on its way and satellite caught the perpetrator heading towards Durango, final destination perhaps New Mexico. Drones and roadblocks are being deployed as we speak."

"Sir, it could be a fabricated decoy," Gary countered.

"Acknowledged, but we can't take any chances." Gary conceded the point. Digitally-created images in place of public figures and private citizens had become common, and it was nearly impossible to tell between real and fake.

"What did you order?" Gary asked him.

"For Janet to have her team leave the Ouray area or resign her position. She agreed since her analysts believe the perpetrator is on the run. On another subject, do you think it means anything Brayden was the one to be contacted?" the President asked.

"Sure it does," Gary replied. "They are sending a message loud and clear that we have been made vulnerable and they are monitoring the situation."

"Taunting us."

"If taunting is equivalent to watching, then yes. But I have bigger issues on my hands because what I hypothesized during our meeting is now a much likelier scenario."

"And what's that?"

"That the coder with a conscience wants to make money off the information," answered Gary. "As an update on that side, we're already working on a strategy which includes changing passcodes and data for the hundreds of millions of vulnerable accounts prior to digital Armageddon. I've put Brayden as the task-force lead for the financial side."

"You think that's wise?" questioned the President. "He's already been compromised."

"Being used by Janet as bait or being chosen by the hacker to convey information?" Gary challenged, offended on behalf of both Brayden and his organization. "Look, Scott," he continued, purposefully using their personal connection. "You and I both know Brayden has put the government and above all else in his life for a dozen years. If he were going to compromise us, he's had plenty of opportunities to do so. However, there's not one piece of data to suggest that is the case, and in truth, he's been the closest to this situation from the beginning."

"You'll be giving him carte blanche to do what's necessary?"

"And the ability to leverage every underground, undercover and dirty-world connection the FBI has to get what we need."

"Do it." It was all Gary needed to hear. His next call was to his best agent in the country.

CHAPTER 21

Brayden changed out of his sweats and into jeans and a button down, all thoughts of a romantic evening with his wife gone. He'd accepted the assignment without hesitation.

When Laura walked through the door, the New Year was well underway. He was on the phone with a member of his elite team. She waved, walking up the stairs as he ended that call, then began another conversation.

"More news," said one of his computer analysts. Brayden listened, his eyes on the cars going down the slick street. One swerved, narrowly missing his mailbox.

When the call was over, Brayden called Gary back.

"Sir," Brayden began, "our worse fears have just been confirmed. Word of the availability of the cubes and, more importantly, that of the masters, is already on the dark web. It's a small, isolated thread, but it's there. My guess is that was enough to attract the attention of whoever hacked into the satellite and saved Janet's people."

"So the hunt has already begun," Gary said grimly.

"Yes, sir. But one question which is unanswered: what about the theft earlier today? Do we know yet what was taken?"

"We're waiting on that."

"Then let me ask you this," Brayden continued. "Were the cubes left in the mine shaft decoys or the real thing?"

"Real."

"They never thought the perpetrators would get this far in other words?" Brayden asked, incredulous. "Wonderful. Does Janet believe the same group or person who perpetrated the theft the first time is the same as the second?"

"That's the conclusion of her analyst, yes."

"Unbelievable," Brayden muttered.

"Agreed."

Brayden knew his boss thought he was referring to the cubes being live and not fakes, but his thoughts weren't on the storage devices at all. They were on the only person Brayden knew who could ascend, steal and get away with another theft of the century.

When Kyle arrived at the back door of the bar, Ty apologized for punching him. It was clear Ty had more questions than answers, but for now, he offered to help Kyle when it was required.

Kyle accepted the food then took him up on that, asking Ty for a favor. While Kyle waited, Ty placed a call to the owner of the Weisbaden: would Linda allow a private soak for the most beat-up and misunderstood kid in town, who was persona non-grata on everyone's list, including his? Linda was sympathetic, requesting Kyle to use the entrance near her home at the rear of the springs.

Once there, she took Kyle into the dark vapor room which was empty except for a honeymooning couple who paid no attention to him. Kyle went further back into the darkest region of the 109 degree space, waiting until he was alone and it was dead silent. He'd slipped all fifty cubes and the masters into the highest and deepest crevices. There was no way even the best investigator would think to explore the vaping cave or the thousands of tiny bore-hole areas.

The next hour was spent detoxing, physically, mentally and emotionally. Linda checked on him, offering a bottle of cucumber and lemon infused water.

"It's not easy to be the standout in a small community," she said. Kyle nodded. She probably knew all about that. Linda had been the original rebel decades before his own mother had arrived in town. Her flowing grey hair and single status as unsettling to the ranchers and conservative townsfolk who'd dominated the area. But she'd purchased a run-down shack and transformed a natural rock formation into a world-class destination while keeping it small and unpretentious. It was hard to think anything bad about her now.

"I don't suppose you could use any help around here," Kyle offered, already prepared for rejection.

Linda smiled, her thin, wrinkled face naturally elegant. Kyle briefly imagined how stunning she must have been as a twenty, thirty or even forty-year old; a woman in her seventies who looked that good had to have been a knockout.

"Ty suggested that you might be available," she answered, her voice kind.

"I won't be visible," he offered. "I'll stay out of sight, cleaning and doing the water pumps—I'm pretty good at that," he added with a light smirk.

"I couldn't rightly have you be at the front desk anyway," she said with a genuine smile. "Come back tomorrow morning at seven, using the back entrance like you did today. We'll work together and no one will ever know." Before he left, she touched his arm. "It's going to work out Kyle. Being on the receiving end of judgement and losing things you care about is hard in the moment, but worth it in the long run."

Kyle felt a little less lonely as the snow pelted him on the way home, waiting until he heard his parents go to bed before he called Billy with the burner phone.

"This better be an emergency," she grumped.

"The emergency has come and gone..." As Kyle spoke, he heard the sounds of movement, the computer firing up and the clicking of fingers.

"This is not good Kyle," she said now sounding wide awake.

"You're kidding right?" he asked with slight exasperation. "I did what you asked, now one or more men could be dead, my ATV is gone and Mark is completely involved—"

"No, not that," she interrupted, not unkindly. "Serious congratulations on the cubes—you went above and beyond. I'm talking the satellites. We should have images of you leaving and what you described, but there's nothing. As in, we aren't the only ones with access to the satellite feeds. Someone went in and overwrote their own data..." She trailed off, and Kyle finally got her line of thought.

"Are you telling me you might have competition for the cubes?"

"Well, I doubt that someone is tracking the activities and overwriting the videos for fun and enjoyment," she suggested.

Kyle abruptly changed the subject. "Are you still going through with it?" he asked.

"Yes. Only a few more days. Nothing more to say on the topic Kyle, and I'm sorry but I've got to go. I have to see if there's a way to track who is tracking *you*."

Kyle wasn't sure how long it took him to fall asleep, but when the alarm went off at six-thirty a.m. he felt drained. He'd had dreams of racing down from the mountain but not being able to leave the town, every road cut off, then hitting the metal bars and landing in the frigid water. By now, the men had most definitely come down from the mountain and were perhaps already searching homes.

He caught himself looking to the street for signs of new vehicles. Stu was out shoveling the snow, chipping the ice from the path to his home.

He could ride into town...no he couldn't. The snowmobile was in a barn south of town.

Crap. His parents would have seen it missing from the carport when they arrived home. His adrenaline spiked as he tried to think of a lie—

No. No more lies, he'd promised them.

That was before I broke another promise, which was not to steal again.

He'd prepared himself for a confrontation, entering the kitchen to see his dad with his back turned pouring a coffee.

"Morning," his father said, looking over his shoulder.

"Hey dad." Kyle took the orange juice and milk out of the fridge, avoiding his dad's look by opening the cereal cupboard.

"I saw Mark on my walk. He told me about the ATV being stolen. Unreal." Kyle turned at his father's tone of voice.

"We've been down this road with Mark before it seems, him telling us one thing and then finding out the reality was another." Kyle drew in his lips, licking the cracked flesh. "No one steals anything in this town and we all know it. Not a car. Not even a bicycle, but then mysteriously, your brand new ATV is taken the very night something big happened—*again*."

Kyle sidestepped his father to sit at the table, talking as he poured the cereal.

"Something big, huh?" Kyle asked, glancing up.

"Yeah. A dead body found near the lake." Kyle's hand shook until he put the spoon in the bowl. "And a few snowmobilers got stuck up on the ridge, just below the mine."

"That's a whole lotta gossip for a single New Year's Eve night, especially when you were out for most of it."

His father sat, the grey eyes dark with worry. "Kyle, I don't give two rats asses about the ATV. Men are in the hospital and another is dead. Please don't tell me you've gone and killed someone."

Kyle wanted to be the honest son he used to be.

"You haven't gotten over whatever hooch you drank last night," Kyle said stood, feigning laughter. "I was here then I went out..." he said, reciting the story he and Mark had created. As Kyle did so, he wrote on a piece of paper.

We can go for a walk later

"…so then I come back and it's gone," Kyle said. "Aren't I the lucky one? I should have bought a lottery ticket but since Stu had me fired, I don't have that kind of change."

Kyle sat back down and pretended to read the newspaper as he pushed the piece of paper toward his dad; his father's wide eyed stare only broke when Kyle used a hand gesture to implore him to speak.

"It's all the town can talk about—well, those who weren't so hung over that a bomb could have gone off. But you," said his father, scouring his eyes, returning to normal. "Your face looks better—and worse."

"I noticed. Thought you should know I'm going to help check the water for Linda starting this morning." At his father's raised eyebrow, he continued. "She took pity on me. Something about understanding what it's like to be a pariah."

At this, the wariness in his father's eyes abated. "She'd know. You gonna keep that on the down-low?"

"Of course. No point in having Stu blackball her establishment like he did with Barrett's." After turning a page or two of the paper, Kyle asked his father if anything else had caught his attention.

"Nothing much other than a few of the early season ice climbers arrived today." Kyle nodded. It wasn't unheard of for the professionals to pay a few visits to Box Canyon ahead of the actual competition, participating in the pre-season climbs.

"Sean been working the lines?" he asked.

"Trying to but he got a late start. His crew found the snowmobile up by the higher platform and it took 'em a while to bring it down. Looks like the body they found downstream belonged to the rider." Kyle met his father's eyes for a split second before his father continued. "The railing has the skid mark, like he tried to stop but went over, the snowmobile staying on this side."

"Must have fallen straight over," Kyle said, taking the note he'd written over to the sink. "That's awful," he added, turning on the water. It *was* awful, but he wasn't responsible, he told himself. He didn't push the guy, nor had he done anything…except steal more government property. "

"What'd mom say about the ATV?"

"What do you think? Once again, Mark was put in the position of calming her down."

Kyle got his coat. "Walk later?" he asked.

"Later."

He took the alley all the way up to town, past the school up to the Weisbaden, arriving at seven a.m. sharp. He called for Linda who came around back, a cleaning box in her hand. "The chemicals are nearly identical to what's used at the springs…" she began, motioning for him to follow. It took only fifteen minutes of explanation to understand what variations she used to check the quality of the various water pools and her preferred cleaning methods. Discussion of money and hours was saved until the end of his first shift, two hours later, just before opening.

"You tell me what you were getting with Barrett and when you need it." Kyle told her, thanking her again and promised she wouldn't regret it.

CHAPTER

22

Box Canyon was quiet, the small ticket building empty, the waist-high metal gate open. Kyle held the rail, descending down into the canyon itself. Above and beside him the grey rock provided covering from snow and rain, although today was full sun. Near the bottom he saw Sean Volant, the city parks and recreation manager who held a long, industrial sized metal rod. Kyle came up as Sean directed his assistant to hold tight. It was aimed at the very spot where the snowmobiler had been the night before.

"I thought you'd be up at the ice park," Kyle remarked.

"Trying to see if we have any lasting damage from the event last night," explained Sean. He turned back, grimacing with the weight of the rod.

"Yeah, Dad said someone ended up in the river," Kyle remarked, coming alongside him, keeping a distance just in case the heavy metal rod got squirrelly. "Is that for real?"

"Unfortunately. Took them nearly two hours to get the snowmobile unstuck from the railing up there on the higher platform. Poor sucker went right over and bam. End of the line. On the bright side, the firefighters who were supposed to be up at the Ice Park today shooting water did search and rescue this morning. Maybe they'll find your Christmas gift." Kyle stared at him. "You know, the stolen ATV? Mark thinks whoever was drunk enough to fall over the edge might have taken your ride in the carport when you were out. It's easy enough to get generic keys and ride off with machine. Easy come easy go, eh?"

Kyle mustered a dry laugh. "Is that supposed to make me feel better?"

"Not really," Sean told him, smirking. Kyle saw the man struggling and offered to help, but was declined. "This town can't afford the liability if you get hurt."

"I'm already a liability, in case you hadn't heard."

Until that point, Sean had done a decent job of avoiding looking directly at Kyle's face, but at the remark he stared right at him.

"I have, and no offense, but I'd like to keep my job," continued Sean, groaning with effort as he extended the metal until it hit the platform.

Kyle grimaced. Everyone knew or guessed Kyle had been fired by Barrett due to Stu, and no one was safe, city employees included. Only Mark seemed immune to Stu's influence, and who knew how long that was going to last.

"Is the Ice Park going to be ready on time?" Kyle asked, changing the subject.

"At this rate, probably a week early for the pre-event climbs for the locals. At least if the weather is cooperating. And on the upside, you'll handily win your age group again."

"Unlikely," countered Kyle. "I'm going to be placed in with the adults."

Sean grunted. "Good, you need some competition. Maybe one of the foreigners I've already seen scouting the area will give you a run for your money." The manager jerked his head towards the ice park. "They were out there inspecting the runs when I came down. One mentioned taking some lessons and I offered up your name. Stu can't fire an out of towner, right?"

Kyle's stomach clenched even as expressed his thanks. Visitors the day after the accident? Too coincidental.

Kyle walked the ten minutes up to the ice park, but instead of using the main road, he took the short cut up the side of the hill. Sean and his guys did a pretty good job of keeping the steep path clear, and today it was nearly down to the stone.

As he reached the crest of the highway, he noticed a group of guys standing at the end of the ice park. Thoughts of FBI, NSA or the Patrol vanished as he approached the group. Two of the four had shoulder-length hair poking out of caps, their accent Eastern European. A third had the top of his curly, black hair in a man-bun. Definitely not a government look.

The one closet to Kyle sported razor cut sides, a matching scruff along his chin and slicked back hair. Kyle thought he looked like the cooler, European version of himself.

Kyle heard the men talking, recognizing the language but not understanding the words.

"You guys here for the ice climbing?" Kyle asked. He saw their eyes search his face and couldn't help touching his nose. The brace was still there, but maybe in another day he could finally remove it.

"Yes," answered the one with cropped, sandy blond hair and a five-o'clock shadow, his accent English. "But the city manager told us we're too early."

Kyle nodded. "Sections aren't as thick as they need to be. They'd never support a grown man."

Kyle walked a few feet, looking up and down at the face of the ice wall for his own edification. He imagined the four spending a lot of money coming from overseas only to hear the news they'd arrived half a month early.

"What else can be done in this area in the meantime?" the same man asked. "Other than avoiding whatever happened to you, that is."

Kyle turning with a smirk. "Why is it that foreign accents make insults sound like a compliment?" he asked in response. "Kyle," he said, belatedly, making up for his comment which might have come across as rude.

"Philip Rush, but my friends call me Rush." He put his hand out. Kyle shook it, glancing at the other guys who had gone quiet. "Marcus, Alexie and Raze," he said, each man nodding as Rush said their name.

"This wasn't done by a visitor by the way," Kyle explained. "Just a pissed off guy who wasn't getting what he wanted." Saying the words gave Kyle a release he didn't know he needed. The ability to speak with people completely unrelated to the town, without preconceived notions of him or his background, was liberating. The guy with the man-bun asked what there was to do around the area.

Kyle named off the local attractions like Barrett's spa, the vapor cave of the Weisbaden, and the hiking trails around the town.

"You could also rent snowmobiles," he added as an afterthought, "but really, if you're not into the outdoors you're sort of stuck. Not much nightlife outside Telluride, and Silverton is pretty sleepy. Durango's not much better."

Kyle was hoping the guy would ask about hiring him for ice climbing, but he couldn't think of a way to bring it up without coming across as needy, so he kept his mouth shut. If the time was right and the guy mentioned it, so be it.

"What about girls?" Rush asked, his expression changing.

"You'd be best served importing your own," Kyle answered with a smirk. The others grumbled in Russian.

"Guess that didn't go over well," muttered Kyle, earning a laugh from Rush.

At that moment a red Jeep drove by and slowed, the window going down along with Kyle's mood.

Speak of the devil.

"Hey Mr. Winner," Marty greeted, slurring the words. He leaned back in his seat, more than enough to reveal Ashley who raised an eyebrow, her pouting, red lips visible to all. Her focus slid from himself to Rush in the querying way a female does when she sees an attractive man. In his peripheral vision, he noticed Rush look back. The moment was over as Marty scowled and drove away. Kyle almost felt sorry for his former friend. He still didn't get that Ashley only ever wanted what she couldn't have.

The group had gone quiet, then Rush spoke. "If that's an example of the locals, I'll take two," he observed. "She available?"

"Might want to wait a few months until she graduates from high school or her dad will make sure your passport is stripped and never returned. That said, she's eighteen and legal, so go for it if you have that kind of game."

His comment set the group laughing, and Marcus, the largest of the three, looked at him.

"Since I take it you're a climber, what's your favorite climbing runs?" The guy's accent was thick, his glacier grey eyes having a unique dark rim.

"Chocolate Salty Balls and Mr. Hankey, but Not Without My Balls is a good one two," Kyle informed him. "And yes, those are the real, American names but only used by the locals. The seven others are equally hard, but neither the names nor the climbs are as good."

"They'd be hard enough for you," Rush said, slapping Marcus on the shoulder.

Alexie uttered more Russian that got the others laughing, but were quieted with a comment from Rush.

"I'll be climbing against you then," he said, looking at Kyle.

"Probably not," Kyle admitted. "I turn eighteen next week and my guess is you're classed above me."

"Nope, I'm twenty-five."

Kyle eyed him. "You're right. Same class. I'll be seeing you on the ice then." Kyle raised his chin up in an acknowledgement.

"Or before," interjected Rush, "because I was wondering if I could hire a local to show me some of the best climbs around. You interested?"

Kyle pondered the offer. It was one thing to coach a visitor, but another to show a potential competitor the best tricks and techniques for this particular area.

"Come on," chided Rush. "You have to be confident you're going to kick my ass regardless of what you show me."

The challenge was all Kyle needed.

"Sure. Seventy-five an hour," proposed Kyle without hesitation. "Travel time on top of that."

Rush snorted. "They charge $125 in Telluride. I'll give you a hundred an hour cash, so you won't have to declare it if you don't want to." Kyle nodded an agreement. "Tomorrow?" suggested Rush. Kyle looked at the ice again with a discriminating eye.

"Too early," he restated. "Not even us locals would try this ice. You're going to be stuck here for at least another week," Kyle said, his voice turning serious at the statement. Someone else's life was going to be in his hands, and he needed to exercise more caution, not less.

"No problem," said Rush. He pulled out his phone and asked for Kyle's information. "Sending you a text right now." A vibration in Kyle's pocket notified him of the receipt. "Just call or text me when you think we can get started," Rush said.

They shook hands and Kyle left, enthused about the prospect of earning some extra money. Between his new job with Linda and this one, his daylight hours would be filled, the evening or early mornings spent in the vapor room.

Good. Less time to obsess over things he couldn't change, like when Billy was going to be back. What were her last words? Use the masters as leverage? What could be more valuable that a person's own DNA?

CHAPTER 23

Rush and his men stayed silent until the kid was out of earshot.

"That was the one, correct?" Marcus asked him.

Rush nodded, turning around to look over the valley. The town was everything the brochure presented it to be: circular by design, contained and picture perfect. And Kyle Smith was all that Rush had not expected. The newspaper photos presented a self-confident jock, the prototype Rush instinctively loathed. But the kid wasn't a douche-bag like the one who drove by with the explosively-hot girlfriend.

"We can do this tonight and get out of here by daybreak," said Marcus with anticipation. Rush didn't need to look at his bodyguard to know he was hunching his shoulders against the wind, his massive fists two mounds in his down-coat pockets.

"Problem is we don't know the whole story," Rush replied. As he began walking, the others followed, closing ranks on either side of him. "According to my source, that face was caused by a beating from the NSA, one of whom is now dead, and it doesn't even prove he has what we came to get."

Marcus made a guttural sound of interest at the challenge the situation presented. "But your source said he was mentioned on line and in association with the cubes."

"Correct, but if he'd had them, he'd be in the government's custody, locked away in some cell, not here. That means he tricked the polygraph, then he proved immune to the chemicals they injected."

The bigger man scrunched his thick lips. "Then he's not our guy and we keep looking."

"My source showed me the face and it belongs to Kyle Smith. He's the one."

Even as Rush said the words, he tried to punch holes in his own thesis. Kyle had been injected and beat up. He had withstood each. The kid either had balls and brains of steel, or someone had helped him out. Or both. And even though Kyle had looked straight out of a fight movie, he walked like a lean, upright cat, smooth and with a strong body. Match that with growing up at 8,000 feet and he probably had the lungs of mountain lion. Rush guessed that his skills were unlikely to have been the result of fancy instructors or lessons, or attending weeklong basketball camps in the summer or ice training seminars in the winter. Rush intuitively knew the kid had likely worked himself from the ground up.

There was something else. Rush had noticed the kid checking out his clothing as he'd approached; the millisecond observation and resulting expression. It had been one of understanding about money; Rush had it, Kyle did not.

"Everyone has a weak spot," contended his most reliable enforcer.

Rush glanced around the street, knowing what his man was implying. "What are you going to do him that hasn't already been done?" he asked rhetorically.

"The family angle."

The hard snow crunched under their feet as they walked. "As much as I like seeing you in action, your skills aren't going to work."

"How can you be so sure?" Marcus asked.

Rush kicked a ball of ice with his foot. "Because you can't take anything from a person who has nothing to lose in the first place." Rush had once been exactly like the kid who was now in the distance. "We have to find another way."

Rush came to the corner where the edge of the ice park met the main road. He paused, taking a moment to absorb the rim of the city, the diagonal light hitting the front of the inner bowl as the sun moved higher in the sky. It might require a month, but he had that kind of time. Each day would be measured in billions of dollars to himself, his patience well rewarded.

Once they returned to the car, Rush accessed the local city directory, getting Kyle Smith's family information, address, parents' name and high school transcripts. No police arrests or violations, but lots of press mentions. He'd won the ice climbing competitions in his age group since he was twelve and was one of the top basketball players in the state for the size of school and region.

"Let's go into Telluride and load up on some ice climbing gear." Turning to Marcus, he added another stop. "On the way back, I think we should check out some stained glass windows."

Brayden lay in bed, savoring these moments with his wife. Her chest rose and fell in rhythmic patterns, the peaceful look on her face one he never saw during her waking hours.

Last night after his phone call, Laura had come to the den. Her touch had taken the place of words, his tentative response followed by a passion he'd been forced to keep dormant. Knowing that they would soon be separated magnified their intimacy. Yet somehow, they both seemed to be okay with it, as if they each recognized their tie was tenuous, the invisible spider-like thread strong in the moment.

Now she was on her back, staring at the ceiling while he was turned toward her, tentatively stroking the inside of her arm. True intimacy was much harder than the rough pleasure. Alone, they managed. Together, they had faltered.

"I can feel you looking at me," Laura said quietly, her eyes shut.

Brayden's lip curled in a smile. "Surgeons are like that. Eyes not just in the back but on the side of the head."

Her eyes fluttered open. "I could be blind and still feel your energy."

Brayden tenderly stroked her skin, the caress causing her fingers to twitch in appreciation. He didn't know where to begin, worried that a conversation would open doors neither of them could safely walk through.

"I spoke with that Deputy," Laura disclosed. "He was concerned about Saachi." Laura lifted her hand to his cheek, the touch including a love that he'd not felt since their son had died.

"But I'm more concerned about you."

Laura turned her fingers, the outside of her index finger sliding down his jaw, pausing on his chin.

"You are a very handsome man." Brayden closed his eyes, moving his face so her touch was on his lips. He kissed her fingers, brushing the skin back and forth. "Is there a message you'd like me to give Mark when he arrives this weekend?"

Brayden hummed. The Deputy had been pretty obvious about his feelings for Saachi, but they were a fraction of his own for Laura. Brayden answered her question by leaning close, causing her fingers to move through his hair. When he spoke, his voice was so low, he knew not even the best listening devices would pick it up.

"You can tell him someone is tracking all the movements around Ouray, and he must be very careful." Brayden paused, nuzzling her ear with his nose. "Kyle is the young man who found the cubes."

As he spoke, Laura's fingers dug into his scalp, the words causing a physical reaction. "Tell me about him," she asked quietly.

"A high school senior," Brayden answered. "Eighteen next week. Tall. Handsome. Clean cut."

"Brayden, it's t's already happening," she revealed. "Even as we speak. The first faces will be done this week. Do you know what that means?"

Brayden squeezed his eyes hard, fighting back the tears. "Change," he finally got out.

Then he felt the shift of her chest from easy breathing to tremors, the kind that came with sobbing. This was what he'd been expecting and remained quiet.

"All the pain can and will be put towards a better future. It will never be the one we imagined, but it can be beautiful Laura. It will be."

She sniffled, nodding her wet cheeks against his skin. When he'd first started to believe what Kyle had told him, he'd indirectly asked his wife about it and she'd acknowledged she'd played a role in their daughters' disappearance. In the last two weeks, he skipped right over anger moving to gratitude to have the strength to do what he could not have done: protect their daughter from the government. In the time since, it was clear she'd be leaving Denver not to get away from him, but to eventually reunite their family.

"I'm worried about Kyle." Her words were uneven, trembling with the emotion. Brayden knew it was as if he was her own son, not just some stranger in a mountain town who had stumbled into a crisis. "You take care of him, okay?"

Brayden promised. "Soon we'll have Sasha back with us."

"She's been raised by another woman since she was three," Laura murmured. "She won't even know us. Fourteen years is a long time to be away from your parents. She's a young woman now, with her own life and thoughts and ideas."

A visual of Billy came to mind. It was the moment he'd been waiting for.

"Another young woman has been missing her mother for that same amount of time. The woman who disappeared happens to be of Native American background. Laura, is it Billy's mother who's been raising our daughter?"

Brayden felt Laura's head nod and arms tighten around his body, an admittance of her role in Sasha's pretended death. He had no words at her response. He'd already gone through the anger and resentment he felt at the acknowledgement, her years-long deceit and the ruse of putting their daughter in the grave unforgivable.

It was through her wisdom and yes, premeditated deceit, that their daughter had been spared the DNA-changing virus affecting the rest of the country. It was because of Laura's internal strength and protective mother's drive to keep her daughter alive that they now had a future as a family.

His voice was rough with emotion when he spoke.

"I love you Laura. With every ounce of my being, and for doing what I could never have done."

Jagged sobs came again. "Can you forgive me?"

"I already have, and then some. We're going to be okay, Laura. We're going to make it."

She nodded again, holding him so tight a gasp of air escaped his lips. "I hope so, Brayden. I really do."

Brayden heard the doubt and fear in her voice, taking comfort that her emotions were now laying on the surface, when for so long they'd been deep underneath, cold and dark.

He stroked her hair, periodically kissing her forehead until he felt the muscles in her back release. Then her shoulders went, followed by the rhythmic breathing of sleep. Brayden continued his movements as he thought about Kyle. He was sure the young man was working with Billy, a plan likely already in place to leave town or spirit away the cubes to a safe zone.

It's me who should be worried. He knew the perpetrator, the goal, and was now complicit with his wife in defying the very thing his government had mandated. They could both be arrested under the terrorist act, jailed indefinitely.

The best terrorist is the one least suspected. For who in their right mind would believe that he, Brayden Cox, lead agent for retrieving the stolen cubes, would be the very one helping hide them? And who would possibly think that his wife, one of the most respected research scientists in the country, would have included her own daughter in avoiding the system she herself had participated in?

Brayden closed his eyes, the image of holding both his girls in his arms. He'd do anything to make that image a reality.

Anything.

CHAPTER 24

Friday morning, Linda met Kyle at the back gate, handing him a key.

"You'll need this for when I leave town," she said, adding that she'd told the manager Kyle was on staff for the spa, pool and cave area. "Fortunately for you, Tyler dislikes Stu's wife on account of her being uppity at the grocery store one day. No need to worry about you getting fired here." Kyle wasn't worried about losing his job, but Linda losing her business, and said so. "It's fortunate for me then that most of my patrons are out of towners, people who would look down their own noses at a person who was once a mere vice president of a mining firm."

Kyle caught her wink.

"There's a wide world out there that's a whole lot bigger than this itty bitty town and the few people here who have outsized importance."

It was something he tried to remember as he finished his morning tasks. On the way back home, he stopped at the grocery store and was in the candy aisle when he heard her voice.

"Mom, just get it and let's go." The statement was followed by Ashley's familiar huff of impatience.

"Excuse me, could you recommend what you think is the best hot springs experience around here?"

Kyle didn't need to look around the corner to recognize Rush's voice. It was smooth and elegant, exotic and unique, all that Ashley pined for.

"Yes, of course," Ashley answered immediately. Had Kyle not known her, he would have sworn it was a different person; the alter ego of an individual who could be both petulant and sulky or sensual and inviting. Kyle paused in the aisle. There was only one door in and out of the store, and the two check-out lanes had people waiting. He returned his cherry pie to the shelf and went around the meat section to the dairy aisle. With any luck, they'd keep talking and he'd avoid a scene.

Ashley was in the midst of giving Rush a dissertation on her favorite spas when Kyle walked by the furthest lane.

"What about the Weisbaden?" Rush asked, cutting off Ashley's answer. "Hey, Kyle."

Kyle lifted his chin in acknowledgement, the look of shock on Ashley's face rewarding. Yeah, Kyle had friends from cool places.

"How do you know Kyle?" Ashley asked, her innocent question indicating what Kyle knew was complete annoyance.

"He's my ice climbing guide," Rush replied.

"Oh, you could have someone better," Ashley told him.

Rush cocked an eyebrow. "Who's better than the number one competitor in the area, according to the papers?" Rush asked, waiting for her answer.

"Well, the papers don't always tell the full story," she replied with a coy lilt in her voice.

Ashley turned the conversation to Rush's jacket, a conversation Kyle was happy to avoid as he scooted out of the store.

At home, he found his father. "Want to take that walk now?"

Outside the front of the house, they paused momentarily, each of them looking across the road.

"Looks the same as it did last night," his dad said dryly.

"And it's not gonna change," Kyle answered, thinking of Ashley's interaction with Rush. "Left to Cascade path or do you think it has too much snow?"

"We'll see when we get there."

Together they kept right on their property line until the sidewalk ended.. In silence they continued until the path connected with Oak Street.

"Left," suggested his father. They'd end up at Box Canyon, hang another left to the top of town and then wind their way back down Main to home. It would be long enough to tell his father the entire truth, not just a part of it. Heck, if his father had been able to live within the government system for his entire life while not being a part of it, he might actually have insight.

At least that was Kyle's hope.

"Dad, I don't know where to begin, so I'm going to start with the fact I haven't been entirely honest, which you probably guessed—"

"I did," his father interrupted. Kyle swallowed and kept walking. Despite having shorter legs than himself, his dad kept up a brisk brace.

Kyle elongated his stride and began with old D's confession. He told of the trip to the mine, made possible by Joe who drove him, his theft of the cubes, then his slide down the mountain. His father remained silent as Kyle related the ensuing cover up, first with Brayden, who'd found him out, and then with Mark's help, having escaped the Naturalist who turned out to be Billy's Uncle Roy. When Kyle revealed Roy was actually one of the good guys, his father started humming.

"I know what that means, but I'm almost at the end," said Kyle. "Hang with me just a little longer."

"Good, because my legs are fine but my brain is about to explode with commentary."

Kyle told him what he could remember of the government shake down, and finally, the second theft at the mine. When he finished, Kyle didn't have to wait long before this father started speaking.

"But that's not the entire truth is it?" his father asked rhetorically. "You left out your new job up at the Weisbaden and there must be a reason for that. You storing the cubes up there?" Kyle hmm-mmm'd his answer. "When are you planning on leaving us?"

"What?" he exclaimed. "I'm not planning on leaving at all."

"Well you should. If you watched Forensic Files, you'd know in a heartbeat the minute they find that ATV, they'll be able to match the tracks on it with those that ran over the snowmobile. You're toast." That was not the upper Kyle wanted to hear. "Tell me this son. Did you intentionally kill that rider?"

"No, absolutely not, but... he was shooting at me, Dad. I had to get him off my back and there was no other way given the direction from which he was coming."

Kyle explained how he'd hit the rails himself and knew the guy wouldn't be familiar with the canyon or the platform. "I did it precisely in front of the platform so he'd fall over it and land on the metal grate."

"But he overshot it and fell to his death."

Kyle wished there had been another way, but there wasn't. "I was either going to end up dead or caught, which would have ended up with me being dead anyway. What would you have done?"

They had walked a distance and were turning back into town. The sky was cloudy and the overcast shadows were turning the town from a full-color picture to a black and white frame. Winter was usually Kyle's favorite time of year.

Not this time around.

"You want to know what I would have done?" his father said, jerking his head to follow him across the street. "I'd have left school and gone straight to those Naturalists, handing them everything you had on a silver platter, me and your mother be damned." Kyle felt a sliver of cold air shoot down his windpipe, searing his lungs. "And then I would have come back home, gone over to Stu, told him to screw himself and his daughter, and waited out the rest of the year. Yes, I said that."

It took a few moments for Kyle to process his father's comments, but then relieved laughter traveled up his chest and erupted into the air.

"Just why in the world you didn't actually tell me all of this before you made such a bloody mess of things is—well, totally typical I guess," his father muttered.

"Now that's not fair," Kyle started to say.

"Of course it's fair," his father argued. "You wanted to remain the kid we raised you to be, not the ones *we* were when your age. Heck, Kyle. Your mother got pregnant at sixteen, I came into her life when you were four and together we tried to figure out how to raise a child while we were still doing drugs that were illegal."

"I've never heard you describe my youth in quite that way."

His father grunted. "Because in between working I was drinking and doing other things which shall not be mentioned, but I can say I'm pretty sure they all went against the government. We moved out here to escape all that, the confines, regulations and monitoring. Of all the people in this town, Kyle, you live with the two adults who would have supported you most of all."

"Yeah, but you know Mom would have gone ballistic and rampaged against the machine because it validates everything she's ever argued."

"She might have killed you herself," said his father, keeping Kyle's laughter going.

"But Dad, you can't lie to save your soul. I'm not even sure it's a great thing to have told you, because you can't pretend to be the ignorant, former hippy everyone thinks you are."

His father gave him a sly, sideways glance. "I play a great ignorant hippy because you think I can't lie. Shows how much you know." Kyle's reality as he knew it was going through a catastrophic upheaval which kept him silent. "And post script: I'm not going to change now."

They continued down the street, Kyle still chuckling to himself. Once they reached the Stagecoach Hotel, Kyle thought of Brayden and his family situation. He'd not told his father about that part and did so now.

"You think they linked the two of you and that's why he was arrested?"

Kyle shrugged. "Maybe they learned he was protecting me, but if they knew that, they would have turned right around and picked me up."

"Yep, and that's another reason you get your ass out of this town and deliver those cubes where they belong."

"But that's the problem," Kyle hissed, exasperated. "Billy won't tell me where she is. I'm only guessing Laura knows something, but I can't show up at her hospital and ask. So what should I do?"

"Spare me."

"What?" Kyle exclaimed.

"I said: Spare. Me. Grow up and do it fast, Son. This government has been lying for decades and using innocent young men and women to cover things up. That guy who flipped over the metal railing and floated down the river was just one of thousands to die serving the government this year. You think he cared about you? Not for one second would he think about your death, so don't you think one more about his." His father grew quiet again as they came upon pedestrians slowly strolling in front the shops.

"Furthermore, how many people are going to die as they endure experiments for new faces?" he asked. "Dozens? I bet hundreds. On top of that, you're going to have a bloodbath for those who won't accept the facial transformation. I'm talking real-life, normal people who don't want the world to be natural and normal. They want fake and artifice. Any names come to mind?"

"Yep," Kyle said, thinking they all had one thing in common: affluence and position.

His father nodded. "I have always thought you have it worse. Me and your mother are both wrinkly and unattractive, but you're a handsome Roman statue, stuck here in this one-light town."

Kyle wedged his fingers in his coat pocket; they felt cold when they should have been warm. His father had never revealed so much in their twelve years together.

"I thought..." Kyle trailed off, unsure of his emotions. His father was encouraging him to do exactly as Billy had suggested. It almost struck Kyle as if he were now engaged in an act of resistance his own father would have wanted, even looked for when he was a kid.

"You really want me to do this, don't you?" he asked.

His dad didn't answer until they reached the bridge, and paused to look over at the rushing water below.

"It's not me wanting you to do it. It's you getting the chutzpah to see through what you started."

Kyle gripped the ice covered railing, watching the river. His father was challenging him to go the distance, no differently than Billy or Mark had done. If Brayden were here, Kyle knew he'd say the same thing.

"I realized when I went up the second time, that was it," Kyle admitted.

"So now what?" his father pressed.

Kyle already knew the steps he had to take, and he didn't like a single one of them. "You want to know or should I keep it to myself just in case you get arrested?"

His father looked down the road to their home. Mark had just pulled up in his patrol car and was getting out, his hand on his holster as he approached a group of men in front of their house.

"Why don't you just keep that under your hat for the time being," suggested his father. "And if one day you disappear, I'll know you're doing what's necessary, you got that?"

"I wouldn't do that," Kyle contested.

"Son, you do whatever you have to do, and don't think twice about your mother and me. We've had our life. It's time for you to live yours."

CHAPTER 25

Mark saw the group of men standing outside the Smith home. He was ready to go, his toiletries for the weekend in the back of his personal vehicle, just waiting to drive to Denver, the agenda including two women with very different situations, yet somehow tied together. His departure meant he was leaving Kyle here alone, but what more could he do?

Mark slowed in front of Stu's home and did a U-turn, parking feet from where the men stood. As he stopped, the four glanced his way, taking long drags on their cigarettes and holding them between their forefinger and thumb. Along with that mannerism, uncommon for Americans, was the unrecognizable clothing brands they wore. Too trendy. Too loud to be from the States.

Foreigners.

International visitors were certainly common enough during the ice cleaning season, but their presence now was a bit too unsettling for Mark.

He had one gloved hand relaxed by this side, the other resting on his holster. Never hurt to install a sense of authority, Mark thought, especially when two of the four looked as though carrying weapons were second nature. The tallest one of the bunch with the man-bun met his eyes, his sharp chin and narrow gaze matching his broad shoulders. Mark approached, listening to their conversation. He thought about the possibility of his own government recruiting Russian nationals for internal situations. Perhaps in the big cities where the Russian cartels ran the fencing trade, but here?

"Gentleman," Mark greeted them. "My name is Officer Hancock of the Ouray police force. You all visiting? Need directions to somewhere in particular?"

"Hello Officer," greeted the blond. He stood eye height with Mark, his grey eyes clear and bright. "Yes, we are visiting. Here for the ice climbing but we arrived too early, unfortunately," he continued, motioning up to the canyon. "We just learned of that."

Mark nodded. "What inspired you to visit the Windows to the World?"

The man shrugged. "Nothing actually. We have made one half the loop of this town and think this is the end. Now we are going to turn back up."

"Do you have some identification I can take a look at?" Mark asked.

"Sure Officer." As he reached behind his belt, Mark's grip became firmer on his holster and the largest man watched him, muttering quietly in Russian.

"Here you go." The others followed suit. Just then Mark saw two figures he recognized walking towards him, one of whom being Kyle, the very person who should be the furthest away from unknown individuals.

"Where are you staying?" Mark asked the men, his voice stiff. The tallest of the four took notice of the change in his tone, immediately nodding to the other two who formed a semi-circle around the spokesperson.

"Hey Rush," called Kyle. "You guys having a social outside my house or what?"

Mark glanced down at the IDs. Philip Rush. When he looked back up, he took in the three who were standing guard around him. "Kyle—hold up," said Mark. "You know one another?"

"Yeah, they're ice climbers and now clients," Kyle answered congenially. "They causing problems already?"

Mark wavered in his response.

"Oh, hey," Kyle said, finally catching on. "You think...Mark, these guys are cool. Ice climbers from Denver most recently, but London and Russia before that. Hey Marcus," added Kyle, nodding to the largest.

Kyle had come around to the other side, shaking Rush's hand.

"I didn't know this was your home," Rush told him casually.

That told Mark something else. The guy was either really rich who needed bodyguards or was a member of the Russian mafia. And yet he and Kyle were talking like old friends.

"Kyle, can I speak to you for a moment?" He'd directed the question to Kyle although his eyes never left Marcus, whose silver orbs were steady. Mark hadn't been around a lot of killers, but he sensed this man had hurt others before and wouldn't hesitate doing it again.

Ed, who had been standing silent, muttered, "See ya kid," and with a nod to Mark, he went around the back, through the carport.

"Don't go anywhere," Mark told the four. He touched Kyle's arm, leading him several yards away from the men.

"Hey, Mark, ease up," Kyle told him when they were out of earshot.

"Are you freaking kidding me?" Mark hissed. "You think it's some coincidence that after what went on yesterday we have strangers in town under the guise of ice climbing?"

"Mark, I guess they could be FBI agents with faux English and Russian accents, but why?" Kyle contended. "I mean, if they were after me, why wouldn't they just take me? Why bother renting a place in Telluride and sticking around for weeks?"

Kyle had a point, and it made Mark ponder the scenario for an elongated second.

"It just doesn't sit easy," grumbled Mark. He gave Kyle a once over, then did the same to Rush. The four were speaking Russian, standing casually and relaxed.

"Tell me how you met." Mark listened to Kyle's story. "Well, this is crappy timing. I'm leaving for Denver tonight. I'll tell you about it later."

Mark turned back to the men, unhappy about going away for the weekend, but he couldn't babysit Kyle every hour of the day.

"Here you go gentlemen," he said, returning their identification. "Enjoy your stay and if you're going to ice climb, let one of the local boys scurry up the wall first, like this kid."

As Mark drove up the hill into town, he watched Kyle point to the hot springs across the street, then he went into his house while the group crossed the road.

False alarm. Perhaps his instinct was wrong on this one, he thought, looking at the clock. He hoped so, because if he wasn't, Kyle was on his own.

CHAPTER 26

"Those the men your mother mentioned?"

"Yesss," drawled his younger daughter. Stu watched the men head towards the hot springs. Older, much older than he'd ever want his daughter to date, but not just in age. They might only be a few years older than Kyle and Marty, but in terms of experience...

"Stay away from them," Stu warned Ashley.

"Oh dad," she retorted, pouting in her flirtatious I-wouldn't-do-such-a-thing way, which meant exactly the opposite. She'd already crushed Marty's self-esteem and it had only taken five days.

It made Stu despise Kyle Smith more than he already did. Had that kid stayed on the path laid out for him, his daughter wouldn't have the predatory wandering eye she did now. It was Kyle's perennial aloofness that had kept Ashley chasing him.

Or chased him off.

Stu roughly pushed the thought away. Kyle could have acted with class, but he hadn't. Now the out of towners were arriving for the ice climbing and they had given Ashley attention she craved.

Not that she needed any.

"How are those college applications coming along?"

His daughter laughed. "They aren't. I stopped at UC Boulder, where we thought idiot was going."

"Kyle may have acted foolish, but we both know he's anything but an idiot." Stu hated saying the words, but the young man had been a good influence on his daughter, especially as it related to college. "That said, if you're not inclined for Boulder, perhaps CSU in Montrose is an option."

"Oh, now that's funny," his daughter retorted. "What? A crappy little college like that?"

"Yes," he said with prescriptive cadence. "One that has a global reputation for graduates going on to top schools. One that perhaps you should consider with your grades and...acumen."

His daughter's bottom lip dropped, the perfectly red, heart shaped mouth half open at the implied insult.

"Are you telling me I got into those colleges because you helped out?"

"I'm telling you," he said with forced patience, "that without a study partner, or the motivation to stay on the right path, you might be best served to stay close to home, where weekends can be spent here, with us."

His daughter's mouth remained ajar but she added a rolling of her eyes. She was beautiful no matter how sullen she behaved, but it wasn't going to get her far in the real world.

"In four months' time, you are going to be out on your own—"

"Finally!" she interjected, crossing her arms.

"And you will need to take on the responsibilities of a young adult. At present, none of your friends are going to college, and you will be without—"

"Someone to watch over me? I get it dad. Geez. Why are you acting like this? All I do is talk to visitors who are way more handsome and far more elegant and sophisticated than Kyle ever thought about being, and now you're suggesting I stay here?"

Stu didn't have to pretend surprise. "You always maintained to Kyle that you wanted to be close to home the entire time you were dating. It was one of the things that drove him away."

"Wait a minute," she argued, jutting out her chin. "I never *drove* him away. He left with that crazy, computer weirdo, and I said I wanted to come back *after* college, not before."

In other words, his daughter wanted to exercise her freedom to do what she pleased for a few years, have it all paid for, then when she'd finished getting the wild years out of her system, settle down with a house and have kids, just like her mother.

In that moment, Stu thought of Ruth, his older, less attractive but far more responsible daughter. Stu hadn't endorsed her choice of nursing, so she'd gotten a job and a loan to pay for it. He'd resented her for the duration of her college years, the feeling eventually evolving into respect. Something he wondered if he'd ever have for the daughter standing in front of him.

"I said it before and I'm saying it again. Stay clear of the visitors coming to town over the next months. Stick to school and your grades." His daughter met his eyes, her chin raising up slightly in defiance. "I mean it, Ashley."

"Or what?"

Stu slowly inhaled, realizing that this was the moment he'd been dreading since Kyle told him he no longer wanted to date Ashley, the real reason why he'd been so pissed at the boy. "Don't talk to me that way young lady."

"Like I said, or what?"

The slap cracked across Ashley's face, the force of his backhand pushing her off balance. He flipped his right wrist, feeling his college ring on his knuckle. The B on the ring had blood, as did the small diamonds around it.

His daughter turned, holding her face. Where he expected tears and an apology, he saw cold rage.

"I'll do what I want dad, just like Ruth."

Stu watched her go. Ruth appeared from the kitchen, looking at his hand and face.

"Better get some ice for Ashley or her cheek will be black and blue like Kyle's," he said.

Ruth nodded. "Sure."

Stu knew his reaction hadn't made things any better for his daughter. He'd likely made it worse.

Wednesday night, Kyle helped his father inlay the glass into seven different projects, his mother returning from Montrose in time to solder the final lines in place. They were an efficient line of productivity, the hours passing until the sun set, the steady stream of lights into town invariably turning at the hot springs.

At a quarter til ten, Kyle headed to the Weisbaden, saying hello to the manager on duty who happened to be in the back room where the testing supplies were located. He completed the water sampling from the outdoor pools as the last of the bathers were exiting, changing into his own swim trunks before going into the caves. Since Monday, he'd been churning over his conversations with both Mark and Billy. First, he had to identify what states were on the cubes he had and which, if any, were still missing. Then he had to get those cubes to Billy.

Kyle felt in his swim trunks for the permanent marker and did a final pass through of all the caves before telling the manager on duty he was going to soak for a while in the vapor cave before shutting it down.

Once inside, he did just that, for exactly fifteen minutes. Then he retrieved a single master cube and the original three he'd taken, double checking each state. Colorado, California and New York. Then he began the arduous process of taking one cube and matching it with a master, refamiliarizing himself with the magnetic pull which occurred when connecting the state and master cubes. It had to be the correct side of one aligned with the right side of a master. As he slowly rotated the state cube forward, the flat digital image of data appeared in front of him, hovering in the vaporous air.

One by one, he identified the states, writing the abbreviation on the side. At first, he didn't concern himself with placing other sides of the masters against the state, but twice he slipped, connecting two flat surfaces.

The first time, bank accounts, IRA and 401K records showed totals, transfers and account holders. The second time, divorce filings, settlements, liens and warrants appeared. He was sidetracked by the information, seeing DUI's, the outstanding arrest documents and then payments made in a civil case.

He immediately disconnected the cubes, pulling at the magnetic force.

Stay away from the details. Millions of records existed, not one of which he cared about right now. He just had to finish the task, and that meant telling Billy exactly what he had. Then figuring out how to get the cubes to her.

"You in here?"

It was Linda. Kyle glanced at his watch. It had been nearly an hour. Far too long to be in the vapor cave.

"Just relaxing," he called back. "Be out in a minute."

"No rush," she called back. "Just checked on Susan and she's left for the evening. Lock up the back when you go."

Kyle promised, waiting a few minutes before he resumed analyzing the cubes.

Just stay focused on the DNA. The other stuff is noise, and unnecessary.

Working quickly, Kyle matched the remaining states. He grouped the cubes logically and replaced them in the crevices, then changed and locked up. As he walked home, the biting wind felt like a thousand pin pricks on his face. It hurt like hell.

But the face is mine, and no one can take that away from me. Ever.

CHAPTER 27

"How's the development coming along?" asked the President, the lines crackling. He was calling from Air Force One, the others dialing in on the secure line.

Gary's colleague running the CIA had nothing to report.

"The lines have been quiet," Pete informed the group which included he and Janet. "Nothing internal or external, anywhere from our sources, but as you can imagine, we aren't raising the topic ourselves, just keeping our thousands of units."

"Janet?"

"No news." The cubes were still missing in action, the drones, roadblocks and satellites yielding nothing.

"Gary?"

He cleared his throat. "The first mention of the cubes has appeared on the dark web." He explained that his team technologists were working around the clock, devising and implementing the back-up systems.

"Five banks control fifty-six percent of all money in America. JP Morgan Chase, Bank of America, Citibank, Wells Fargo and Goldman Sachs. The task force lead personally contacted the chief executives, financial officers and technical director. Everyone else was excluded, including the regulatory personnel, who would have alerted entire departments within the government. What we are doing never to be exposed to the general public, the coding completed by engineers who work independently so no one person knows all the parts."

"Can they be trusted?" questioned Janet.

The gall of the question was laughable. "My team hasn't had any breaks Janet," he replied evenly. "Clean slate," he said. "To continue...."

He explained that while the majority of the country's financial accounts would be covered, the remainder of the country was at risk and vulnerable to financial espionage.

"Not enough to decimate the economy, but the executives agreed the criminals will go for the biggest accounts first, not the smallest, which were sure to be held at the credit unions and smaller, local banks. Those 6,799 financial institutions are just going to hope for the best," Gary finished.

"The chief executives of these five had to be thrilled," said Pete in a dry tone.

"Of course," Gary confirmed. "The government is protecting them and their assets."

"Bring me in at any time as required," volunteered the President, ending the call.

Gary was in the top twenty percent of the country's bank accounts but in the bottom seven thousand. If Brayden's team didn't do their job, he'd lose everything he had along with the rest of the country.

Brayden's concentration was complete as he scanned the latest email thread with Danny Amato. It included the details he'd withheld from Gary, justifying it as an act of national safety. The fewer who knew the particulars of what was being conducted, the better. If questioned, Brayden would say that even he wasn't exempt from special precautions. Danny and his group of consultants had done the work for the FBI when their own groups were compromise; an external agency with a fat government contract were motivated by greed and a long-term payout schedule.

In its favor, Danny's firm had been on the government payroll for fifteen years, enough time to establish the credibility to ensure a job like this would get done on time, the budget irrelevant.

As Brayden watched the screen, instant messenger popped up

Framework for changing configuration scheduled for next Friday

In a world where every day counted, each day was one away from the cubes being taken from Kyle and havoc wreaked on the country.

Any way to move it up? Typed Brayden.

Not without risk of mistakes, Danny replied. *After the configuration, testing required. Five banks, millions of accounts. We need to test at least five percent.*

Brayden's fingers tapped the keyboard impatiently. That sounded like another week, which is what he guessed.

Yes, seven to ten days, responded Danny.

Approximately the middle of January. Could Kyle make it two weeks, or would Janet's team send someone in to finish the job they'd failed at twice before?

Brayden used his internet connection to route and reroute his next phone call.

"Ty, Brayden," he began. "I need you to get word to Kyle…"

Ty promised, asking once again about his daughter.

"I'll tell you the minute I do, I promise."

"I'm trusting you," Ty told him.

So were a lot of others, Brayden knew. And a few were going to be let down, no matter what he did.

Kyle lay in bed, exhausted, eyes staring at the ceiling. His mother had called Ruth asking if his nose brace could be removed. She laughed as she relayed Ruth's words.

"If Kyle can keep from hitting other people or hitting himself in the face, then yes, it's fine."

The words brought a slight smile to Kyle's lips. He wasn't a light sleeper, and he could just see himself turning over and pushing his nose sideways. That he didn't need, so the nose brace was still on.

He adjusted his legs and body, doing his best to lay on his side while keeping his head up, dialing the burner Billy had given him.

Easier to talk at this angle anyway.

"Hey cube master," Billy greeted, her voice low and husky. He closed his eyes at her tone, then popped them open. This wasn't a call to put him to sleep.

"I have news for you, good and bad," he began.

She chuckled. "More of the same. Let's hear it." He told her of his progress on determining what information he had on the cubes, then she related her experience of having new skin placed on her face the day prior. The description was as revolting to Kyle as the experience apparently had been to Billy.

"But they wouldn't let you see how it looked on you?"

"No, because it wasn't fully finished and I might have freaked out."

Kyle snorted. "You think? And they need you and Roy to see if this is going to work."

"I'm not worried about me handling it. It's the others."

Kyle guessed the comment was directed at him and chose his next words carefully. "You are going to be perfect Billy. An exact replica of what you are now."

"In theory, yes."

He understood what she was saying and his voice instinctively lowered. "I didn't think I needed to tell you the feelings I have aren't going to leave if your looks change."

"Not even a little?" For a girl so perennially in control of her emotions, it was comforting to know he wasn't the only person periodically afflicted with doubt.

"Don't go getting insecure on me," he said.

She laughed, breaking the moment.

"How am I supposed to get you these cubes you wanted to badly? Where are you Billy? Tell me now so I can come to you and see you one last time before---"

"Sorry, doll. I can't. I'm going to come to you when this is over."

Kyle paused in surprise.

"You just called me doll?" he laughed. "That's a bit emasculating isn't it?"

"I don't conform to such archaic thoughts. You are a gorgeous doll to me, even if you are all knocked up."

"Billy, you can't come back here only to leave again. That will rip Ty apart."

"I disagree. It might actually be better, but I'm not going to debate it with you. Go back in to the caves and see what else you can find on the masters."

For Kyle, that triggered a reminder of an earlier conversation. "You said the satellite was hacked and someone might be infiltrating your organization. Did you ever find out what had happened ?"

"Yeah, nothing," she told him. "It looks like it was someone inside the NSA who accidentally overwrote the code, because we found it in one of the deleted folders. No biggy."

Kyle didn't know much about computer engineering, and Billy sounded confident it was an aberration. He let that particular worry go.

"So nothing else up at the mine is what you're saying? No activity."

"It's dead up there. In fact, Roy showed me how to track the NSA using their own intra-net. Most of their effort has gone back to Durango and into Denver. They believe the cubes are on their way into town, or already there."

Kyle thought about that. "What's in Denver?" he wondered aloud.

"Apparently, the engineer who created the cubes lived in Denver before he went underground, and rumor has it his son is still there."

Kyle thought that through. "So the feds are running around in Denver, leaving us alone for the time being,"

"Affirmative. Now I must get back to work and you get to sleep. Be safe."

Had Billy stayed on the line for another thirty seconds, he might have become sentimental, but her abrupt hang up prevented it.

Perhaps that was her intention. Keep him focused on the task in front of him and making it through the weekend.

On Thursday, Kyle began the day by testing the water a full hour before the caves opened, giving him plenty of time to fiddle around with the cubes. He lined up the masters, wondering if they had a physical difference in coloring or anything else. He pulled out Colorado again and placed it against a random master, using his fingers on the digital screen in the air to select names, scanning the data.

Criminal records? He'd missed that before. Juvenile crimes were included: assaults, robberies, it was all there.

"No such thing as a truly exonerated person in this country," he muttered to himself.

The thrill of the discovery was as exciting as it was scary. Billy had said leverage, but she should have said profit. If Kyle had half a criminal bone in his body, he'd already be selling the cubes piecemeal to the highest bidder.

He was on his way home when his phone buzzed. It was Rush, wanting Kyle to look over his gear.

Pick you up in thirty? Rush texted.

With nothing to do and nowhere else to go, Kyle texted back an affirmative. It would give him time to get home and change. His short-term side job was going to start benefiting him now.

CHAPTER 28

"Billy, you ready to send the data?"

"On your command," she replied eagerly. When she affirmed her uncle sent it, she peered closer, exclaiming.

"Is that right?" she whispered. "109 total?"

"That's the number of reservations with hospitals," he said. "Eighty-seven of those have surgical capabilities," he added. "More than enough to accomplish what we need. Get ready to send…and, now."

She pressed the key then waited, knowing he'd tell her when he received the confirmation receipt.

They came in seconds, each physician on the other end identifying they'd received the DNA profiles of individuals in their region.

When the last screen closed, Billy turned to him.

"Can we do New York now?" she asked, feeling the delight that came with activity. She and Kyle were doing their respective tasks equally; he on his end, she on hers. They were partners separated by states and hundreds of miles, but working for the same goal.

"Only fifteen reservations there," Roy said, "but the population they will have to cover is enormous. California was spread much more evenly."

Billy wondered aloud if it would be enough.

"Enough to do what we require," he answered, opening a new window. "Ready Billy, and...send." As with the previous set of reservation-based surgeons, those in New York confirmed the receipt of the data.

"But after they go through all the records," she started, "how are they going to approach the outside world, anyone not on the reservation? 'Hey, we're growing your face in a lab. If you want to change, we'll show you a before and after, then strip your old one and pop in a new?'"

He chuckled. "Well, it's going to be a gradual approach. We expect that since we are starting with those on the reservation, then those natives not living on the res, then graduating to anyone with an iota of Indian—the numbers are significant. Since your dad is white, you probably didn't know that in 2008, the country had just over one percent of the population with some amount of Native blood, or three million people. Today, that number is double."

"Six million?" she asked, skeptical.

"And using simple math, we think maybe one percent, or six hundred thousand in the country might say yes, hand me my original face. Who else would have the most pride in their history other than us?"

"How many surgeries do you think can be conducted?" Billy asked.

Roy snorted. "A few thousand tops before government officials find out what's going on. Word will get around."

"Then what?"

"The government will have to step in, and they could do several things. Try and stamp out those who have proved the mutation was a lie, but if that doesn't work, they could make changing faces illegal."

"Which means arresting all of us, which is impossible, or arresting those with new faces."

"That's right. And what are they going to do? Arrest tens of thousands of people who are doing the morally right thing?"

Billy was quiet for a moment. "So you think they will eventually roll with it, and accept the surgeries are here to stay?"

"Yep. You might as well try and strip out the right for all citizens to vote."

He noticed when she went quiet, asking her what was on her mind. Billy didn't immediately respond. "I'm not sure what the new me is going to look like," she admitted. Part of her was extremely excited, the other afraid her body would reject the new skin and she'd be left with scars and a lifetime of taking anti-rejection drugs.

"You have a lot of your mother in you; an unbelievable strength."

It was not what she expected. "Right. Leaving me high and dry as a three-year-old was not strength. It was weakness and running away from a situation she didn't want."

His darks eyes bored into her. "There's more to the story than that, Billy."

She felt a tightening around her lungs.

"Are you going to tell me then, or just press the hammer to my chest, expecting me to believe what you're saying? I mean, not a word in fourteen years. And what about you?" she continued. "Where have you been my entire life? It wasn't like she was the only one to leave me. The entire family was gone overnight." She felt a crack in the thick dam holding back her emotions, and it hurt.

"It had to be that way," her uncle finally said. "And the answers to your questions aren't mine to provide. They are your mother's."

"Well, assuming she's still alive, I guess that's a reunion that will have to wait."

The grey, Land Rover Defender 110 screamed understated cool and Kyle wanted to spend more time checking it out, but he noticed two figures in the house across the street. The one in the living room was Stu, the other on the second floor was Ashley. He held in a pleased smirk; neither Ashley nor her father had better things to do with their lives.

A strip of white caught his eye, and he couldn't help but look up at the second floor window. Ashley had a patch of gauze on her cheek and her left eye looked bruised. As much as the girl annoyed him and had poured salt in the wound with Marty and Rush at the store…

"Hey guys," Kyle greeted, closing the door behind him as he sat down in the back seat. Rush sat in front with Marcus executing a U-turn in the center of the road, heading out of town. "The other guys skiing?"

"Can't come to Telluride and not ski," answered Rush. "The place where we are staying has ski-in ski-out so they started early."

"You evidently rented near Oprah and Tom Cruise then," Kyle guessed, though he didn't really care. It was only a diversion tactic, his mind elsewhere.

On Ashley specifically. Despite everything that had happened, he couldn't help himself. He typed out a quick text and waited for a response.

"Kyle, did you hear me?"

"I'm sorry, no," he apologized.

"I was asking if the local girls in Telluride were different than in Ouray."

Kyle laughed. "Different yes, and more of them. They are older and have been around the block a few times, usually with people like yourself."

Rush half-turned and looked at him closely. "And by that you mean?"

"Us locals hold no appeal against the hot, wealthy out-of-towners." He'd purposefully half-grumbled, causing the two in front to laugh good-naturedly. "I don't mind tho..." his comment trailed off when he read Ashley's text.

I'm so sorry, he texted back. *Honestly.*

I don't need your sympathy

So Ashley.

"Everything okay?" Marcus asked him. When Kyle looked up, he saw Marcus' eye had seen him in the rear view mirror, probably catching the sour expression Kyle felt on his face.

"Yeah." Kyle watched the snow covered fields go by, the three-foot high fencing mostly covered by the hip-height drifts.

He found it hard to believe what Ashley had written. Her father hitting her because she wanted to go out? Stu worshiped the ground she walked on. And go out with whom? Kyle wondered. Marty wasn't a problem, and no one else in the town had the guts to ask that girl on a date.

Kyle's gut gave him the answer. "Rush, you see Ashley again?"

"Trying to," he answered his response causing Marcus to laugh. "I got a yes then a no for tonight, so suggested meeting at the hot springs but the jury's out on that. Put in a good word for me, will you?"

"Mmmn," hedged Kyle, the non-answer causing Marcus to give him a look in the rear-view mirror, one that conveyed Kyle should be more open to his boss's suggestions.

"I'm thinking you're not on anyone's good list right now, except mine." Marcus' brows furrowed, and Rush turned further in his seat. "Evidently, Ashley asked to go out with you, or at least be in your presence. The result of that was getting her face slapped by her dad."

Rush's grey eyes went black at his words. "She told you this?"

Kyle lifted his phone, turning the text screen so Rush caught a glimpse of their exchange. "When I walked to the car I saw her in the upstairs window, a patch on her face and a bruised eye. Regardless of how it ended between us, she's a decent girl. Not right for me, but—anyway, I sent her a text when I got in the car and she let me know what happened. As

I said, she wanted to go out with you and her father said no. When she argued—"

"He hit her because of me?" Rush asked, incredulous.

"Looks that way. Ashley's biggest problem is Ashley— she's beautiful and gets what she wants—"

"What beautiful woman doesn't?" Marcus interjected, a knowing smirk on his lip.

"Is this behavior normal?" asked Rush.

Kyle looked at Rush. "No. Not even a raised voice, and I've known them practically my whole life," he emphasized. "She's not perfect, but she didn't deserve to get smacked." Kyle broke away from Rush's gaze, looking out the window. "But it's a small town," he added, watching the desolate landscape turn mountainous as the car climbed. "Just one more reason I want to get out of here."

Rush's elbow was now up on the window sill. "It's beautiful to be sure."

"Yeah, from a distance."

"College for you, then?" asked Marcus.

"Supposed to be until a week ago. I had a few scholarships and a job for that matter, then I broke up with Ashley," he continued, bitterness creeping in his statement. "Stu, Ashley's dad, ruined both of those for me."

"Her father has that kind of pull?" Marcus asked.

"And then some. All it took was a few calls and my three scholarship offers and job were gone. It's one of the reasons I directed you to Barrett's place. Stu tried to ruin his business by bussing all the clients to another town."

"No kidding," Marcus said, glancing over his shoulder.

That kind of action was probably mice nuts from where these guys came from, and Kyle hoped he wasn't coming across as a whiner.

"Doesn't matter," Kyle replied evenly. "If I can't get into college on my academic record, screw them. But the whole point of this is to let you know we aren't all jerk-off Americans, that some of us are decent."

Rush put up his middle finger. "This is what I give the parents of girls I want to date."

That set Kyle laughing. He was glad Rush had a sense of humor.

Entering Telluride, Marcus turned right, heading up the hill to a gated community. Soon they were in front of a modern-styled mountain retreat. Rush said he had to take care of some business, and Marcus showed Kyle the gym where the climbing gear was laid out and ready. It took Kyle slightly less than an hour to go through each item. It was all overpriced of course, noting the tags that were still on the apparel, but standard.

"Well," said Rush, who had come up behind him. "Did we do well enough to climb in Ouray?"

"Brands don't make the climber," Kyle remarked dryly.

Rush clapped Kyle's back and grinned. Kyle much preferred that look to the one Rush had given in the car when he'd learned about Ashley.

An hour and a half later, they were back in front of Kyle's home. Rush asked him about the schedule for the following week. Between work and school, Kyle told him only afternoons would work.

"But even then we have to get clearance from Sean," he said. "I once climbed before the official opening and got fined, but another guy did it twice and they banned him for the entire season. It's a death thing," he added with a smirk.

"Got it. Text me when you think we can begin. I'll ski in the meantime. And here." Rush had three, hundred dollar bills in his outstretched hand.

"Too much," Kyle said.

Rush raised an eyebrow. "You got change?" Kyle shook his head. "Then take it. You saved us from potential death by inspecting the gear and it would have cost me double with someone else, right? Good. See you later this week."

Kyle pocketed the money and avoided looking at the Fine residence as he entered his home.

Easiest three hundred he'd ever made, and it didn't take two and a half weeks to do it. The prospect of more inspired Kyle to call Sean and he was bummed when he learned the ice wouldn't be ready for another few days.

Kyle texted the information to Rush, then glanced outside, seeing the Defender was still parked out front. It could have been Kyle's imagination, but he thought he saw both Marcus and Rush's heads turned towards the Fine home. A moment later, the Defender left, going up towards town, leaving Stu in Kyle's direct line of sight.

Kyle let the curtain drop. He was the least of Stu's problems now.

CHAPTER 29

Monday morning, Kyle carefully removed the bandage from his nose and cheeks. In the week since the interrogation, it had become a second skin. Now the absence of the metal and plastic made him feel oddly naked.

It was pitch black outside, only five forty, but he'd gotten up ten minutes earlier. Now that he'd made it through the weekend without getting arrested, the tension moved into excitement over what he was going to learn next from the cubes.

Cube Master was a bit grandiose, he thought, but maybe he could discover things that would help Billy and in a big way.

He was out the door by a ten to six, finishing his water testing thirty minutes later. He stripped into his swim trunks and went far into the vapor caves, inhaling deeply.

Kyle worked with the cubes for nearly an hour, but didn't learn anything new. Frustrated, he replaced the items, got dressed and made it to school with twenty minutes to spare.

He was at his locker when he felt a presence rush up to him just as he smelled the familiar perfume.

"How could you?" Ashley hissed. When he met her eyes, he scanned her face.

She looked terrible.

"How could I what?" he asked, glancing over his shoulder, and seeing Samantha, Ashley's best friend, at her own locker. "I just got here."

"You called the cops and repeated what I said," she said, her voice rising hysterically.

"Come on, Ashley. Leave him," Samantha suggested, touching Ashley's arm.

"Ash," Kyle said, his voice low. "No, I didn't call the cops. I haven't seen Mark since he left on Friday."

She shook her head as he spoke, her lips trembling, a pale, uneven pink lip adding to her splotchy face.

"Her dad was arrested thanks to you," said Samantha. "Making out with Billy in the gym wasn't enough?" she spat. "Come on Ashley. Let's go."

Kyle was still digesting the words when he touched Ashley's arm, hoping to stop her.

"Don't you touch me," Ashley half-sobbed as Samantha lead her away. In the meantime, Ben and Marty had approached, pausing as the girls walked by.

"Good going, Kyle," Marty said.

Kyle didn't bother respond. Whatever was happening didn't include him.

He took his books and made for first period. In class, he pretended indifference to the others, but it was tough. The entire senior class only comprised twenty-eight people, half of those were in one of the two classes held each period.

Throughout the class, Marty made snide comments. It wasn't until the teacher asked Marty if he'd like to be excused did he shut up.

Ashley was with him in math, the two of them sitting near one another. Her face was less red, but her eyes were puffy.

Mr. Jenkins was having none of Marty's comments, excusing him half-way through. As Kyle walked out after class, Marty was waiting outside the door, and said nothing until Ashley emerged.

"You really made up a story to Mark because Stu called you out at the basketball game?" Marty asked. Ashley bit her lip, closing her mouth to the truth which would have exonerated him. Kyle stared at her. She was going to let everyone believe he had lied.

He turned away, not dignifying the question with an answer.

Marty was close enough to his back that Kyle felt his breath. "Not going to admit the obvious? One girl was too good for you and the other one left after a week. Stellar boyfriend."

Other students had slowed their pace, loitering to observe the spectacle of two former best friends going at it over a girl. Kyle turned, looking down a half-inch at his former friend.

"Since you're believing a lie Marty, why don't you ask Ashley how'd she come by that knock on the face? You going to suggest I did that to her as well?" Kyle glanced at Ashley, her face grey. "Hasn't it occurred to you Stu would have shot me right then and there if I'd touched her?"

Ashley had started to squirm. "Come on Marty, he's not worth it."

Kyle nodded. "Nope, but you know what Marty? Neither are you. The whole reason Ashley looks like she does is she wanted to date someone other than you and her dad said no. Chew on that."

Kyle shut his locker and started to walk away when he was slammed forward into the wall, his books scattering as his hands and elbows went up to protect his face. Before he could turn, he felt a sucker punch to his kidneys, the pain excruciating.

He turned just as Marty threw another punch, missing Kyle's stomach by an inch, hitting the locker instead. Marty yelled in pain, and the next second he was hurtling to the floor after Kyle pushed him with both hands.

"Break it up," yelled Coach Harrison who glared at Kyle. Of course he didn't see the first part of the fight, only the second. "You're gone," he told Kyle.

All the unjustified jealousy, anger and fear Kyle had been harboring welled up within him. "You going to expel him too, since he started it?"

"Anyone else back that up?" the Coach asked, looking around. Kyle was still bent over, fighting to catch his breath, but looked around at the group. Every student in the hallway stayed quiet, even Ben.

"Looks like you get your things and sign out," Coach Harrison said without sympathy. "The Principle will give you three days at least, so that means you're gone until Thursday."

Kyle gave a single head nod and stood up straight. Seeing the Coach wasn't going to leave until he did, Kyle took his things out of his locker. He turned to see Marty wearing a victorious grin on his face.

"Truth is persistent Marty. You just remember that when all you learn about Ashley comes back to this moment in time."

Her bruised, plumped mouth spewed forth a line of curse words that would have made her mother faint, but Kyle only stared at her.

"You guys deserve each other," he said to both of them. "But she doesn't want you anyway, so I guess you're on your own Marty."

"Now, Kyle," ordered his coach.

Kyle walked at a normal pace to the front office. They would have the rest of the day to gossip and point fingers, Marty now doubting Ashley, and she doing her best to deny or lie, both traits she possessed in equal parts.

As for himself, he effectively had three days to kill.

And he had to come up with something so that he didn't worry himself sick over Billy and her upcoming surgery. She'd not told him when it was, hanging up before he had a chance to ask.

That girl had a mind—and face—of her own. It was her right and her will to do what she wanted.

Would he like the new her? She was going to be beautiful no matter what happened, and still the same Billy.

Kyle made uneasy peace with the situation, deciding activity was the best solution. What could he do in the middle of the day or evening?

He looked to the mountain on his left. As he walked home, he sent Rush a text. He hadn't had a ski buddy in a while.

"Let's go through line forty-one," Brayden said to Danny. The elite task force of fifty had been working around the clock. He didn't care what they used to sleep on or for that matter, to stay awake with, legal or not. His job was to protect the financial security of the top fifty-six percent of this country from ruin.

"Let me get there," requested Danny. As Brayden waited, he mulled over the fact that his own status wasn't to be included in the tax bracket of this group. As a career FBI agent, this was just one more instance of putting the good of the whole before himself and family.

"Line forty-one," said Danny. They snapped to the details, Brayden questioning specifics as Danny gave clarity. Bank account managers were going to wake up one day soon and receive passwords for system accounts, believing it nothing more than an organization-wide upgrade. The passwords provided would be the trigger for a complex series of protocols that automatically closed accounts and opened new ones, all done without the knowledge of the customer, preventing the hackers from gaining access to the money. Danny's elegantly sophisticated program didn't even require the numbers of the checks to be changed; it was all done in the background, additional tags on the accounts revolutionary in banking history.

"Too bad it took an imminent catastrophe for this type of uber-change," remarked Danny.

"Not as bad as you not receiving the credit for it," replied Brayden. "The blessing and curse of the brilliant white-hatter."

"Eh, don't worry about me. You guys pay pretty well."

Not as well as the bad guys, Brayden thought to himself, thankful people existed who still wanted to do the right thing for the right reason.

An hour later, Brayden tapped into Kyle's files. The NSA was continuing to populate it with new information, each piece a digital ingredient Brayden feared would eventually make into a recipe of disaster for his teenage friend. Bit by bit, the NSA forensics teams were recreating what Saachi had almost figured out.

Brayden could only watch, since any interference on his part potentially seen as obstructionist. Worst case? He might be the one called upon to bring Kyle in, and he wouldn't have a choice.

CHAPTER
30

"It all went down this morning, probably when you were at the Weisbaden," Mark told Kyle, who was sitting on the other side of Mark's desk at the police station. "And it was a woman who called me by the way, which I first thought was Ruth who was there when I showed up."

Kyle couldn't imagine Stu being handcuffed and forced to sit in the back of the patrol car.

"He wasn't," Mark corrected. "I took a gamble he wouldn't bash through the plexi and make a run for it, so I gave him the courtesy of allowing him to move in and out on his own volition."

"Did he appreciate the gesture?"

Mark snorted. "Of course not, but then he didn't threaten to have me fired again. Anyway," he continued, sighing, "for now he's got a bigger problem."

"No kidding. Ashley's going to be the wild child we all suspected her to be."

"That's not who I was referring to," corrected Mark. "Ruth. She's been disowned, or so I hear. No longer welcome in the house."

Kyle cocked his head. "Why? Oh, Stu thinks it was Ruth who called the cops?"

"Apparently."

"They need to get their story straight," said Kyle. "Ashley accused me of doing the very same thing today at school, which led to the fight with Marty, which has gotten me suspended."

Mark put an ankle on his knee, hands on his belly. "You're turning out to be a right delinquent," Mark complimented. "Never thought you had it in you."

It was a compliment Kyle could have done without.

"How's Saachi?"

"Beautiful and messed up," Mark answered, a pained smile on his face. "She wants to keep her scars because she says it's an authentic representation of her life and experiences, which I can respect. Her arm's a complete mess; the burn went to the muscle. I disagree with the doctor about the use of it; she'll inflict her will on her arm, eventually making it work."

"Mark, would you be willing to leave Ouray to be with her?"

Mark eyed him, the patrolman's gaze intense. "Am I that obvious, or is it because that's what you'd do for Billy?"

"Both," answered Kyle seriously.

"Then we each have our motivations don't we?"

Kyle nodding, standing. "I'm heading home. More to chat about later if you want to stop by." He didn't have to look at the cameras in the corners to know they were there and operational.

At home, his mother gave him an earful for how he'd reacted to Marty, the call from the school Principle alerting her to the situation.

"I think Marty asked for it," his father chimed in. "What were you supposed to do?" he'd asked. "Make it acceptable for the guys to go sucker punching you?"

When Mark showed up after dinner, he revealed why the government hadn't come back into town. "The NSA was told to leave the area. Brayden says they're gone and won't return."

"Do you believe that?"

"Neither me nor the Sherriff have been told otherwise, and I trust Brayden."

No investigation meant the marks on his ATV wouldn't matter. "When can we get back my ATV?" Kyle asked

Mark grunted. "What are you doing now?"

Ten minutes later, Mark picked up Kyle beyond the hot springs and together they rode to the abandoned building. On the way, Mark told Kyle about Laura's message.

"They're both concerned about you and want you safe."

Kyle pushed the fabric of his snow pants flat. It wasn't a big leap to think they were hoping he wasn't going to meet the same fate as their son.

When they arrived at the old mill, Mark told Kyle to find several rocks. With Mark's guidance, they inflicted damage to the panels that would be consistent with encounters with boulders.

As they worked, Mark educated Kyle on paint chips, depth and degrees of damage. "The key," he said, pausing with effort as he scraped, "is to make an existing mark much worse, then elongate it so when the FBI forensics team does their weight and ratio calculations, it doesn't match." Kyle watched as Mark took a quarter inch scratch and turned it into one over six inches and a centimeter deep.

"You sort of mauled my machine," Kyle said, depressed.

"That's the art of disguising a criminal act," Mark replied. "You have to think like a criminal in order to catch one, or in our case, avoid being caught."

With that in mind, the two of them went over the ATV inch by inch, inspecting and changing any fault, creating new ones along the way.

"Then the ultimate trick. Be back in a sec." Mark returned from his car with a can he shielded from Kyle. "When the whole shooting accident happened with Roy, I didn't want you to know too much about outsmarting the detectives. This next act is included in that. Turn around."

Kyle did as he was told. Spraying was followed by a rough, abrasive scraping sound. "Can you tell me what you are doing?"

"Sure. It's a rust accelerant used overseas to patina copper, but it does so in a way that appears natural. It's almost foolproof in the US"

Kyle's nosed twitched. "It reeks."

"It should," Mark laughed. "It's essentially bottled urine with some chemicals." Kyle looked over his shoulder. "I didn't say you could turn around," Mark scolded.

"While your making my pristine vehicle look used, it would be a good thing for you to hear about Billy. She ah…" he hesitated, "she's one of three guinea pigs for the new faces." Mark's scraping stopped as he looked up. "Her, her uncle and Joe. All three going under the knife this Friday."

Mark looked a little pasty grey even in the weak light. "Turn around!" he ordered, as if he just noticed Kyle had been looking at him. "She okay with it?"

"She volunteered. Wanted to be a part of the history-making effort to ensure this all works."

"Wow Kyle. That girl…"

"Yeah I know. As soon as I get the transfer pad I'll be sending the 47 other states along. They'll have everything."

"When?"

"Friday, the same day as the surgery."

Mark whistled in appreciation. "Ok, I'm finished. You ride that around for a while then go home," Mark advised.

Kyle did just that, taking the long way on Oak Street that paralleled the hot springs until he hit the Box Canyon turnoff where he went left, then right up to the ice park. He got off the ATV, walking the length of the park, examining the various courses as he went. Some spots were a dark grey, a sign the ice was thick enough to climb. It was the translucent areas that meant risk.

Kyle shivered, getting back on the ATV. It was in the teens, the temperature dropping quickly. A cold wind was picking up. It was like his life, he thought, every aspect hard and cold.

Except the vapor caves. Secure and private, hot and soothing, it was the one place where he could escape the forces of this town, all that seemed to be closing ranks against him.

It was just what his mother had predicted after the game. He was the least popular person in town, but he was going to use that to his advantage.

Rush sat in the den of the rental home, his concentration on his laptop fierce. A novice engineer he'd hired had taken it upon himself to customize the Bulgarian's supply chain management software tracking all the legitimate product parts imported from foreign distributors. The idiot had thought he'd improve the system, combining the US-based inventory systems with what came in from overseas; problem was, the American side was completely illegal, the products flowing from sources who preferred to remain anonymous, the originating destinations off the back of trucks and literally, in most cases, off the actual automobiles.

"What to do with you?" he said to himself. The kid was a talented MIT grad who they were paying one-twenty-five a year, covered for his moving costs to Denver and planted him in a high-rise not far from where Rush knew Danny lived. Alexis' notion of making the kid disappear didn't work for Rush; the business needed talent of the upstanding kind as well as the non.

No, this was a simply business process discussion between manager and employee. The trick was trying to explain why the systems shouldn't have been merged in the first place without revealing the darker side of the business.

That's when you learn if someone is smart enough to figure out what is going on for themselves, and then you watch and wait to see what they are going to do about it. Nine times out of ten, a smart newbie will decide to keep his or her mouth shut and collect the paycheck. But in the few cases where morals get the better of the person…

Rush picked up the phone. "Yeah, get Sandy to have the conversation with him," he told Marcus. "She'll come up with the reason for the separation if that's the direction he heads. Yeah, correct." The call was short and pointed. They'd been down this path before. Movement outside caught his eye and he looked up. A group of Elk grazed in front of the ridge in front of him, a bull with seven cows and two calves. He'd never seen a herd in real life, and the moment stuck with him. It took coming to the back corner of the state to track down one Kyle Smith to see it.

Rush got on line and typed a short note to Danny. No cubes from Kyle yet, but it would happen soon.

He left out the play he'd made with Ashley, smiling at the thought. He'd been around worldly women for so long, he'd almost forgotten what a pseudo innocent girl could bring to the table.

And Rush had no doubt that Ashley was a virgin, despite her efforts to come across as sophisticated and in control. There was no question she was the top of the female food chain in this town, but she'd be eaten alive outside Montrose. Still, his time in Ouray was going to be short-lived. He was going to make the most of it.

CHAPTER 31

Rush was supposed to be partying in New York City with friends one week after New Years' Eve, not parked out front an eggshell blue home in Ouray, Colorado. But when the door of opportunity gets a knock, one must answer, he mused.

When Kyle returned from the Weisbaden, Rush was already out of the car as Kyle reached the freshly shoveled path.

"It's going to be some killer snow today," Rush predicted. Kyle nodded, glancing beyond Rush's shoulder.

"No Marcus?" he asked.

"The guys headed back to Denver for a few days, but Marcus will return this weekend. You want help getting your gear?"

"Nah, but you're welcome to come in if you want."

Kyle had spent the night thinking about what the cubes revealed about Rush. By the time he fell asleep, his fear had morphed into a slight interest, then fascination and fear.

Finally, it had transitioned into a bit of jealousy. He lived what seemed like a glamorous life with cool cars and girls; everything the movies made it out to be.

Well, they had to get their ideas from life, and truth was always the basis for most fiction anyway.

In the house, Rush greeted his father who'd returned from his walk. His dad looked up, gave his standard, "Hey there," and returned to his work. Led Zeppelin played in the background, a fact that must have amused Rush because he was nodding his head and humming as he poked around the living room, touching the hummingbird feeders and glass ornaments that hadn't sold over Christmas.

"You do all of these here?" Kyle heard Rush ask his dad.

"Every last one."

"These Tiffany replicas are pretty impressive," Rush complimented. His father grunted a thank you then asked where Rush was staying.

"Over in the Telluride community."

"Ready if you are," Kyle said.

"Watch the powder," his father said as they walked by the office. "No off trail."

"Promise."

His father grunted. "For whatever that's worth."

Kyle shot him a look, hearing Rush chuckle as the door closed behind them.

Kyle knew restored Defender 110's topped a hundred grand, and this looked worth every bit of it.

"Bullet proof glass?" Kyle asked without thinking. Rush shot him a look of curiosity. "Well, if you're going to be a full Russian gangster, what use is a tank without bullet proof glass?"

Rush laughed. "That is definitely a necessity," he replied, the response giving Kyle a smug sense of satisfaction.

"I hope it didn't bother you that Mark asked for your ID the other day."

"Not at all," Rush replied, taking a left at Ridgeway onto Highway 62. "People don't realize that geeky coders can drive hot cars."

"Coders?" repeated Kyle.

"Yeah," said Rush, glancing over with a smirk. "As in, software engineer."

"Seriously," he deadpanned. "You're a coder."

"What? This isn't what you imagine for a coder? We too can be hot my friend."

"No offense of course, you just seem too...cool to be sitting in a cubicle somewhere banging out a million lines of code for a banking application."

Rush nodded. "Not the image I'd really want to cultivate anyway. Doesn't work with the ladies."

Kyle smiled, shaking his head. "Any particular area of expertise, or just a little of everything?"

"You could say I'm an opportunist," he answered. "Since I freelance, I pick and choose the projects that are the most lucrative."

"That must be nice." His phone buzzed, and Kyle's heart bounced. It was the burner phone Billy had given him.

"You going to get that?" Rush asked him. Kyle was in a tight spot, the waves of uncertainty going down the back of his legs. He couldn't ask Rush to pull over so he could get out, but each ring could be the last one before she was incapacitated for a week or two.

"Hey," Kyle greeted, somberly.

"What's up Cube Master?" Her voice was light and happy, not what he'd expected. "You sound busy."

"The short version is that Marty sucker punched me at school yesterday because Ashley said I called the cops on Stu, who was arrested. When I let Marty have it, Coach kicked me out of school until Friday. Just another day in high school."

"Sorry Kyle, but why would you call the cops on Stu anyway?"

"Ashley wanted to date an out of towner, a good guy actually, but her dad said no. Apparently she defied him and he hit her."

"Wish I could say she deserved it, but she probably didn't. You say out of towners?" her voice wary.

"All good," Kyle said. "Going skiing right now with him. What's going on with you?"

She took a breath. "They are doing the final prep today and tomorrow. Even though I shouldn't have rejection issues, they aren't taking any chances."

"So that means…?"

"I check in Thursday afternoon, and I'll call you right before."

"Billy—" he hesitated, unsure of how to say it. "Can't Roy just overnight what I need? I saw him hook it up and use it. Just send the directions. It could work."

"Except for the masters."

"Yeah, but you'd have all the rest.. There's no risk. If anyone opens it up, they'll have no clue what it is."

"I knew there was a reason I called you the Cube Master."

He laughed. "Hardly. Data transfer master maybe."

"Okay, I'll get on it. Love you."

"Love you," he said right back.

"See how easy that was?" she gloated. "Automatic and real, just like an old married couple."

Kyle's grin was unmanageable. "Real, but not old." She hung up, but Kyle was still smiling wide.

"That sounded cool," Rush said. Kyle nodded. "And sorry for overhearing, but is she having surgery somewhere? Is everything okay—she's having a boob job, not going to die or something is she?"

Kyle laughed out loud. "Billy is a snowboarding, computer genius, with a body curvy and hard, requiring no modifications."

"In other words, the exact opposite of Ashley," Rush added. "But back to your girlfriend. I'm serious. Is she okay?"

"Yes, it is serious, and no, I honestly don't know if she's going to be okay, but she's strong willed and determined. I'm supporting her in the best way I can, which is to be here doing my thing."

They were the first ones in line when the lift opened, the powder deep and trails ungroomed. It was the best Telluride skiing had to offer; zero crowds and perfect snow.

No wonder Billy always made fun of him for not taking a day off here and there when she was always off boarding. *And still getting better grades than me.*

On the lift ride up, Rush asked Kyle about his family.

"If you don't mind me asking, if your parents' work is so good, why do you live where you do?"

Kyle shrugged. "They do it for the love of the art, not to make money. So the rich make them sign confidentiality agreements so the general population can't know how little mom and dad are being paid. Ergo, we live in our micro sized house and live project to project."

"And that whole business with losing the scholarships and your job didn't help matters."

"Nope," replied Kyle pragmatically. "But that's not stopping me from leaving here in a few months."

Rush nodded his head. "Anywhere in particular?"

"That is to be determined," Kyle hedged, thinking about Billy. "What kind of money do you make coding?"

"You thinking about it?"

Kyle smirked. "Hardly. My skills are more in line with physical science than computers. I was thinking of my girlfriend. She's a natural."

"Unlike Ms. Fine."

Kyle looked over, raising his eyebrow. "Ashley could probably tell you what kind of computer looks the prettiest," Kyle snarked.

"So I learned last night."

Kyle stared at him. "Seriously?"

"I wanted to see how far that girl will go to piss her dad off, and the answer is pretty far."

Kyle closed his mouth, wondering if…

"Don't worry," Rush laughed. "I'm not going to get the girl pregnant or give her some disease. But between you and me, she's the cougar on the prowl looking for some red meat, not the other way around."

Kyle laughed with satisfaction. "Her dad always told me I kept her on the straight and narrow."

"That girl is neither straight nor narrow. Race you," Rush challenged as the chair came to the platform. "First one down wins a hundred."

Kyle thought about the hundreds in his wallet. "Make that three."

"You're on."

CHAPTER
32

Danny intercepted the email just as it reached the computer of Agent Brayden Cox. He read it once, then read it again to make sure he didn't miss a critical element. The FBI woman currently in the burn unit had known the name of the kid in Ouray and had covered it up. Or rather, hadn't been given the chance to expose it before the lab blew.

It was all there. Kyle Smith's DNA had been inside gloves discovered in a dumpster outside town three days after the break in at the mine. They were found by the NSA forensics teams who had come up after the incident and recreated all her work after she was in the hospital. The same residue had been in his locker and also on each one of the file cabinets in the mine, despite attempts to wipe down the surfaces. Kyle's blood had been found in the sink at the hot springs, and while it didn't link him directly to the mine or the blood on the ground at the base of the mine, it was another piece of circumstantial evidence from that Friday night. The first evidentiary items were going to be enough to nail the kid, the second were backup points.

But Smith had passed the polygraph then the injections, two more data points that the NSA teams had considered as reasons to hold off taking him in. They'd concluded Smith had help from either a governmental source like Saachi or the Naturalists. Either way, he was just a way to get to the cubes, not the person he was presumably working for. That was the primary target.

Danny looked at the time. 5:08 p.m. He typed out an email to Rush. It was nice of Rush to take it slow, but that luxury was gone. Any day, the NSA could pick up that kid and their once-in-a-lifetime opportunity would be gone.

Danny cracked half a Vivarin caffeine tablet and washed it down with Mt. Dew, which was the second worst thing he could do to his system after alcohol. If his doc had been a witness, Danny was sure he might have suggested crushing and snorting the tablet, or mainlining the liquid caffeine straight into his veins. Both were equally toxic to his stomach, exacerbating the ulcer, but he had to get the job done.

"And that job is staying awake until I find you again," he said to his screen. Sunsetmoon had been communicating with Kyle Smith in Ouray, and Danny was willing to bet it had been Kyle on the mountain New Year's Eve. It was too coincidental that the last interaction between the two parties was just hours before the incident on the mountain with four snowmobilers.

As Danny waited for Rush to respond, he checked in with the fifty white-hat coders he had working on the FBI project. Ironically, Danny's efforts would protect the majority of citizens against financial devastation while leaving a few billion around for Rush to siphon. When you have a single guy like Bezos worth a hundred on any given day, a percentage loss was large enough to be noticed. A better strategy was to take it in piecemeal from business accounts tied into the markets, as well as retirement funds where the rise and fall could be manipulated, the extraction taken on the spread. No one would ever know, and by the time it was discovered, the traces would be long gone and the money spent.

But it was now 5:31 and his task wasn't to preserve the financial wealth of the country, but to track Sunsetmoon who seemed to know a lot more about the missing cubes.

Danny had been watching Sunsetmoon's activity, wondering why she'd not used her account to contact Kyle Smith again. She certainly didn't know about the NSA email to Brayden or the wires would be burning with the information.

Could be using phone lines and that was a lot harder to crack, especially if they were using burners.

As Danny watched the lines of code, he felt like a fisherman casting his net to the digital ocean. With each current of information, his mutating code would extend its coverage. If and when Sunsetmoon appeared, his software program would capture the IP addresses and interaction.

Thirty minutes later, he'd not heard from Rush so he shut down his computer and left. His fancy apartment building offered a hot yoga class, promoting its cleansing, detoxifying attributes in a 104 degree room while burning 1,200 calories.

Any little bit is going to help.

An hour later, as he lay flat on his back, marinating in his own sweat, staring at the ceiling as the instructor said to keep his eyes open, he thought about Rush and whether he'd made much progress with Kyle.

The two skied until closing, Kyle easily beating Rush to the bottom because Rush made the mistake of cutting through the trees, his wide skis perfect for the deep powder but slower than Kyle's older model which were designed for speed.

Rush handed over another three hundred, the remaining stack undented by the loss of three bills. Putting his wallet back in his pocket, the buzzing of his phone went off and he paused to check it.

After he replaced the phone, he looked back up the mountain then to the town. "You interested in dinner?" Rush asked him. Kyle had nothing better to do and at least now he had money in his pocket to pay his share.

On the way back to Ridgeway, Kyle listened to Rush describe the nightclubs in Moscow compared to London, his mind not on the girls or the music, but why being with a person of Rush's background didn't bother him. Was it because Kyle himself was immune to the underworld he knew existed but didn't impact his daily life, or the reality that Rush was just an opportunist as he said?

The American way of life, thought Kyle. It's what draws the courageous and enterprising from around the world, those who have the balls and the brains to come and make something of nothing.

When they reached Ridgway, Kyle told him to stay left.

"You're going to see some old time western Americana," he added, pointing to the wooden walkways with overhangs. A sign dangling read *True Grit*.

Rush hadn't been to the John Wayne themed restaurant before, or even heard of it. Kyle was amused to learn that in Russia, for all its seeming anti-Americanism, John Wayne was an iconic hero.

"The Wild West," said Rush with unabashed enthusiasm. He knew more about the movie star than Kyle would have imagined. Kyle knew the bartender from climbing, and he gave the man a nod and a head jerk to Rush.

"Anywhere," the bartender called as he turned to make a drink.

"I can see the locals get treated well around here," Rush observed, ordering a dark ale.

"True story, but it's only a chapter. The backstory is everyone knows I don't drink, there are only two cops on duty at one time and he knows my dad."

"A veritable criminal playground," Rush joked.

"You're not too far from the mark," said Kyle. He pointed out the signed pictures on the wall, the movie props used by John Wayne close enough to touch. Waitresses yelled the orders from the tables, the country music so loud they could barely hear one another.

"I love this," Rush said, taking a sip of beer. "So would Marcus."

They looked at the menu, Rush asking what Kyle would recommend.

"I haven't been here a ton," he admitted, "but have heard everything's good." Kyle kept his eye on the menu, figuring that Rush would be wondering why a local didn't come to a restaurant like this. It all came down to money, and Kyle never had much. "I can pay for myself thanks to kicking your ass on the hill," he said, preempting Rush's attempt to pay for the meal. One thing Kyle didn't want was a pitying look from anyone.

"Who said I was going to offer?" Rush countered. When the bartender came by, Kyle ordered the chicken fried steak with Rush requesting a filet mignon.

Over homemade bread with honey butter, Rush asked about Kyle's preferred tourists.

"Californians are obnoxious but rare," said Kyle as he took a bit of bread. "They think Heavenly in Tahoe is good, but it's nothing compared to the powder of the Rocky's. Telluride itself attracts eastern Europeans for some reason, and I avoid Aspen and Vail like the plague because that's where the posers from Hollywood go."

"Where's your favorite skiing then?"

"Crested Butte," he answered without hesitation. "It's got a vertical drop almost four thousand feet higher than Heavenly and two more than Vail."

"Real skiers go there," Rush surmised.

"Serious. The girls have more hair under their armpits than the guys, but skiing is tops."

Rush rumbled a laugh. "Speaking of girls, I'm not from small town in Colorado, so tell me how it goes down with a guy like you. All-state basketball and his pick of girls but ends up with someone into computers?"

Kyle's left shoulder was against the wall, the vibrations of the country beat pulsing through his arm. "How is it that a guy like you who could have any hot girl in that state could even be interested in someone like Ashley?"

"Touché," Rush answered. "In a word, curiosity."

"You're amused."

Rush tilted his head. "And a bit intrigued that you dumped her for Billy. What's up with that?"

Kyle didn't know where to start, having never been asked the question.

Rush took a drink, scanning the bar crowd. "It's okay. I can see you don't want to talk about her, for whatever reason."

"Sorry if that came off rude," Kyle said, trying to regain his equilibrium. What would it matter if he told an out-of-towner about Billy? It was no state secret. "See, up until three weeks ago, we were competitors in the academic and life sense of the word…" Kyle told of their rivalry starting in the seventh grade, her outsider status as the only child of a man who owned a bar and whose wife left him.

"A loner," interjected Rush.

Kyle nodded somberly. "Hidden under her thick snowboarding outfit is an amazingly gifted person who is--- well, she came into my life and saved my ass at the same time. She and I—we just happened, totally unexpected for both of us. Then she's always coming up with hilarious witticisms to describe herself, which is totally sappy and not her at all, making it all the funnier."

"And you're totally hung up on her."

Kyle cast him a sideways glance. He probably came across as a complete shmuck, but just thinking of Billy's comments and comebacks, sheer will and determination made him surf the wave of desire all over again.

"Have you ever had a female in your life who was so completely brilliant and strong that you'd pretty much walk over nails to reach her?"

Rush's eyes canvassed his face. "Once and was burned in the process."

The salads came, halting the conversation for a moment. "So what's up with her surgery?" Rush asked. "You implied it wasn't required but she was doing it anyway."

Kyle chewed, thinking of her pre-preparation injections. "She's a guinea pig for an experimental type of skin," he revealed, considering the information benign.

"And she had to do it now?"

Kyle buttered a piece of bread. "She had some incentive. Billy left after I kissed her in front the entire town, her life going immediately downhill due to Ashley's torment and Stu's influence. The timing worked out."

"She coming back after it's over?"

Kyle didn't know. "Unsure. She says in a few weeks or less. We'll see."

"But you'd do anything for her."

Kyle snorted. "I've already done almost everything humanly possible, not all of them great."

Changing the subject to London and Russia, Kyle asked if Rush missed either. Before he could answer, Rush's cell phone buzzed. "Hold that thought." Kyle ate as Rush scanned the screen. After a few seconds, he put it away. "London's a lot of fun but seriously expensive," Rush told him. "Russia is seriously corrupt. Even I have a hard time keeping above water."

Kyle got a laugh out of that. "Denver is your criminal utopia?"

Rush had a piece of steak on his fork and pointed it at Kyle. "That's the second time you've mentioned me and criminal in the same sentence," he said, taking the bite.

"Yeah," interrupted Kyle, "but just a minute ago, you mentioned it yourself."

"Fair enough," Rush acknowledged. "I will tell you the coding activity does tread a fine line of grey. But I don't have any convictions on my record."

"Not yet, anyway," Kyle wisecracked. Rush turned to him with a look that made Kyle's chest go hollow. "What? I thought you'd take the whole criminal thing as a compliment, not getting caught anyway. That's not easy to do, especially with the FBI and all."

Rush started eating again, but Kyle felt the weight of the conversation shift, as if heavier air had entered the room, sucking part of the oxygen out with it.

"And would it make a difference if I told you I was a part of organized crime, and that I do unsavory things all the time?"

Kyle kept eating. "I'd respond that I'd already guessed that part."

"And what if I said that I know you're a criminal just like me, except worse. Just now, I learned your name is being circulated within the FBI and the NSA. Quite an interesting development."

Kyle stopped chewing. His only recourse was to joke. "Losing the big game caused that type of uproar?"

With precision, Rush cut a piece of steak then dipped it in horseradish.

"Your DNA was in gloves retrieved from the dumpster outside town after the mine was broken into. Trace materials from that same glove was found on the file folders up at the mine. Additionally," he continued, "your blood was at the base of the mine, and in the sink at the spa, and despite the fact that you passed the polygraph and the truth serum, the NSA is convinced you are the one they need to get. And here's the kicker," Rush continued, cutting another piece of meat. "That FBI agent, Saachi Gupta, knew most of this and nearly got herself killed because of the information. The government thinks it was the Naturalists who blew up the lab in order to protect your identity from being revealed within the agencies. The NSA thinks they can catch a Naturalist when they meet up next."

Kyle had unconsciously put down his fork. Now he was afraid his hand would shake if he picked up the glass of water to take a drink.

"Then on New Year's Eve," continued Rush without pause, "I'm sitting by my white-hat adversary as he taps into a satellite. We watch real time as a person outruns four snowmobilers. That person was *you*."

The air caught in Kyle's throat. Rush's commentary had been so matter-of-fact, devoid of judgment or threat.

"The saving grace is that no one has put together the fact that you and your Internet conspirator who I believe to be Billy are connected; except me."

Kyle thought about all that he'd unwittingly disclosed. Running wasn't an option. Kyle had no car, and where was he going to go where Rush wouldn't find him? A person who could make money and people disappear, unburdened by the law or morality was far more dangerous than Lex or Jim.

"You're the people Billy said were snooping around the satellites."

Rush gave him an admiring nod. "Just like Billy did herself. Smart girl, like you said."

"What are you going to do?" Kyle asked.

Rush took a swallow of beer.

"*We*," he emphasized, "are going to finish our meal and talk about how you're going to help me get what I came here for."

"Then what? You turn me over to the government and I get killed anyway?"

Rush paused, looking around the room. "I have no incentive to aid the government, but I don't mind helping others like myself."

"A fellow criminal?" Kyle joked, only half-kidding.

"Those of us who have to work up from the bottom should help one another, don't you think?" Kyle felt a bit of comradery, the comment of starting from humble beginnings not lost on him. "Finish your meal and take your time. I'm not going anywhere and neither are you."

CHAPTER
33

Brayden's heart raced as he read the email. The NSA forensic work had finished, and they'd nailed Kyle for the initial break in. Saachi had intended to pass on the information so the Naturalists tried to kill her through the lab explosion. Brayden and Mark's involvement were completely missing in the picture.

Thank God.

The modified video satellite of the latest break-in was the second part of the issue. Someone had determined it had been tampered with, but *who* was an open question. The NSA ruled out incorrect settings or accidental handling of the technology.

Janet's team now felt the Naturalists were in possession of the cubes, first and second set. They doubted Kyle had the skills to evade, and or kill, the four agents sent to the mountain.

It was a miscalculation, and Brayden was glad of it. Gary informed Brayden that although Janet's team was told to stand down in Ouray, those orders were now void. Janet's teams were scouring the entire southwest corner of the state for the Naturalists and watching every cell and Internet activity for clues.

Kyle was safe, *for no*w. But Brayden knew that didn't mean he was going to be completely left alone. If the NSA got desperate, they'd arrest him in a heartbeat and try to break him.

It didn't hurt to check on the kid. Brayden used his burner phone to call Mark's cell.

"Hancock here."

"It's Brayden."

"Brayden!" Mark exclaimed. The enthusiasm gave Brayden a much needed lift.

"You free?" he asked, barely waiting for the confirmation. Quickly, Brayden shared the essentials of the email he'd received.

"If you're worried about Kyle, he's working at another spa, and now that he's out of school for a few days, he's skiing and teaching visitors to ice climb."

Brayden barely heard the first part but stopped at the last. "Visitors rock climbing?" he repeated.

"Yeah, guys from Denver," Mark said dismissively.

Brayden looked up, focusing on the wood paneling which covered the sloped ceiling. He decided to tell Mark about Billy. The revelation drew a chuckle. "You knew?"

"Kyle told me."

"Did you know hundreds of faces are being grown in three states, multiplying to thousands within the month?" Brayden asked.

Mark didn't. "Well one person who's not taking advantage of that is Saachi. Unfortunate, but a reality. Will you be leaving this weekend?"

The change of topic caught Brayden short. "Where would I be going?"

"With Laura? Moving?" prompted Mark.

Oh right. "I'm not sure if I'll be following her or when."

"Hey, sorry buddy," Mark cut in. "I didn't mean to intrude on your personal life. No explanation necessary."

"Don't worry about it. Kyle is a lot more important than my marriage at this moment."

"Actually Brayden, I'd say things here are pretty mellow. I relaxed after you said the NSA wasn't up here, and they haven't returned. Now that you've redeployed, we can go back to the Ouray version of normal, which I will welcome after all of this."

Brayden listened to Mark's expressions of relief, even as he examined the source of his unsettled emotions. It wasn't Mark raising the subject of Laura's move.

The visitors from Denver. He pressed Mark for more the details, but the Deputy was calm.

"I had the exact same reaction," Mark admitted. "What were the odds, right? But I checked their identification. They are just visitors renting a place in Telluride. Ice climbers and skiers. Three left already, headed back to Denver, as the ice won't be ready for another week, leaving one guy in town. If they had ulterior motives, I don't think they'd hang around for another week just to kill time."

Neither did Brayden. That wasn't government protocol. They came, they investigated and they acted. More so in a situation where time was of the essence.

"You remember this guy's name?" Brayden asked.

"Gonna do a check on him?"

"Doesn't hurt."

"Rush is his last name. I looked at his ID but don't recall the first or middle."

"When you have a minute," requested Brayden.

"Sure. No problem. As soon as I get it."

Brayden thanked him and hung up. One person he wasn't going to call was Ty. If his own daughter was keeping her location and situation invisible to him there had to be a reason.

Billy walked to the post office, the non-descript yellow padded envelop in her hand. It would be received by Kyle's mother. If she opened the package, she'd probably give a little smile. It was a red, metal coaster with four corners, each with small round rubber dots. The top had a heart outline around the words "Stick Around."

Perfectly tacky, Billy had told her uncle. The device was a replica of what he'd used to transfer the data from the first three cubes. Each transfer took only minutes.

But what of the masters? she wondered. It was a question neither she nor her uncle could answer. Billy was determined to go back to Ouray and pick them up herself. She knew it was risky to have them on her person—or anyone's person—but that was only a part of it. She wanted to get back to Ouray to see Kyle…and her dad.

In the two weeks she'd been gone, thoughts of her father had been put in a drawer, shut tight against the pain she'd caused him. When she returned, he'd be angry, hurt, resentful but ultimately she knew he'd forgive her for leaving.

But will he accept my new face?

Billy paid the amount requested by the cashier and left without a backward glance. On Friday, Kyle would have the envelope, probably opening it as she was nearly done with surgery. When she returned to the clinic, Dr. Pike was waiting at the receptionist area.

"Ready to see how far we've progressed?"

Billy nodded, excited and nervous.

"It's changed a lot since we placed the biomesh on your face," he said, gesturing for her to follow along.

"They stood outside an incubation lab. Seeing Dr. Pike, the technician opened a large fridge in the back, returning with a metal cookie tray. On it were three nearly completed faces, the newly grown skin adhering to the biomesh.

Billy involuntarily swallowed. "It does look slightly better," she admitted.

"It's graduated from the cross-work pattern to a completely smooth surface," he pointed out. "It's still alive, feeding and growing, and will continue to do so even as it's connected to you through the nerve endings."

"Media is food," Billy said, repeating the lines used by her uncle.

"Correct. So while I'd like to wash off the red media, that could damage the final cell growth phase."

"I'm just going to have to wait until it's on to see the end result," she said, resigned and relieved. Although curiosity consumed her, seeing the final product before it was put on might be too….real at this point.

"Between now and Friday, get lots of rest," he advised. "Take only the prescribed vitamins and relax. The cells respond as much to the mental and emotional state of the patient as the actual skin we are using. You need to be in top condition in all aspects of your life for optimum recovery."

Billy nodded, understanding the gravity of his words. Any distraction would hurt her potential for healing.

"It's my face doc. I have lots of incentive."

She returned to Roy's house, the door unlocked and the house was empty of human presence, as always. The one-story ranch style home was nearly identical to the others scattered around the reservation; only the materials and color of the outside made it unique. Inside was another story, just like her own home. Intricately carved wood pieces formed the furniture, the worn leather or skins used as the surface pieces, authentic and rich in heritage.

Unable to sit still, she walked the small room, moving between bookshelves full of leather-bound copies of the classics. Most looked worn on the outside and barely touched on the insides. Not much use for Shakespeare when the majority of the tribal members were out hunting in the winter or gaming in the summer.

Although that was changing. On the other side of the reservation, the lodge-like casino employed thousands of tribal members and regular citizens alike; the world-renowned spa and golf course drew visitors from all over the globe. They invariably got sick from overindulging, the need for a hospital necessitating a modern medical facility. As her uncle had said, the forward-thinking leadership anticipated a day where the tribe required more than just financial independence. Setting aside profits from the gambling, they now had a world class medical facility.

Running her finger along the dusty ledge of the bookshelf, she stopped at an old wooden box. Curious, she opened it, expecting to see old driver's licenses and a few gambling chips. Instead, the top photo was one of Uncle Ray as a younger man, perhaps in his late twenties. A woman stood beside him who she assumed was his wife or girlfriend. She picked it up, staring.

It was her mother, a much younger version. Jet black hair, wide, high cheekbones and equally broad eyebrows. Her face was thin, accentuating her collarbones poking out of her u-shaped white t-shirt. "Unique," Billy said to herself, thinking of Kyle's words to describe her own beauty. Although she hated her mother for leaving, the resemblance between the two couldn't be denied, nor did Billy really want to. Her mother was beautifully exotic, her charcoal-colored eyes gazing intently at the camera, as though she knew the picture was important and didn't want to ruin the moment with a smile.

Billy's fingers were shaking when she replaced the photo. There was another picture underneath. With trepidation, Billy lifted it close. Her mother stood beside another woman, fair and blond. In her arms was a little girl with dark hair and wide eyebrows, the skin coloring matching neither woman. The blonde's lips were closed and her eyes were sad, in opposition to what a mother holding a child usually displayed. Her own mother held a little girl, cradled protectively. Her eyes were closed, the little poke of hair dark and faint.

The truth dawned on Billy like the sun over a dark horizon. What Kyle had found on the cubes had to be... .

Still holding the photo, she went to her computer, accessing the files Kyle and Roy had transferred. There, she looked up Brayden and Laura Cox. Billy placed the picture on the laptop, resting the frame against the screen.

Billy's mother had disappeared at age three, leaving Billy with her father in Ouray. Kyle had said the Cox's daughter had died at age three, but Kyle remained convinced Sasha was alive.

On the surface, and by virtue of the pictures, it appeared as though Billy's mother had been raising this child for Laura and Brayden, leaving her real daughter alone for fourteen years.

Billy sat back, consumed with bitterness for her own situation, the seed of resentment blossoming into a nuclear explosion of anger and hate.

Why would the Cox's daughter get the benefit of having a mother when I was stripped of one?

Billy closed the laptop and replaced the photo to its original location. She sat on the couch, one leg under the other, feeling her chest pounding from the center outward.

This is not going to help my mental state for the surgery.

But neither was the knowledge that her mother was living with and raising another girl.

Kyle had said Brayden almost punched him for suggesting his daughter was alive, which meant he didn't know. Laura had acted on her own, without his input or knowledge.

Now Billy knew the truth and wanted it confirmed. She wanted to see her mother…to yell at her for choosing another little girl over herself and to tell her to go to hell, or to cry and ask her to come back into her life.

She went to her room, and sat on the bed. She effectively had a day and a few hours before she went under, so the question was whether it would be worse to see her mother now and resolve her issues, or if she should do it afterwards when she was beginning to heal.

Billy didn't have the perfect answer, but knew who would.

CHAPTER 34

The moment with Rush was interrupted by the buzzing of the phone.

"Bet that's Billy."

Kyle pulled out his phone, debating leaving the restaurant and going outside. In a split second, he decided to stay. *Safety in visibility.*

He put the phone in his left hand and turned to the wall, talking low. "Have they moved up the surgery?"

"No, it's scheduled for Friday morning but I want to talk about...my mother, actually."

That was not what Kyle expected. "Your mom?"

"This is what you thought, and this is what I now believe." Kyle listened as she related discovering the pictures, hearing the anxiety in her voice. "But given what Dr. Pike said, I'm sort of screwed, because I'm going to be completely stressed out if I don't at least talk to her or get some resolution---"

"But if you do, you might be setting yourself up for something worse," he finished for her. Kyle wished he had an easy answer, but it didn't exist. She was ten steps closer to the truth, than she'd ever thought possible in the last fourteen years, but it couldn't have come at a worse time.

"Well, what do you think?" she asked. "And where are you by the way? It's so noisy."

"At True Grit just finished with skiing. Billy, I agree. You're screwed." Her laugh was dry and bitter. "I can't imagine what it was like not to have a parent, then find out all you'd known was a lie. You must feel betrayal, anger, desire—all mashed up into one. A little forgiveness too, maybe?"

"Not sure on that one."

Kyle breathed in deep, the exhale silent. He didn't want to offend her, but she'd called for his advice and he was going to give it.

"Then I recommend you don't do anything," he said with conviction. "It's not worth the turmoil and upheaval you're going to experience. At least now you know what you have in life. Me. Your dad, and in forty-eight hours, a fresher, newer, version of you. Leave it at that."

"Deal with one major life event at a time then."

"Don't you think that's wise?"

"Yeah Master of more things than just a cube. I do think that's the wise approach."

Kyle's relief was infinite. They didn't need any more drama or literal trauma in her life than what they now faced. And for that reason, he justified not telling her about Rush. She would be pissed off and mortified if she learned that Rush's guys had discovered her digital tracks, leading Rush right to Kyle.

"How are things with you and the town we know and love?" she asked, changing the subject.

"Mostly normal," he lied. "I've picked up some ice climbing clients by sheer luck and they are keeping me occupied and in the money until the runs are open." Kyle felt himself talking faster, in an effort to avoid not telling the truth.

"That's great," she said with distant enthusiasm.

"Look, I know you're still thinking about your mom. Don't. Focus on you, the revolutionary surgery you're about to have and glory in that," he said with real enthusiasm. "You're going to be in the history books—"

"Yeah," she interrupted. "But for what? As a terrorist or a hero?"

"Let's hope the latter. Billy," he paused. "I'm really proud of you for going through with this…it's," he stopped, searching for the words, "amazing. I really don't think I could do it."

She snorted. "You say that, but you don't give yourself enough credit. You found a way to get the cubes, escape and keep on going like it was no big deal, all bashed up and now an outcast."

He laughed. "Now that you put it that way, maybe I should be the hero."

"Well, if you want to swap out your face after you see me, I'm sure they'll take you as a volunteer."

Kyle hesitated, once again feeling like he had so much to say, but knowing she was going to cut him off before he got sentimental.

"Kyle," said Billy, her voice uneven. "I'm scared."

His voice was now barely above a whisper. "Visualize yourself in my arms, holding you tight, my lips brushing your forehead, caressing you to sleep." He thought he heard her hum, the sound comforting and sensual.

"I like it when you talk to me like that," she murmured.

"Yeah, but since I'll be eighteen Friday, I'll be an adult and you won't. I could therefore get in trouble."

"Only if we go too far," she retorted with a laugh. "But speaking of your birthday, you're going to be receiving my gift Friday." Kyle started to protest but she cut him short. "It's addressed to your mom, but it's for you and holding your drinks."

Kyle was disappointed to have his almost-intimate moment broken by the transfer pad. "Useful but less than hot."

"Like your birthday celebration," she observed.

"Yeah. I'm going to try to not get arrested, accidentally kill anyone or get fired."

"Aim high baby. Love you."

"Love you too."

Kyle replaced the burner in his coat pocket, feeling his face warm. Thankfully, Rush wasn't staring at him, but checking his own phone.

"Were you saying she's screwed figuratively?" Rush asked making it clear he had listened to the entire conversation.

"Her mother abandoned the family when Billy was three, and she is now learning the truth of why her mother left and where she is—or so Billy thinks." Kyle inhaled deeply. "It gets back to what you want: the cubes. But not that you'd care about any of that information. I take it you just want everything of the financial side? Simple theft."

Rush grinned. "It's not like it's all that simple," he said. "We have to decipher the information, get the bank accounts, the passcodes—there's some actual work to be done here."

Kyle chuckled. It was funny—and the entire situation as…horrible and about as real as you could get.

"Money is money," Rush continued, stabbing a French fry. "There will always be more to make and take and we'll get to that. On a serious note, I actually like you. You seem decent, which I can't say about the rest of the people in your town. Tell me more about the cube."

Kyle assessed him and the question. What was the worst that could happen? The government would take him, kill him and life would be over. Rush had a few questions, was a thief at best and a killer at worst. Either road could be a dead end.

As Kyle spoke, Rush leaned close, listening carefully.

"The cubes are different," Kyle began. "On the state cubes are the DNA…" Kyle held nothing back for the next twenty minutes as he disgorged all he'd learned. He and Rush had two different agendas and desired outcomes, his layered with emotional issues. "What you want are the masters, because the state cubes are simple data," Kyle concluded.

"Hey big boy!" Their conversation was interrupted by Ruth. Kyle quickly returned her hug. She leaned in, kissed his cheek and looked him over, simultaneously putting her warm palms against either cheek.

"Not too bad," she assessed, turning his face in her palms. "I do good work. You'll go right back to being the handsome specimen you were before."

Kyle cleared his throat, uncomfortable as Rush scrutinized Ruth's backside. Her figure had curves in all the right places, unlike her sister, and Rush noticed.

"Ruth, this is Philip Rush, one of my clients from out of town."

She turned her gaze to his friend. It was then that Kyle realized she was slightly off balance. She'd been drinking, but not overly so. Kyle just realized he'd never seen her out on the town.

"You sure you aren't Kyle's older brother, the hotter one with a beard—" she stopped, her eyes focusing. "Philip Rush? Oh, man. You are persona non-grata around here." Her words were disapproving, and her smile was downright malicious.

"Ruth is Ashley's sister," Kyle interjected, raising an eyebrow at Rush.

"Ah, well, I promise I didn't do—"

"Oh, don't worry about it," Ruth cut in, a lopsided smile on her face. "Ashley got herself into her own trouble with my dad. I was there and I heard it all. Dad doesn't want her dating anyone who's not a priest like Kyle here. Ashley was a rude b—well, I'd have smacked her too if it were me, so don't you worry. Kyle's moved on to better things, haven't you?"

On a whim, Kyle touched her arm. "Ruth, answer me this. If you could, would you change what you look like—your face that is?"

Ruth gave him a hard stare like he'd lost his mind. "And look like my sister? For shame little brother. A good man has to work for this kind of lovin. Wouldn't know if the love were real otherwise." Before he had a chance to respond, Ruth planted a kiss to his cheek and started to leave.

"You're not driving are you?"

She waved her hand. "Greg is already in the car. Thanks to my dad, we're now living together because where else was I going to go?" She gave them a wink and a grin.

"That was Ashley's sister?' questioned Rush after she'd gone.

Kyle nodded. "The cubes contain pictures of individuals with and without the transmutational gene. What they would look like as natural," he clarified. "The first thing I did was look at Ashley, then Ruth. Any guesses?" Rush's eyebrows furrowed. "Ruth is hot, body, mind and face. Ashley is like the ugly stepdaughter, with everything that entails."

Rush got the bartender's attention, ordering another drink.

"So not everyone will be in favor of the change." He paused to take a drink, lifting the glass in the direction of an attractive couple. "What do you think should happen?"

"I think it's only fair people have a choice," Kyle answered in an unwavering voice. "No one had the opportunity before. They should have it now."

"Government's don't operate that way, you know. They make a decision then enforce it."

Kyle felt his lips tighten in response. "Then we have to make sure that doesn't continue to happen."

A chin nod was Rush's response to the statement. "You and I aren't so different Kyle. We have diverse goals, but we don't have to kill each other to get what we both want and need to be satisfied."

"Yeah, but my files don't say *suspected in the disappearance of...*"

Rush clapped his back. "That's what you learned on the cubes?"

"And a lot more."

"Do tell." Kyle listed off every item he could remember, waiting for Rush to dispute one or all. He didn't, smirking instead.

"Ten-to-one bets your files, had they been updated, would now say the exact same thing. Tonight we'll retreat to our corners, both considering our situation. Tomorrow we'll ski."

Kyle couldn't hide his shock. "Why? I mean, it's obvious you only hired me to get to know me."

"True, but you do need the money and for the ice climbing advice it's deserved. You bettered me in skiing, which isn't easy to do and my ego chalks that up to you living in the mountains like a goat---"

"And your excuse is you were raised in the city?" Kyle bounced back.

"It's the only thing I got. But neither are the reason I want to hang with you. It's simple. I have something you don't. *This.*" Rush pulled back the ride side of his jacket, revealing two guns, one with a silencer, the other without. "My constant companions."

"But—" Kyle started, the comment cut off by Rush's severe smile.

"Not for you," he confirmed, dropping his jacket. "After what I just learned from my informant, I find myself in the ironic position of being your protector until these cubes are figured out, decoded and transferred. Until then, I can't let anything happen to you, because if it does, I'm screwed, just like you and Billy."

Kyle blinked. "You…we're working together?"

The side of Rush's lips pulled up with humor. "Think of it more as bodyguard to client."

Kyle choked on his sip of water. "I think you just gave yourself a demotion. Not sure Marcus will be too happy about that."

"Marcus would be angrier with me if I let you get killed."

So would Kyle.

CHAPTER
35

Mark placed his last of nine phone calls to the Ouray hotels and another four to Ridgeway. On the surface, they were simple civic duty conversations, checking on the visitors under auspices of those who might raise alarms as boisterous partiers.

That reminded him of his promise to get identification on that Rush guy for Brayden. Kyle was still expelled from school and would either be up at the Weisbaden or skiing.

Or ice climbing. Mark looked at the clock. It was half-past ten.

He picked up the phone and called Denver General, asking for Saachi Gupta. The restriction for callers had been lifted for him after Brayden called in a favor on Mark's behalf.

"How's my favorite small town cop?"

Mark smiled at Saachi's greeting. "I'm wondering if your words are slurry because the drugs are working as they should, or because you are woozy with affection for said cop."

Saachi emitted an uncharacteristically girly laugh, another indication she wasn't entirely lucid.

"How's the arm?" he inquired.

"I can't put it around your full waist, if that's what you're wondering." Mark snickered. The way she said it made him feel like she appreciated there was more of him to love. It had also opened the door for him to say things he otherwise might have held in had she been in a more logical state of mind.

"You're so tiny I'll wrap both around you—"

"And you can have my one good side, face and arm."

Mark's face flushed, the visual a nice one. "How is it healing?" he asked. Flirtatious banter was wonderful, but he still wanted to know her situation. "Seriously."

"I'm good. Ser-iously," she drawled, clearing her voice as though she knew he expected a legitimate answer. "My skin is crumbly, like the crust on an apple pie that doesn't stay where it should."

The image caused Mark's nose to wrinkle. "That sounds sort-of awful," he confessed.

"It *is,* but it's also normal. The skin goes from gooey to hard and crackly, if it's not kept moisturized and apparently I removed some of the gauze during the night. It dried out and now I'm crackly like a piecrust."

Mark couldn't help but laugh at her horrid description. It was so brutally honest and one hundred percent Saachi, through and through.

"I really like you Saachi."

"I know," she quipped back. "Over our conversation eating jalapeno poppers... I knew it then."

Mark laughed. "You think you could ever ditch the big city life for a slower paced venue?"

He heard her scoff. "You mean a place that's far more dangerous than the backstreet sewers we have to deal with? Not a chance."

"Oh," he responded, utterly deflated. Yeah, he was a small town cop with the subtlety and manners that go along with it.

"Marrkk," she said, her voice prescriptively paced. "You asked if I could *think* of doing that, and I said not a chance, because I don't have to think. I know."

A slow smile pressed Mark's lips flat. They'd skipped right past going out on a first date, circling the bases and sleeping together.

"Do you want me to come help out with your healing?"

The giggle returned. "No, that would be annoying. Stay there and keep those people safe. Our time will come."

"Not fast enough."

"Let's take a walk, Dad." Kyle stood at the open window, tapping his fingers.

"I'm working," responded his father without looking up.

"No. You're *walking*. Let's go."

His mother and father both raised their eyes, their expressions different. His mother was a variant of annoyed while his father had a tinge of curiosity. "One sec while I solder this in."

Kyle went for his coat and hat. The black sky was littered with stars, always an indication the temperature was in the teens.

They left out the backdoor, walking around the car port and up the alley.

"The bears are going to be insane this summer," said Kyle making small talk. Dan and Susan were smoking on their back porch and gave the two a wave as they went by.

"You become a National Park Ranger with all your spare time?" snipped his dad.

"Just saying they've been coming further down the mountain each year. You remember how close the bear scat was to the back door by July. You might as well plant huckleberry bushes and put out a sign."

They cut left, the deep trails now packed from snow shoers and cross-country skiers.

"What's this really about?"

"Things have gotten a little squirrely and I wanted you to know. I also need your advice." A cough exploded from his father's chest, the exaggerated effort annoying Kyle. "I'm serious."

"And so am I. Not once in your life have you really, sincerely asked for my advice."

"It's because this involves criminal activity, and you've been boasting of all your past escapades you can't or won't talk about. Can we start already, or are you going to keep giving me grief?"

His father shut up straight away. As they walked, Kyle first told him about Billy.

"Ty is going to freak when he sees her," said his dad, "but then again he might be so happy to have her back he won't notice or care about her facelift."

"Not lift," Kyle corrected. "New *face*. Anyway, she's ignoring me and will do what she wants. But I have other news and this is not good. You know that guy named Rush you met? He's his own brand of criminal. He wants the masters for the financial data."

His father's toe kicked a pile of ice as they walked past. "And once he has them, what then?"

Kyle glanced sideway. "In theory, I'd be alive, the cubes and the risk to me gone."

"Hardly. Billy wants the masters for leverage, a safeguard against people who would harm her, the rest of the Naturalists and their efforts. Rush wants the masters for financial gain, pure and simple."

"But once I transfer the data off the individual cubes and given Rush the masters, I've lost my only leverage."

The snow crunched louder as they walked. "Rush will only be incentivized to kill you if he feels you are a threat and will at some point expose him. He knows better than most how torture can extract information from even the most reluctant witnesses. Truth be told," his father continued, "American forces are seriously wimps when it comes to torture. The Russians and Chinese do it really well."

Kyle admitted he hadn't spent a lot of time considering Rush ending his life if Kyle turned over the cubes. Rush seemed so…gentlemanly about it, if that phrase applied, like he respected Kyle enough to take what he wanted and leave him alone afterward.

"I don't think he's worried I'll expose him."

"You *think*," emphasized his father. "You don't know. Criminals are brilliant," he said with obvious respect. "They know how to do things the rest of us can only read about in fiction."

Kyle considered what his father wasn't saying. "Let me see if I can interpret your comments. You aren't morally opposed with me giving Rush the cubes or him extracting a few billion here and there—"

"Nope," affirmed his dad. "The country has trillions in the accounts. It won't even be noticed."

"But you are worried I'll be a corpse when it's over."

"Which you may be anyway, regardless of who ends up with the cubes: the Naturalists, the US government or Rush. What's more," his father continued. "You wonder why it's only him who's here? From the moment you told me about the cubes, I've been waiting for this town to be swarmed with locusts, all vying for the chance to get the data first."

Kyle had wondered this himself. Rush had implied Billy wasn't real good at covering her tracks.

"Oh man," Kyle said aloud.

"Exactly. But look on the bright side kid. Maybe Rush is so feared in the criminal underworld that the rest of his ilk are waiting in the wings to see if he makes it out alive. If he doesn't, they swoop in like vultures. And if he lives…"

"He can sell the information to the highest bidder," Kyle finished. "I bet wealthy people would be happy to pay a lot of money to keep their data secret."

"Eh, but why? That's messy and gets cops, FBI and God-and-country involved. Simply stealing is so much easier."

"Geesh dad," hissed Kyle, bumping him with his shoulder. "You're so callously pragmatic about these things."

"And you're acting like this is devirginizing your pure ears," his father teased. "For decades your mom and I have been saying the government is more corrupt than the citizens it's supposed to protect. Now we have proof it was all true."

Kyle grunted. "So that justifies me working with a bad guy?"

"Bad how?" his father countered. "You said you saw what they had on Rush for yourself. He's been accused of a lot of things, convicted of none."

"Which means what? He's innocent?"

"Or so smart they can't catch him. I think the latter."

They walked the next block in silence; Kyle trying to get his head around what he instinctively felt was his only recourse. It wasn't like he was going to call up Brayden and tell him that he already had an organization at his side, offering an alliance.

"You alright?" his father asked midblock.

"I had a crazy thought," Kyle admitted.

"Hit me. We've haven't talked our entire lives like we've done in the last week."

"What if I told Brayden the secret's out and Rush is here?"

His father didn't immediately respond.

"What do you think the man is going to do?" his father asked. "Arrest him? For what? The guy has done nothing wrong. *You* are the criminal in possession of the cubes, and as much as Brayden saved your ass before, he's under no obligation to do it again. Taking it further, Rush won't actually be guilty of a crime until he takes possession of the cubes, but even then, the government would have to prove he took something he knew was already stolen. Also hard to prove. Rush is guilty of nothing until he crosses the line and actually starts stealing."

Kyle inwardly moaned at the situation. "You are awfully smart for a law abiding citizen."

"I told you I have done many things that I'm not going to talk about."

"Maybe I should go back and look at your profile on the cubes," Kyle threatened.

"Maybe you shouldn't," retorted his father. "Still, you get what I'm saying."

"Yep. Loud and clear. I'm done for."

"Pretty much. And you're on your own until you get the data to Billy and figure out how to manage Rush."

They crossed off the path, walking down the empty street, directly across from Box Canyon. The lights were shining on the ice, the shades creating iridescent greys and blues.

"You think I should trust him?" asked Kyle, wanting assurance.

"What does your gut tell you?"

"That I can," he said without hesitation.

"Then what're you asking me for?" his father demanded with annoyance.

"Because I'm second guessing myself. Maybe you can see something I can't."

His father stopped dead in his tracks and turned. "Well I'll be damned right here and now. I never thought this day would come."

Kyle wanted to laugh. His adopted father, who'd been an active part of his life from the time he was five, treated him like his own and had never displayed an ounce of undue emotion, now he was the rock that Kyle never knew he had.

"If anything happens, you're going to be okay, won't you?" Kyle asked.

His father's lips moved slightly, giving Kyle the distinct impression he was holding back strong emotions.

"We are going to be just fine and will take care of you no matter what." Then his father smirked. "Your mother may go straight to heaven when she eventually learns all she's ever believed was a conspiracy theory is truth. Heck, the town may implode as well."

Kyle didn't say a word. He just put his arms around his dad and gave him a hug, their first full-bodied embrace ever.

"I love you dad. Thanks."

"You're welcome. Now get off me before people think we are having an unlawful moment in the street."

Kyle gave him one last squeeze, happy and oddly at peace. He'd told the truth, all of it. If Kyle were going to die or end up in a compromised position, his father supported his path, and that was all he needed.

CHAPTER
36

Billy was up at five Thursday morning, realizing this was the last full day she was going to wear her face. She'd never been vain about her appearance, knowing that her body was strong and lean, and her brand of pretty wasn't typical. But it was *unique*, especially to the only person who mattered.

As she showered, she debated calling Kyle, and managed to wait until a quarter till eight to phone him.

"Don't say it," he preempted. "I'm Kyle, not cube master."

She laughed, grateful for the sassy tone full of affection. That was exactly what she wanted to hear to start her day.

"Kyle just sounds weird," she said with a smile, "you know what I'm saying?"

"I do. Are you checking to see if I learned anything new or do you want some reassurance without admitting that you, the strongest person alive, actually need it?"

"All of the above." Her initial happiness faded as she confided that yes, she just wanted to speak with him once more before her surgery.

"I'm going to be confined to a bed after this, hooked up to IVs around the clock. I have my music and a few books, the television has cable so I'm going to get my fill of shows I wouldn't deign to watch before now."

"And afterward?" he prompted. "Will you return to Ouray and graduate from school?"

"Oh, ye of little knowledge. I had enough credits last semester to graduate because of all the college courses I've taken—"

"What?" he exclaimed. "You aren't serious."

"Very much so. That's why it wasn't all that big of a deal to leave when I did, at least from an academic perspective." They spoke of the Native American scholarships available to her and she asked the obvious question. "And what about school for you?

"Still expelled until tomorrow. But going back to our college efforts or lack thereof. Since you are a proficient hacker, what would stop you from getting other scholarships granted and entire transcripts wiped clean?"

Billy caught herself on a laugh. "My turn to ask if you're serious."

"As much as you were about me siphoning off some money. I mean, where does the line of integrity and morality begin or end?" he wanted to know. "When it's convenient?"

"How about when we get back what was due us in the first place?" Kyle didn't immediately respond, and she took a breath. "Doing that kind of thing has been an option for me since about tenth grade," she said with no false modesty. "But I really do like to go to school and learn about different subjects. I enjoy getting A's on the tests for the competitive pleasure of it. Cheating didn't occur to me because I haven't needed to, but even then," she paused, thinking, "I wouldn't. Me and dishonesty don't go on dates together."

"And now you're seeing things differently?"

"I'm seeing things for how they really are," she answered, "and I don't like it. I want change, but I have this part inside me that wants to get even as well." She paused for a moment. "Something is odd, talking about school when we've already determined our lives afterward are sort of shot. Is there something you aren't telling me?"

She heard him sigh. "A few things, yeah."

"Well, I'll make a few assumptive statements, and you can confirm as you see fit, sound good?"

Kyle laughed, the sound filled with a bit of relief. "Things are going on with people you can't talk about," she began.

"What--??" he exclaimed.

Billy smiled to herself. "And you are being forced to make decisions that might compromise data on the cubes. Is that right?"

"Okay, Billy. Do you have cameras placed around my house as well as your own?"

"No," she said smugly. "But I am a realist. Anyone with half a brain was going to track you down. Maybe even someone from inside the government who is a greedy turncoat and wants the cubes for themselves, have you thought of that? There are literally legions of people who will look the other way if it doesn't directly hurt someone."

"Do you think that's entirely wrong?" he asked, feeling the hard edges of his morality going soft.

"I'm not going to make a judgement call on whether it's bad or good, right or wrong. It's not my immediate problem, and likely as not, won't be yours either."

"I'm just a pawn," he said factually.

"Pretty much. Are you still going to transfer the data?"

"Billy!" he hissed, sounding offended.

"Okay, fine. But if you happen to slip off some data that helps others along the way, or keeps you and me alive, what's the harm?"

A pause followed his response. "Sheesh Billy. You sound almost identical to my dad."

It was her turn to hesitate. "You told him about all of this?"

"Yes. I just couldn't take it anymore and honestly, I needed some perspective. Believe you me, dad has a lot. I had no idea of his past and I don't want to dig for more."

"We all have something crummy in our backgrounds," she said with a tinge of bitterness. "Well, except you. You're all in the present. Kyle, I just looked at the time. I have to hustle to the medical center."

"Will you have the burner with you?"

"Yes, and will probably be stressed out and bored in equal parts. I'll look forward to hearing your voice."

"Me, too."

Billy hung up, sitting on the edge of her bed until she couldn't delay it any longer. She assembled her few personal items and took a look around. It would be the last time she'd see this room and her things with the face she was born with.

Gary assessed the notes from the NSA and CIA. The kid in Ouray wasn't even an object of consideration right now, at least not for finding the cubes. The Internet chatter bubbled with talk of their existence, the source in a remote mountain town, the connection between the Naturalists and the government confirmed. Brayden's first alert of word on the darknet was like a giant wave hitting the shores of Waimea Bay.

He called Pete.

"We've got known points of contact between the North Koreans and their Asian sources on the mainland," Pete elaborated. "The Latin American cartels have aligned with the brutal faction of Hungarians and Ukrainians on the east coast, and it's coming west."

Gary understood the implications. "Any teeth to Janet's theory that the cubes were going to be taken overseas?"

"We've seen no evidence supporting that theory, which I believe was flawed from the beginning. It only made sense for the items holding the financial data. I'll send you the analysis now, but there are no patterns for attaining the target, only a hypothesis."

"They know someone's out there, but not who, not yet anyway."

"So it seems. Sending you the analysis now." Gary held his finger stiff, waiting for the materials. He scanned everything and then said, "Sunsetmoon wasn't real smart in his communication, was he?"

"Nope, and it's no wonder someone picked up on it last week. Perhaps we should all be thankful it took another week for the rest of the world to catch on."

Gary sent a note to Brayden, receiving a status update in seconds.

On track isn't good enough, Gary typed. Seconds after pushing the button, Brayden was on the phone.

"Thirty days was always a pipe dream," he stated. "But throwing more bodies on the project won't increase the speed of completion," Brayden said.

"The NSA wants the head of the snake, not the tail."

"Kyle's on his own," Brayden confirmed.

"Unfortunately. He made the choice to do someone else's dirty work and will pay the price. With luck, if he is tracked down, he'll expose his lack of knowledge before too much pain is inflicted."

Gary encouraged Brayden to get back to task.

"I'll see what we can do to collapse the schedule further," promised Brayden.

Gary thanked him and hung up, then called Pete back. He wanted the CIA's perspective on Kyle, verifying that protecting him wasn't the best use of manpower.

"A teenager in a town five hours from the nearest city isn't a strong motivation for an organized crime syndicate," Pete said. "It would be much easier to wait until they see movement on the darknet than to act presumptively."

Gary disagreed, thinking a five-hour drive was a small investment for a huge financial payout. "The Hungarians are especially brutal," he remarked, already pulling up Kyle's picture again. They'd force him to talk.

"Then he won't stand a chance," predicted Pete. "Let the situation with the kid go. The best of your mobile SWAT teams will be needed for the ground wars that will inevitably break out."

Gary looked at the image on his screen. The kid's eyes, intense and competitive. His lack of fat a sure sign of an athlete. His hair, short on the sides and long on top, trendy yet conservative. Any junior profiler at the academy could tell you someone who cared about their physical appearance on the outside wasn't going to hurt it from the inside. Probably clean of drugs and alcohol.

Pete, never having been at Quantico, wouldn't know that whoever had put Kyle up to the challenge of getting the cubes had relied upon one thing: the element of trust and morality. Kyle would be counted on to turn them over to the right people who could take them forward.

The FBI profiler in Gary kept going with that line of thought. What if Kyle had changed his mind and decided to keep the cubes to himself?

The pencil stopped twirling as Gary rotated his chair to the window, looking down at snow-covered ground. While he'd accepted Smith's ability to pass the polygraph and the injections, they were two different levels of sophistication. One could be foiled through caffeine pills; any junior pharmacist or avid watcher of Forensics Files knew that. But getting past the chemicals by the NSA? That took help. *Real* help from blocking chemicals.

Only a limited few people in the medical and intelligence community even knew what kind of blocking agents to acquire. Then the person on the receiving end had to inject them, also at the right time.

Gary took a deep breath of reality. Going backwards up the food chain, there was only one person who was with Kyle before the polygraph, and that person had the ability to give him the blocking agents which had to be provided by a member of the medical community. That person was his very own special agent Brayden Cox.

The timing aligned and the motivation as clear as if Janet was repeating her earlier words. Brayden could have been acting out of sympathy for his own son's suicide, the desire to keep a normal kid put in a compromised situation rational. Not even Gary wanted the kid strung up, beat up or killed to get the cubes.

But ultimately, Pete was right. He was just one kid in an inconsequential town of five hundred. What was the FBI going to do? Send in a force of twenty to protect the high schooler from every criminal in the country?

But Brayden...Gary instinctively knew all that he'd strung together was accurate. Janet had tried to tell him as much but Gary didn't hear it. *Didn't want to hear it.*

He turned back to his desk, thinking that whatever Kyle Smith did from this point forward was on him.

CHAPTER 37

Danny was living on Red Bull and Mountain Dew, copious amounts of caffeine pills and smokes, he and his team successfully writing in three days what would take salaried developers three weeks. He read Brayden's latest email.

Danny knew all that Brayden wasn't telling him; the darknet was alive with the chatter of the cubes and the data suspected of being on them. Danny had predicted that Sunsetmoon was going to make mistakes and she had. Danny's only advantage was that he'd seen it a week before everyone else. Now the FBI and NSA knew.

It only took one determined black-hatter to make the connection between Sunsetmoon and Ouray, then Kyle...

He switched screens, sending a note to Rush.

And then what? Danny wondered. Rush was working against a timeline of Danny's own making.

He's got to finish his job before I complete mine, Danny thought, the irony of the situation as great as the good and evil cat and mouse game he and Rush played on a daily basis.

But this will be the one and only time Danny hoped Rush would in fact beat him to the finish line.

Thursday morning at the ski mountain meant near-empty lines, skiing right up to the lift and loading without a wait. Kyle and Rush hit moguls and after lunch they had an impromptu race, a challenge Kyle had won. Where Rush caught up was in mid-mountain. They crossed over to the free style area, and Kyle showed off his aerial skills. He came off the first jump, doing a backscratcher, the second jump high enough for an easy 360. But no amount of tucking in pole position was going to catch up with Rush, who hadn't bothered with more than a daffy when he'd hit his own jump, the skis landing straight and his heavier weight easily carrying him in front of Kyle.

Late afternoon, they had just loaded on the chair lift when Rush's phone buzzed. He slid his poles under his outside leg, removed a glove and checked his phone. He cursed, the guttural word low and fierce.

"You want to know what that text was about?" Rush asked.

"Not if you're going to have to kill me afterward."

A bark of laughter rang down the mountain. "I don't relish physically damaging people the way Marcus does. Hurt reputations and lost money are far more impactful than a broken bone which eventually heals."

"So what's up now?"

"We are running out of time," Rush answered directly. "You tell me what you need. A million. Ten million. Won't matter. Four business entities alone control about three trillion in assets. We are literally talking billions—hundreds of billions taken without materially hurting the economy. For you, I'll set up an overseas account under a corporate name, and it will be shielded within a Foundation with you listed as the trustee. All legit and clean. One day and you're done."

"Then what?"

Rush lifted his skis up, clicking the ends together. Clumps of snow dropped on either side, falling silently to the ground.

"I transfer a token amount, ten percent say, then verify the data is solid and accurate. If it is, you get the rest. If not, call it non-refundable earnest money. You keep it regardless."

Kyle glanced at him. Even through Rush's goggles, Kyle could see his eyes were clear and bright.

"Why would you do that?"

"It's only reasonable," Rush said with a shrug. "You didn't place the data on those cubes, and if all this is for nothing, and the information isn't legit, I've spent a week of my life with great skiing, and you're a few million richer."

Kyle chewed on the inside of his cheek. "Other than taking money, what do you plan on doing with the information?"

"Unsure, actually. But from what you've explained, it's the motherload." Extortion came to Kyle's mind, the dirty details of every single person in the country.

"You go after all the people you hate and make their lives miserable?"

Rush's lips curled. "The notion had occurred to me."

The eight-foot drop below them was soon covered with the protective netting, designed to catch overzealous disembarking skiers.

"Kyle, I'm not sure how much longer I'm going to wait to get these things."

"What sped up your timeline?"

Rush turned his head, looking him straight in the eye. "Rivals."

The hollow sensation in his chest wasn't fabricated. Kyle had the sense that not all people searching for the cubes were going to be as...civil as Rush.

"Look, I'd give them to you now just to be rid of them, but the transfer pad arrives tomorrow. I can't do anything without that first."

"I could take them all and do the work for you," Rush offered.

"Very gracious, but no." The chair started vibrating as they reached the turnstile. As they lifted off, Kyle gestured for them to turn to the right down the double black diamond. Rush slowed to a stop.

"I'll make you a deal," started Rush. "I win, you give me the financial cubes tonight. You lose, you get another twenty four hours."

Kyle's adrenaline shot up the back of his legs. "Plus a grand," he boldly proposed. If he lost the cubes, a thousand wasn't going to begin to cover the guilt he was going to feel about forfeiting the cubes and lying to Billy, if that was even possible.

Rush smiled in predetermined victory. "Deal."

They both shoved off, launching themselves down the steeply fierce run. This wasn't the race of Kyle's life. It was for the lives of millions of others as well.

CHAPTER 38

Brayden thanked the waitress, barely able to appreciate the smell of the homemade garlic bread and clam linguine. Laura's salmon Caesar would be soggy if she didn't arrive in ten.

Impatient, he checked his phone, finding an update from Danny, nothing from his wife. He read the content, as satisfied as he could be. Another twenty-four hours had worked software miracles, but would it be enough?

The door opened and through it walked Laura. She saw him, and came over immediately, kissing his cheek. Instead of sitting across from him, she took the seat next to him.

"I only have a half an hour," she said breathlessly. He slid the salad in front of her, encouraging her to eat. He leaned closer into her ear. "I have the micro table blocker on," he said in a whisper. "It will be our exercise in a romantic lunch time conversation."

Laura spoke in a low tone. "Dr. Pike reconfirmed Billy and the others are in for surgery tomorrow," she revealed. He raised his eyebrows, but kept his gaze focus on his food. "The teams around the country are awaiting the results, in place and ready to start additional surgeries if successful."

Brayden felt full with satisfaction which had nothing to do with the food. Three centers running full time. He envisioned dozens of facial transplants within a week. A hundred in a month.

"What about the rest of the DNA?" he asked.

Laura took a bite. "Friday we should have everything for everyone in the country."

He pressed her left leg, feeling an electrical current move between them as though every step of progress forward was that much closer to a reunion with their daughter.

"If I can find some reason to visit the center in Coeur d' Alene after I'm settled in, I will."

He gave her an inquisitive gaze. With their daughter, Sasha, presumably at one of the reservations near Coeur d'Alene, it was only an hour away from her new hospital.

"How are you going to be able stay away?"

Laura's lips curled, the pensive look that evolved into one of determination.

"I'm going to exercise a lot of patience and wisdom," she quietly replied. "To have come this far...I'm not going to risk anything."

He gave her a soft kiss to her cheek. "I love you."

They discussed how they were going to stay in touch, her worries allayed when he described the communication blocking devices he'd already installed in her car. "And this," he said, reaching within his coat pocket. She took the two phones, not even asking. It had been years since they first talked about all the ways to get around the constrictive government protocols for communicating, but not since their son's suicide had they had a reason to use them.

"And you? When do you think you'll be able to visit?"

"Not until this immediate deadline is over." Laura didn't know the details of the masters, only that the information was separate from her work on the identity cubes. "We were targeting thirty days, but reality is if this isn't buttoned up in the next few weeks, I'm afraid it will be all over."

Brayden told her about the financial exposure for the country, and themselves. He felt her warm hand on his right thigh.

"We are going to be fine, no matter what happens."

Brayden nodded, appreciating the sentiment, but knew that as a pragmatist, their emotional health had nothing to do with the possible financial hit that might be coming. But she was a strong woman, who had held a secret for fourteen years, defying all he stood for, the government and even her own physician code of ethics for the good of their family.

Now it was his turn.

Mark thanked Ed for the information and returned to his patrol car. Kyle was skiing in Telluride. Ed said it was with that guy Rush. Mark would just have to wait to talk to Kyle.

Bored, he grabbed a sandwich, watching the steadily increasing traffic through town. Sean had put out the word that the ice park would be open to locals tomorrow, but Mark could see others were hoping to sneak in on the action. License plates from Denver were on every fifth car, not unheard of but unusual this early in the season.

He caught a glance at the occupants: long-haired or short, bearded and not, they looked a little on the rough side. Typical outdoorsy ice climbers, certainly not government employees.

Reaching Box Canyon and seeing it empty, he went up to the ice walls. Sean was there with three volunteer fire fighters. Sean directed the areas and angles and the three held and sprayed. Only the industrial tube of water could get enough layers of ice in time for an early opening.

"You took out the big guns, huh?" Mark asked, coming beside the city manager.

"We had some avid climbers who are itching to get up here," Sean explained, not taking his eyes off the spray. "They made a few comments to the city council and here we are."

"You catch their names?"

"Nope."

"Accents?"

"Yep."

Mark could only guess who the guys were. Rush and his crew were probably spreading around money at the local stores to make his point.

Mark watched in silence as the spray shot up fifty feet in one area, seventy-five in another where the climb was steeper.

"You ever have the hankering to climb up here?" asked Sean, his head directed to the sheet of ice.

Mark snorted. "Not on my life. And I've never seen you up there either."

"The best view is from the ground in my opinion." Clapping him on the back, Mark asked him to keep an eye out for anyone who struck him as odd.

"It's the younger generation with mullets and perms," Sean retorted. "They're all odd."

Mark had nothing else to do but go back to the station and wait.

CHAPTER 39

With keeping the cubes another twenty-four hours as his motivation, Kyle had pushed himself to the edge of crazy to make it down the mountain first. He and Rush were tip to tip as they'd neared the bottom of the run, Kyle tucked tightly has he knew how, keeping his knees fluid over the bumps, crushing out every space of air that could have slowed him down.

It was enough. When he finally stood, his thighs burned, the lactic acid build up requiring him to shake out his legs, barely holding off a major hamstring spasm.

"You've been letting me off easy," Kyle stated. "But I have my grand plus another twenty-four hours."

Rush lifted his goggles, his chest heaving with effort. Rush had tried and lost, and he was not entirely happy about it.

By the car, the first thing Rush did was check his phone. He put it to his ear, his face hard. "How long ago?" he asked.

Kyle removed his jacket, changing out of boots as quickly and quietly as he could. "Keep me updated," Rush requested.

Once on the road, Kyle couldn't help himself. "Anything to do with us?"

The muscles under Rush's cheek tightened as he turned on the music. "My sixth sense tells me it is. Raze and Alexie were ambushed. Marcus got caught in the firing line."

Kyle new nothing about city violence, gangs or random. "What now?"

"Marcus is already on the road back to Ouray."

Kyle watched the lights of the approaching car come and go. "Is that smart?"

Rush's eyes lowered, thin view of his grey eyes scary. "He doesn't have a choice. I need him here."

"I think what you just said is that this is about the cubes, and your guys got shot up because somebody thinks you have them."

"Or we are going to get them first."

Rush accelerated, moving in and out of traffic. "The State Patrol officers aren't as congenial as Mark, the deputy who looked at your identification."

Rush slowed to five miles an hour above the speed limit.

"Kyle, we'd be naïve to think others aren't going to want in on this opportunity. Now we all have to be ready, because we don't leave without those cubes."

Ergo, they weren't leaving without Kyle.

A beat started blasting out of the speakers, and Rush turned it up louder.

"This song is ironically appropriate," said Rush, his head moving. The deep base was augmented with an electronic melody. Kyle recognized it from a movie but couldn't recall the name.

"It's called Battle Without Honor or Humanity," Rush informed him. "The artist is Japanese and carries his guitar like a samurai sword. The movie was Kill Bill Volume 1, where the female Yakuza leader gets her ass whipped by a white girl played by a very pissed off Uma Thurman."

"And this song is appropriate because for us, there's no honor or humanity in battle?" Kyle suggested.

"Among us amoral black hats who'll do just about anything for money? Nope."

And myself? thought Kyle. There wasn't going to be much honor for himself or dignity for his parents if he ended up in jail.

Thirty minutes later, Kyle walked straight through the front door, stopping in front of the open window.

"Dad. Now."

His mother couldn't even get a smart retort, her eyes wide and mouth open as his father followed him into the bedroom.

Kyle turned on the music loud enough so the next door neighbors could have sung along.

"You and mom have to leave town. Today."

"I'm not going anywhere," his dad protested.

"Dad, you don't understand. People like Rush are going to be coming after me. I can't have you stay here and risk your lives."

"Then give Rush what he wants. He seems willing to pay you a pirate's bounty for the cubes." As Kyle debated the insanity of his father's words, for a minute he thought about walking up the Weisbaden and doing just that.

"I can't Dad. Billy sent me the coaster for the file transfer. It's doesn't arrive until tomorrow. Nothing can happen until that occurs."

His father scrunched his mouth to the side, the look unattractive. "That *is* a problem."

Kyle sighed. "You think? Dad, I have to stay here, but you don't. Go visit Aunt Ernie in Mississippi or head to the beaches of Florida for a few weeks. You do vacationing really well."

"Not when we have clients and projects pending, we don't."

Kyle groaned with exasperation, running his fingers through his hair. "Are you kidding me?" he hissed. "Do you even comprehend what I'm saying? His guys are Russian bodyguards and they got shot up, all because other criminals from the underworld think Rush has what's in my possession."

"Another reason for you to give them up," he continued, toning it down. "Besides, Rush is assuming they are going to come straight here and that's a stretch. Honestly, I'd be more worried about you giving Rush those masters. He could raise holy hell, extorting good, innocent people like me for the remainder of their lives."

Kyle cocked an eyebrow. "You mean *not-so-innocent* people like you. Look, if I could somehow block out the information, I would."

"That's a great idea," his dad said, jumping on it. "Kyle, even the most basic of things have a locking mechanism. Remember those ancient floppy disks from decades ago, then the hard, smaller ones. Then we had CDs then the itty, bitty smart cards you use? They all had a way to lock the data, either by a passcode or by a press of a button. The genius who created these things had to think of that. You better get your head in the game and figure that out."

Kyle reluctantly agreed, his focus still on getting his parents out of town, an argument he continued.

"I said no," stated his father, ending the conversation by leaving the room. "And turn that crap down!" he yelled.

Kyle spent a few moments on his bed trying to slow his heart rate. He couldn't call the one person who'd understand the situation: Billy. She didn't even know about Rush and the danger he represented. On the evening before her life-changing surgery, this was not what she needed.

He thought about calling Mark, but what was he going to do? He couldn't arrest new visitors for being in town, and Rush admitted he didn't know what these guys looked like; all these people worked behind the dark veil of anonymity.

No, he and Mark were in the same boat. They were going to have to wait until something happened.

"I'm going out for dinner," Kyle informed his parents when he returned to the living room.

"You have school tomorrow," said his mother, looking over her glasses.

"I do," he agreed, heading to the front door.

"Hold on now," she said, stopping him with her tone. He stood in front of the front window. "Your ATV," she said. "Mark said he *found it* in an abandoned building."

Kyle caught her emphasis on the words found it, but let it slide. "Yeah, and whoever took it scratched it up. Don't go look, it will just make you mad," he said.

He saw his mother's shoulders go stiff, the lines around her lips going deep.

"I'm already mad. No," she said roughly. "Your father told me some of what's happened. What's next, Kyle?"

He glanced at his father, who remained quiet. "Apparently, you two are going to stay put, I'm going to continue on with life and at some point, we'll all go back to our boring selves. How about that?"

His mother scowled, leaving Kyle to brace for a stream of obscenities. "I'm getting real tired of you lying to me."

"Then don't make me by asking questions you know I can't answer."

They stared at each other, the mother-son glare of obstinacy in full force.

"Get going," she grumbled.

Kyle bit his upper lip. "I love you mom, and I'm sorry. Again."

"I know."

Billy pulled the second blanket closer to her chest, watching the quiet interaction between Dr. Pike, Charlotte and another technician. They'd checked her in early afternoon, the preparation work the same as any other medical facility. Her height, weight and blood pressure were taken, then she'd changed into a gown and assigned her own room. Armed with books and a flatscreen television, she'd been given the first series of anti-rejection drugs.

Billy was careful not to pull out the IV in her left arm as she adjusted the blanket. It wasn't the temperature of the room which made her cold, it was the circumstances. She would have preferred checking in at five the morning of the surgery and go straight under, but that was never going to happen. This wasn't just about anti-rejection drugs: it was about using her, Joe and Uncle Ray as a teaching opportunity for all the other surgeons who'd be involved in facial operations.

A staff member wheeled in a portable screen, setting up and testing the connection. "Just a minute now," he said to her. Billy watched him silently. He used his phone to operate the screen. First one window appeared in the upper right corner, then another just below it.

"Dr. Pike, we're ready." The physician turned and nodded, coming to Billy's side. "It's on mute for now," said the technician, who then moved aside.

"Billy," Dr. Pike said, "as I'd mentioned earlier, this is the final conversation we're going to have before the surgery tomorrow. Ask if you have questions," he encouraged.

Dr. Pike used the remote control to turn on the sound. Immediately, Billy heard voices she recognized; her Uncle Roy and Joe. Screens were adjusted, and the upper right box was filled with Joe, the lower with her Roy. Each were in hospital gowns identical to what she wore. A woman and two men were beside them, presumably members of their respective surgical teams.

"I'd like to begin by thanking each one of you…" Billy listened and nodded, as Dr. Pike expressed his appreciation for their willingness, bravery and self-sacrifice. He couldn't promise it was going to turn out perfectly, but the effort by all would be worth it.

"Now let's go over the practical items," he continued, changing his tone. "You've all been given the anti-rejection drugs, Joe having a bit more, since unlike Billy and Roy, he has the transmutational gene. Whereas Roy and Billy have the autologous cells, meaning they came from the person they are going back to, Joe is the reverse. His mutated cells may reject his natural cell structure. That said, each one of you could experience the exact same post-operative side effects. I'm going to list them once again."

Billy had heard this twice now, the simplified version from her uncle, the detailed one from Dr. Pike. "…the main reason for the length of the surgery is we are trying to reattach the blood vessels. That's the lifeline for a successful face transplant. As far as nerve regeneration is concerned, it's vital, but the data from the cubes provided us critical information that was previously missing in the world of medical science," he continued. "Look to your screen and you will see what I mean."

A three-dimensional image appeared which Billy immediately recognized as her facial structure. Chin and jaw, cheekbone and forehead. On top of this, a single piece of skin was overlaid.

"Now these connection points are the nerves." Hundreds of red dots appeared on and around the face. "These are the nerve endings, unique to your own DNA. They send the signals back and forth to the brain; lift your eyebrow, twitch your cheek—whatever muscle movement you want to take place, the nerve endings make it happen. And they are only moving because the nerves are telling the muscle to move. The dead nerve would make it look like it was paralyzed." Billy thought of his previous comments about the watering hose to the grass that was the face.

"That being said," he paused, "there are always new advances in those areas. The CAD drawings show where the blood vessels are to attach, and where the nerves are. The biggest thing we don't know and can't verify—and I want to be very clear on this—is if what's provided on the cubes is accurate. We have made the assumption it is, but to be sure, we have the full surgical staff required for three days of activity instead of using the optimist's view of a twelve-hour operation."

"It's a roadmap to my face." It was Joe who had made the comment.

"That's correct," affirmed Dr. Pike, "and we hope it's precise, but we must be pragmatic. We might encounter bumps along that map, or some of the nerve endings could be damaged during surgery. If a nerve doesn't reconnect, you might end up with a section of your face that doesn't respond, and while nerves have been known to work around what we call a dead spot."

"Say that again, doc?" asked Joe, who squirmed a little in his bed.

Dr. Pike nodded with patience. "Your nerves are made of neurons, which means they *do* regenerate," he emphasized. "However, despite the body's best intentions, not all do, for reasons we don't fully understand. We can take two perfectly healthy nerves, reattach them, and they won't work. Nonetheless, the body is pretty incredible. As I just mentioned, if a nerve is damaged, it can reroute itself around the damaged area—it just takes time."

Billy thought about the worst case. A part or all of her face wouldn't move. She'd be a walking Frankenstein albeit with pretty, wrinkle free skin.

She listened as Dr. Pike introduced the members of his surgical team. Roy's operation would be happening simultaneously, and in the same building as Billy. Joe's team up in Coeur d'Alene was headed by a female surgeon.

Each theatre would have a total of three surgeons, along with two anesthesiologists, and a full surgical technical team to handle every aspect of an operating room. Joe was insatiably curious, asking about the roles and tasks of each person in the room. Billy thought Dr. Pike was more than patient as he willingly identified all the tasks, from suctioning the blood to handlined sutures. Dr. Pike finished the call by talking about the skin glue used for the top epidermal layer. This would cover the internal sutures put in place by the attending plastic surgeon.

"No stitches," said Joe, who seemed positively enthusiastic about the operation.

Unlike me, thought Billy. She'd gone from a willingness to being involved in a history-making achievement to the hesitation of one realizing she didn't have it so bad. Her face was pretty, it was without a major blemish or flaw, and worked as it should.

What if her nerves didn't reconnect after the recovery? Yet it was too late to go back. The physicians desperately needed her now, to show others the surgery could be done; that the three-dimensional CAD drawing of the nerves would in fact reduce the operating time from three days to one. If the doctors didn't have at least three as their first sample set, how many others would sign up? Not many, was her guess.

Dr. Pike had stopped talking, giving the floor to the other surgeons. Joe had a few more quippy remarks about his forthcoming look. Billy smiled. The middle-aged man was overweight, his weather-worn face lined with vertical creases, sun spots and one scar she could see on the high-definition screen. He was going to be completely unrecognizable after the surgery.

Perhaps that why he's doing this. His life might be better in every respect; self-esteem, luck with the ladies.

But changing his rough exterior wasn't going to soften his interior. And for Joe, Billy hoped it wouldn't. She liked his craggly personality. It was what made Joe *Joe*. She hoped that no amount of predictive analysis or new skin would change that.

CHAPTER 40

"I bought you a day, no more than two." The man's voice came through loudly over the speaker. It wasn't Marcus or Rush's other associates. This guy sounded straight up American.

"Tell me," Rush requested.

"I tapped into NSA security. They are setting check points at the state lines and drones are flying. I've already inputted the license plates and descriptions Marcus gave me for the top suspects coming out of Denver."

"My competition," Rush mouthed to him. "Good job and thanks."

"What about your side? Any progress on the cubes?" the man asked. "Tell me something I want to hear."

Rush looked at Kyle. "You want to say anything to Danny?"

"I'm receiving a transfer pad tomorrow," Kyle began. "But that's only used to send the data on the identity cubes, and that's not what Rush wants. The Naturalist I was with couldn't get anything off the masters themselves before, so all I can do is try."

"Not promising," intoned Danny. "Rush?"

After a moment, Rush said, "We give him the chance." The audible sigh on the other end wasn't an enthusiastic endorsement and the line went dead.

"What can I do for you?" Rush asked him. "I may have some technical skills that might prove useful."

The statement got a slight laugh from Kyle. "I'll need a laptop that can't be traced for the transfer."

"That's easy," Rush told him. "My house, my computer."

Kyle watched the overhead lights flick on his face as they passed the intermittent poles. "Why haven't you just demanded the cubes or threaten me and leave?"

Rush laughed. "You'd resist, I'd have to torture you, your parents would be devastated and I'd feel guilty for the rest of my life. I can tell you are their entire world. Even if that didn't bother me in the slightest, as brilliant as I like to think I am, there may be something you have uncovered that I won't or can't."

Kyle felt the sick relief that came with knowing Rush's word carried the truth.

"You have one clear advantage over me," Rush continued turning serious. "You don't operate like a developer, a breed who are always trying to outsmart and outthink everyone, sometimes making a mess of things."

"You believe simple is better?" Kyle suggested.

"Sometimes it is. You don't always need to bring a gun to a knife fight."

When they reached the intersection of Ridgeway, Kyle expected Rush to turn left, heading to True Grit. Instead, they continued straight.

"We are going to Montrose," Rush informed him. "It's been noticed how we look alike. We're going to take that a step further."

"Seriously? How?"

"You'll see."

Two hours later, it was Rush who had been transformed, not Kyle. Rush's hair had been cut to the shorter, trendier look sported by Kyle, the front sections blonder, mirroring Kyle. Next the barber expertly shaved off Rush's facial hair. Only then did it dawn on Kyle what Rush was attempting to do.

"You think they are going to go after you?" Kyle asked with concern.

"I *hope* they come after me," Rush responded with emphasis. "It may be the only way you and I make it out of here alive, with or without those cubes."

At the Mexican restaurant, Kyle ignored the twenty-something hostess who hit on both of them. Only Rush played it up.

Over tacos and queso, Kyle did his best to listen with interest as Rush talked about his family still in London and divulged what he meant when he'd referred to broken reputations.

"Put my old man in jail on fabricated charges of child trafficking after he left me and my mother," Rush confided without remorse. "He'll be out in a few years and I'll put him back in jail for something else completely false. Something that will keep him in for a while."

The bad guys are just like us, thought Kyle. But then as his father would often say, even the most awful people had good sides. Mob bosses took care of their kids, drug lords paid rent for the poor.

"You want to see the cubes?" Kyle asked him once they were in the car. "Meet me at the back of the Weisdbaden hotel and spa. It's in the rear with a gate and fence. Bring your swim trunks."

"Is it hot?" asked Rush. "I'm not really good with the heat."

"Like a frog in a pot of boiling water hot. But if you want to see the cubes for yourself, you'd better learn how to deal with it."

Kyle arrived home to find the front porch lights were on, the low fluorescents illuminating the eggshell blue siding. From the street, Kyle could see his mother bent over her workspace, his father absent.

Probably up at the Elks Lodge. In a small town, the weekend started on Thursday.

He went inside and gave his mother a kiss and one armed hug.

"You're prickly again," she grumped, squealing when he brushed his cheek against hers even more. "Get away!" He chuckled, closing the blinds. "Said it before and I'll say it again, that's not going to help."

"Nope," he retorted. "But it certainly isn't going to hurt. Stu has long since stopped watching my ins and out."

His mother snorted. "You wish. How was dinner?"

Kyle sat on the stool, moving the strips of metal solder around on the table. "Dinner was tacos in Montrose. Where's dad?"

"Where do you think?"

Kyle stood. "I'm going to chill before heading up to the Weisbaden." He had another two and a half hours before he needed to leave.

In his room, he stared at his burner phone.

Kyle sat on the edge of his bed and punched in a number. Billy didn't pick up. Was she already asleep at eight p.m., or in the middle of conversation? She'd said the phone would be by her side. Had her plans changed?

He lay down, wondering about his decision to show Rush the cubes.

No, I told myself I'd trust Rush. If he took the masters by force, Kyle wasn't going to lose his life over it. The DNA cubes....well, he hoped it didn't come to that.

"They're asleep," Charlotte informed him. Dr. Pike thanked her, going through the plan for the following day once more before he went to bed. The entire team were going to be on their feet for hours, and the start time was five a.m. It had been two weeks since they'd received the DNA, and it was finally happening, thanks to the brave young woman asleep in the pre-op room.

"Can I get you another cup of tea?" she said.

"Yes, thank you," he said, looking up. "This time no honey at all. Just lemon." Eric wasn't going to risk even the slightest amount of nervous hand movement during surgery.

When she returned, he was concentrating on the figures before him. Tomorrow morning, they'd be up just long enough to be put to sleep yet again.

Eric accessed the secure site for surgeons from around the world who were involved in the movement. Hundreds of men and women all seeking the same thing: the chance to change the face of the United States' citizens. And with each operation, the surgeons would be honing their skills further, increasing their own value which would one day be open to the highest bidder.

He knew that not all surgeons were doing this work for altruistic reasons. Many expected or hoped the government would eventually be forced to pay for the corrective surgery, but rules would likely regulate the fees actually paid. That left an opening for the affluent to cut the line by virtue of wealth. It was morally and ethically unfair, but it was life, and applied to everything from boob jobs to kidney transplants. Those who had the funds could do what they want, and the surgeons providing the service were going to become multi-millionaires.

Eric posted his update to the board, along with the before photos of Billy and Roy, their eyes blackened out to keep them anonymous—for now. He uploaded their respective CAD drawings and resultant biomesh, along with the final skin.

He saw Joe's physician had done the same. From Jakarta to France, New York to California, the medical world was already watching.

It was going to be the show of a lifetime.

CHAPTER

41

Kyle saw Rush and Marcus waiting by the Weisbaden's back entrance as he approached. Marcus' face appeared to be scratched, but as he drew close, Kyle saw it was stiches along his jaw.

Like a bullet graze.

"This way," Kyle said, unlocking the back gate. They passed the heated outdoor pool and soaking springs that were a quarter full of guests, some of whom were getting out. He gestured for Rush and Marcus to wait a moment as he spoke with the front desk manager. His friends were given a guest pass and he walked them to the changing room. It was Thursday night, the evening when most out of towners arrived for a four-day weekend. A lot of folks were still on holiday from New Year's, but now the ice visitor's intent on ice climbing were starting to arrive.

Marcus had a patch of gauze on his chest, the diagonal strip giving Kyle a queasy wave. Did Marcus blame Kyle for his wounds? If it weren't for him and the cubes, there would have been nothing to compete for, but then it was Rush's choice to come here. It wasn't Kyle who made that decision.

"You won't want to get that wet," Kyle told him, his eyes going to the chest. "The sulfur will sting the shit out of you."

Marcus grunted. "Might disinfect me."

"That too. Still, its house rules a person can't go in with an open wound, so wear your t-shirt."

Fortunately, the vapor room was only occupied by an older couple who left shortly after Kyle and his friends entered.

"Follow me," he said, winding his way to the very back. "Hold on." Kyle kept his side turned to them as he reached up into the deep crevices, then realized his dilemma.

"You might as well help," he said to Rush. "Take these." Kyle dropped two sacks in Rush's hands who commented on the weight. "I got the others."

Kyle crouched as he went to the ledge and sat on the smooth surface. His legs were in the water as he set aside the masters, gesturing for the cubes in Rush's possession.

Marcus found it difficult to sit on the thin ledge, opting to stand in the water facing Rush and Kyle.

"Am I going to have any hair left on my legs when this is over?" the big man asked in a dry tone.

"Maybe," Kyle smirked. "You're a hairy guy."

It took a few minutes, but Kyle found the Colorado cube. He placed it on top of the two others he'd chosen at random, the green, digital information immediately appearing. Marcus leaned back an inch while Rush leaned forward, examining the data. Kyle was silent as Rush reached out to touch it, the same as he and Billy had done. When Rush's finger connected and moved up, the list scrolled in unison. When he touched on a single name, the data expanded.

"This is a gold mine," Rush murmured.

"Actually, it's not," corrected Kyle. "It's more like the map to the gold mine. Pull up a record and I'll show you what I mean."

Kyle went through the list, asking Marcus if he could see the data as well.

"It's backwards," Marcus told him. He got out of the water, crouching beside Rush. "That's better."

"Found me yet?" asked Kyle, two master cubes already in his hands. He leaned close to Rush, seeing what was in his sights. "There. Press on me."

Kyle's parents and relatives appeared, his net worth, which was practically zero and... "there," he pointed, reaching over and touching the line. "That's what the Naturalists are after. The DNA threading. See how this area is blank? I'll help you out here." He quickly found the Fine family. "See this section—that's the TMG, or the transmutational gene mutation. It means Ruth had a foreign gene added. And now watch this." An image of Ruth appeared. "Now this is what she'd look the way God and nature intended her to be."

"Holy shit," Marcus muttered.

"Exactly. And you remember Ashley of course." Kyle touched on her name, and soon, side by side images of Ashley appeared.

"Just like you said," Rush observed. "Less than good."

"You two are foreigners and aren't tied to the issue, but it's why the country is up in arms over these cubes. It's because we have had nearly forty years of lies, and it looks like this."

"Go back to the financial data," Rush requested. "Look at the Fines, shall we?" Kyle touched on Stu's line. It had a line listing a financial institution, but no details under it.

"That's uninspiring," Marcus drawled.

"It's because this is the DNA identity cube. What you are after are one of these." Kyle showed the cube between his forefinger and thumb. "They look the same from the outside, but watch." He brought the Colorado and master together. "What you don't see is an invisible, magnetic pull. They want to be together. Try." He handed it to Rush, who nodded as he felt the magnetism. He handed them back to Kyle who said, "You remember what you saw for Stu? Now watch this."

The two were silent until Kyle rotated the master. The explosion of data appeared. "This is the health side," he said informatively. "Here you can see all the medical stuff, but now let's zero in on the Fine family in another category." Kyle rotated the sides again.

"Stop," requested Rush. "What's this?"

"The criminal side. You want to see if Stu has a record?" Kyle didn't have to look to see Rush's head nodding. Kyle touched and watched what appeared on the screen. It was empty, save for a speeding ticket four years prior.

"You," Marcus said. Kyle obliged. His record was clear. Having indulged their interest, he found what they were all looking for.

"This is the money side," he began. "Any and all of what would come up for the treasury of the United States, and it's pretty broad. Watch." He first pulled up his mom and dad, unashamed at how little they had in the bank. "The system has no way to track cash," he pointed out, "only the accounts through the banks. Now compare us to the Fines and you'll see one major reason I was unattractive to Ashley."

Kyle was quiet as the air seemed to fill up with lines of assets. Checking and savings accounts, 401K for the entire family, IRAs and bonds.

"Even the stock accounts," Rush pointed out.

"Watch here." Kyle touched on the alternative assets. Up came a link to estates. "If you look on the other side of the cubes, it's family things. Wills and trusts, divorce decrees and payments. All sort of things. Property and real estate."

Kyle noticed Rush's eyes flitting at the data. He was probably wondering how many property deeds he could transfer into his name.

"You really need more property?" Kyle asked him, genuinely curious.

"It would look a little obvious if people's homes started being taken away from under them," Rush responded. Seeing that Kyle wanted a better answer, he shook his head. "There's enough illegal activity already happening in that area, I don't need to add to it. What are the other sides?"

Kyle ran through each one, pausing again on the criminal side. He pulled up Rush's sheet. Both he and Marcus' eyes narrowed as they scanned what the feds had on them.

"Could be worse," snorted Marcus.

"Yeah. They don't know half," agreed Rush.

Satisfied they'd seen enough, Kyle separated the cubes, the green data disappearing.

"Okay, you need the individual states to activate the masters," Rush said. "What do they do on their own?"

"That's the problem," admitted Kyle. "As I told you before, Billy's uncle was able to transfer the data off the states in minutes. But the masters just kept hanging, is what he said."

Rush pressed his lips out in thought. "Can I see them?" Kyle handed over the cubes without hesitation. He'd not locked any of the sides, thinking that Rush could replicate that feature of the devices himself. He was certainly more brilliant when it came to technology. All it would take is curiosity and time.

Marcus leaned in as Rush connected the cubes, the data appearing as Rush rotated the sides, pulling them apart and reconnecting with the other four surfaces.

"Better than we thought," murmured Marcus.

Thinking of his father's words, he spoke. "Tell me you're not going to use these things for extortion or....whatever," Kyle said to Rush. He had no right to be issuing any type of warning; his comment more of a plea to do the right thing.

"Answer me this," Rush began, pointing to the digital screen that hovered on the vaporous air. "Would you like to get some sort of recompense from Fine for nixing your scholarships and putting you out of a job? And what about getting some compensation for the spa owner, who had all his business at the highest season of the year go elsewhere?"

"Who wouldn't?" Kyle answered, "but I'm not a modern day Robin Hood. Go around getting back or even with everyone, trying to right all the wrongs? I mean, where does it end?"

"Socialism?" Rush suggested.

Kyle snorted. "Seriously?" Then he saw Rush's look. "You came from Russia where the entrepreneurial billionaire was practically invented. You thrive on the capital market. Wealth redistribution would pretty much crater your work."

"Not if I already had so much it didn't matter," he replied, handing back the cubes.

Kyle returned the cubes to their hiding places. "Are you seriously suggesting you'd be the do-gooder and make everyone even?" he asked, dubious. Even Marcus was looking at his boss skeptically.

"No, but it is entertaining to think about. Imploding the United States of America without having to elect a new president to do it for them."

The world of politics and money was not his issue or priority. "Not sure you answered my question. Extortion?"

Rush only laughed. "My skin's melting off. Let's get out of here."

Changed and outside the fence, Kyle shifted on his feet, wanting assurances Rush wouldn't go back and take the cubes, but having no guarantee or threat to stop him.

"Look Rush, I promised Billy—"

"Don't say it," he interrupted. "Tomorrow you get the pad, transfer the files and we are good to go, right?"

Kyle swallowed hard. He was taking money and the promise of security for the secrets and assets of peoples lives, those he hated and loved. "That's the plan," he finally said.

"Then just call when we can pick them up, and then we are out of here. Your life goes back to normal."

What was normal about his life anymore? Nothing. Not with his parents, his long-distance girlfriend or his future plans which were anything but set.

"How are you going to kill the time between now and then?" Kyle asked out of curiosity.

Rush gave him a mischievous grin, which Kyle knew would slay just about any female alive.

"I'm going to have my way again with your former girlfriend, who has proved herself to be rather adept at escaping that prison of a home."

Kyle raised an eyebrow. "Again?"

Rush clapped his shoulder, his smug look of victory reminding Kyle of the handsome Russian bad guy in a James Bond film. "See you tomorrow."

On his walk home, Kyle chose to focus not on Ashley and what she was doing with Rush, but instead on the words he'd said: back to normal. That's exactly what Kyle had to ensure: that life for those he cared about would do just that.

If it were even possible.

CHAPTER

42

That thought was the first thing which came to mind when Kyle woke Friday morning. It was five forty, and Billy was already in surgery. Her phone wouldn't be answered and there was no point trying.

He didn't bother showering, heading directly to work and doing the testing quickly before heading straight to the vapor room. The cubes were right where he'd left them.

Thank God.

Kyle had a mental list of those friends of him and his parents and a few relatives he didn't want Rush to touch. Their tenuous relationship could go sideways at any time, and Kyle had a very good idea of what Rush might do.

But maybe I can prevent that.

Kyle first accessed his family, and was just about to swipe away the data when he hesitated. His father had hinted at his past misdeeds.

He couldn't help himself, deciding to satisfy his curiosity. Criminal files, he thought. His father's record came up, the list long and varied. Petty theft. Auto theft. Forgery. DUI. No violent assaults or armed robbery with a gun, but it all had to do with one thing: money, or lack thereof.

Now it made sense why his father had no real issue with Rush taking money. He wasn't hurting people—not in the physical sense. But stealing a person's property was a violation on its own.

Kyle thought of the timing. The dates were decades prior, before he was born. No, wait. For a period of about five years, until Kyle was about ten, his father's law-breaking activities continued. Then he stopped.

Something must have happened to cause the change. His mom putting her foot down or threatening to leave?

Without another thought, he erased the file. His fingertip hovered over the Fine Family. With one swipe, their family records were eliminated. Kyle would get a scholarship on his own or not at all, and Stu wasn't that bad of a guy. He was a dad who has—or had—a favorite daughter, and a misdirected wife, but he wasn't some child abuser. In hindsight, Ashley might have crossed a line in the sand she didn't really know existed, and as Ruth said, had deserved it. But the family shouldn't have to suffer if Rush went sideways with Ashley.

One flick of his finger and the family had digitally evaporated.

Kyle then thought a bit broader. He swiped away the records for Mark, Saachi, Brayden and his wife—anyone who could be blackmailed, extorted or ruined. Ty was next on his list, as was Sheriff Deardon, Barret and Linda from the Weisbaden. He even included Sean and a few others in town he liked. Not that Rush would care two shakes about the people, but it didn't hurt to protect them.

But was he going to go through the entire exercise with the other five masters?

Kyle sighed. It would be nice if they all synched…

"No way," he whispered. Kyle took down all the masters and used the Colorado cube to test it out. It didn't work. They were still there. Kyle hesitated, unwilling to go through the list of people five more times.

Kyle popped his eyes open with an idea, scratching his itchy facial hair as he clarified his thoughts. He held all six between his thumb and ring finger, holding them tight for three seconds with no other logic than the fact that it had worked on the other set.

Carefully but quickly, he took a different master and placed it against Colorado. His breathing had gone shallow as he waited to find his own name. It was missing. So was Stu, Mark and Brayden.

Kyle picked up another master and repeated the process. Sure enough, the data was gone.

I did it.

Erasing the information on one master eliminated it on all the others, the aggregator effect complete. Kyle smiled to himself. He found Rush's name and swiped right to left. He then placed the masters together, ensuring he was off every cube. Sure, these were only back-ups to what was already on other systems, but if those were gone, Rush would be starting with a clean slate.

If there really was a universal Karma God looking over the present world, Kyle hoped it would inspire Rush to do a few right things along with all the bad he planned.

"A third of the way," whispered Charlotte. Dr. Pike had not had sugar or caffeine for a week, long enough to lower any microscopic shaking in his hands. The delicate work of removing the young woman's face had been done by an associate physician, ensuring Eric was fresh and ready to begin the laboriously vital task of reconnecting the nerve endings. He had another surgeon working as directed, the two of them a choreographed symphony using the nerve CAD imagery on the monitors around the room as their sheet music.

So far, Billy hadn't displayed any signs of rejection, although that usually came later. So far the nerve reattachment was going smoothly—better than even Eric expected.

"The data was accurate," Eric said to the team. The other physicians murmured their agreement, the happy reality boosting the excitement in the room. Never before had a major operation been conducted with the dot-to-dot imagery afforded by the cubes.

During a moment where the lasers weren't connected to the tissue, Eric was asked about the status of the remaining cubes.

"This afternoon," he replied. Eric knew Billy's contact was receiving the transfer pad later today, and that she'd included the instructions on how to make it work. The data would be sent directly to the dark net, which Eric would access after the surgery was complete. He'd then disseminate it across the country, the other surgeons who were likely already watching the three transplants on line ready to receive it in their in-box.

"Unbelievable," murmured Charlotte. That's exactly what Eric thought.

It was ground hog day for Kyle as he made his way to his locker. Students looked at him before glancing away, as though acknowledgement was a contagious disease. Marty breezed by, knocking into his previously injured shoulder. Kyle thought to tell him it no longer hurt and he was an idiot, but he did the opposite. He dipped his shoulder an inch, lifting and twisting, catching Marty off balance.

Kyle sniggered as Marty knocked into a girl passing by. By the time Marty righted himself, Kyle was already walking into his first period classroom. Ashley was sitting in her usual seat, as were Ben and Samantha behind him. Marty came in as the bell rang, answering the roll call as he sat. When it came to his own name, Kyle didn't even get a chance to respond.

"Facial hair isn't allowed in school," said his first period teacher. "That means you're either going to shave it off or make a trip to the principal's office."

Kyle was dumbstruck. "Carrying sharp objects like a razor isn't allowed according to school rules Mr. Williamson."

"Neither is facial hair."

Ashley started to laugh. Kyle turned in his seat, unable to contain his rage at her and her father.

"You're laughing because you've been sleeping around with strangers?" Her mouth was still open when Samantha told him to shut up. Kyle ignored her, but did cast a look at Marty. "And not by you big guy. Too bad," he said, grabbing his books as he stood up. "You weren't big enough on the basketball court or in your pants." At that, he heard Ben cough over a laugh.

He paused just a moment by Ashley, leaning down. "And tell your father that getting me fired and blowing my basketball scholarships is nothing compared to what's coming his way. Paybacks are a bitch Ashley, just like you."

In his peripheral vision, he saw Ben's wide eyes, mouth open. Never had Kyle uttered a disrespectful word or threat in his life, and the entire room knew it.

What had possessed him, he wondered, knowing the answer before his mind formed the words. He'd had enough of being the poor kid, the one who wasn't good enough, the one who had uncool parents living on the fringe.

Kyle went straight to the front desk, saying he was sick. Ms. Beyer called his home and his father answered, excusing him. On the way, Kyle took the main road, thinking more about the scene he'd just caused. Stu would no doubt file a restraining order against him for threats to his daughter and himself. Ashley would blow off Marty's questions about her sleeping with someone else, because Kyle was sure of one thing: Ashley wouldn't deign to get naked with Marty. And Rush? Kyle had no idea if the guy had been successful with Ashley or not, and he didn't care to find out. Just saying the words and seeing her response was enough to confirm if they hadn't reached their destination, they'd gotten pretty close.

A black Chevy blazer approached and passed him, then pulled a U-turn. Kyle glanced over his shoulder. It had parked in front of the Stagecoach. Three men emerged, each looking as casual and touristy as the next.

Just more out-of-towners, he told himself. I'm being paranoid.

Nonetheless, Kyle bent down, pretending to tie his shoe. He saw two enter the building, while the third paused to check his phone. By the time Kyle stood, he too was gone.

It hadn't occurred to Kyle that he'd increased his pace, but he made good time to the grocery store and then the police station. Mark's car was parked out front. Kyle saw Mark inside, phone to his ear, pencil in his left hand. He looked up as Kyle walked by, gesturing him in.

The click and clang of the bell on the door accompanied Mark's gesture to sit and wait. "Brayden," Mark mouthed, hand over the phone. Two head nods later, Mark asked him to pause. "What was the name of that Rush guy?"

"Philip Rush," Kyle answered. Mark relayed the information to Brayden, telling him he'd wait to see what came up.

Kyle's stomach clenched. He knew what was happening. Brayden was pulling up the FBI information on file, the same that was on the cubes. Then Mark would tell Kyle that Rush was a suspected criminal, that Kyle had to cut ties with him and that he was going to get Sheriff Deardon to tail him until he left town.

Instead, Kyle heard Mark say, "That's great news. Tell Laura hello for me."

For the second time in an hour, Kyle was dumbstruck.

"What's up?" he asked innocently.

"Just being prudent and checking on your new friends," Mark replied. "Brayden had asked about them, thinking the timing of their arrival after the break-in was coincidence, and this proved it wasn't. All clean."

It took a moment for Kyle to find his voice. He'd been so prepared for the indictment on Rush, that a clearance caught him off guard. There was only one way that could have transpired, and it was through hacking the internal monolithic government systems.

"Glad to hear it," Kyle responded. He felt a bit of sweat materialize on his lower back, a physical manifestation of the guilt associated with lying to Mark again after he'd promised no more.

"What are you doing out of school?" Mark asked.

"Got bounced because of my facial hair."

"They keep kids in school after they've toilet papered the teacher's car and then kick you out for facial hair?" Mark shook his head with wonder. "The star has really and truly fallen to Earth."

"Causing a massive crater in the town's social system, I know," Kyle added. "So I'm going fill out more college applications and see what happens."

Mark nodded, his lips jutting out in thought. "Isn't a loved one having surgery today?"

Appreciating the wording, Kyle told him that was correct.

"Not sure when it started, but hoping to hear word soon. A package is arriving in the mail today which is going to help me out a lot, so until then…" he let the words trail as he stood.

"Mark…" he began, then hesitated. By tomorrow, Rush was going to be long gone, along with the master cubes, headed to Denver or wherever he kept his base of operations. His presence wasn't going to be missed by anyone, including Mark. "Enjoy an easy Friday."

Kyle went home and did exactly as he told Mark. He looked up another half-dozen colleges, all top tier engineering schools, editing the cover letters with the right names, attaching and sending the materials required by admissions. The registrar at his school was going to be responsible for supplying his formal transcripts, and even if he'd somehow managed to alienate her as well, she'd have to comply with the process.

Seeing the time, he called the post office. The boxes were being stuffed, he was told. Give it another hour or so.

Kyle went back to the college process, this time looking at the second tier schools. They were generally smaller, most lacking basketball teams. He'd have to rely on his grades and essays, hoping for the academic scholarship angle.

Too nervous to stick around the house, he walked up to Ty's. The eatery was mostly empty, except his preferred table at the front. Kyle had wanted the closest reminder of Billy he could get, which were the seats where they'd had the fateful discussion which had started this entire chain of events.

But it wasn't meant to be. It was occupied by the men from the black Chevy who'd recently arrived. Their conversation was animated, but in low enough tones Kyle couldn't catch it. He sat at the counter instead.

"Hey, kid." Ty placed a water in front of him. "The usual?"

The familiarity made Kyle chuckle. He was half-tempted to ask for a beer, just to see what Ty would do. "A Coke and potato wings?" Kyle suggested.

"Coming up."

Kyle glanced at the flat screen, catching the reflection of his own face in the mirror. The purple around and under his eyes had faded to greyish circles, easily attributable to a late night out and not enough sleep. His well-filled in facial hair covered the cracks on either side of his lips and late stage bruising on his jawline. All in all, Kyle didn't think he looked too bad.

"Is this a lunch break or what?" Ty asked him, sliding the Coke across the counter. After a drink, Kyle told him what had happened.

"That makes for an entire week out of school?"

Kyle nodded. "On the upside, I applied to another dozen colleges today, give or take."

"And working hard growing a beard," Ty added dryly. "You look like yourself, but not."

"That a good thing?" Kyle asked.

"It's an older thing. You remind me of a guy I've seen around here few times in the last week. English guy. Hold on. I got an order. I'll be back." Ty took the order and then returned. "Any word from Billy?" he asked Kyle, in an undertone.

"A few words. She's gonna look a little different when she comes home," Kyle said, knowing he was walking a very fine line. Ignorance didn't cause harm, but the truth could. "She asked me not to say much more than that."

Ty was resting against the bar counter, a glass in one hand, a dishtowel in the other. "You've seen her?"

"Only on the computer, a couple of times. She's where she wants to be, doing what she wants to do."

Ty's eyes were down. It gave Kyle the distinct feeling her father might give too much away if he looked at up. "You said she's gonna look different. How? Boob job?"

Kyle practically spat out his Coke. "Not Billy," he laughed. "She's perfect the way she is and that's what I told her but..."

A pause followed, Ty placed the glass rim down, picking up another. "She ignored you."

Kyle grinned. "As usual."

Shaking his head, Ty left, returning with potato skins. As Kyle ate, the noise from the other table increased, and he heard a name he recognized. Kyle turned, looking over his shoulder.

"Yeah, I'm talking to you," said a dark-haired man. His yellow, Moncler jacket was the only thing louder than he was.

"You sure?" retorted Ty, his voice gruff and protective. It stopped the stranger, who peered at Kyle with a narrowed gaze. Kyle didn't break eye contact with him, still chewing as he shook his head then turned back to the bar. It was the only thing Kyle could do: his stomach bile had gone straight up to his throat, where Kyle swallowed it back down.

"I guess not," grumbled the man. The noise at the table picked up again but it was more subdued.

"Keep eating," murmured Ty, staying in his position behind the counter. Kyle sensed a figured coming up behind him to his left. He forced himself to take a drink of soda, extending the slurp until the man positioned himself to his left.

"You need something?" Ty asked, placing his hand on the counter.

"Not from you. Him."

Kyle raised his eyebrow, looking at a different guy, this one with closely shaved sides and a mop of blond, curly hair on the top.

"And?" Kyle asked with the attitude of a teenage kid. "I'm not into men, or out of towners." He said it loud enough to get a guffaw from one of the others in the corner, and a smirk from Ty.

"You have a problem with Kyle or just looking to start trouble?" Ty asked. "We don't have tolerance for that kind of thing around here."

The man ignored Kyle's insult and Ty's threat, continuing his examination of Kyle as though he didn't trust his eyes.

"Can I see your identification?" asked the stranger.

Kyle laughed. "Sure, if I can see yours first. Or better yet, we can call Deputy Hancock who can ask for both of ours at the same time. Would you like that?"

The threat wasn't empty. Ty picked up his phone.

"Come on Greg," called one of the others. "It's not him. Let's eat."

"Not who?" Ty asked.

"Yeah," joined in Kyle, taking another bite of potato skins. "Who am I supposed to be that clearly you don't like?"

"No one," said the guy with finality. Ty put the phone down. "One question. You got a brother?"

"Look guy," interjected Kyle. "I'm a kid who grew up here, still lives here, no brothers or sisters. I already established I'm straight and uninterested, plus today I turned legal so if it's alright with you, I'd like to finish my meal."

Even Ty laughed at that one, joining the group who teased the man who returned to their table and sat down. Kyle removed his wallet but Ty moved his hand flat across the counter.

"It's covered. Happy Birthday. Go home, or wherever. You seem to be attracting trouble like a flower attracts bees."

Kyle thanked him, glancing at the table near the door on his way out. He took a mental snapshot of all three men, knowing he'd be able to describe them to Rush.

The post office was halfway between the bar and his home, but just to be sure he wasn't being followed, he looked over his shoulder several times. He went in, picked up the package and kept going, calling Rush on the way.

"I'll be at your place in five," Rush told him casually.

"Change of plans," Kyle started. "A group of guys thought I was you, and had it not been for Billy's dad, I probably wouldn't be talking to you now."

A foreign word was followed by Rush's command. "Tell me where."

CHAPTER 43

"I thought you told me they'd be delayed a few days!"

Danny winced at Rush's controlled anger but was analytical in his response. "Everyone Marcus gave me was tracked," he replied evenly. "A few slipped through. What can I do? Put a flag on every criminal organization in a six state radius?"

"Wouldn't be a bad idea," grumbled Rush.

Danny was sitting behind his computer, doing double duty as a legitimate, law-abiding citizen and a grey, black-hatter working with the enemy, one who was going to take the bullet during this effort, not himself. Perhaps he should be a little more patient with Rush.

"You have a description?" he asked. "Anything I can use?"

"Maybe in five minutes when I get Kyle in the car."

"But you don't have the cubes yet?"

"He just picked up the transfer pad from the post office. We'll head back to my house and I'll call you then."

SARAH GERDES

"Watch him," Danny warned.

"He's the least dangerous one of us, Danny. You included."

"I'm not suggesting he's going to physically harm you," Danny said, changing his tone. "His girlfriend is having her face peeled off and a new one put on today, in case you've forgotten. All I'm saying is he might not be in the best frame of mind."

"Look, a high school senior who can outrun four snowmobilers and deal with Marcus is a pretty even-tempered kid. Even with the new guys in town, he didn't seem riled up."

It was Danny's turn to scoff. "People keep things inside, Rush. That's why we have a police offer going to Disneyland one day with his wife and two kids then killing them and himself the next day."

"Yeah, I saw the news."

"All I'm saying is you might need to be a stabilizing factor in the kid's life at the moment, which is ironic to say the least. Did you know today he turns eighteen?"

"Nope," said Rush. "Talk to you in a few."

Danny had a Red Bull pressed to his lips the moment the conversation stopped. Danger to him had nothing to do with guns and bullets, but his heart stopping from adrenaline overload. The new computer systems for Brayden and the FBI were now in the testing phase. Using 10,000 dummy accounts within Chase, data transfers had started, the information to be stored and then random transactions made. Saturday night, after 11 p.m. Eastern, when the least amount of activity occurred, the other four banks were going to sequentially replicate the exercise. If that worked, the next step would be to start backing up the live accounts on the new system, transferring the data to the new structure, all of it to be completed by Wednesday. Now that Rush had his competition in town, Danny feared it wouldn't take them long to identify and isolate Kyle. But they were going to make the transfer Friday evening, and Rush could start manipulating the files immediately thereafter.

Barely enough time for Rush to do his magic with the cubes.

Danny had done his job too well and was now pissed at himself. He could however, slow things down just a little bit by throwing an error or two into the system. If even a minor hiccup occurred with the new financial systems, it would delay the completion.

Feeling comfortable the timing would be close but doable, Danny finished off the soda, the caffeine and sugar jolt on his empty stomach causing heartburn. Not much longer now. From what Rush had communicated after his session with Kyle and Marcus in the vapor room, Danny was soon going to get the chance to see what his natural face looked like.

"And this effort would either be worth it, or a complete bust," he muttered to himself.

Laura smiled uncomfortably, her very real sadness at leaving the hospital mixed with the hope and fear of heading to a new job and a future without Brayden, at least for a little while.

She sensed a figure to her left and smelled the cologne.

"I'll miss you, Laura," Torben said.

"And you, Dr. Natter," she bounced back, returning his hug with brevity. "I understand the new hire starts on Monday," she continued, making small talk as she picked up a plate. She wasn't going to indulge his overlong stares or the impression he would like something more than a going away hug. It wasn't entirely his fault. She'd not done a very good job hiding the cracks in her marriage, but had never acted on his invitations to dinner or night caps at conferences.

"There was always a rumor of you being on the government payroll, some deep state secret going on about DNA. Was there any truth to that?"

Laura raised her eyes to the sky. "As if they didn't have more brilliant people to choose from." The comment didn't create the reaction she wanted; instead of laughing along, he looked more inquisitive. "Don't believe anything you hear, Torben."

"I didn't have to hear it. I saw it with my own eyes. You've been a consultant for years."

"Consultant yes, rocket scientist no."

"Smart enough not to answer the question, however. What about DNA and transmutational genes? Growing new faces?"

The innocuous conversation was starting to both annoy and worry her. What did he care if she were on the payroll? Every surgeon who could get a good paying gig with an outside entity took it, as long as no conflicts existed. The open questions left her unsettled and wanting to end the conversation.

"Making the leap from consultant to genetic scientist then top secret work is quiet a stretch," she said good-naturedly.

"It could happen."

"Sure," she said, her eyes roving around the room to express her disinterest. "I think what you're really saying is the government needs a man of your talents and skills, and now that I'm on my way out, you can take my place."

"It's a good idea," he agreed, watching her reaction.

Laura threw her plate and fork in the trash. "Then I say go for it. I'm leaving both the position and paycheck behind, just as I am this hospital."

"And me," he interjected.

She touched his arm. "We work together, Torben. There was nothing *to* leave behind." With a stiff smile, she left to chat with a few of the nursing staff. As they talked, she felt Torben lingering in the background. Could he have really thought he had a chance with her, and that his final play was going to produce a different result than the previous months? And what was with all the questions about government work? It was innocuous and normal in their field. If he really wanted a position, all he had to do with talk to the medical director and he'd have a straight line path.

She didn't think further about Dr. Netter as, a little later, she held the small box of personal items from her office and shut off the lights for the last time. Tomorrow she was going to be driving to her new home in Idaho, one that would be the residence for her family.

All three of them.

"Your assessment?"

Gary's forefinger was at his lips, the action ensuring he had a moment to consider his words. Janet was sitting across from him, the attempt at cornering his agent's wife unprofessional, unwarranted, and in his opinion, amateur.

"What exactly were you expecting?" Gary asked her. "She was going to divulge all to Torben after a year's worth of flirtatious attempts failed?" Gary flicked the papers in front of him, the transcripts of all Torben's interaction with Laura given to him only in the last hour, and only done when Gary demanded the President force Janet to reveal her surveillance of his team.

"First you went after Brayden, who came up clean. Then you turn on your own research scientist, and why? I mean, I just don't get what your beef is with a family who lost two children." The woman was unperturbed as usual, requiring Gary to use every ounce of self-control he possessed.

"You going to sit there or take your conversation logs and get the hell out of my office?"

The woman's hands were folded on her lap, the skin absent of age spots. Laser treatments could remove the dark freckles but so far, medical technology hadn't created a hand lift. Gary was sure once they did, she'd get the work done.

"There's a reason for our continued interest in Brayden and his wife Laura, well, two in fact. One was accidental, the other intentional. He wouldn't have been involved in any of this had it not been for his wife." Janet paused, removed her phone from her briefcase, and began typing. "I'm sending you an email now with her files. The short version is Laura was one of the researchers selected to work on the transmutational gene project while she was in medical school. She's a brilliant scientist, and we needed her work on the next generation, if there was going to be one. We also wanted her involved to ensure we could reverse the code in case a President elected to do so."

Gary held up a hand. "I'm assuming Brayden had no clue about this."

"Correct," she affirmed. "And he still might not. It was part of the confidentiality agreement she signed before they even knew one another." Gary nodded and she continued. "When her daughter died, we were of course, sorry for her, expecting her to resign or draw back her position, but she went ahead with a zeal we attributed to shock and loss. For years, nothing untoward occurred, but she was on our watch list—"

"For vulnerabilities, sure," Gary said, understanding. As much as he was personally appalled at all that Janet had done in her role at NSA, she had been working under the direction of the President, and moved forward accordingly. All agents were vulnerable to outside attempts at bribery or extortion particularly in times of shock or grief, and the death of a three-year-old daughter certainly counted.

"Over a period of years, we noticed certain anomalies. Rare, perhaps once or twice a year, a woman who'd been under Laura's care would experience a child mortality within six months of birth. To our discredit, we really didn't look into it until Laura's son Jarod died. It was only then that my analysts looked back at her files. Over the years, Laura signed off on a number of mortalities. By Jarod's death, we are talking nearly three dozen mortalities that she signed off on, and in each situation, the mother and daughter had visited Laura about six months prior."

"And she's not an OB," Gary said.

Janet was somber. "And what self-respecting surgeon bothers to deliver babies when they get a million saving lives?"

Gary agreed, unsettled at where the conversation was going. The loyalty he had for Brayden had always applied to Laura by association. Even so...

"Murder is murder," he said flatly, "so it can't be that, because she would have been arrested immediately."

Janet pursed her lips. "The bodies were tracked and exhumed from the grave. All were individuals who had died of natural causes, with no missing organs so it wasn't organ trafficking."

"You saying she certified each death?"

"Yes. She accessed the medical records and changed the notation for the transmutational gene." She paused, waiting for his reaction.

"Not getting it," he admitted. "The one you had inserted into all of us, vis-a-vi the HPV shots in pre-pubescent girls and then later, through flu shots and the like?"

"These women all had two things in common. The first thing was that they were all outliers: women who didn't have the gene administered, according to their files."

Gary finally saw where she was going. "The Naturalists," he guessed. "All of them?"

"Every last one. I mentioned a second element they had in common. All the mothers had young daughters they brought in. The records show exams, but nothing else. No shots or follow-ups."

He pondered that, in shock and with a certain amount of awe and respect. "You think she was giving them the reverse gene, whatever terminology is used to negate the original?"

Janet rewarded him with a nod. "Ensuring they would turn out to be Naturalists in the truest sense of the word."

Gary's mind raced with the implications. Laura could have spread the reverse DNA to hundreds or thousands of girls if she had a big enough network, with the reverse gene being passed on to their children. Even those who weren't naturalists could become so.

"Do you think she was sharing her work with others? And if you found this out---what, three years ago, why didn't you do anything before?"

Janet cleared her throat. "As I said, we didn't really notice until Jarod died, and that's what stimulated the surveillance on both of them."

"Which I never understood."

"Jarod didn't commit suicide Gary," Janet corrected. "He was murdered. We, the NSA, covered it up and changed the files. Brayden never knew the truth, and as far as we can tell, neither did Laura."

The cold heat of fury moved through Gary.

"We never did find out who perpetrated it, but we hypothesized it was one of Laura's clients, friends or associates who she dealt with and they were angry. In any event, her side work at the hospital ended shortly thereafter."

"No more visits and changed records?"

"Not that we could tell. So ironically, what started our investigation ended with uncovering the data, watching her and Brayden and coming up with nothing and no crimes proven. Falsifying records will get you nothing more than a warning."

"But that's not the case is it?" he asked. "Otherwise you would have kept all this information to yourself, never revealing any of it. And taking it a step further, you only reveal something to me when you need some type of authorization, except when you want to set up my agents and arrest them as part of a plan."

"We are all cogs on a very big wheel called the United States of America, Gary," she replied coldly. "I could have kept going without your input or involvement."

"Scott said he ordered you to stand down or resign, yes or no?" She hesitated, clearly caught off guard he'd known that detail. "Yes, it might help you to remember he and I served in the Marines while your elegant ass was upon the Hill, brown nosing every president since this travesty occurred. Cut the bull. What do you want?"

"I want to know the real reason Laura's moving to Idaho, why Brayden let Kyle Smith go when he's the one most likely to know where they are, and I want Laura to give me the names of every Naturalist contact she has."

"Why are you talking to me then?" he retorted. "Why don't you just arrest them both?"

"You're not seeing around the corner, Gary," she said contemptuously. "This doesn't have a thing to do with professional courtesy. It's because our systems have been hacked to a level that even I've never seen before. Files are being manipulated. Data is disappearing. We take Brayden, and Kyle will disappear before we step foot in Ouray. Something happens to Laura, and those we want on the other end—the ones master mining what's going on--will go deeper underground than they already are."

Gary's paternal instinct for Brayden and preference for a duped young man in Ouray Colorado was strong. Still, he was the Director of the FBI. His obligation was to his job and country.

"You left out the part where Brayden is leading the financial safeguard, which I might point out, worked well today. Without adverse events, the financial system will be safeguarded by the middle of next week."

For once, Janet was without a quick comeback. "Congratulations."

"I know that was hard for you Janet, but not everyone is entirely corrupt. I suspect Brayden has no idea of what's been transpiring, but even if he has been, he's staying the course for the job at hand."

"And if he's like Laura, involved to a degree where it can't be managed?"

Gary thought of what he suspected about Brayden's assistance with Kyle Smith. "Then we consider the evidence presented therein and make a decision. Given all you want to accomplish, we, the FBI and NSA, have no choice but to play this out."

Janet leaned forward, and at first, Gary thought she was going to stand. Instead, she put her elbows on her knee, interlacing her fingers.

"I'm glad to hear you say that, because it's already started. Yesterday, a group of known criminals in the Denver underworld had a shootout, which normally wouldn't have attracted any attention, except they all have been known to traffic in anything digital, from financial accounts to identities, to the highest bidder. Gary," she continued, her stare narrow and intense, "there is such a thing as information futures, just like commodities—"

"Selling future data at existing prices—" he broke in.

"Yes. Now we have two opposing entities, one dead man, and two wounded. We tracked them over their cell phone conversations, honing in on key words."

"Where are they now?" Gary asked quietly, guessing the answer before she said it.

"That small town where it all started. Each criminal entity searching for one person, Kyle Smith, who will either be taken or maybe working in concert with either. It's unknown."

"And you couldn't have revealed all of this before? No wait," he interrupted, stopping her from speaking. "You want me to let Brayden and Laura continue their efforts, unaware of what's happening, so you can nail those in Ouray?"

"Correct, and let's be clear. We don't have to like or necessarily respect one another to be on the same page. I had to take it on the chin for Saachi because your group didn't know about the lab. Ergo, I have a traitor in my organization. But this—"

"Is probably coming from my organization," he finished for her. "I'm assuming your people are already on the way?"

"Three hours out give or take. One is from the second incident on the mountain who administered the injections."

"And presumably can identify Kyle Smith by sight."

"Correct."

Gary looked at the clock. It was nearing two p.m. Kyle would still be in school, and they'd take him into custody before anyone else had a chance to hurt him. The NSA would do that job themselves.

CHAPTER 44

Kyle shuffled from side to side as he waited for Rush. It being a Friday, the bus activity to the springs was increasing. He was hopeful Stu's ploy hadn't inflicted permanent financial damage on Barrett's business.

Billy had been in surgery six, maybe seven hours now. In the best case scenario, they'd be done with the nerve reattachment around three or four p.m. All he wanted was her back in his arms.

But not here in Ouray, he thought to himself, seeing the grey Defender approach.

Kyle got in the back seat. "Tell us what they looked like," Marcus demanded.

Kyle detailed the three down to the goatees and moles.

"Accents?" Rush asked.

"None I could make out. Honestly Rush, they were flipping out because they thought I was you."

"Not as good looking though," Rush remarked. Kyle wanted to smile, but couldn't. The oppressive feeling of confinement increased with every day, and would continue until Rush had what he needed and left.

"Guys, turn around," Kyle requested. "The cubes are still in the caves. Sorry. It doesn't take very long for the transfer, a minute or so for each cube. In roughly an hour, you get out of here."

"We are going to be cutting it really close," Marcus muttered.

"We'll make it," said Rush. "Won't we, Kyle?"

Kyle had a sudden understanding of what was going on. "Those guys are the ones Danny mentioned would be coming?"

"One batch of them, anyway," answered Marcus.

Given that increased threat, Kyle wasn't going to risk changing when every minute counted. He ran from the car to cave, violating every single spa rule when he didn't even bother to remove his shoes as he waded into the hot water. A rotund older man opened his eyes wide.

"Forgot my water bottle," Kyle said as he delved into the furthest corner. He put the sacks under his sweatshirt before he turned around. On his way out, he pulled on a white bathrobe and grabbed an extra towel. He sloshed and slipped past the pool, apologizing as he got in the car. He put the towel beneath him before he sat down.

"Sorry about the water, but you said time was of the essence."

"When you're dry enough, open the package from the Post Office. Let's see if all of this was worth it."

To Kyle's surprise, Rush hadn't opened it while he was gone. He would have thought.... Inside, Billy had included a new burner phone, the transfer pad and a note.

"Can I see the item?" Kyle handed the pad to him while he read Billy's note. "A benign device," Rush observed, "but some of the best technology usually is."

"Here," said Kyle. "Read this."

They exchanged the transfer pad and paper, Kyle putting the new burner phone in his jacket pocket.

"Billy is thorough and funny," Rush commented. "But are you sure she's your girlfriend?"

Kyle chuckled. "This is a love letter compared to what she normally writes," he said dryly. It was Billy at her objective, intelligent finest.

"Why Billy?" Rush inquired.

It took a second for Kyle to catch on. "Oh, because in seventh grade, me and the guys made the mistake of calling her by her given name, Elizabeth and we got a smackdown. It's been Billy ever since." He smiled now at the memory.

When they arrived at Rush's house, he directed Kyle upstairs.

"Change everything, top to shoes," said Rush. "I'll set up the transfer. You have the cubes, together we're golden."

Kyle picked black jeans, and a grey mock turtleneck, the top edge hitting his growing facial scruff, then went back downstairs.

Rush was at the desk, the laptop open and transfer pad coaster to his right.

"I connected the two devices as Billy indicated," said Rush. "You can finish the process."

Kyle took a cube out of the sack, placing it on the pad. A blue light on the transfer pad turned on as expected, and a bar icon in the center of the screen began moving slowly from left to right, the indicator data was being transferred.

"And it appears to be working," Rush said. The transfer picked up speed half way through the exercise. When it was completed, about a minute later, the blue light went out.

"One down," Kyle said with satisfaction. He emptied the entire batch of cubes onto the desk.

"Kyle," Marcus said. "Your cell phone is buzzing."

It was the new burner, but a call from Billy was impossible. The surgery still in progress. He stared at it for a moment, finally deciding he had to answer.

"Kyle," a woman said. "We are receiving your data at this very moment. Thank you."

The air he'd been holding in went out with an exhale of thanks. "That's awesome," he breathed.

"Billy gave us instructions to let you know the data is going into the secure site for physicians and centers around the country. You'll continue uploading until it's done?" she asked.

"Yes. All of them. Before you go—how's Billy? Any word?"

"The operation has gone wonderfully," enthused the woman. Kyle could almost hear her smiling on the other end, as pleased with the results as he was. "In a couple more hours they'll be finished. I'll call you then."

Kyle thanked her and hung up. Billy was already special; she might just be heartbreakingly beautiful after her face healed from this surgery. Though he hadn't been kidding before when he told her he'd miss the smile lines and her freckles. It's what he'd fallen for.

I'll just give her a lot more to smile about, recreating those little wrinkles, and soon we'll be back on the mountain, giving her new freckles.

Strangely, his thoughts turned to Ashley. "Rush, you meet with Ashley last night as planned?"

"Sure thing." Kyle looked over his shoulder. Rush was placing the cube on the pad, his gaze focused on the process before him. "Do you think she was smart enough to use birth control?"

"No need to worry about that," Rush replied. The answer relieved and annoyed Kyle. On one hand, Ashley wasn't as easy as he assumed, but on the other, he wanted to be vindicated he was right.

"Guess you can't always get the girl," he joked.

"Oh, I got the girl alright," corrected Rush. "But years ago I had myself snipped as a safety measure against unwanted pregnancies. But that was after I put a whole lot of baby-making juice away in a cryogenic holding tank just in case I do find that person I want to procreate with."

Kyle wished he hadn't asked. His comment in class had proven accurate, but it didn't give him the satisfaction he desired.

"You get an update on Billy?" inquired Rush.

"It's all good so far. They expect to be finished late afternoon. Just about the time you'll be on your way out of town."

"Nope," said Rush. "We are going to hit that ice wall we've been waiting for all week."

"Boss, not sure that's a great idea," Marcus interjected.

"I have to best Kyle in something before I leave. Besides, it's below ground, not the most visible place in town, am I right Kyle?"

Kyle confirmed the statement, adding that the ice park was a lot longer and varied than most people knew. "You can't even see ten feet below the edge unless you are standing right on the edge of the crevice."

The information didn't seem to allay Marcus' concern. "Still don't think it's a great idea."

"We're doing it," said Rush, ending the conversation.

Marcus left the room to pack.

"FYI, I did you a solid," Kyle started, sensing the tension. "Your data files have been wiped out everywhere. All the masters are clean of your existence." Rush glanced over his shoulder. "And that was *before* I won that grand," he added with a smirk. Rush pushed the chair back, pushing his hands into his pockets. He held a wad of cash, counting out ten bills.

"Thanks for that, and the reminder. Given my imminent departure, here you go."

Kyle accepted the cash. "No worries. I'm doing what I can to ensure you don't have a reason to come back—ice climbing aside."

Rush had turned back around, moving the next cube on the transfer pad as Marcus excused himself to pack the car. "I disagree. You were just being nice."

His comment caught Kyle off guard. "How can you be so sure?"

"Because you're one of those rare individuals who doesn't have any guile. You have no ulterior motive. Not sure you know how. You didn't have to delete my files, you just did it."

Kyle wasn't sure what to do with the compliment, so remained silent. It bothered him that he would come across as so...either naïve or easy to read.

"What's Marcus' last name?"

Rush provided it and Kyle looked him up on the cubes he had in hand. He scanned the page, feeling the skin of his forehead pushing up. "How is he not in jail?" Kyle wondered aloud.

"The American judicial system is the world's most amazing thing for a criminal," Rush said. "So much has to be proven in such a short period of time, all with witnesses and evidence."

Kyle looked back at the list. These were violent, ugly incidents of assaults and suspected murders. But like Rush, nothing was proven.

"Hard to convict without witnesses," he said aloud.

Kyle wiped the data out without another thought, connecting the masters between his fingers, ensuring it was done across all six.

"Marcus is in the clear," he announced. Rush thanked him, but Kyle barely heard the words. His concentration was on the cubes, which were only a few inches in front of his eyes. In the light, he saw very fine vertical ridges on the sides, as though they were laser cut, not molded.

"Rush, don't bullets have striations from the gun barrel, and each are unique?"

"Yeah. Why?"

"Just thinking out loud." Kyle was no metallurgist, nor did he have a magnifying glass, but he wondered if there was something to the micro ridges.

"I suppose if they're laser cut, the sides might match up," Rush told him, "but in the gun world, all that connects is the bullet with the gun, and who pulled the trigger. In this case, does it matter who manufactured these things?"

Kyle didn't think so and kept playing around. He had the surface for genealogy and family ties for lack of a better word. Since he could lock out certain data sets, he could do that now; every side could be locked except for the financial side.

Would Rush get furious at him? Uncertain. Would Rush make him undo what he'd done, guaranteeing their continued relationship? Most likely.

Kyle lifted his eyes, seeing Rush only had a few more cubes. If he were going to do this, he had to do it now.

With one eye on Rush, Kyle methodically aligned each side of the cube he wanted locked out, holding the cubes for three seconds each.

Kyle checked that the actions of one would carry over to the rest of the masters. He held all six between this thumb and fourth finger as he had in the past, counting to three. Kyle took the last cube, placed it against Colorado and waited. Every side was now locked out except the financial side.

Kyle stood with purpose.

"Here you go," Kyle said, putting all six masters on the desk. "It's all up to you now."

"All ready to go," Marcus said from the doorway. Rush lifted a finger, indicating one more moment.

"We're done," replied Rush, scooping the cubes into the Ziploc bags. Kyle followed him out. In an hour, they would be gone. Kyle was going to have a new normal for sure, and in four months, he'd be gone himself.

CHAPTER 45

Mark had just finished his grilled cheese when the phone rang.

"Hi boss," he greeted jovially. The day had been uneventful. Rush had checked out as a non-entity and Saachi was healing and obviously interested in him, their flirtatious banter about her giving up the city life for small town encouraging. "You ready to come home yet?"

"Mom is doing better, thanks for asking, but I'm not calling about that." Mark immediately sat straighter in his chair. This was not the tone he used when it was a social call. "O'Connell called me from state. Kyle's mom went past Maury and up to the governor." Mark groaned. "I take it you didn't know."

"And I suspect neither Ed nor Kyle do either. What does that mean for us?"

"More headaches if someone shows up. Maury didn't want to tell the governor to go to the Feds, but the complaints forced his hand. Now it's the FBI's problem."

The Feds trumped even the head of State police on any subject for any reason. "It's not like we are going to have US Marshall's showing up because one mom is pissed."

"No, but some investigative journalist might pick up the chatter on police stations as they always seem to be doing."

"In other words, we have to keep our eyes open."

Dearden grunted. "The last thing we want is a bored reporter out of Montrose coming to town looking for a story."

"Gotcha. Anything else?"

"Yeah. There was a gang altercation yesterday in Denver. One of Brayden's internal guys got wind from the FBI that it was over something to do with the mine."

"How's that even possible?" Mark asked.

"The items stolen were never recovered. Rumor is that they are either in Denver or possibly still here in Ouray."

"Then why the scene in Denver?"

"Maury said that according to the Feds, word about the items has gotten out, and now criminal organizations are heading your way to see if there's any truth to the matter. The shootout in Denver was the prelude."

"Actual guns?" Mark clarified. He immediately thought of Rush and his friends who looked like they could handle a weapon. "We've had an increase in visitors over the last few days," he said, "but there's no way of knowing whether they're carrying without a door-to-door search."

"And that's not what Maury is advocating."

"In other words, we are going to sit tight and wait."

"That's about it," confirmed his boss. "I'm just sorry you will be handling it alone," said the Sheriff. "Call Montrose or Ridgeway if you have any issues, but this is hopefully a stretch," continued Dearden. "Nothing came of the mine break-in anyway."

Not that you ever knew of.

"Oh, one other thing. If you have to call in for back-up, you're not to mention the mine, the Feds or any other details." Mark was astonished, starting to argue. "No discussion."

"Yes, sir."

Mark hung up and tapped his fingers on the desk. In theory, he was to do nothing more than monitor and respond, no different than any other day on the job. The next moment, he grabbed his coat and locked the door on his way out. The Feds knew that something had gone down in Denver relating to the mine, and if anyone had it correct, it was them. Brayden must not have known what happened when they last spoke or he would have given Mark a heads up. It gave him some degree of comfort knowing Kyle was out skiing...

The cold outside hit him as hard as another thought. What if those guys with Kyle weren't what they purported to be? Bad guys slipped through the system all the time, the very best never getting caught.

Mark got in his car, wondering where to start. Flipping a U-turn in the road, he decided to head to Ridgeway and work his way back. He'd also give the local Deputy a call. He could discuss suspicious activities all they wanted within the bounds the sheriff had given him; the line of truth was black and rigid, but that didn't mean he couldn't walk right up to the edge.

"What's this song called?" asked Kyle, his voice loud enough to be heard over the thumping beat.

"Omnipresent, by Leroy Moreno," called Rush. Kyle couldn't help but move at the electronic beat, envisioning a packed club in Budapest with girls wearing barely-there clothing and bouncers with biceps the size of boulders. It was a life he'd never thought about before, but did now. The clothes borrowed from Rush fit in all the right places, the shoes were comfortable and trendy. With the jacket Rush gifted him, Kyle was now part of the club with outerwear the value of a car payment.

Or a mortgage payment.

Kyle had been doing a lot of thinking over the last few days. He could take the good parts of Rush--the car, clothes and high-priced lifestyle--without the associated bad. Engineers were well paid, and if Kyle joined a start-up, he'd get stock and if he were part of the lucky few, it might eventually be worth a few million.

Kyle snorted to himself. Who was he kidding? Billy wasn't into that scene, neither was he. They were two, small town young adults who just wanted to be free of the constraints of life where everyone knew their business. Someday they could travel together and see the world. This was almost over.

"Kyle, you said my files were gone," began Rush. "Can you show me?"

"Sure." Kyle asked him to pull out the Colorado state and a master. "Doesn't matter which one."

There was still plenty of daylight, the sun high in the sky as they drove the windy road between Telluride and Ouray. He leaned forward, holding the cubes between this hands.

"Not sure if you both can see this."

Marcus was behind the wheel and glanced as he could, but Rush moved closer. Kyle pulled the files, showing the list of names in the R section, the green lettering hovering in the space between them.

"Like I said, you aren't there," Kyle stated, manually scrolling up and down the list. Kyle handed the cubes back to Rush and sat back. "Did you think I hadn't done it?"

"I told you before you don't know how to have ulterior motives," answered Rush. "This exercise was called being prudent. I set up the account for your windfall this morning. You are the proud owner of a bank account in Switzerland."

"I'm not giving these to you for the money."

"No, but you're getting some anyway. You want me to tell you how much or let it be a surprise? Scratch that," he said, his accent strong. "I'll do both. I made your upfront payment an even million. Wiping out the records for me and Marcus is worth at least that amount."

"Thanks but..." Kyle began. Two men had died so far, old D, who had first shared the secret with him and the guy on the snowmobile. Kyle had gone to write a forty-year wrong, not profit.

As if sensing Kyle's discomfort, Rush turned to him and said, "You keep the money. Full stop. If Fine manages to kill your scholarships, how are you going to pay for college? That's fifty G's a year for a half-decent school, and you're way too short to jump from high school to the professional basketball league. Take the money and feel justified knowing that you and your parents will be taken care of for a few years."

The car was momentarily quiet. "These cubes are only backups to bigger systems," Kyle began uncomfortably. "Your data has to be somewhere else, at least, I imagine it is. What if...what if the stuff I erased is still in other places?"

"Shows how much you don't know about government systems," Rush responded. "Half the time, the backups and existing systems are synched like a contract address book on your phone. New, replaced or edited information is automatically corrected. I'm running with the assumption that at some point, I'll give these masters back through my internal, black-hat means, and they will perform the synch. My data, and Marcus' will be gone everywhere." Kyle could only nod. Rush was right: he knew nothing about systems. "As to the size of your commission check, that's going to depend on how much money I'm able to scrape off of these things. And even if you want to give it back, you can't. I'll just call it a birthday gift. Happy eighteenth birthday Kyle."

"Thanks," he mumbled without much grace. It didn't seem real—*wasn't* going to seem real until life was back to normal. And then what was he going to do, show up in a new Maserati when he came home from a college?

By the time they reached Ouray, it was two-forty five. Driving up Main, Kyle saw Ben and Samantha on the east side, walking away from the other students. School had just let out.

"If you're serious about climbing, we'll have time for one or two quick trips up," said Kyle.

"Great," replied Rush, his eyes focused on Ashley who gave him a smile of recognition. Kyle directed Marcus to the ice park office. Sean was down in the Gullies and that's where they headed.

Kyle had Marcus take Camp Bird Road back down to the lower parking area, loading up the gear between he and Rush.

"Where are you storing the cubes?" Kyle asked Rush, envisioning a secret lock box inside the tank-like vehicle.

"On me," Rush replied. He opened his jacket, revealing a thin black vest. It was a cross between a fishing jacket with lots of zippers and pockets and the Teflon type worn by military. Efficient and effective.

On the walk over, Kyle hung behind Rush and Marcus and called home.

"Just wanted to let you know I'm up here at the ice park with Rush and Marcus," he told his dad.

"Mark has been looking for you," said his father. "Everything all good?"

"Dad, I wouldn't be calling you if it wasn't," he chided. "And on that note, all that we talked about has happened. The info is all gone. It's done. Rush is leaving after we take our first and last climb together. We get to go back to our exciting life, just like we talked about."

His father cleared his throat. "Mark indicated that the town might have some visitors, also looking for a few of the things rumored to be here—or others who might have them."

Kyle guessed his father was being subtle because his mother was nearby. "Then the good news for all of us is that these guys will be gone in ninety minutes or less."

"Mark won't be the only one in town to be relieved," said his dad. "Stu has literally worn a groove in the front room pacing back and forth."

Stu wasn't Kyle's issue any longer. He caught up with the guys at the staging area, where he heard them talking to Sean.

"Thought you were going to be here earlier," Sean told Rush. "Oh, wait—sorry. I thought you were Kyle Smith." Kyle laughed, and Sean did a double take. "That's your doppelganger," he said.

"My English older brother from a different mother," Kyle joked. "Can we still climb?"

"For approximately forty-five minutes or until the sun hits the ridge, whichever comes first. Cowboy up, Lower Bridge and Scottish Gullies are my recommendations," said Sean.

Kyle nodded, already slipping on his gear. "Marcus, you not climbing? Oh, right," he said, correcting himself. He'd momentarily forgotten about the wound. That reminded him of something else. "Rush," he said in an undertone. "You ah, still packing?" The word sounded stupid when he said it, but it was shorter than 'carrying a weapon on your person.'

"Always," Rush said without hesitation.

Kyle took a deep breath and eyed the steep wall of frozen water.

"Let's go then."

CHAPTER

46

The man made park had evolved over the years Kyle had lived in town, the convenient rock slabs transformed into challenging venues for strong-armed thrill seekers. The three ice faces Sean recommended could be perfectly viewed from the road.

Kyle walked along the edge, pointing out the options. They didn't have much time, and it was only going to be he and Rush anyway. After checking out all three, Marcus pointed out his preference.

"That one," he said.

"Scottish Gullies," said Kyle. The long stretch had seven primary climbing routes, and the bottom was accessible by a rough walk path or rappelling.

In two more weeks, these empty paths along the ridge would be lined with display tents occupied by global brand names like Patagonia, Arcteryx and other festival sponsors. Locals and big name climbers would mix over beer and wings at Ty's after a day on the ice.

But today it was quiet.

"Mixed climbing isn't as challenging, but that's all your gonna get if you want to leave on time," Kyle predicted.

He walked to the edge. He was thinking the Optimator route, where half the terrain was actually ascended by placing legs on either side of the ice which was great for inner thigh and core strength. Then it became a more traditional straight up climb. He and Rush were discussing either a rope or belaying style when Kyle pointed.

"Someone's already been up there using the twin rope system." That made the climb a no-brainer. It was safer, faster and easier for the multi-pitch climb.

Marcus stayed in place and lit up a cigarette as Kyle led the way to the edge, the decision to rappel down made due to the time constraints. Rush had his helmet already when Kyle's phone buzzed.

"Yes?" Kyle answered. The news made him smile. "Can I see pictures? Yes please. That would be great." He put the phone away, his heart light.

"Billy's out and it was a success," he told Rush. "I might be able to speak with her in a few days, they'll keep me informed."

Kyle fastened his helmet, energized by the news. Kyle led the way down, and at the base they put on ice cleats. Kyle asked if Rush wanted to take the lead.

"Yeah, for once," Rush joked.

Kyle watched him harness up, eying the placement of his foot. "Hold on," he said. Kyle pulled the harness, tightening it half an inch, clapping Rush's shoulder when he was done. "That matters when you are falling," he said, tongue in cheek.

As he watched Rush start his ascent, Kyle glanced up at the hardened sheet of water above him, then to the light blue colored sky above. This three-week period of his life was almost over.

Kyle inhaled the cold air, not minding the sting in his lungs that continued as he prepared for his own climb. Ashley had defied her dad and received the attention of a worldly guy. Her ego bucket should be brimming over until the end of the school year. Marty would remain bitter, but his ATV and his father's money might make him less annoying to be around. Billy would heal and in a couple of weeks, they'd be together. Most of all, their mission to spread the DNA of the countries' citizens was now being disseminated to centers around the country, landing in the hands of surgeons who would be on the forefront of undoing the damage inflicted by the country's leaders.

Mark, his father and even Stu would return to their normal patterns and routines.

"You coming or what?" Rush shouted down.

"Right behind you," Kyle called.

Rush scoffed and kept moving. He had quite a head start on him now, and Kyle would have to scramble to catch him.

Mark was at the Post Office when he got the call from Ed. Kyle had returned and was up at the ice park with Rush. Timing was good. Mark would stop at the Stagecoach then Ty's one last time before heading up. He looked forward to updating Kyle on the events and essentially baby sit him until this blew over.

The hotel was busy. Guests were checking in every hour, many of the early birds stating they were heading directly for the hot springs before hitting the bars.

At the bar, Mark took a quick look around. Locals were mixed with a few familiar faces from Telluride. He gave a head nod to Ty, declining a drink, and was about to leave when the sports channel came on and he paused, waiting for last night's score. In his peripheral vision, he saw a black Chevy blazer, recognizing the occupants. Mark lifted his chin, catching Ty's attention. "You see these guys in here?" he asked.

"Yeah, from Denver and they're pricks to boot."

"Do tell," Mark requested.

Ty wiped the counter. "They mistook Kyle for another visitor that's been here this week, and I *know* he is from Denver."

"And the prick part?"

"One zeroed in on Kyle, thinking he was that Rush guy with the English accent," Ty explained. "Had to threaten to call the cops while verifying Kyle was a local."

Two groups from Denver. Just as Mark had been warned.

Mark leaned forward, the intensity of his expression causing Ty to do the same. "Call Ed, find out where Kyle is exactly and have Ed take Kyle's ATV up there, *now*," he emphasized. Mark didn't add that the kid's life might depend on it. He hoped his eyes and the fact that he walked purposefully out the door carried the point across.

Rush was lean and muscular, making easy work of the ice. As they climbed, Kyle used the pauses to satisfy his curiosity. Now that the end was in sight, he might never have another chance. He asked Rush when he was going to start his own work with the cubes.

"Tonight when we get back," Rush answered. "You making conversation so I'll slip a grip and you can pass me?"

"Maybe," Kyle laughed, taking another long stride, closing the distance between them. "But I'm also intrigued by Danny and why he's so interested in the cubes. Is he just in it for the money?"

A moment went by as Rush kicked the toe of his boot into the ice, stabilizing his position. "Danny is actually a free-lancer who works with many clients, one of whom is the government. He's like you: not after the money, but the righteous nobility of having a natural face."

Kyle hammered the pick into the ice. The tip stuck nicely.

"I do think that's noble," he said, using his arms while pushing his thigh muscles to raise himself up the ice. His breath left him as frigid air hitting him in the face.

They made good time up the wall, almost at the mid-point. Rush was about eighteen inches above him now. Kyle found no fault with his technique or movements.

"You're a good climber," he complimented Rush, giving another push, this time feeling the burn in his left calf muscle.

"Russia has a lot of ice my friend."

"Just beyond that mound is midway," Kyle told him, looking up. "Marcus should just about be able to see us."

"Good," Rush grunted. "I told him to take some good glory shots."

Kyle laughed, the sound overshadowed by the thud of a gunshot. Rush slammed against the rock, blood from his right shoulder splattering against the wall, his helmet cracking against the ice.

Kyle lurched over and jammed his right toe into the ice, simultaneously looping his left wrist with the twin rope, reaching for Rush's harness. Kyle caught Rush's strap with his right hand just in time, gritting his teeth against the sensation his arm was going to pull out of his socket.

"I got you," he said through clenched teeth, hoping that Marcus was taking care of the situation above. Another thud hit the ice, barely missing Rush's left cheek. Kyle had no choice but to lessen the grip on his twin rope, lowering them both. He extracted his toes, using the sharp ends to slow rather than stop his descent.

"Rush, can you hear me?" he whispered as he lowered them both, the effort straining his lungs and thighs. Rush mumbled, but it was enough. He hadn't been hit in the head, neck or middle back, the wound on his far shoulder hopefully dulled by Rush's foresight in wearing his Teflon-like vest. Kyle could lower him down to the ground but then what?

Mark hadn't seen the black Chevy on his way up Main Street, his close observation of every passing car a distraction. Were there only one or two other groups coming in to town, or were they already here?

He went straight to Sean's office, learning he had directed Kyle to the Gullies. Seeing Rush's big friend standing on the side of the ridge, Mark was just about to speak with him when he heard the echo of shots ricocheting in the valley below. The man at the edge ducked, and reaching inside his jacket, pulled out a gun.

"Hold it," yelled Mark. The man spun around as another shot went off. It was coming from somewhere else.

"Stand down," Mark screamed, crouching low as he crossed the street. The man evidently saw Mark wasn't the threat, and immediately turned, looking up and down the ridge. Mark watched as the man crouched low, preparing to fire. Only then did Mark see the intended shot.

"Stu! No!" The thin man had a rifle on his shoulder, pointing downward into the gully. Stu ignored him, adjusting the weapon on his shoulder. "Stu! Hold your fire!" Mark yelled. Two shots rang out; but only one from Mark's gun. Who shot the other bullet he didn't know.

Stu fell to the ground, the gun slipping off his shoulder and into the ravine.

Mark called for backup. Ridgeway and Durango Sheriffs were on their way. He'd also requested additional units to block off traffic incoming and outgoing.

He ran to the edge, fearful of what he was going to see below. Two men were at the bottom, both wearing helmets, one helping the other. A trail of blood started halfway up the ice wall and continued down to the bottom.

"Kyle, that you?" he yelled, praying to God he wasn't the one who'd been shot.

"I'm fine," he yelled. "Rush isn't. Can you…"

A series of shots rang out again, this time behind Mark. He instinctively fell to his knees. Kyle was fine, but Stu…Ashley's father lay motionless as three men ran towards him.

The screeching sounds of tires and bullets blended together as Mark positioned himself behind his car, taking aim at the three who were headed towards the ice wall. They'd shoot Kyle and Rush into oblivion if they made it.

Mark aimed for their legs, hitting the lead runner. He fell, his gun skimming across the icy road. The other two turned, heading back to their car. He went for the legs, each time missing. The men made it to their vehicle and took off too quickly for him to catch the entirety of the license plate. He called in what he could see, putting out a region-wide APB. The next moment, he called Brayden's cell. The FBI's reach was far longer and forceful than the locals.

"I'm on it," Brayden said quickly. "Find and hide 'em," were his last words before hanging up. Mark knew exactly how to interpret the words. Keep Kyle safe.

Mark ran to the ledge, looking down. Kyle and Rush were gone, the blood ending at the corner of the basin. It wouldn't have taken long for them to go that distance, then up the metal steps at the end.

Ed would meet them, but what then? Where were they going to go? How could they possibly make it out of town? The local police were setting up stations at either end of Ouray within minutes.

With a groan, Mark realized his massive error in judgement: the authorities would block the roads on either end of the small town, and they'd be catching the good guys along with the bad. Kyle would be done anyway.

CHAPTER 47

"Come on," Kyle encouraged, half pushing and pulling Rush through the narrow ice passage. It was growing dark. Rush was dazed, but other than his shoulder wound, not seriously hurt.

"I'm going to kill that guy," Rush promised. Kyle heard the high pitched hum of an ATV. It was above and to the right of him. Kyle kept Rush going as fast as he could. Maybe it was Mark coming to his aid, or even Brayden who might have been tracking him.

The pitch lowered to an idle.

"Get my gun," commanded Rush, pulling Kyle to a stop. "Here."

Quickly, he unzipped the jacket and removed the gun.

"Kid!" Kyle looked up, putting the gun away. It was his dad.

"Help me," Kyle requested. His father scrambled down, slipping several times on the way. Together, they helped lift

Rush the final twenty feet. "There's shooting up top—" Kyle said.

"I know. The town's panicking."

Together, they got Rush on the ATV. Kyle sat in the front.

"Marcus," groaned Rush, his voice slurred, the injury taking its toll. "Get him now." Kyle rifled through Rush's pockets, giving Rush the phone.

"Where can I go?" he asked his father.

"You won't be going anywhere very far with the gas you have."

A visual appeared to Kyle. "The Idarado."

"Good thinking. I know the security guard. The guy's an Elk and we stick together. I'll make some calls. You just get to the entrance using the back roads."

Rush nudged his arm. "Here," he said, giving the phone to Kyle. "Tell Marcus where."

Kyle gave point to point directions. "Get off Main, turn left onto Oak. Drive slowly, head all the way down and you will pass the hot springs. Just after that is a trailer park and wooden bridge connecting the road and park. Its dark and dingy, no one will notice if you take it easy. We'll be there in less than two minutes."

"What about Mark?" his father asked. "What do I tell him?"

Kyle didn't hesitate. "Only things that they can't extract later."

His father grumbled. "Nothing then. Go."

With a pause, Kyle leaned in. "Thanks dad."

"You're welcome. Remember what I told you about us. This is about you."

Kyle gave him a quick hug and left.

Mark heard the car peel out of the lower parking lot, unable to stop Rush's friend as he received constant updates from his counterparts in Durango and Ridgeway. Mark couldn't leave the scene: Stu Fine was in bad shape. His shot in the back of the leg was either from Mark or Rush's friend, but the one in the front, that was from the guys in the Chevy.

He called Ruth, the closest medical personnel in the area. The town never did have a doctor, always relying upon one in Montrose or Durango. Then he called emergency services and lastly Sean, requesting he close down the area.

"What were you thinking, shooting Kyle?" Mark muttered more to himself as he attempted to stop the bleeding from Stu's stomach. It was pretty bad.

"Wasn't....Kyle..." gasped Stu.

"What? Then who?" Mark demanded.

"The other one. The guy Rush," Stu choked. "Been messing with Ashley...told her I'd kill him if they fooled around."

Mark worked furiously on the man's wound, in disbelief Stu would throw away his entire life, and someone else's, for a girl who was hardly a saint.

"Ruth will be here soon," he told Stu, trying to comfort him. He felt for the pulse. It was weakening. "Shit..."

In the distance, Mark heard the whaling of sirens. Ruth's silver Honda approached and he waved at her. She was out and running towards him. Mark hoped Ruth could keep her father alive until the ambulance arrived.

"Get a satellite on Ouray now," Gary ordered. Brayden had called right after talking with the Deputy. Gary now stood in a control room within the FBI headquarters. By protocol, Janet should have been handling this directly, her team already on the way. In fact, Gary was surprised they hadn't been present when this went down.

"We see nothing, sir," said his lieutenant. "No heat blooms. Regular traffic."

Gary knew that was incorrect, and he knew the reason.

"We've been hacked, God dammit. The spool is a decoy. Spin up a new sat or drone, whatever we have in the area and at our disposal," he ordered. "And if we don't have one of our own, commandeer another one. Now."

Janet had been right about two things, both of which pissed him off. The first is that the activity was in fact playing out in Ouray as she'd anticipated. The second is that they might actually catch all of these people at once, including the teenager who started it all.

As Gary waited impatiently for a new satellite in the area, he thought of Brayden. His wife Laura had left town, her move to the northern Idaho town of Coeur d'Alene official. Brayden was focused on his task and undeterred. Gary knew that if the other agent had deviated at all from his present mission, Janet would have known and taken action.

No, Brayden was on course and vigilant. He wasn't involved in the hacking.

Then how had the satellite been blocked? The question plagued Gary. Only a person on the inside knew how to pull this off—repeatedly.

But who? And what was the motive, he wondered, staring at the panel of screens before him. It must be a Naturalist sympathizer, one who could also share in the financial gain from the masters or both.

The only way to ferret out the internal traitor was to shut everything and everyone down, then prescriptively give out access, monitoring activity by each and every keystroke. But the risk of that was those taken off then put back on were alerted to the issue.

Gary processed all of this in a minute, infuriated. He had no choice but to wait until the person or persons made a mistake. Everyone did, it was only a matter of time, something they didn't have much of.

"Sir, we have one up," said his lieutenant. "On visual now."

Gary looked up, the middle screen on the wall a clear visual of the town. Traffic moved slowly southward, with an ambulance and two patrol vehicles at the north end. That had to be where the shooting took place, the ice park.

"Zoom in," he requested, looking for any signs of unusual movement in the area. Nothing there. "Zoom out."

The cars entering town moved north, pulling into hotels and restaurants, others turning either east or west to homes. On the right hand side of the screen, a lone car traveled the speed limit. The map identified the street as Oak. Gary watched it proceed, before merging on to Highway 550.

Something about that triggered a factoid. The last home in town belonged to the Smith family. It had been in Brayden's report. Across from the large hot springs, impossible to miss because of location and color.

"Pull that home up lieutenant," he requested. "Can you identify a color?"

"Looks light blue," said his direct report.

Gary looked back to the vehicle moving south. It had gone back on to the freeway for another mile, then turned west, avoiding the checkpoint. Intentional or coincidence?

As much as Gary wanted to keep Janet in the dark, his professionalism over road his instinct for paybacks. Once she was on the phone, he gave her the update, suggesting her team go directly to the ice park.

"We will be in place within the hour."

By that time, it will be too late he thought. He hung up, his eyes wandering back to the car which had turned west. A few homes were scattered near the turn off, but after that, only one major entity had lights. The screen identified it as the Idarado Mine.

The car turned in and parked. *A worker on the night shift.*

"Sir, you have a call from Agent Cox."

Gary took it. "Hancock sent me a photo of the downed man in Ouray," began his agent. "He's a known figure here in the Denver digital underworld, Jlubo Rakev, his group a combination of on-line theft and brute force killers. What's strange is not that he's involved, but that he went in himself. No one does that."

"Unless they don't trust anyone else with what they want," Gary added. "Anything else?"

"Yeah. They didn't do the initial shooting. Stu Fine is a local who thought his daughter was sleeping with an out of towner," explained Brayden. "Rakev and his guys were after the same person, who happened to be with Kyle Smith ice climbing."

"And?" prompted Gary.

"And now they are both together and missing."

"Your guess?"

"No guess," the deputy confirmed. "It's Phillip Rush who's with Kyle. I'd previously looked him up and the file was clean. I looked again on another system and we can conclusively say that Rush is not a Naturalist. He's a suspected cybercriminal but no convictions. Ergo, he's doing it for the money."

"The masters and all it entails."

"Our worst fears realized. And since I know you're going to ask, we are still a week away from total transfer, and yes, I've already asked to move it up but got an absolute no. The final five haven't completed their test runs."

"Then let's hope their car overturns or we catch them first."

Gary called up his regional leader for the SWAT. Where Brayden was a great field agent, the SWAT were a different breed. Brutal, efficient and without fear of the Patrol, the deviant group was also controlled by Janet. She'd not brought them up at all during this effort, but Gary knew they were out there.

Gary debated calling the President. His order for containment was still in force. If this got out of Ouray, or Colorado....

He picked up the phone guessing what Scott would say. After listening to Gary describe the situation, he was given his orders.

"We have no choice," said Scott, using his formal tone of the Presidential office. "The FBI SWAT, Janet's group at either end, and the Patrol is going to swoop in on the borders of that town. There's absolutely no way anyone is going to get in or out of that community without us knowing."

"And what do we do if we catch them?"

"We need to know what information they have. If they resist, proceed accordingly."

Gary hung up, relaying the orders to his team and Janet without emotion. They had to finish this, and it was going to happen tonight.

CHAPTER

48

"Here, drink this." Kyle handed Rush an energy drink, steadying it under his lips. They were in the back seat of the Defender, Marcus driving, his left arm injured from a bullet which had grazed him. They'd met him on Oak, transferred from the ATV to the Defender, with Kyle guiding him on the outskirts to the highway, then on the turn to the Idarado Mine.

"It's shit," Rush muttered. Kyle smiled. Rush was wounded but not dying. That was left to Rush's rivals.

Kyle showed him the text from Mark.

"Rakev," identified Rush.

"Well, he's dead," said Kyle, adding that the two others hadn't been caught. "Turn left at the light," he told Marcus.

"Where are we going?" asked the bodyguard.

"We're going to take a very scenic sixty mile road under some very tall mountains," he explained. "It's a former mine road for silver, gold and other metals and it's been closed for years but kept in good shape. It comes out at the Pandora Mine in Telluride. I'd recommend you booking a private plane to get you out of here," continued Kyle. "The strip is right by your rental home and the one used by celebrities. The air traffic controllers are used to anonymizing their passengers, a perfect cover for you guys."

Marcus slowed the car, seeing the security guard in the distance.

"Don't worry. My dad was supposed to have talked with him," Kyle assured Marcus. "Drop me off, drive through and be on your way."

Kyle felt a massive amount of relief as he said the words. The security entrance was waving them in. "How much cash do you have on you?" he asked Marcus.

"How much do you need?"

"Enough to incentivize this guy to let you through and keep his mouth shut."

Marcus drove up slowly, extending his arm as the window lowered. As the man looked down, his eyebrows went up at the same time as his hand stretched out. He returned to the security shed. The next moment, the gate retracted.

"Marcus, slow down so I can get out." Kyle put his hand on the door.

The car accelerated instead of slowing. "Sorry, Kyle," said Marcus. "You're staying with us."

Kyle's hand was still on the door. "You're serious?" He was prepared to jump out the car and roll for it. Rush couldn't run after him and Marcus' number one objective was getting his boss out of the area with the cubes.

The car picked up speed. Kyle saw the entrance about a hundred yards up and gave himself a countdown to dive and roll.

Kyle's regular phone rang, and he stopped cold. No one had called him on that since Billy left. The seconds became a minute as he hesitated. He took the call, his right hand gripping the door, ready to bail out the moment it was over.

"Kyle, Mark—"

"Mark, I don't—"

"Kyle!" Mark said loudly. "Look, I don't know where you're at or what you're doing but…I'm sorry to tell you this but—your house was…it's gone Kyle. We won't know what happened until forensics arrives, and Brayden said a fleet of FBI and others are on their way—"

"What do you mean?" demanded Kyle. "Gone? How is my house *gone*?"

"Kid. Kyle," said Mark, his voice low. "I'm sorry. They…the house had an explosion. Set from the inside or out, we don't know. We won't know—"

"Stop!" Kyle commanded. "Are you telling me my parents were inside the house? Dad didn't leave us more than ten minutes ago."

The pause was eternal. "Then it must have happened right after he arrived. And yes," Mark continued, his voice rough. "Both your parents were inside." Kyle choked on his anger, shock and rage burning hot. "Kyle, you there?"

"Yeah," he said harshly.

"I don't think it was the guys at the ice park. Another group maybe---"

Kyle hung up, shoving the phone in his pocket. He leaned against the door, his world shattered. He felt a grip on his arm.

"Don't," warned Rush. "Losing the use of your legs is not what you need right now."

In the swirl of pain and fury, Kyle looked at the man.

Rush's eyes were a mix of compassion and ruthlessness. "You have to be where the cubes are," he said. "I can't risk it at this point."

Kyle didn't need to have a gun pointed at him to know that even he were to escape, there was no place he could go that Rush wouldn't find him.

As if understanding the inevitable, Kyle nodded.

"You'll be a part of us until your life gets settled. As to the group who just killed your parents, I'll do that part for free."

Kyle leaned back into the leather, the colors of his world fading   into   black   like   the   tunnel.

ACKNOWLEDGEMENTS

A special thanks to research scientist Shay Wallace, who was instrumental in helping educate me on the world of gene therapies, DNA and the process and stages of cell growth. A further debt of gratitude for her patience and humor as she helped clarify and simplify a very complex subject. I hope I've done her, and her fellow researcher scientists in the field justice.

ABOUT THE AUTHOR

Before she began writing novels, Sarah Gerdes established herself as an internationally recognized expert in the areas of business management and consulting. Her novels are published in over 100 countries and translated by publishers in three languages. The Cube Master is her twentieth novel. She lives with her family in Northern Idaho among a menagerie of farm animals.

BOOKS IN PRINT

SARAH GERDES

Romantic Suspense

Global Deadline

In a Moment

The Danielle Grant Series

    Made for Me, book 1

    Destined for You, book 2

    Meant to Be, book 3

A Convenient Date

Action Adventure

The Chambers Series

    Chambers, book 1

    The Spirit Warrior, book 2

The Incarnation Series

    Incarnation, book 1

    The Cube Master, book 2

Non-Fiction

Author Straight Talk: The possibilities, pitfalls, how-to's and tribal knowledge from someone who knows

Sue Kim: the Authorized biography

The Overlooked Expert: Turning your skills into a Profitable Business, 10th Anniversary Edition

Navigating the Partnership Maze: Creating Alliances that Work

REFERENCES & RESOURCES

Web site: www.sarahgerdes.com

Instagram: Sarahgerdes_author

YouTube: Sarah Gerdes author

Facebook fan page: Sarah Gerdes author

To sign up for Sarah's newsletter, go to her website www.sarahgerdes.com.